THE MASTER AND THE MAID...

They crossed the rigid bounds of class to satisfy a hunger that knew no limits!

Houston Lamont hesitated, glancing at the open door of Mirrin's room. She was seated on the bed, the spotless white sheet drawn up to her waist. Within the scant cotton shift her breasts were free and heavy. Her hair draped her shoulders. She looked straight at him.

"Mirrin?"

She smiled, not in calculation, not lewdly. She smiled warmly, and gave a slight apologetic shrug as if to ask forgiveness for the theatricality of her invitation.

"May I come in, Mirrin?"

"Please do," Mirrin said.

The master entered the bedroom and with rueful formality closed the door on the outside world. . . .

Strathmore

Jessica Stirling

A DELL BOOK

Published by
DELL PUBLISHING CO., INC.
1 Dag Hammarskjold Plaza
New York, N.Y. 10017

Originally published in different form by
Hodder and Stoughton Ltd., London, under
the title *The Spoiled Earth*

Dell ® TM 681510, Dell Publishing Co., Inc.

ISBN: 0-440-15971-7

Reprinted by arrangement with Delacorte Press

Printed in the United States of America
First Dell printing—April 1977

Strathmore

Part One

CHAPTER I

THE cellars of the Consort Hotel, like the dungeons of a castle, were dark, dank, and malodorous. If the canny Scottish businessmen who thronged the gaily decorated supper rooms could have glimpsed the squalor below stairs it is doubtful that they would have tackled their meat with quite so much relish. Stone corridors, strewn with rubbish, led from the kitchens and larders. Through this maze, in daylight hours, victualers' lads stumbled in from the lanes of Hamilton Town with the quantities of provender needed to keep the hotel's many guests comfortably gorged. It was by the Judas door to the left of the cavernous coal hole, however, that Mirrin Stalker made her discreet nightly sorties to dole out scraps to the shivering urchins who congregated hopefully under the back arches of the grand brick building.

Mirrin had forged no relationship with the children. Her acts of charity were performed without that grace and leisure that marked the philanthropic excursions of most fine Victorian ladies. Mirrin Stalker was no fine lady. She was only a collier's daughter, a scullion, who understood exactly what it meant to go to bed hungry.

In the four months since she had come to work in the Consort, Mirrin had hardly missed a single noctural run. Her generosity was perfunctory, hasty but unselfish. All she gained from feeding stale bread to skinny youngsters was the practical satisfaction of redressing a social injus-

tice—and of putting one over on the hotel's miserly proprietress, Mrs. Agnes Grogan.

Inevitably, Mirrin had grown careless in slipping away
from the sinks, in pilfering moldy broken loaves from the
wicker dumps in the pantry, in her negotiation of the
warrens that led out into the yards. She had evaluated the
risks, considered them worth it, and would rely on her
quick wits to talk her out of serious trouble if ever Agnes
Grogan should catch her in the act.

It did not occur to Mirrin that other hazards might
lurk in the empty cellars or that her career as a lowly
servant might be cut dramatically short through no real
fault of her own.

Closing the low wooden door behind her, she nudged
home the rusty bolt. Turning, she began to grope her
way along the tunnel toward the main corridor.

Flame flickered abruptly. The lucifer's aura illuminated
a man's face. He was leaning against the big oak door
that defended the wine vaults, an area religiously locked
against thieves. How he came to be there, Mirrin could
not imagine. She recognized him as one of the younger
coalmasters from the convention of mine owners and
engineers who had taken over the Consort for one of
their infernal conferences. A thin cigarette jutted from the
center of his crinkly, sand-colored mustache. He touched
the match to the tobacco as if lighting a fuse, tilting his
head cautiously from it.

By the lucifer's waning glimmer, he studied Mirrin
keenly.

It was not the first time that Mirrin had attracted the
attentions of males of the species. Her dark hair, good
figure, and handsome bearing made her a natural target.
Only her father's reputation had saved her from the
strenuous assaults of the young men of her home village,
and even as a kitchen drudge in Hamilton she had caught
the interest of cooks and boots and footmen, regardless

of age. She was not vain of her appearance and possessed the kind of arrogance that protected her against flattery and made her well able to defend herself when the occasion required it.

Buried down in the bowels of the hotel, she had thought herself safe from attention. Twice in the last two days, however, she had been ordered to squeeze into an ugly bombazine uniform and wait table in the luncheon room. It was there, she assumed, that the young coalmaster had singled her out as vulnerable, available, and a possible source of diversion.

She recognized him as Ross Finlay, owner of the notorious Blairbeth colliery, an antediluvian pit on the far north spur of the Lothian seams. He had come into possession only recently, on his uncle's death, and had not yet started on the improvement scheme that new government regulations demanded of him. Even before she had left her home village of Blacklaw there had been much gossip about the foul conditions at Blairbeth. Only yesterday a fellow waitress had pointed out weak-chinned, glabrous Ross Finlay and commented that he had an unwholesome passion for whiskey and women. Even so, Mirrin experienced no sense of danger as the match spluttered out. She was only impatient with this gentleman lout. He had no right to invade the scullions' province, let alone spy on her. She did not doubt that he had seen her take the bread outside.

Wiping her hands on the bib of her apron, she said, "You're in my path, sir."

Finlay laughed huskily.

His breath smelled of whiskey.

"Slipping out is a bad habit for servant gels," Finlay said. "Got yourself a lover out there? If so, he must be as fast as a whippit to attend your needs in such short order."

"I'm required in the scullery," said Mirrin stiffly. "Please let me pass, Mr. Finlay."

"So—you know who I am, do you?" He lit another match. "What's your name?"

"Stalker."

"Very well, Stalker, give me a nice warm kiss and I'll let you through. That's my toll—a kiss, and a promise."

"You're mistaken if you think I'm that sort."

Finlay chuckled, amused by her lack of humility in confronting a coalmaster. "Where are you from, gel?"

"Blacklaw."

"Houston Lamont's place?"

"That's right."

"Have you a husband?"

"No."

"Family back in the village?"

"Yes, sir."

She was tempted to tell him to mind his own damned business, but if he did know her secret, then he might report her to Mrs. Grogan and she would be dismissed. She could not decide whether or not she would welcome dismissal. The work in the Consort was not so amenable as she had anticipated.

Four of her eighteen years had been spent at Lamont's sorting troughs, the best job for women in a colliery, and she had lived with her family in the narrow house on Blacklaw's main street. Impulsiveness and a vain inclination to better herself had coaxed her into quitting the security of her home to travel the six miles into Hamilton in search of a job. Six miles did not seem far, yet she was as effectively cut off from Blacklaw as if she had crossed the Atlantic. The hours she was expected to put in at the Consort were even longer than her colliery shifts. So hard did Mrs. Grogan drive her staff that Mirrin had had only one day off in all her time at the hotel. Summer had come and gone, and the autumn had advanced into October, and Mirrin had been as unaware of the seasons' passing as a convict.

Finlay crabbed down the tunnel.

Now that the second match had gone out, his position was telegraphed only by the glowing tip of his cigarette.

"You're a collier's daughter, are you?"

"Aye, and proud of it."

"Proud and handsome, that's how I like my women."

Finlay reached for her.

The Judas door was too far for her; besides, the bolt was rusty. She inhaled a deep lungful of air and affected a coy and winsome tone, saying, "I see you've got me at a disadvantage, Mr. Finlay. All right, then, I'll pay the toll. Just one kiss, though, that's all."

"With a promise, Stalker?"

"Ah, now, sir, none of that. No promises."

Finlay tossed the cigarette aside and moved against her. Executing a neat side step, Mirrin avoided him and found position on the outside. She could hardly make him out in the gloom. Only the stink of whiskey, French tobacco, and pomade told her where he was.

"Come on, gel, don't be difficult."

Stretching out, she caught the end of his mustache, rough as a length of old hemp rope, and pinching it, brought his face down. She administered a brusque kiss on his brow. His arms flailed in an endeavor to ensnare her, and his wrist brushed her breast. But she was too nimble for him. Tweaking his mustache in a parting gesture, she snaked past him, scampered down the tunnel and along the wider corridor to the kitchen door.

Behind her, Finlay cursed and blundered in the gloom.

The latch clacked under Mirrin's hand, and she slid into the safety of the steam-filled kitchens.

Two bedraggled young girls drudged over the huge oval tub in which the barroom glasses were rinsed. The hatch from the carpeted lounge stood open in its alcove, and she heard Kane, the head publican, roaring irately down the shaft, demanding more clean pots. Through the arches, in the hot area of ranges and stoves, autocratic cooks were fussing over pans and casseroles. The Irishman, who claimed he was a master chef, was sizzling a dozen pork chops over a trench of small coals. From the inner depths, by the service stairs, male and female waiters clamored for their orders.

Savory odors, light, heat, and noisy hubbub enveloped Mirrin. She heaved a sigh of relief at being clear of the dank corridors and the slimy attentions of the amorous coalmaster.

Until the convention ended—after luncheon tomorrow —and the villains had departed for their various wee empires, she would be extra careful not to encounter Finlay again, or any of his dirty-minded friends.

Dabbing her brow, she edged toward the ale hatch to unload its cargo of glasses and pots. She did not even notice Agnes Grogan, silent and motionless in the corner. The woman's eyes were watchful, speculative, the color of chipped flint. In her hand she held the iron key with which she had unlocked the wine vaults to allow Ross Finlay access to the outer cellars and the opportunity to seduce the arrogant Stalker girl.

❧

It was very late on that October Friday before the senior staff were released from duty and allowed to stumble off to snatch a few hours' sleep in their homes in the town or on the iron cots of the hotel's attic dormitories. The Irish chef was first away; the youngest scullions were last. In the ground-floor salons convention guests were still drinking, gambling, and arguing boozily about the state of the market and the innate idleness of the Scottish labor force. A night clerk, with keys to the bottle cupboard, had been installed in the foyer cubby to attend the clients' needs until dawn. Outside in the town's squares, Presbyterian clocks solemnly declared the first hour after midnight.

The child-servants were asleep on their feet. Bread and dripping and a cup of watered milk was supper for each of them. Mrs. Grogan dispensed the largesse herself; no motherly gesture, only a sure means of ascertaining that the servants' greed did not bring her to financial ruin. She eked out the pallid milk as if it were the best brandy, defying the girls to ask for more. The girls were too exhausted to be hungry and chewed the bread as mutely as cattle in a barn. Setting down the cups, they gave the proprietress a curtsy, and with one penny dip to lead them all, trailed up the narrow back stairs to the attics.

Mirrin was the last to leave the kitchen.

She put down the cup and turned away.

Mrs. Grogan said, "You're not finished, Stalker."

"But . . . ?"

"The guest in room fourteen, in the third-floor wing, wants a warming pig. Fill one and take it up to him."

"That's a chambermaid's job."

"Are you arguing with me, Stalker?"

Mirrin bit her lip. "No, Mrs. Grogan."

"The pigs are in the cupboard. There's hot water in the kettles."

"Yes, Mrs. Grogan."

The hatchet-faced proprietress watched as Mirrin found the heavy stoneware bottle, filled it, wrapped it in a towel, and with the bundle in her arms like a foundling infant, set off through the kitchens for the maids' stairs. There was nothing evident in Agnes Grogan's expression to indicate deception, though she gave Mirrin a brittle smile by way of good night. If Mirrin had been less weary, it is possible that she would have been more suspicious of that smile. As it was, the heavy work of evening and night had dulled her like the others and nudged the memory of Ross Finlay's ambush out of her thoughts.

She trudged up the carpeted staircase to the ground-level foyer. Laughter drifted faintly from the forward salons, but the hall was deserted; even the night clerk's cubby had been temporarily abandoned. From the supper room came the harmonizing of a group of jolly engineers, the lyrics audible and ribald enough to make Mirrin grin to herself as she climbed out of earshot to the second floor and then onto the musty landing at the end of the third-floor wing.

Gas mantels were dimmed. Sounds of slumber—snores, stirrings, the creak of bedsprings—leaked from behind the heavy varnished doors. She found the brass numerals that identified room 14 and knocked gingerly. A smothered, mumbled voice told her to enter.

She pushed into the bedroom, leaving the door ajar behind her. The glass-globed oil lamp was on the dressing table away from the bed, its wick low, the flame hardly more than a faint blue ribbon in the shadows. The quilt and sheets on the bed had not been turned down. There was no sign of the room's occupant, though the curtains of the dressing alcove were parted.

"Your warmin' pig, sir," Mirrin said.

"Put it in the bed," came the gruff instruction from behind the curtain.

Mirrin moved around to the side of the bed. On a chair a gentleman's clothes were neatly set out, the hard collar lying on the clean striped linen shirt, the elastic-sided boots beneath the chair, pointed out, already polished by the boots boy before retiring. She deftly turned down quilt and sheets, making a crisp white V, slid the wrapped stoneware bottle into the middle of the mattress, and plumped up the pillows.

Drowsy, hardly even concentrating on her work, she did not hear Finlay's approach. The first she knew of the guest's identity and intention was when he clasped her from behind and cupped her breasts in his hands.

She squealed and struggled involuntarily, but Finlay had already transferred one hand from her breast to her mouth. He pulled her back against him. His silk robe was open, swirling about him, and even through her coarse skirts she could feel the urgency of his unclad body. His mouth, buried in her hair, muttered obscene threats for her earlier rebuff. The whiskey reek was sharp and sickly sweet about him. His fingers hooked into her bodice and tore off three or four buttons, exposing the fullness of her breasts above the camisole. He stroked and caressed her, then, fumbling at her skirts, shoved her against the edge of the mattress and thrust her down full-length across the quilt.

Though years of hard work had made Mirrin strong, she was no match for the ardent young coalmaster. To him the conquest was half game and half obsession.

Brown eyes blazing with fury, Mirrin arched her back and struggled to throw him off. But his strength was greater than hers, and he smothered her struggles easily with his weight. She could see nothing but his naked chest, sprinkled with fair, babyish hair. Shifting attack, his hands moved away from her mouth. She gave one quick, strangled scream of rage, fear, and revulsion before he stopped her cry with his forearm.

Above her, on the cream ceiling, she watched the gigantic shadowgraph of her downfall.

Then, unaccountably, the weight was gone from her. She jerked upright immediately, thrashing out with her feet. Enveloped in the silken robe, Finlay had been dragged from the bed. The door was wide open, pallid gaslight making a carpet across the bedroom floor. Outlined against it she saw a second man, taller than Finlay but thinner, and as broad-shouldered as a collier. She did not recognize him at first. She rolled across the bed and reached the floor, crouching down out of the way.

"Get out of my room, damn you," Finlay cried petulantly.

"We're respectable gentlemen, Finlay. I beg you to remember that, at least while we're in convention."

"You . . . you *prig*," Finlay bellowed.

"Do what you like with your trulls at home, but . . ."

The blow was wildly aimed, and obvious. The intruder blocked it easily. Parrying it aside, he brought his right fist up in a curt arc and clipped Finlay on the point of the jaw, felling the young lecher effectively. Finlay dropped back as if poleaxed, sprawling across the bed end, wallowing, and slipping onto the floor. He lay on his back, the robe spilled around him, his weak mouth open. The man stepped over and deftly flipped the silken folds to cover Finlay's nakedness.

Hesitantly Mirrin said, "Thank you, sir."

The stranger stepped away, eyeing her coldly.

"You should be more careful, girl," he said. "Still, I suppose in your trade you must encounter this . . . this circumstance fairly frequently."

"My trade?"

"Get out."

Mirrin shifted her position. She recognized her rescuer now. Indeed, she should have recognized him earlier. He was Houston Lamont, the Blacklaw coalmaster, owner of the colliery in which her family had worked for thirty years. She had seen him often enough, though usually from afar, and had even heard him address meetings once or twice.

"No, wait," she said. "What d'you mean, 'my trade'?"

"I think you understand."

"If you think I'm a . . . a trull, as you called it, then think again, Mr. Lamont."

Houston Lamont raised his eyebrows. "You know me?"

"I should." Mirrin felt no awe. Some of her fury at Finlay simmered still in her veins. "An' I'll have you know, sir, that your precious young coalmaster started this . . . folly without any encouragement from me."

"That, at least, is your tale."

"To hell with you then," Mirrin snapped.

Lamont had come closer now, head cocked, intrigued.

"Who are you?" he asked.

"Just a kitchen skivvy."

"Yet you recognized me?"

"Before I came here," said Mirrin, "I worked in *your* pit."

"What's your name?"

"Stalker, Mirrin Stalker."

She could not be sure if the taciturn features registered surprise or wry amusement at this information.

Lamont said, "Alex Stalker's daughter?"

"Aye."

He nodded. "Then, Stalker, I apologize for the behavior of one of my fellow owners. I see now that I was wrong to leap to a hasty conclusion."

"Why?"

"Because I'm sure Alex Stalker's daughter would not lie."

"You know what m'father thinks of you."

"Politics," Lamont said, "are one thing. Deceit is quite another matter."

Mirrin gestured at the unconscious figure on the floor. "What about him?"

"Leave young Mr. Finlay to me," said Lamont. "I suggest you go immediately to your room and say nothing of this to anyone."

Mirrin hesitated. She was full of inbred mistrust of the coalmaster's motives and searched for cunning in Lamont's suggestion. It would be a cover-up, of course. There would be no public scandal to besmirch the honor of the owners' convention. In fact she realized that the Grogan woman had intended her to be Finlay's victim, that she had been set up like a lamb for the sacrifice. Anger welled in her once more. She felt the hot smarting of tears in her eyes.

Controlling herself, she grudgingly gave Lamont thanks

once more, then hurried out of the bedroom and along the corridor to the back stairs.

It was not until she was huddled under the blanket of her hard cot in the attic dormitory that she allowed herself to weep. Burying her face in the straw pillow, she sobbed brokenly to herself. She did not know why the incident pained her so much now that it was over. She had never been naive in the ways of the world. Perhaps it was being in Lamont's debt that disturbed her most of all, the reluctant acknowledgment that even in the most powerful men there can be compassion of a sort, even a prudish gallantry.

The clocks of the town struck two, and shortly after, worn out and exhausted, Mirrin Stalker fell asleep, the doubts in her mind still unresolved.

✐∾◑

It was just after seven o'clock, and the focus of activity below stairs in the Consort was concentrated on preparing and serving the large and varied breakfasts that early birds among the coalmasters and engineers demanded. Since five, a dozen of the youngest had been up and about, raking and resetting the grates, cleaning and firing the cooking ranges, fetching in the day's milk and bread supplies from the drays in the lane, generally laying the groundwork for the arrival of the cooks and serving staff at six forty-five. Mirrin had risen with the other scullions at the stroke of six and after a hurried breakfast of bread and tea had been fully occupied with shipping crockery from the cellar closets to the dining room via the hatches. Last night's events still haunted her like a vivid nightmare. Her mind was only half on her chores as she decanted hot water into the washing tubs and lathered the soap. Soon the first greasy plates and cups would be dropping down from the salons, and the seemingly endless routine of fetch and carry, wash, dry, and rack would be in full swing.

"Stalker."

Mirrin had not noticed Mrs. Grogan's arrival.

"*Stalker*." The tone was more imperious than ever, a savage bark. Mirrin swung around from the oval tub, sleeves already rolled up and cap over her hair.

Agnes Grogan looked more like a prison wardress than the manager of a large hotel. Her day dress was severely cut and whaleboned, black as a funeral plume, unrelieved by any form of trimming. Her hair, iron-gray and lank, was scraped back into a bun and skewered by a long steel pin. Knotted with righteous spleen, her face reminded Mirrin of a boxer dog's, particularly the pouched and sallow jowls. Mrs. Grogan did not intend that her insolent scullion should escape humiliation. She did not approach her across the flagged floor of the kitchen, merely raised her voice so that everyone, from chef to potboy, could hear her clearly.

"Stalker. Is this not a respectable hotel?"

Activity diminished, the rattle of pans and plates ceased, and the chatter throughout all the nooks and crannies of the basement area stopped, leaving an echoing silence. Male cooks and even haughty waiters sidled to the arch-posts, watching with cynical interest.

"Aye, Mrs. Grogan," Mirrin answered, toweling her hands on her apron.

"Then what right have you to ply your disgusting wares under my roof?"

"I . . . I don't understand, ma'am," Mirrin said, though an inkling of the truth had dawned on her.

Waiters smirked and exchanged knowing glances with the cooks. In the pantry two striplings sniggered.

"Last night," Mrs. Grogan announced with all the discretion of a town crier, "last night when we had retired to our beds like good Christians, you, Stalker, *you* crept into a guest's private room and there solicited a highly respectable . . ."

"That's a damned lie."

". . . a highly respectable gentleman to pay you money to have relations with you."

"He . . . he attacked me—aye, an' well you know it. You put him up to it."

Mrs. Grogan looked to her senior staff for support, her expression one of total moral outrage.

"Oh, *I* put you up to it, did I? *That* is your feeble, your puny excuse. *I* am now to be accused. . . ."

Mirrin tugged off the cotton cap, pulled the bow of the apron, and let the buckram garment drop.

"Think yourself fortunate," Mrs. Grogan said, "that I do not call an officer of the law."

"But then a charge would need witnesses, for proof," said Mirrin. "An', as it so happens, I have a witness to what really went on upstairs last night."

This obviously came as a surprise to the woman, whose manner changed instantly, losing its theatrical ease and becoming more cautious, more openly venomous.

"A witness? And who might that be? Another of your kind, another lying servant?" Mrs. Grogan cast a scowling glance around the kitchens, making the young scullions quail.

"A gentleman," said Mirrin boldly. "A guest."

"His name?"

"You can whistle for his name," Mirrin said.

"Hah! There is no such person."

"Summon the law officer and we'll see," Mirrin said.

Murmurs of contention ran among the onlookers. Mirrin paid them not the slightest heed. It was tempting to blurt out her version, to involve Houston Lamont, to save face; but something stayed her. For once, she felt her impetuosity fade into calculation. She had known all along that the Grogan woman resented her and that with those odds against her, her tenure in the Consort could not last long. Sooner or later she had expected to be dismissed for some minor infringement—though not on a trumped-up charge of soliciting.

"Do you deny," Mrs. Grogan cried, "that you have stolen bread from my pantries to feed your begging friends?"

"Do you deny that you encouraged that rabbit-chinned wonder, Finlay, to have a shot at seducin' me?" Mirrin retorted.

"I . . . I . . . I absolutely . . . deny it."

"Right!" said Mirrin. "Make a liar out of yourself if you like, but you won't make one out of me. Aye, I took a few handfuls of moldy bread and gave it to the poor wee starvin' wretches who haunt your yards like rats. Aye, I did that—and I think I did your fine guests a favor, 'cause all of us here know where that bread goes."

"That's *enough*, Stalker."

"Into the puddings, blue mold an' all," Mirrin yelled. Shamefacedly, the cooks inched back out of sight.

"Deny *that*, if you dare." Mirrin crossed the breadth of the kitchen and dumped the apron and cap into the astonished woman's hands. "To save you the bother of dismissing me, ma'am, I'll take my week's wages and resign."

"What do you think you are, you brat, you collier's slut," the proprietress hissed. "You'll get no wages from me."

Mirrin paused, then nodded. "Fair enough! Chalk them up as payment for the few rotten loaves I 'stole' from you and thank me for bein' generous enough to keep my mouth shut about your catering methods."

She stepped past the seething woman. The gaping servants parted before her as if she were a carrier of plague as she strode to the door to the back stairs.

As her position of authority demanded that she have the last word, Agnes Grogan called out, "Don't imagine that you will find another job in hotel work, Stalker. I'll put

out the word on you all through the county *and* into
Glasgow and Edinburgh. You won't work in *this* profession again."

Mirrin's answer to that was terse, rude, and telling.

She left the kitchen in a stunned silence and less than
five minutes later was out on the street with her scant
belongings wrapped in a shawl.

Cutting left at the arch, she passed the front of the building. Its facade was all brightwork and fresh paint and
neat red brick. She knew now what lay behind such
sophisticated trappings. The doorman in his bottle-green
uniform looked down his snoot at her, giving her no
more acknowledgment than if she had been a stray alley
cat.

Mirrin did not care.

For the first time in months she felt light again, free,
whole, and without rankling resentment suppressed within.

Hoisting the shawl, she headed southwest up the Hamilton hill, steering for the back road to Blacklaw. She
would say nothing at home about the reasons for her dismissal. Her family would accept and respect her reticence.
Her first bid to shake off the ties of the colliery village
had failed. But she did not grieve much over the failure.
Her brush with town life had taught her many valuable
lessons. She would return to her dull job at the colliery
troughs and to the security of the narrow house at the
main street's end changed in several subtle ways.

As the square sandstone houses on the outskirts of
Hamilton dropped behind her and she looked ahead to the
open fields in their auburn colors, toward Blacklaw, she
felt cheerful enough to whistle to herself and call out
cheery greetings to the carters and drovers who trundled
toward the town.

If she stepped lively she would be home in time for a
late breakfast and to register again at Lamont's pit before
the hooter sounded noon.

CHAPTER II

ONCE more the swan had spread its wings across the ceiling. This morning it was yellow with brown edges, which meant that the rain in the night had been heavy, seeking out the cracks in the attic walls to paint the damp patch on the back-room ceiling. The swan shape meant rain, rain meant mud, mud meant boots—and boots meant skinned heels. Mirrin sighed and peeped over the patchwork quilt to see what time it was. Kate, the family's most reliable clock, was half through dressing. Mirrin watched her loop her hair into a trim coronet. Never any rush with Kate. She envied her sister's tidiness but knew better than to try to emulate it. She wriggled down under the bedclothes to lie snug for another few minutes. Kate was in one of her brisk moods, however. "High time you were up, Mirrin."

"In a minute," Mirrin murmured.

"Now."

Stoically, Mirrin slid from under the quilt, pulled into a sitting position, and stretched. In the faded pink nightgown she looked younger than nineteen.

Yawning, she said, "Not much of a mornin'?"

"At least it's dry. It rained itself out early," said Kate. "Now hurry up. Things are all behind this mornin' as it is. Da, James, and Dougie were late leavin'."

With sudden vigor Mirrin said, "Right!" rolled from the bed, and peeled her nightgown over her head. She padded naked to the dresser, poured water from an iron jug into a tin basin, and bathed her face and body, hissing with the cold.

From the single cot by the wall, Betsy Stalker complained, "You're not at that again, Mirrin?"

"Toughens you up," Mirrin shivered.

"Aye, you're tough enough already." Betsy turned her face to the wall. All that could be seen of her were the sausage-shaped ringlets that she tended with such care that even in sleep they retained their bounce and curl.

Betsy was fourteen, and like her twin brother Drew, still attended parish school. Nobody grudged her her extra hour in bed. With the end of summer term Betsy too would be committed to early rising. By now Alex Stalker and his sons would be creeping along the bottom level of the pit for ten hours of toil at the coal face. In a half hour Mirrin would also be at Blacklaw colliery, and another workday would be in full swing for them all. It was the sameness of it that dismayed Mirrin; her experiences in the Consort Hotel, in Hamilton, five months ago had taught her that many kinds of work can be drudgery. She did not regret her return to Blacklaw. At least she was with her family, not at the beck and call of every snot-nosed "gentleman" with the price of a night's lodging in his pocket; free too of petty tyrants who because they wore black dresses and chignons thought themselves better than they were. At least she knew where she stood with foremen and masters at the colliery. Hopping, she pulled on a clean shift and furled black stockings over her shapely legs.

"I don't see why you can't have a warm wash at night like everybody else," said Kate.

"I don't mind cold water."

"Must you be so shameless about it?"

"I'm not ashamed of what I've got."

"Mirrin, really!" Kate exclaimed. Betsy giggled.

"Kate," Mam Stalker called from the kitchen. "Are you about ready to serve this porridge?"

"Coming," Kate answered.

"Make sure it's not lumpy," said Mirrin.

"Just for that," said Kate, without malice, "I'll see to it that your share's like a turnip field."

After Kate had gone, Mirrin knelt before a square of mirror and combed her thick, dark hair. She wasn't vain, like Betsy, but enjoyed the sensual satisfaction as a bracer against the harsh day ahead. Casually, she studied her features—the straight Stalker nose, the determined chin, and the wide, frank mouth that she shared with nobody. Impudently, she stuck out her tongue at her image and went through the low doorway into the kitchen.

The room was already warm and bright, fire burning in the stove, reflecting on the brass tea caddy and the willow-pattern plates on the dresser shelf. A scrubbed pine table stood in the middle of the room. Of the seven chairs around it, only one, her father's special place, had a crocheted wool cushion. Bowls and mugs were on the table, and the porridge pot bubbled on the hob. The sodden smells of sweat and steam mingled with the aroma of stewing tea, smells common to every collier's house and quite unnoticed. Kate had ladled out porridge, and standing, was spooning the oatmeal into her mouth. Drew had come down for breakfast. He had taken his bowl to the window where he peered at a newspaper as he ate, a typical pose, absorbed, almost secretive. Ignoring the boy, Mirrin moved to the stove. Toasting her rump at the fire, she ate without real hunger. There had been many days in the past when, with Alex's bare wage pared to meet "economies" at the pit, a simple cup of porridge had seemed like a feast. But things were not so bad for the Stalkers now with four wages coming in and the prospect of Betsy and Drew adding to the communal purse before long.

Flora Stalker still complained, though. She was no Tartar, like some village wives, and chivvied the family from a position of strength, secure in her husband's loyalty and her children's love. In the past year or two she had grown stout, her brown hair flecked with gray.

"I don't know what's wrong with our Dougie these days," Flora said.

"He's learnin' not to like the early rise," Mirrin said.

"Dougie never complains," said Flora defensively.

"He'll learn that too, soon enough." Mirrin would argue at any time, morning or night. "He's realized how little he's got to get up for. My God! A coal-face shifter at sixteen. He should still be at school."

"Dougie didn't take to school," Drew said from behind a back issue of the *Glasgow Herald*. "He once told me he thought schooling was for sissies, an' education a waste of time."

"Pay no heed to him then," Kate advised.

Secretly Flora Stalker was inclined to share Dougie's suspicion of book learning and resented the priggishness in Drew's remark.

"Dougie's doin' a man's job now, an' it's a mercy for you that things are not as they were when I was young," she said, "or you'd be underground too, howkin' coal in baskets or tollin' a vent rope for fourteen hours a day."

Drew sighed, not audibly. He had heard this litany a hundred times before.

"Oh, aye, things are just wonderful now," said Mirrin sarcastically.

"Don't give us a Socialist sermon," Kate warned.

"I haven't time," Mirrin replied, swallowing tea, and sitting, reaching for her boots. As she laced them up she said casually, "Hey, our Dougie's started shavin'."

"How do *you* know?" Flora was disappointed that she had not been the first to learn the news.

"I saw him, late last night," said Mirrin. "Da was

instructin' him, only the old man kept laughin'. Finally Dougie got annoyed and sliced a piece off his delicate hide."

"Is that what the blood was?" said Flora.

"Aye, you'd think they'd butchered an ox between them," said Mirrin. "Still, whatever the rest of us say, it seems nature is catchin' up with our Dougie. He'll be chasin' the girls next."

"Mirrin, that's enough!" Flora Stalker resented the need to give her strapping sons into some other woman's charge. There would be weeping and wailing when James got himself caught, even louder lamentation when wee Dougie took himself a wife. Finishing her lacing, Mirrin stood up and experimentally drummed her boots on the floor. Indefatigably high-spirited, she changed the rhythm into an impromptu dance, kicking her heels, shaking her skirts until even Drew glanced up and grinned.

"Aye, miss," said Flora, "we'll see if you're as bright at the day's end."

"Hard work never killed Kelly's donkey," said Mirrin.

"Huh!" said Flora Stalker, then, relenting, gave Mirrin a hug to send her on her way to work.

The door closed behind the girl, and her footsteps died away. Wiping her hands on her apron, Flora glanced at the clock.

"Four out and two to go," she said. "Kate, away and dig Betsy from her bed."

"Yes, Mam," Kate said and for the first time that morning smiled.

Within the Stalker house the day at last had steadied to an even keel.

❧

The rain, which had swept intermittently from the west for days on end, had finally dwindled and died out. The blustery wind was more persistent, though, and continued to rattle slates, slap ropes, and clatter the rusty scraps that blew into the village from the pit head. Milky light bathed the low hills of the neighboring county—but that was cattle land, and colliers claimed that farmers always had the best of the weather. Closer, at Northrigg and the home pits on the edge of Blacklaw, slag heaps kept watch on the sky, bald-crowned and dismal. Rain or shine, thought Mirran, there was little enough glint in Blacklaw.

The village comprised two rows of brick cottages, a brace of shops, a thriving public house, and in a lane stemming from the thoroughfare, a red sandstone kirk and its graveyard. The Stalkers' house was the last in the row. The street lifted ahead of Mirrin, climbing gradually to the colliery gates. Many women were out and about. The first haul of the day would be up soon, drawn on slender cables from the bowels of the earth. The women worked at the sorting tables and long troughs down which the coal harvest was poured. It was rough work, a far cry from being a hotel maid, but it seemed, strangely, more honest. It was a damned sight better than being stooped over a mule all day with a hundredweight creel strapped to your back and ten flimsy ladders between you and daylight—a murderous sort of slavery that had ended only a few decades ago. The troughs were bad enough, thank you; out in the open yard with only a leaky tin roof to umbrella the rain, and a filthy river of coal endlessly flowing from the upstairs wagon tips.

Coal—hard, gritty, clinging coal—was the source of all their fulfillments, element of their needs and supplier of their comforts. It infiltrated everywhere, into the pores, nostrils, lungs, hair roots, eyes, fingernails, even into the most secret and tender parts of the body. It was the main chemical in the air they breathed, and tainted the water from the taps and pumps. The streams were coal-black; the Shennan coke-gray; the tree buds uncurled from winter's sleep with coal grit embedded in their tiny folds.

And all day long, week in, week out, Mirrin and forty like her pored over the tables sorting the valuable stuff, cleaning out stones and clay and bits of rusty metal that adulterated the pure black mineral on which all their lives depended. Fit work for women? So the menfolk thought. But the men had it even harder. By now the day shift would be cramped against the seam, the change shift tucked in bed, sleeping the sleep of sheer exhaustion.

Hennigan's shop was open for business. Women crowded its doorway, buying a pie or a quarter loaf for the midday meal. Kate, as always, had packed a bannock and cheese into her sister's coat pocket. Mirrin joined a stream of women making for the gates. For the most part their spirits were high. Too bold to be popular with many of her co-workers, Mirrin's quick wit could not be ignored. She came up behind a bunch of former schoolmates huddled sniggering over a furtive postcard.

"Showin' off that smutty picture again, Maggie?" said Mirrin in passing.

Flushing, Maggie Fox glanced up. Mirrin glimpsed a sepia-colored card showing what looked like four rolls of uncooked dough engaged in hand-to-hand combat. Maggie palmed the card and tucked it away.

"Tut-tut," said Mirrin, "and you a Sunday-school teacher!"

Deirdre Collins and her aunt Essa, both twenty and as alike as two peas, emerged from a doorway and fell into step beside Mirrin.

"Here," Essa said. "Did you hear about Janet, Big Tam's daughter, her that worked in the Lamont house, in Strathmore?"

"What about her?" said Mirrin.

"Walked out."

"I thought she needed the work."

"Couldn't stand it there," said Deirdre.

"She's only been there since Christmas," said Mirrin.

"Expected too much of her, if y'ask me," said Deirdre, confidentially.

"Who?" said Mirrin. "Lamont?"

"The master himself."

"Have you spoken to Janet?" asked Mirrin.

"No chance," said Essa. "Packed her bags on Saturday and left Blacklaw on the night train."

Mirrin did not doubt the Collins girls' word, only their interpretation of the facts of the matter. Janet Mackenzie wasn't the first local girl to quit domestic service in the coalmaster's house, but for all her dislike of the man, Mirrin did not believe the rumor that Houston Lamont was a lecher. He was married to a wife who would keep a sharp eye on servants' behavior; besides, the coalmaster was hardly the sort to demean himself by tickling the maids—especially maids like the Mackenzie girl, who had a face like a surly sow. The chances were that Janet had been caught pilfering.

Hesitating, Mirrin glanced back down the long scoop of the main street. In the distance, a full mile from the village, a high dike and a wealth of handsome oaks marked Strathmore, Houston Lamont's estate. Many villagers considered it right and proper that Lamont's property should have more than its fair share of greenery. He *was* the mine owner, and being rich, educated, and powerful, should attract such favors naturally. Mirrin did not subscribe to the theory that coalmasters were God's elect. Her political fervor was something of a joke among the men, an embarrassment to the women of her family. She was astute enough not to have mentioned her confrontation with Lamont in the Hamilton hotel. She thanked her stars for her caution now as the Collins girls prattled on about the habits of county gentry and the Lamonts in particular as they hurried through the gates and along the crowded lane under the towering winding gear.

All around her now were Lamont's men, Lamont's machines, the black dross that fertilized Lamont's wealth. For all that, she could not help but feel secure within the confines of the pit head. It was every collier's steading, their estate, and they had as much pride in it as if their names were scribbled across the deeds and contracts. Beneath her feet seams of coal radiated out across Lanarkshire, deep, rich, and inexhaustible. The raddled landscape was not without a certain weird appeal—bogies shone like pewter, corrugated iron sheds were rufous red. The coal stream itself, beginning to ripple down the chutes, had an iridescent sheen. Blacklaw must surely be one of the ugliest spots in all Scotland; yet even here, sometimes, there was evidence of a kind of beauty.

As they hung their coats in the shed and wrapped stiff canvas aprons around their waists, the girls continued to gossip.

"Janet would've done better to stay on the troughs, if you ask me," Deirdre said.

"She was always as lazy as sin," said Essa, giving Mirrin a sly nudge. "But then you don't have to be a worker to get on in this world—not if you're a lassie."

"What's that supposed to mean, Essa?"

"If Janet had had your looks, Mirrin Stalker, she. . . ."

"My looks!" Mirrin said. "What do you need looks for in this job? All you need is a strong pair of arms."

Before she lost her temper at the jibes Mirrin turned and strode off to her place at the troughs. Her appearance had been used against her before by women who called themselves friends. But their nasty taunts meant little or nothing. Her season in Hamilton had taught her that Blacklaw was the place for her. She was strong, healthy, and young, had her family, her politics, her steady job, even a *beau* of sorts, if you could call Rob Ewing that. No, there was precious little wrong with being nineteen and a sorter in Lamont's pit.

Mirrin Stalker started work at five minutes past seven o'clock. By noon that day, Monday, March 19, 1875, she would wish herself a thousand miles from Lamont's colliery and everything it stood for in the tragic history of Blacklaw.

⤬

The schoolhouse was to the west, between the village and Strathmore, a tight, hunchbacked building with a spit of sparse grass for a playground and an iron bell in the tower over the dominie's parlor. At eleven on the dot the bell clanged, and boys and girls rushed yelling from the doors to take advantage of ten minutes' break from the rigors of free education. Three boys walked soberly through the middle of the bedlam and stopped by the school gates. The tallest, Henderson, had the startled expression of a snared jackrabbit; McLaren was moon-cheeked and sly-eyed; the youngest, Drew Stalker, was solemn and emotionless, a fact that riled the bullies considerably.

"So you told old Guthrie on us, you rotten tyke," McLaren snarled.

"I didn't tell him," answered Drew calmly. "He's not blind, y'know. He saw you squintin' at your crib of the test answers. You're lucky he only took the crib away."

"Lucky?" said Henderson. "I flunked the last three tests. If I fail this one my old man'll murder me. He wants me to stay through to fifteen. The school board won't accept me if I fail again."

Drew said nothing. He was innocent—not that that would save him from their anger. Henderson in particular was jealous of his brilliance; envy bred injustice.

"Kick his head," McLaren advised.

Though most of the senior school knew what was going on, nobody would stand up for Stalker. Even Betsy had hidden herself away in the lavatories. Secretly Drew was delighted that Henderson and McLaren had been caught cheating. Where had they been all those nights when he was crouched over his books in the backyard shed? Chasing rats over the shale hills, laying traps for hares, or kicking a cloth ball about the yard of the pub, most like; while he'd been camped on top of the washtub peering at print by the glimmer of a penny dip. He knew that they would not respect him for fortitude and diligence; he did not expect it. On the other hand, it was grossly unfair that he should be punished for their ignorance.

McLaren pinned him against the gatepost.

"Give him the pincer," Henderson said.

McLaren's fat fingers reached for Drew's nose. But Drew, light and fast, ducked and darted away. McLaren was after him at once.

Many children were watching now, forming a slack ring around the fighters. Stalker was always fair game and put up a good show, though the fun really started when Henderson had him down. The bouts had the inevitability of ritual. Drew crouched, arms out, to parry any sudden rush. Provided he kept his head the bell might save him from too much punishment. He faced the back wall of the schoolyard and the grass slope above Poulter's burn, the landscape no more than a screen to which Henderson and McLaren were pasted like paper scraps. Then something twitched on the edge of his vision. He glanced up, startled, and his hands fell slackly to his sides. Henderson's knuckles bled his mouth. Drew did not move, blood dripping from his swollen lip, eyes round as marbles. On the slope above the burn the big chestnut tree quivered again. Drew shook his head incredulously. The barren tree had developed life, swaying nervously from side to side. He lifted his arm and pointed. "Look at that."

Everyone turned.

As if to entertain them the tree danced faster.

"Da!" Henderson murmured. "Daddy!"

A rumbling roar filled the air, and a series of shocks vibrated through the ground beneath their feet. In the dominie's tower the bell clanged tentatively, then hung silent. A low moan rose from the schoolchildren. The chestnut tree shot out of the ground, trunk, roots, fibers, as if punched from below. For a moment it hovered, then arched up and plunged into the stream fifty yards away.

Nobody in the yard moved.

Dominie Guthrie flung open the main door, and followed by the other teachers, ran out into the playground.

"Attention," he shouted. "Attention, children."

His reedy command was lost in confusion; his appearance had broken the spell. Girls and boys fled in all directions, wailing. Only a few seniors stood stock-still, not knowing what was required of them.

"Please, children, *attention*."

. There was no apparent focus for their fears, and the children had just begun to gather around their master when the ground shuddered even more violently than before and a sound like cannon shot rolled overhead, prelude to a deafening fusillade of explosions. The children scattered again in a frenzy of terror.

Blood dripping from his mouth, Drew ran too, caught up in the crowd that streamed through the gate and along the footpath into the kirk lane. The colliery hooter blared as Drew rounded the gable of the kirkyard. He saw smoke, all peppered with sparks, coiling darkly over the pit head. Suddenly the pall burgeoned into a roaring column that jetted two hundred feet up from the top of the winding shaft. Drew shied and screened his face against the dike. Henderson overtook him. The bully was reduced to a tearful lad crying, "My daddy's on the shift, Drew. He's in there, on the shift."

. It was Alex Stalker's shift too; Drew's father and

brothers were deep that morning, all the way down at the bottom level.

Without a word Drew ran on.

ᕦᔦ

The first tremors rattled table and hob, spilling rivers of tea from the mugs. Kate gripped the table to stop its tilting and looked to her mother in the corner chair. Every bit of color had drained from Flora Stalker's face. Kate stepped around the table to reach the woman. Three blasts battered the narrow room. Pictures dropped from the walls, dresser dishes chattered against their rods, a bowl hopped from the sink and shattered to fragments on the floor. Flora Stalker hauled herself from the chair and reeled toward the door.

"Alex?" she cried peevishly. "Alex?"

Kate snatched a plaid shawl and threw it over her mother's shoulders. The woman sounded more vexed than alarmed. "Not *my* laddies. Not *my* boys."

Every door of every house in Blacklaw was wide to the wall. Women clasped bairns or tucked toddlers under their arms and hobbled like cripples into the middle of the street. Young men not long off night shift fumbled to buckle on their broad leather belts as they ran. Elderly colliers who had many nightmares locked in their memories traveled more slowly as if reluctant to crawl beneath that spreading canopy of smoke.

"It's Number Two pit. Number Two."

Kate gripped her mother's arm like a vise and steered her uphill into the back of the crowd that already thronged the gate area. The lunatic howl of the hooter fluctuated and died away, leaving a babble of voices drifting up from what remained of the surviving pit-head blocks.

"Kate? Mam?"

Kate caught sight of her sister in the crowd.

"At least Mirrin's all right," she said. "Thank God."

Flora Stalker brushed the hair from her eyes and seemed to indicate by that gesture that Mirrin had no claim on her concern. Mirrin burrowed through the crowd, eyes wide and unblinking, a stiff white ring around her mouth.

"How bad, Mirrin?" Kate whispered.

"Bad." Her fingers dug into Kate's shoulder. "Know what they're saying caused it? Firedamp. Hear that? Firedamp. It's only two months since Daddy and the Ewings reported damp in the pit, but nobody paid a blind bit of notice."

"Stop it, Mirrin."

"The bloody bosses were warned, and they did nothin'. Now my father an' brothers are. . . ."

Kate shook her sister vigorously. She had no time for Mirrin's tantrums. She had too much to do, too many people to look after—Flora, Betsy, Drew—to get through without Mirrin's help. "I need you, Mirrin. Pull yourself together."

Mirrin's lips were tight and hard. "What d'you want me to do?"

"Stay here with Mother," Kate said. "I'm going back to the house for blankets. They'll need all the blankets we can spare."

"And we can spare plenty, now, can't we?" said Mirrin bitterly. "All right, I'll stay with Mam. Where is she?"

"There."

Mirrin nodded and thrust deeper into the crowd. Kate watched her make contact with their mother, then pulled back and set off down the main street again. She was shivering with shock. Hugging her arms to her breast, she hurried in search of the youngsters.

School pupils were milling up from the kirk lane, some sobbing, some grim, made adults in the season of a single hour. Drew and Betsy found her at the same moment. Betsy's black eyes had the luster of tears. Drew, though pale, was calm. Though the boy and girl were twins their temperaments were opposite. Betsy lunged into Kate's arms, craving attention. Drew stood back, waiting, silent. Kate allowed the girl a minute's comfort, then gently disentangled her. "No time for crying now, Betsy. We don't know what's happened yet."

"Mr. McCausland told me that Number Two pit's gone up, and everything in it," said Drew.

Checking her mounting hysteria, Kate steered the twins down the length of the street away from the horrors of the colliery yards.

She said, "I've something special I want you to do. Promise me you'll both stay at home, indoors."

"What do you want?" said Drew.

"Have hot water on the hob and tea in the pot. Make sure there's milk, sugar, and bread in the house. You'll find a shillin' in the pickle jar if you need to go to the store. Drew, if you must go out, you go—straight to Hennigan's and back. Betsy, put the warming bricks in the beds."

"But . . . ?"

"Don't argue, Betsy," she snapped.

"We'll do it," Drew said.

Kate trusted him. He would keep his head and calm Betsy down. She had never been able to evaluate her brother's intelligence, could not come as close to him as to James and Dougie. In the house she quickly collected a half dozen worn woolen blankets from the attic and with the stuff in her arms left again, alone.

A fine rain mist varnished cobbles and slates now. When she did not look up at the pinnacles of smoke, the street seemed oddly peaceful. This would be the last moment's peace she would know for some time. Then she heard music. Pausing, she peered curiously down the tunnel between the rows into the back lots. The tune was sweet, harmonious, the trenchant pathos of the daftie finding voice in the tines of the old mouth organ. Lauchlan Abercorn was a young, broad-shouldered man with a face as frank as a ham. He sat on the midden heap like a king on his throne, enraptured by the music he blew for himself. But when he noticed Kate spying, his features contorted and he leaned forward and played a ranting two-note complaint that mimicked the call of the colliery hooter.

Poor Loony Lachie, butt of cruel village jokes, never dangerous, seldom sad, just prone to be irritated at intrusions into his privacy. What would he make of this day's events? Not much, Kate thought. At least for a time he would rule over an empty village and have it for his innocent kingdom.

The noise of the mouth organ sawing in her ears, Kate turned and ran, anxious to submerge her fears in those of the multitude who waited in hope at the steps of the colliery shaft.

CHAPTER III

BLACKLAW colliery was one of a hundred such mines sunk deep into the rich lode that slanted west from the Lothians and earned Lanarkshire the doubtful crown as the blackest county in Scotland. Situated astride the main Glasgow to Hamilton road, the workings were divided yet again by an ancient bypass that staggered in from low ground and lost itself in the wilderness. The pits, known simply as One and Two, were seventy yards apart, both opening north of the bypass. Offices, workshops, and sheds sprawled south, linked by a spur of the Hamilton branch line to an artery of the Caledonian railway. The pits were prone to dampness. Minor injuries from spurt fires were frequent occurrences, and Alex Stalker had sued loudly for more thorough inspection. To give him his due, Lamont did not let the complaints pass unchecked. Only that morning, at 4:30 A.M., firemen and an underground manager had given the pit safe clearance. No trace of gas had been found. At 6 A.M. a full day shift had started work. At 11:15 A.M. a massive explosion had ripped the guts from Number Two pit. The source of the blast was unquestionably firedamp. The toll obtained from the pay office set the number of colliers underground at 115 men and boys.

Rampaging from the shaft aperture, shock waves wrecked the cage and spewed boulders, coal, girders, and wooden props over a huge area. The offices and workshops, which suffered the brunt of the detonations, were speared with flying debris. Worse, though, was the fate of the surface squad. They had been drawing hutches from the pit head to the coups, directly in the line of the blast. The squad had been ripped apart, workers tossed like dolls over the scorched ground and plastered against the iron hutches. A few survivors still stumbled aimlessly around, oblivious to the cause of the calamity. Railway gangs rushed down the embankment to lend aid, and the first organized platoons from Northrigg had just arrived to swell the ranks.

Numb with horror, Kate gaped at the hellish scene. Every animate and inanimate object was coated with slimy black dust. It clogged her nostrils and made her eyes smart like salt. A boy not much older than Drew swayed past, face covered by his hands. Blood welled through his fingers. Impulsively Kate stepped toward him. Roughly he thrust her aside and blundered on in search of daylight.

"Don't stand gawpin', girl." A ganger waved angrily. "Away t'the joiners' shop and help the doctors."

Kate spun around. Hummocks and mounds were all around. Stretcher-carriers bent over them, prying with their hands. Women scurried from barrow to barrow, anxious yet afraid to confront the faces that emerged from the mud.

"My laddie, just a wee laddie wit' red hair. Have you not see my laddie, him wit' red hair?"

Women keening like beggars congregated by the manager's office not far from the blown shaft. Kate drifted toward them.

A shout went up: *"All clear of Number One pit. Number One pit all clear."*

Kate caught sight of one of her father's mates.

"How many in Two, Mr. Pritchard?"

"They'll be postin' lists shortly, Katie. That's all them dirty blackguards are good for—postin' bloody lists."

"How many?" she pleaded.

"Sixty."

A slight figure topped with flame-red hair was rolled into a stretcher, a clean sack drawn up over his crusted face. At the back of the crowd she could still hear the woman's voice crying, "Have you not seen my laddie—just a wee laddie wit' red . . . ?" Weeping, Kate moved on.

Mirrin had found her mother a place on a bench by the workshop wall. Flora's face was chalk-white, but she looked inquiringly at Kate, who, stooping, told her that she had delivered the blankets to the gatehouse. Her mother nodded. Mirrin said, "You'll have heard—none of our folk came out of Number One."

"What else have you heard?" Flora asked.

"A crew's headed into Number One pit. They were hardly on the level before they got a whiff of gas, but they're still pushing on to try a breakthrough into pit Two. If they can clear the shaft, they'll put down a kettle." Miners' jargon came easily to Mirrin, though she had never seen the barrel-sized contrivance—the kettle—in which men could be lowered through a blocked shaft in an emergency. "Old man Ewing was for goin' down, but Rob got his cronies to hold him back."

There was no trace of derision in her voice today when she mentioned Rob Ewing. Flora could never understand Mirrin's taunting attitude to the young collier. Even now, in the center of disaster, there was something so challenging in Mirrin's stance that Kate was glad they were out of the crowd. Scorn mingled with grief in Mirrin. Clearly she detested the pompous details with which Lamont's minions pegged the tragedy. On this day of all days Kate prayed that Mirrin would guard her tongue. But Mirrin said not a word during the quarter hour it took for a cage to grind down Number One shaft and for news to reach the surface that two men had been found at the bottom.

"Who are they?"

"Have they any news of Two?"

The crowd surged forward, children shrieking as they were jerked from their mothers' sides.

"For the love of God, stand back!" Donald Wyld, the manager, shook his fists, and men already drawn for the search party shouldered the mob into some semblance of order. *"Give us room to bring them out. We'll be able to post names all the quicker. It's a living hell down there. Don't make it worse for us."*

The crowd quieted and ebbed back a little as the cage gate was raised and two of the rescue squad slouched out. The crowd growled in disappointment. Where were the rescued? Only the underground shift could bring forth the morning's darkest secrets. The growl changed abruptly to a fluting sigh as the rescuers lifted a blanket on which lay a mud-fouled, charred thing, an object that had recently been a man.

"I thought. . . . Oh, God, I thought they meant alive," said Mirrin softly. "They must all be dead down there."

"Don't say that, Mirrin," Flora reprimanded her sternly. "Your father's not dead."

"But, Mam . . ."

"Shush, I tell you."

An oversman, an uncle of David Henderson, called out hoarsely, "I've . . . I've identified a ring. It's . . . my brother, my own brother, Joseph Henderson." He hesitated, steeling himself. "We can't identify the second man. The wrights' shop will serve as the death house."

The villagers understood. In the wrights' shop the bodies would be laid out, all their personal belongings removed and labeled to assist in identification.

Kate sat with her arm around her mother, not watching, just waiting, hope dimmed. Three of the Stalkers had been in the second pit. It would need a miracle to bring them all up alive. Four times the cage descended; four times it rose to the surface and disgorged its grisly cargo. Mirrin spoke only once: "They've started on the brattice. They'll sink the kettle directly into Two quite soon." But "quite soon" meant hours. For hours the clangor of preparation continued. It smirred with rain, and dried, and smirred again, and at last the first of the list was posted and the worst time of all for the waiting women had arrived.

Handprinted papers were tacked to the walls of the joiners' shop. Women came out of the crowd, read, groaned, wept, and turned away, knowing that the waiting was over—or waiting still. By late afternoon the pit head was packed with miners from neighboring collieries. Chokedamp had taken its toll of the rescuers. It denied them the dignity of heroes, driving them scrambling from the cages to writhe upon the wet earth and cleanse their flesh of the deadly film.

Flora Stalker would not leave the site, sharing in every drama, though on her bench by the wall she appeared aloof. Mirrin went up and read each list and returned, sadly shaking her head. Articles brought to the surface were clerically processed and put in a green tin box that Wyld periodically brought to the crowd.

"If anybody can put a name . . . ?"

"Holy Mary, Mother o'God!"

"A knife, with the tip of the blade broken?"

"Her youngest is only nine month."

"Merchant navy button, from the breeks?"

"Peter!"

"A buckle . . . ?"

"John!"

"A boot with four star studs?"

"Willie!"

"Holy Mary, Mother o'God!"

Tears rivered Kate's cheeks in arid compassion. She was firm in the resolution that she nurtured no false hopes at all now.

"Kate?" Mirrin stood before her, an older Mirrin, no longer bold. "It's James and Douglas. They're named. Our James and our Dougie. Both . . . dead."

Flora sagged. Hand on Kate's arm, she confided, "Douglas was just sixteen, you know."

Kate nodded.

"He was just a laddie."

Kate nodded again. It wasn't true, though. Douglas had been a man, a collier, proud to crawl to the face on his father's heels.

"What about Da, Mirrin?" Kate said.

"We . . . we can't be sure."

"I want Alex." Flora Stalker struggled stubbornly to her feet. "*I want my man.*"

 сево

Donald Wyld had never been involved in a major disaster before. Though he had been well tutored in emergency techniques he cursed the stroke of luck that had taken Lamont out of Blacklaw that day of all days and pushed all the responsibility onto his shoulders. Vast pockets of gas in the low levels had brought operations to a halt. Wyld arranged for hundreds of gallons of water to be pumped down the shaft to help counteract the gas. Pumps and hoses were run out as work continued on the main shaft's pulley. Fresh teams of rescuers were recruited. By now mobs of sightseers had arrived from Glasgow and Edinburgh, drawn by morbid fascination. In the joiners' shed a dozen doctors worked feverishly on the injured. In the timber bay next door a canteen for the rescuers was quickly set up. No one was admitted to the wheelwrights' shop, however. In her heart Kate was convinced that within its sullen walls lay all that remained of her father.

Late in the afternoon Flora Stalker was persuaded that Drew and Betsy had been alone long enough and would be in need of her comfort. Hanging on Kate's arm, she left the yard without looking back.

Mirrin was relieved that Mam and Kate had gone; now she could concentrate on ridding her mind of sentiment. She had worked with men, argued, laughed, traded insults with them; she wouldn't cry now.

Dusk had come down, lamps and lanterns had been lit on the walls. She pushed herself stoically across the mud to the lists. Rain had made the names run; some were almost illegible. Were there no wax crayons in Lamont's office, Mirrin wondered, or had nobody thought that the rosters of the dead deserved permanence? *James Stalker. Douglas Stalker.* The ink had rivered, and the names of her lovely brothers merged and seemed to form a single unit quite separate from the scores of others.

"Och, James," she murmured. "James and Dougie."

Behind her, torrents of water spouted from the hoses. The wheel was turning again. No matter what happened to the men, that damned wheel was seldom still for long. It was a symbol of the coalmaster's power, fetter of them all. Mirrin moved away, marching as if she had a purpose and a destination. She tramped around the abandoned sheds and under the limbs of the troughs, alone in her misery. She could not stand the sight of the crowds at the shafts, fancy dans from the cities in nap overcoats and curly-brimmed hats, gawping toffs, and sensation-seeking reporters. And where the hell was Lamont, that grand man, God on this earth? He'd be cowering in some posh city club, hiding his shame, like as not; or maybe he was already out canvassing his committee pals to find him an excuse for his criminal negligence. She walked faster. It was not properly dark, but she could not bring herself to forsake the arena of lamplit workings, like a moth hovering around a flame. On the fifth stage her feet suddenly became leaden. A hundred yards from the frieze of dark shapes she halted, leaned against the wall of a docking hut, and wept.

For a tall man he moved lightly. Inside the Ulster cape his shoulders were broad. The stand-up collar framed his face. He held his bowler in his hand. When he touched Mirrin she whipped around, burning with shame at being caught in the weakness of tears.

"Miss . . . Stalker?"

She recognized him at once, barbered and neat as ever. A host of furious shouts seemed to clamor into her mouth, choking her.

"Who have you lost, Miss Stalker?"

"If you must know, it was two brothers."

"I am sorry."

"I'll bet you are."

Lamont raised an eyebrow. "I didn't mean to . . . to intrude."

"Aye, it's a bit late. If you'd intruded a month ago, when my father told you about. . . ."

"May I have one of my men escort you home?"

"Home? God Almighty, Mr. Lamont, *this* is home."

Perhaps he would have persevered, but she gave him no opportunity, pivoting and striding away alone. One more moment in his company and she would have gone for him, screamed out that he was a murderer, an assassin. Prudence, product of grief, stayed her rage. Tears blinded her, blurring the red glow of the torches and the sudden excited ripple that stirred through the crowd ahead of her.

Shouts brought her to her senses.

"Alive! Some o' them are alive!"

Mirrin gathered her skirts and ran.

The wives were jammed against the sawhorses. The motion of the mob was like a tidal shift, a massive surge. On a girder rack the last squad slumped, too spent to share the jubilation their efforts had brought.

"They're bringing them up. They're bringing them up *alive*."

Mirrin elbowed her way to the front rank. The trestles creaked and tilted under the pressure of the crowd. A dozen men stood agitatedly on the platform at the lip of the shaft. Light lay in great pallid wedges, shadows of the beams cut again by shadowgraphs of cables. When the cage hoisted into sight, the women fell silent. Ponderously the cage shuddered level with the boards, and rocking, stopped. A dozen men were visible within, like cloth puppets in a candle theater. The gate lifted. Mirrin pushed her knuckles to her mouth. She could hear something, something that made her heart pound. She could hear it, not clearly, but with sufficient clarity to give her hope.

A wounded collier was first out, hobbling between his rescuers. Two surgeons were on hand, frock-coated, tile-hatted gentlemen from Glasgow. Next out was a young man in a blood-soaked blanket stretcher. She could still hear the familiar sound—it was not an illusion. Then she saw. She closed her eyes and wailed.

There was no proper stretcher, only a broken shoring plank supported by two of the relief squad. They edged it gingerly from the cage.

". . . Told the bloody-minded bastards . . . told them months ago. Jesus Christ! One man's greed . . . I . . . ah, God! Listen, Lamont, you murderin' swine. . . ."

Snarling with vitality, that voice had often filled the Stalker house with its mutinous complaints. Mirrin pushed down the trestle and leaped over it, running, calling, "Da, Daddy, I'm here."

Alex Stalker was propped on the plank, head and shoulders bolstered by the bearer. Mirrin would hardly have taken the charred effigy for human if it had not been for his open mouth and the volume of his shouting. His watery eyes scanned the ranks of bowler-hatted gentlemen. Mirrin stopped herself from hugging him. Garments and flesh were knitted by burns, his blistered face caked with dust and his raised fist silver-scaled like a mailed gauntlet. He ranted and raged against the hell's brigade of petty officials whose negligence had destroyed so many of his comrades.

She knelt beside him. "It's me, Da. It's Mirrin."

He peered at her, lips peeling back in a parody of a grin. "Hullo, chick," he croaked. "Where's . . . your . . . mam?"

"She'll be here soon."

"Listen, chick. Listen. . . ."

"Don't try to talk."

"Hell, let him talk, Mirrin." One of the bearers was Rob Ewing, hardly recognizable. His feathery mustache stuck out like a piece of flint. "Your old man should really be dead, y'know. It's pure hatred that's keeping him goin'."

"Lamont . . ." Alex Stalker bellowed.

"Stand aside."

Mirrin was lifted clear of the plank. The doctor was no gentleman surgeon but a sawbones from the Poors' Hospital in Waygate, whey-faced, baldheaded, and brusque. A couple of officials stood behind him, looking duly concerned. The doctor gave Alex a cursory examination. "Take him up to the shop. I'll do what I can for him there."

Rob Ewing steered the plank on a course along the front row of the crowd. Mirrin walked by her father's side. He was gasping feebly, yet still vociferous, his forefinger, like a charcoal stump, pointed accusingly. "You . . . all know . . . who did . . . this. Find him . . . Make . . . him pay."

"Rest yourself, Daddy, please."

"Houston Lamont must face . . . the . . . law. Law's on
. . . our side."

The crowd shuffled restlessly. They had no eyes for the
other rescued man, only for Stalker whose ruined body
epitomized all that the colliers had suffered. His struggles
split the rucked skin, and fissures showed in the tarry
crust. His head fell back, imprecations still trickling from
his lips.

Mirrin gripped the plank, and facing into the crowd,
shouted, "Do you hear what he says? It's Lamont's fault.
By God, we'll make him pay for this day."

Now there was anger, shouting, assurances, threats; the
crowd's response comforted Alex Stalker. He closed his
eyes.

"In the name of God, girl, have you taken leave of
your senses?" The doctor snatched at her shoulder. "This
fellow might be dying, and you call for revenge."

"Aye, it would suit the bosses' purpose better if *nobody*
came alive out of that hole."

"Well, it's Glasgow for him. I haven't the facilities. I'll
arrange to have him sent to Glasgow infirmary—there's
a special train in the siding. . . ." The stretcher was close
to the field hospital now. Mirrin's nostrils cringed at the
hideous stink of the place. She stepped in front of the
doctor.

"No."

"Look here, m'girl, he's. . . ."

"Right. If he's dying, at least he'll die at home. Rob,
find a hand cart."

"I'll take no responsibility for his life," the doctor said.

"Nobody ever did," Mirrin snapped. "My father's a
Blacklaw collier. He's ducked death a hundred times. If
he's slated to die now, it'll not be in Lamont's shed. If he
dies at all, it'll be in his own bed."

"You're a stubborn fool," the doctor said. "All right,
do as you wish. Keep him warm, give him plenty of

fluids but no alcohol or solid food. I'll call in when I can."

"You'll find him in the last house on the main street."

Rob Ewing hurried from the gloom behind the shed, pushing a long slater's cart. "Mirrin, are you sure?"

"I'm sure," she declared.

Later, however, she was to wonder if her impetuous gesture had not deprived her father of many days of his life.

❧

Rob Ewing and James Stalker had been friends all their lives, sharing a school desk and later a pail of beer together after signing one name over the other on the tally for their first day's work at the pit. They were as close as kin. It was really through James's influence that Rob was drawn into courting Mirrin, a relationship that was more like pugilism than wooing. Rob was half afraid of Mirrin, of the hunger he had for her that he could not declare out loud in case she laughed in his face. He could handle other girls, the ones who were prim and proper—but Mirrin Stalker was like whiskey to their milk. There was no great clan of Ewings; they had lost no relatives in the disaster, though the Stalkers' grief was shared by Rob, his father and mother, almost as deeply as if it were their own. Even so, Rob did not feel comfortable in their kitchen, cramped in with the Stalker women, haunted by memories of sons who would never again sit themselves down at the corner table as he was doing and eat the broth that Kate served.

Kate put the plate on the table. Rob wiped his hands on his trousers and lifted a spoon. It was callous to sit in Dougie's chair, using Dougie's spoon. God, but the trivialities hurt most, cut deeper than the mere scale of the tragedy. Still, they had Alex Stalker back, what there was of him; so much nursing would be needed to keep him alive that the womenfolk would have precious little time to grieve for James and Dougie. Kate was busy, busy as always, filling a kettle from the water tub. He reminded himself to fetch coal from the backs and stoke the stove and draw more water for her before he left. He sopped up the broth with a heel of bread and to his surprise ate ravenously.

"Will your mother be all right, Kate?"

"As long as she has my father, she . . ."

Kate's eyes and the tip of her nose were red, which did not make her any prettier. She was more angular than Mirrin and would pass the watershed of twenty-five soon, lucky to find a man to take her. There were too many bonnie lassies in the area, and colliers' sons sought out young, strong girls as wives. Sometimes in the pub it was like listening to farmers discuss cattle to hear the young miners talk of women. Perhaps Kate had already reconciled herself to spinsterhood—it happened frequently to the eldest daughters of large families. A pitiful waste, Rob thought. For a woman a family could be both a consolation and a trap.

He said, "It'll not be easy for you now."

They were alone in the kitchen.

Kate said, "It never was easy, Rob."

Betsy and Drew had been put to bed in the attic, a blanket rigged up as a partition. Alex would need the back bedroom for himself for a long time to come. There was no sound from it now. Mirrin and Flora Stalker would have soothed and settled him and gently cleaned his wounds. Kate poured tea and seated herself at the table. The clock ticked, tin hands showing the hour as near to nine. Rob sipped from the mug, the filthy taste of coal grit seeping from his mustache. He wiped it with his wrist.

"Rob?" said Kate. "Will he die, d'you think?"

"Not him."

"I mean it."

Rob leaned forward. "Listen, d'you know how we found him? Off the gallery in a tight place, with the damned props nearly burned through and a ton of chip rubble down over him, steaming and just ready to ignite. His leg was all that we could see. James . . . James and Dougie were under the chip, buried."

"Go on," said Kate. "I want to know."

"Your old man was lyin' on his back, with his nose an inch from the roof, and a scoop made to his mouth. I'd never ever have spotted him, even with the lamp. But, by God, I could hear him loud and clear."

Kate grinned crookedly.

"He was givin' Houston Lamont big licks. Think of it, down there, buried under a million tons of rock, cursin' the coalmaster blind. It wasn't me that kept your father alive in that hellhole—it was bloody Houston Lamont."

"He's only a man."

"Who?"

"Lamont," said Kate. "He'll have his share of nightmares too."

"His nightmare will come with the inquiry," said Rob. "If your father and his mates have anything to do with it, Lamont could face charges of criminal negligence."

"Lamont will still have the authority to put us out."

"Rest assured, Kate, not even Lamont would dare toss a family into the gutter at this time."

"But after the inquiry he might. It's the rule. And we'll have no man workin' in the pit, not until Drew's of age."

"There might not even be an inquiry," Rob said.

"Mirrin told me. . . ."

"Mirrin's an idealist."

"So you think we might not have a roof over our heads for much longer."

Rob shrugged. He could not help. There was little enough spare cash in the Ewing coffers; even if he offered, the Stalkers' pride would not let them accept charity from a fellow miner.

Kate got to her feet. "I'll need to go in an' help with Father."

Kate's weariness was palpable. There would be many girls and women like her in Blacklaw, forced to suppress their own sorrows for the sake of others in need. Mirrin came out of the bedroom, eyes glittering with tears.

"He's fair quiet," said Rob.

"So would you be if you'd a rag roll in your mouth to bite on," Mirrin said.

"I'm . . . I'm just leavin'," Rob said.

"I'll see you out."

They stood for a moment by the door. The pit head glowed yellow against the clouds, and it was raining heavily now. All the houses were lit, some doors open, as if it were New Year's. Men clustered outside the Lantern public house; a priest strode up the cobbles, and without knocking, entered a house; two Salvation Army women helped a wee old man across the backs. A baby was yelling far up near the Ewing house, and like an echo of that hungry sound, there were impressions of other cries and keenings in the wet night air.

"I'm going to get that man," Mirrin said softly.

"Not now, Mirrin . . ."

"Go on, Rob Ewing, away back to the pit."

He tried to kiss her, but she held an arm across her face and administered a demure little shove with her fingertips. Rob turned and set off disconsolately up the main street. He had gone only twenty yards when he paused and glanced over his shoulder. Mirrin was still standing in the shelter of the eaves. With a quick, graceful motion she passed the palms of her hands back over her hair, then, with odd deliberation, stroked them down the fronts of her thighs. She lifted her hand, and just for a moment

Rob thought she was waving him farewell; then he saw that she was pointing at the high arch of the winding gear silhouetted against the yellow cloud.

"Houston Lamont," she shouted. "I mean, bloody Mr. Houston Lamont, you'll pay for this."

Then she went inside and slammed the door.

❧

"How does it appear, Mr. Wyld?"

The manager pushed papers across the table and yawned. It did not seem right to yawn but he could not help himself. "My figures make no mention of the eighty-three men who returned from Number One pit—they weren't directly involved in the explosion."

The three other men at the table in the temporary office grunted in unison.

"Of the one hundred and twenty-seven men below ground in pit Number Two," Wyld went on, "one hundred and eighteen have been brought to the surface."

"So nine are . . . ah, unaccounted for?"

"I think," said Wyld, "that we may take them for dead."

Nobody bothered to agree.

"Of that one hundred and eighteen, ninety-four were dead on recovery. Of the twenty-four still alive, less than half can reasonably be expected to survive their injuries."

"In other words," said one of the sleek, bewhiskered gentlemen, "virtually the whole shift was wiped out?"

"Aye, sir. A whole shift gone."

For over a minute there was total silence, broken, at length, by the thud of a fist on the table. The man had a rubicund complexion that fury intensified. "Bad. Bad. *Bad*!"

The colliery manager gathered up his papers and got to his feet. He studied the others carefully.

"May I take it, gentlemen, that there will be an inquiry?"

He had his answer at once. "Without question, Mr. Wyld, there *will* be an inquiry."

Donald Wyld bowed and walked stiffly out into the wet and empty dawn.

∽

Edith Lamont was reading her correspondence. She did not raise her eyes at the ominous crack the Sheraton chair made when her husband slumped into it. Common sense told her that a reprimand was not in order. Her pale, perfectly oval face remained calm. When she finally chose to look up at Houston it was with resignation. He had been careless with his grooming. His eyes were dull, pink-rimmed, and his jowls puffy. He looked old. Placing the letters by the side of her plate, she rang the silver bell, saying, "Anne will make you fresh tea."

"She's doing it now," Houston said. "I dropped in to the kitchen."

Edith leaned slightly forward in an attitude of restrained concern. "What is the position at the pit, my dear?"

"Ninety-four dead." He studied the effect of the news on his wife, then repeated, "Ninety-four men dead, Edith."

"We have been associated with the colliery too long to be unaware of its dangers," said Edith. "What was the cause of the explosion?"

"Firedamp."

Edith's eyes narrowed. "The accident that injured several youths just last month, Houston, was that not also attributed to firedamp?"

"Rank carelessness caused yesterday's tragedy," Houston said. "I suspect that one of the day-shift workers ignored the new safety regulations."

"Have you proof of that, my dear?"

"Of course not. I can't be expected to hound them every minute of each day. I can't. . . ."

"Hush!" Edith raised her hand as a girl of thirteen edged cautiously around the dining-room door, trying not to clatter the tray.

The little servant crept across the room, eyes on the carpet, nervous and cringing. Annie—Anne as his wife insisted on calling her—appeared closer than ever to the verge of collapse. As a rule the child's awkwardness irked Lamont, but not this morning.

"Annie, who did you lose?"

"M'brother, sir."

Gently Lamont took the tray from her and slid it onto the table. The girl's cheeks were flushed and tearstained, but she could not rid herself of the embarrassment of showing emotion in the august presence of her employers.

"Annie, you'll have to be brave."

"I'm all that's left, sir."

"Ah, I see. Your father's dead?"

Annie nodded.

Edith Lamont said, "Now, Anne, weeping will not help, but work will. The wages you earn here will be more important than ever. Bear that in mind. It will give you fortitude. Off you go. And wash your face. You may boil yourself one of the brown eggs, as a treat. Then busy yourself with the door brasses."

Lamont might have offered the girl comfort if Edith's rules regarding servants had been more flexible. The girl curtsied.

"Oh, Anne, be sure to offer my sincere condolences to your bereaved mother," said Edith.

"Aye, ma'am."

Wiping her nose on her apron, the servant left the room.

Lamont seated himself before the tray. He had no appetite.

"Brown eggs and brass polish will not mend a broken heart, Edith," he said.

"Food will take her mind from morbid sorrow," said Edith. "Besides, she will be better for the extra nourishment."

Lamont did not speak again.

Edith had not always been so cold and distant. The death of their son Gordon in the great measles epidemic seven years ago had changed her. Until then she had been warm and loving. Rationalization did not change the view he had of her, however; his wife's primness, neatness, presented too vivid a contrast with the scenes at the pit head. He put down his teacup and got hurriedly to his feet.

"Houston, you've eaten nothing."

"I've a meeting in a quarter of an hour."

Edith rose too. "I take it that there will be an investigation into last night's events?"

"Probably."

"Feelings will run high in Blacklaw."

"The colliers are bereft, if that's what you. . . ."

"Would you consider leaving Blacklaw for a few days' rest?"

"Leave?" He blinked. "Leave now?"

The woman lifted a letter from the plate. "The Cunninghams have asked us to visit them in their new domicile in Cramond. You have always enjoyed their company, and Cramond is so beautiful in the spring."

"You are unique, Edith," said Lamont ruefully. "Quite unique."

"I take it you do not wish to go?"

"I can't," said Lamont. "I daren't."

Curtly, he brushed her forehead with his lips and headed toward the door.

"Why not, Houston?"

"I'll explain at dinner," he said, "if I manage to be home for dinner."

"Houston?"

The door closed.

Edith frowned. She put the Cunninghams' letter on the plate again. From a pocket of her dress she removed a second letter that had been delivered by the morning post. It was addressed to her husband. The slanting, overornate script told her that it came from his sister. Embossing on the envelope gave confirmation: MISS DOROTHY ALLERTON LAMONT, WOODBANK HOUSE, MARLEFORD, KENT.

Crossing to the hearth, Edith dropped the letter onto the burning coals and broke down the charred sheets with the poker. That done to her satisfaction, she rang the silver bell again to summon Anne to clear away the breakfast things.

❧

A pale sun shone on Blacklaw and its fields, on slag and coal heaps and the red-stone kirk. It seemed as though every man and woman in the county had turned up to bury the dead. Newspapermen were out in force, from Glasgow, Edinburgh, Newcastle, even from far-off London. The radical presses were well represented too, their cubs badgering civic and mining officials in the hope of catching an inflammatory remark or two to blow up into a banner headline. Northrigg Colliery band played solemn marches and hymns as groups of mourners and shouldered coffins came in endlessly from kirk and chapel, until the whole acre was packed with black-garbed families.

The Stalkers had a quiet corner that fronted the street. There the brothers were buried in one deep grave, one small raw stone standing out among the weathered monuments. Rob Ewing and his father Callum assisted in lowering the coffins, and Drew stood with them. The boy looked taller, more mature—but not like a collier. The Stalkers spurned the services of a minister. Callum read from the Bible, Rob mumbled a prayer, and it was soon over. Kate led Flora away into the empty main street.

The band played distantly. The winding wheels were still. Not even daft Lachie Abercorn crooned on his mouth organ to give relief.

Drew and Betsy walked at the rear of the Stalkers' little procession. Betsy had cried herself out, but Drew had not shed a tear, not even privately. He walked with his head up, lips pursed, a glint of almost disdainful annoyance in his eyes, the Mirrin-thing, that challenging quality that he shared not with his twin but with his middle sister.

Betsy clutched his arm. "Promise me you'll not let them put you to the pit."

"I don't have to promise," Drew said.

"They'll want you signed on soon—we'll be needing the money."

"They'll just have to want," Drew said casually. "I'm not colliery fodder. I'm better than that."

"What a thing t'say!"

"You know it's true, though, Betsy."

"Aye," the girl admitted.

"I'm better stuff than colliers are made of." Drew nodded. "And before long I'll prove it."

"Well, you don't have t'prove it to me," said Betsy, staunchly.

Absently Drew patted her arm and continued to stare down the scoop of the main street toward Strathmore and the full-leaved oaks of Lamont's insular estate.

❧

THE SECRETARY OF STATE HAS DIRECTED THAT A PUBLIC INQUIRY INTO THE CAUSES OF THE BLACK-LAW COLLIERY EXPLOSION SHALL BE HELD BY MR. IAN HUTCHINSON AND AN APPOINTED LEGAL ASSESSOR. PLEASE MAKE KNOWN.

[SIGNED] IAN K. HUTCHINSON
CHIEF INSPECTOR OF MINES

It was a Saturday morning almost four weeks after the disaster when Rob and Callum Ewing brought the good news to Alex Stalker. During the early days of his illness the pain had been too great to allow much energy for talk, and his friends had contented themselves with murmured condolences and blessings for quick healing. In the past week, however, Alex's health had seemed so improved that the visitations had become prolonged and the kitchen put to use as a committee room. Flora Stalker, wrapped in grief for her sons, remained aloof from the activity, and all the arguments and imprecations wafted past her as if she were completely alone in the house.

Rob was drinking tea in the lugged armchair, Callum Ewing at the table. Alex Stalker, recently transferred to the alcove bed in the kitchen, leaned on his elbow on a nest of pillows, speaking rapidly, though his lips were still warped by the burns.

"An inquiry was inevitable," he said, "but there's nothin' cut and dried about its findings."

Callum Ewing was of Alex's vintage, a grizzled, lumpy-featured man, leathery and scarred as a smith's apron, though hardly bigger than a dwarf. "Aye, I never recollect an official inquiry into anythin' improvin' the collier's lot."

"We're not as we were," said Mirrin, who was peeling potatoes at the sink. "The miner's learning he has a voice, an' how to use it."

"But who'll listen?" said Callum.

"Shout loud enough, an' they'll listen," said Alex. "Tell me about the meetings."

"There's unrest," said Rob. "What do you think of these, then, Mr. Stalker?"

He produced a batch of pamphlets from his pocket and passed them to Alex for approval. The hand of the honest militant was evident in the prose, but the effect was somewhat dispersed by blurred print and outrageous spelling.

"Education," Alex said, "is the only answer."

Callum agreed, Rob was less sure, and Mirrin derisive.

Kate, trimming leeks on the broth board, paused and put in, "Aye, but education costs money."

"For the privileged," said Mirrin.

"Define privilege, lass," said Alex.

"Something that should be everyone's right—and isn't."

"Class," said Rob hopefully.

"Class," said Mirrin, "is only an accident of history that's become as . . . as immutable as the law of gravity."

"Laws are never immutable, chick," said Alex.

"Then how can we change them?"

"By process of law, o'course."

"Rubbish!" Mirrin declared.

"So you think we're stuck as we are?" asked Callum.

"Force built walls around the rich," said Mirrin. "Only force will knock them down."

"Just what do you advocate, Mirrin?" asked Rob.

"Revolution."

Rob stroked his feathery mustache to hide his smile. "I see. You'd have us all armed wi' picks an' shovels, storming Lamont's cabbage patch."

"You, shut your mouth," Mirrin said angrily.

"Free speech is the right of everybody, even a humble young collier like me," Rob retorted.

Alex intervened. "Revolution, Mirrin, doesn't necessarily lead to reform."

"Even so," said Callum thoughtfully, "Mirrin's right. The bosses are encounterin' a new breed of collier."

"But change might take decades, centuries," Alex suggested.

"That's defeatist talk, Da," Mirrin said.

"I'm no defeatist, lass, but *I'll* not live to see reforms."

His remark stilled conversation in the room. Kate glanced anxiously around at the bandaged figure in the bed.

Patiently, Alex said, "I didn't mean that. I meant that few of us here today will see justice for the workingman. How many leaders in history have been privileged to be in at the end of any reform they've inaugurated? Precious few."

His explanation was logical. Even so, it somehow smothered the argument. Not even Mirrin had the heart to revive it.

Alex beckoned his old friend. "Come, Callum, tell me what's been said at these meetings an' leave the young folk to their blethers."

Callum pulled his chair closer to the bed. Alex lay back, content for a while to be a listener, to harvest his strength. He would need every ounce of it in months to come when the conflicts between colliers and coalmaster found proper expression and philosophy degenerated into feud.

CHAPTER IV

MARCH limped out on squally showers, and April's early sunshine did not endure as far as the middle of the month. Great herds of cloud drove in from the west and browsed around the low hills, drenching the villages with steady rain. Blacklaw was less bleak than desolate. The closure of Number Two pit meant work-sharing and reduced wages for all the miners. Credit soon ran out at shops and pub. Charitable organizations had a field day. There was much ill-nourishment and bad health, with plagues of influenza and enteritis claiming several victims. Lamont's name was never far from folks' tongues, though he was seldom glimpsed in the colliery or the village. All the talk was of settlements and justice, forms of insurrection strangely at odds with charity and deliverance. Kate Stalker was caught in the miasma that seemed to surround the village. The houses were the same, the street, the pit, all the same—but not quite, for over a hundred men, old and young, had been gobbled up by the past, and the little stooping town was haunted by their absence.

Sunday agitators were out in force. Mirrin was often on the box, shouting and gesturing like a man, egged on by Christy Moran, as close to a professional rebel as you could find, a man who had served time for his convictions —and for clouting a cop at a strike break in Ayrshire.

"Our rights as colliers, that's all we want," Mirrin

yelled. "We don't want their damned charity. Let them keep their handouts, their blood money. . . ."

Kate fingered the two florins she had in her pocket. Rights and justice were fine sentiments, but they didn't put sup in a bairn's bowl. Kate's annoyance fixed on Mirrin. A girl of nineteen had no place on a box on a street corner with her coat flying and her blouse near half unbuttoned. Matronly outrage diluted Kate's fondness for her wild, impetuous sister. She wished that all this talk of rebellion would just die down, that the second pit would open again and Blacklaw get back to normal. But her wish was a foolish one—normality would not come again to the Stalker house.

In the midmonth, however, an event occurred that stirred even Kate's passive nature and led her a step closer to collusion with Mirrin's militant ideas of a democracy.

She came in from the shop to find the house in a turmoil, her father struggling to haul himself out of bed, the Ewings and several other colliers all bawling at once, and Mirrin beside herself with rage. She pushed to Alex's bedside to help Flora hold him down. She recognized all the members of the old gang—the Pritchard brothers, George McNeillage, Donald Ormond and his eldest son, the trusted cronies. She put her hands gently on her father's shoulders and held him against the pillows. His wounds were leaking through his soiled bandages.

He was howling like a wolf. "The blackhearted bastard. He'll not get away with this."

"It's happened before," Callum shouted. "It's the colliery law."

"*Law?*" Mirrin screamed. "*Call it law?*"

"What is it?" Kate asked, then demanded, "What's happened?"

"We're to be put out," Flora Stalker said coolly.

"*Evicted,*" Mirrin yelled.

Kate sank down on the edge of the mattress. "God! No!"

"It's the truth," said Callum. "You and twenty other families."

"Just because my old man can't work in the damned pit anymore," said Mirrin, close to tears.

It was another example of the vicious law that the masters had created for their own protection. The houses were "tied" to the job. Without exception every roof in Blacklaw belonged to Houston Lamont. Eviction! Kate could hardly believe that Lamont would be so cruel or so foolish. Did nothing in the world matter to him but his tonnage and his profit?

"Nothin' we can do about it," McNeillage whined. "What about your precious settlement now, Stalker? Think Lamont'll send it to you in the workhouse?"

"If you don't shut your mouth, McNeillage, I'll brain you," Mirrin snapped.

"Mirrin, that's enough. I'm not too weak to clip your ear for cheek, girl. Now I suggest we calm down and talk this over like sane, sensible, and rational folk," Alex said. His burned flesh had been exposed in the first struggle, and Kate looked with fresh insight into the pain her father must suffer. She flooded with tears and longed to point out to these men the incongruity of expecting leadership from a man who was only half alive. She left them, though, all gathered around the bed, angrily debating the latest outrage, while she and her mother brewed tea and cut bread. At least the threat to the remains of the family had restored some of Flora's competence.

Mirrin was seated on the bed, holding her father's hand, a sign that she aligned herself with his authority. In spite of her avowed love of freedom she would support him as long as he lived; discipline and duty were best fostered out of love.

Kate caught only the tail of the discussion.

"A strike's the only thing he'll understand," Jock Pritchard was saying.

Alex nodded. "Right. Start talking about a strike."

"Are you serious, man?" asked Donald Ormond. "A strike at this time would ruin us all, every one of us."

"I didn't say call a strike, I told you to start talkin' about one," Alex explained. "Put out the word, stir it up, but avoid trouble. And Mirrin, no more of this street-corner militancy."

"Aye, Da. But what's on your mind?"

"Lamont's on thin ice, and he's well aware of it," said Alex. "He's giving the village a fright."

Suddenly Mirrin grinned and slapped her knee. "Two can play at that game."

"Aye," said Alex. "Perhaps we'll be tossed out in the long run, those of us unfit to work again, but that's Lamont's right—once he's made due settlement for his negligence."

"Aye, he won't risk a strike before the public inquiry," said Colin Pritchard. "You're right there, Alex."

"Of course he's right," said Mirrin proudly.

"Do you really think he'll back down on the evictions?" Callum asked.

"I'd stake my life on it," said Alex Stalker.

"We'll filter the word to the night shift," said Rob. "Threaten full strike action."

Mirrin slid from the bed and raised her arms.

"If Lamont wants to play at scarecrows, then I'll scare him out of his breeks. *Boo* to Mr. Houston Lamont."

The men laughed, and Kate saw, with a melting heart, that her mother was laughing too.

◈

"Miss Stalker?"

Hand still on the door handle, Kate nodded mutely.

"May I come in?"

"What . . . what for?"

His carriage was drawn up at the curb. A big glossy

black horse champed against the tie rein, and the bow of the coach door displayed a circlet of gilt letters: BLACK-LAW COLLIERY—PROPRIETOR HOUSTON LAMONT. The curtains of the houses opposite were drawn back, and the few pedestrians in the street at that hour of the midmorning slowed to gawp at the man.

"I wish to speak with your father, if I may," Houston Lamont said.

"I'll see if he's awake, sir," Kate said.

She thanked her stars that she was alone in the house with the invalid. If Mirrin had been at home. . . . It didn't bear thinking about.

"Father, it's Mr. Lamont."

"Aye, I thought I recognized the voice. Help me up, lass."

She propped Alex up and buttoned his nightshirt, then stepped to the kitchen door and ushered Lamont in, murmuring, "My father's still very ill, sir, and should not be overtaxed."

"My business will not take long," Lamont said.

Kate was surprised at his tone. She had heard him only on a few public occasions, when his voice had sounded pompous and booming. Now, however, it was gentle, clipped and courteous. Lamont did not take the chair Kate drew out. He remained standing, towering over the wizened miner, his head a mere half inch from the roof. Colliers' cottages were not built for tall men in tile hats.

"How is your health, Stalker?"

"Fair."

"I'm glad to hear it."

"The rumor I heard about being flung out of my house isn't the best sort of medicine, though," Alex said.

"Perhaps not," said Lamont. "I would point out, however, that much of what's been said and done in Blacklaw this past month has not been truthful, or rational."

"That's so," Alex agreed.

"We're both colliers, Stalker—different ends of the scale, but we are both colliers. We're both interested in Blacklaw, are we not?"

"Aye, Mr. Lamont."

"What's the truth behind these threats to withdraw all labor from my pits?"

"How would I know?"

"Come now, Stalker, let's not indulge in verbal sparring. How serious is the strike threat?"

"Serious."

"A strike won't solve any problems."

"It's the only weapon we have, Mr. Lamont."

"A dangerous weapon," Lamont said. "I know full well that you have influence with the agitators, Stalker. I would be grateful if you would ensure that there are no outbreaks of unrest at this time."

"Before the inquiry, you mean?"

"After the inquiry I'll review the situation."

"How long will that take?"

"Not long."

"Just long enough for a few more families to starve."

"Nobody starves in my village," Lamont said.

"No, you'd send them away first."

"I cannot right all the social evils of the day," said Lamont, dryly. "I came here to ask your help in averting a strike that can only do more harm than good to the community as a whole."

"And to you in particular, sir?"

"I doubt that I'll ever find myself in the parish poorhouse, Stalker. Will you speak to your friends?"

"I'll . . . think about it."

"I'm not an ogre, Stalker. I have the welfare of this village very much at heart."

"Then pull off the eviction orders."

Lamont tapped his hat brim thoughtfully. "There is

no question of *your* being put into the street, not in your condition."

"And the other families?"

"I need the houses."

"Not with one pit closed, you don't."

"Are we bargaining, Stalker?"

"So it seems, sir."

"How many houses are involved?"

"Twenty-three. Mostly widows and injured miners."

"I will need those houses."

"I see you use the future tense, Mr. Lamont."

"Number Two pit will be operational inside a month."

"The public inquiry's findings will be announced sooner than that," Alex said.

"You appear to be setting much store by the board's findings."

"Naive though it might seem, Mr. Lamont, I still have a belief in justice."

"Very well, Stalker, I'll withdraw the eviction notices for the time being."

"And the rental dues?"

"Stalker, really!"

Alex did not push the point, kirk and chapel funds functioned to aid the really destitute. He said, "I'll be seeing some friends tonight, sir. If the subject comes up, I'll mention your kindness."

Houston Lamont grunted in acknowledgment of the veiled promise. He turned from the bed and stepped to the door. Kate opened it. He hesitated. "Take care, Stalker, you're not a well man."

Was it a threat or a clumsy benediction, Kate wondered. She bid the coalmaster a polite good morning and watched him climb into his carriage and take up the reins. The painted wheels trundled over the cobbles. Lamont spared not a glance for her nor for the women who gaped at him, not even for Loony Lachie, who stood to attention like a guardsman and saluted. Kate went indoors.

"You'll be pleased, Da?"

"Aye, I'm pleased, lass, pleased as a tinker's spaniel. Now let's have a cup o'tea to wash the taste of double-dealin' from my throat."

"Then you must rest. Even Houston Lamont said you were sick."

"I may be sick," Alex said, "but Lamont's scared. At long last we've given the coalmaster a fright."

"Lie down, Da," Kate said. "You look terrible."

Chuckling, Alex Stalker slumped back against the pillows.

❧

"Him? Here? Lamont in this house?" Mirrin exploded. "The gall of the man. What did he want?"

"Came to see you, Mirrin, like all the men do," Betsy giggled.

Mirrin ignored her. "Come on, Daddy, tell me what Lamont wanted."

"Trade and barter," said Alex Stalker. In spite of his glee at the triumph of his scheme, pain was riding him hard. He tried to put it out of his mind and gave Mirrin a full account of his conversation with the master of Strathmore.

"One month's reprieve," said Mirrin, "is that all?"

"The settlements will be through by then," said Alex.

"Depending on the results of the board."

"They can't fail to find liability."

"They're an official body and can twist facts as they like," Mirrin said.

"A month's better than a week, all the same," Kate put in.

"Anyway, Mirrin," Alex said, "I'll need to talk to Callum. As soon as you've had your tea will you go and find him?"

"I'll go now," said Mirrin.

"Eat your dinner first, chick."

"Keep it warm," Mirrin told her mother.

"What's your hurry, Mirrin?" said Betsy. "Frightened Rob Ewing won't wait?"

"I'm just doing what Daddy tells me—looking for Callum. Who knows, I might even have to go right into the pub to find him."

"Oh, Mirrin, you wouldn't dare," squealed Betsy.

"Why not!"

Betsy hugged herself in pleasurable outrage as Mirrin caught up her skirts and flirted them from side to side well above the knees. With a suggestive wink she danced into the hall and closed the door.

"That girl," said Kate, only half in jest, "will come to a bad end one day."

"Not her," said Alex, "not our Mirrin."

◦✎◦

The air was not springlike but as cold and dank as October, the sun caught in the Strathmore oaks like a sugary peardrop. As she walked up the main street Mirrin's thoughts were fastened on her father. The outer husk of Alex Stalker was decaying, Mirrin realized, and it was only a matter of time before the man's courage too was eroded by his wounds. Dr. Mackay had predicted it. If time were her father's enemy, it was Houston Lamont's friend. The longer he could stave off strike action, the better it suited him—the impetus of the disaster was already dwindling. God, she thought, how generous it was of the master to let them have an extra month in their dismal, drafty little house, how bloody generous!

"Look at *her* face."

"Who's done it to you, Mirrin Stalker?"

She was near the entrance to the Lantern's yard. Maggie Fox and Jean McCrae were always hanging about here, hopeful that some young buck, too liquored up to be discerning, might give them the eye.

"Since you're nosy enough to ask, Maggie," Mirrin answered suggestively, "nobody's done it to me yet, but when they do I'll be sure to give you all the interesting details."

"Impudent bitch!"

"Bitch yourself."

Mirrin swung into the rear yard, defying the code that prohibited "nice" girls from entering the precincts of the males' drinking preserve. Rob Ewing was seated near the back door in the company of four other young colliers, all with tankards in their fists. All five eyed Mirrin appraisingly as she approached, bold as brass and letting them gaze their fill. She knew the effect she had on them, with her thick, dark hair and generous figure. She was much less embarrassed by their reaction than Rob was.

"What do you want here?" Rob asked.

She delivered her father's message and saw one of the colliers dispatched into the pub to fetch out Callum. She repeated the gist of the day's unexpected events to the old man and watched him hurry off by the back track to consult with his mates. The bachelors had discreetly shifted inside, leaving Rob alone with her. They seated themselves on a wheelless flatcart under the claybrick wall, twilight gathering around them.

"If you ask me," Rob began, "Lamont's trying to shut your old man up."

"I'd guessed that much," said Mirrin.

"We'd best forestall him then. Call a meeting."

"Honest to God, Rob Ewing, if you heard the Last Trump soundin' you'd scurry off to call a meeting to petition the Almighty for fair shares for miners. Lamont's no fool."

"What would you have me do, Mirrin? Throw in with Christy Moran's hotheads and see Blacklaw shut?"

"If it gets us justice, aye."

"That's not the way, not with settlements in the offing," Rob said.

"What if there are no settlements?"

"We'll take proper action."

"And what's that, Rob Ewing, kneeling in the muck to kiss Lamont's boots?"

Rob's hands closed on her shoulders, his face thrust close to hers, so close that she could see the coarse stubble and the dust in his pores. "One of these fine days, Mirrin, that tongue of yours is going to land you in deep trouble."

She tried to pull away, but he held her tightly, one arm about her waist. "Have you taken leave of your senses, Rob Ewing? Damn it to hell, let me go."

"When I'm ready."

"What's got into you?"

"I'm sick of you talkin' to me as if I was an animal."

"Then stop behaving like an animal."

"Och, so you're a lady now, are you, Mirrin? On one hand you want freedom, and on the other you want respect. You can't have both, Miss Stalker. The way you've been carrying on these past weeks, you're lucky to have either."

"Will you let me go?"

"No." Rob laughed harshly. "It's a man you need, Mirrin."

"Who says I need anyone?"

"I'm sick of hearing how the men talk about you, saying things about your . . . your chest, and what they'd do to you if you weren't Alex Stalker's daughter. It chokes me to hear how they talk. It cheapens you, and it makes me seem small."

"Makes *you* seem small?"

"It's no secret that I want to marry you, Mirrin."

"Are you . . . ?"

"I am. I'm asking you to marry me."

"So my 'good name' won't be ruined?"

"It can't go on like this."

"I like my life the way it is, thanks."

"Mirrin, marry me."

"Oh, Rob," she murmured. "Oh, Rob!"

He drew her gently toward him, to take her head on his chest. She allowed him the gesture, then hissed, "Oh, Rob, you stupid, bumptious, conceited pig," and pushed him away. "So you'd marry me just to save my reputation, to make an honest woman out of me, to still the dirty mouths of a bunch of ignorant coal-grubbers? You'd really *sacrifice* yourself for my sake, would you?"

"Mirrin, I don't understand."

"No," she said, "you wouldn't."

He looked so hurt that she almost regretted her outburst. He was not a wicked man, just too earnest for his own good. Suddenly she saw herself as Rob Ewing must see her, and repented a little. Softly she said, "Rob, I can't marry you because I don't love you. I'm not ready to marry yet. Someday, perhaps, but not for a long while yet."

"But you're in your prime, Mirrin."

"Aye, I'm ripe enough, ripe to be plucked and squeezed by some man as if I was a grape, turned into a dried-up raisin with childbearing and worry. No, Rob, I'll see all men in hell before I commit myself to that kind of slavery."

"Mirrin, I never knew you felt. . . ."

"See, Rob, already you're beginning to think you've had a lucky escape. Away you go and have a dram with your mates."

"I'm afraid for you, Mirrin."

"Why?"

"You draw trouble the way jam draws wasps."

She smiled cynically and touched his mustache with her little finger. "You don't mean trouble, Rob, you mean men—men like my father, like you, like Lamont. Aye, life's full of trouble, sure enough. But I'll square up to my troubles as they come, provided they're of my own choosing."

"Is there no chance you'll change your mind?"

She had already risen from the flatcart and begun to drift away across the yard. She felt some sympathy for him and could not wound the big forlorn collier and abuse her power over him.

"No possible chance, Mirrin?"

"No, Rob, none."

"God, I'm a bloody fool," he said.

Mirrin gave him no answer and went out of the yard without another word. It was not until she reached the door of her house that she realized that her eyes, for some unfathomable reason, were brimful of tears.

CHAPTER V

THE gardens of the Kent mansion were brilliant with May blossoms. Cool and gloomy, the drawing room held nothing to engage Lamont's attention, and he passed the time by staring out of the discreetly barred window at the floral display. When Miss Emerson entered he turned almost reluctantly. The woman was short and matronly with snow-white hair. Lamont could imagine no one more qualified than Regina Emerson to manage a residence for Gentlewomen Desirous of Care and Seclusion.

"Ah, Mr. Lamont, I do apologize for keeping you waiting."

"Not at all, ma'am. I trust you are in good health?"

"I am quite well, thank you," the woman said. "And you, Mr. Lamont, are you still engaged with your coal mine up there in Scotland?"

Lamont nodded curtly. On previous visits he had not been averse to a half hour's preliminary chitchat—but not today. The pressure of affairs in Blacklaw, four hundred—odd miles to the north, sat heavily upon him. He came directly to the point. "Your letter requesting me to call had the ring of a summons, Miss Emerson. I take it that it has to do with Dorothy, my sister. Has her condition worsened?"

"Not greatly," said Miss Emerson. "Would you care for tea, Mr. Lamont?"

"No, thank you."

"Have you considered the suggestion I made during the course of your visit here last September?"

"I have," said Lamont. "I would prefer *not* to remove my sister from your care."

The woman said, after a pause, "My concern is only with the well-being of my guests."

"I have always understood that, Miss Emerson."

"As I explained last autumn, Dorothy is undergoing change, not uncommon in women of her age. I think you should take her home."

"But she's been here so long. She must consider this place her home."

"The . . . er, condition that necessitated her seclusion is not dormant."

"What's happened?" said Lamont with a note of panic.

"She tried to run away."

"How did that happen?"

"As you know, she had free access to gardens and grounds. Eight weeks ago she found an unlocked gate and . . . well, wandered off."

"Why was I not informed at the time?"

"I did not deem it necessary," said Miss Emerson. "I read in the newspapers of the tragedy at your pit. Besides, Dorothy did not stray far. She was recovered within the hour."

"But in that hour . . . ?"

"She had gone to the village pond."

"The pond! Good God, think what . . . ?"

"The water is only a few inches deep. She was playing quite happily with the local children. They had a little frog circus on show, I believe," Miss Emerson said. "It's not what happened but what might have happened that spurred me to write to you."

"Is that sufficient reason to request her removal?"

"I do not insist on it," said the woman. "I only suggest that Dorothy might be better cared for . . . elsewhere.

You see, on several other occasions she has tried to leave the shelter of the grounds."

"After . . . what, thirteen years? It seems incredible."

"Change, Mr. Lamont. The equilibrium of the brain changes with age. I can't have her watched day and night."

"Where is she now?"

"I regret that I've been obliged to board her on the second floor."

Lamont blinked. "The second . . . ?"

The second floor was a prison, the stratum of the house where the demented and fitfully violent were incarcerated. Hair rose on his neck at the very thought of Dorothy's confinement in such repellent company.

As if reading his mind, Miss Emerson said, "I do not take in ladies of violent disposition, Mr. Lamont. On rare occasions, however, there is deterioration, weakening of the mental forces, and that makes such a floor necessary."

"But I don't understand why Dorothy has changed so suddenly."

"It isn't sudden. Her wayward fantasies do not preclude feelings common to any normal woman of her age and station. In short, Mr. Lamont, your sister senses that life has passed her by."

"What is the cure?"

"There is no cure."

"But . . . something . . . something can be done?"

"Love helps." The word did not falter on the spinster's lips. "Love and understanding."

"She receives that from you."

"Dorothy is only one of thirty residents. I select my staff with care, but we cannot be expected to offer the equivalent of a real home."

"I take your meaning, ma'am."

"And your answer, sir?"

"I . . . I . . . It's not possible," Lamont said. "I prefer

to have you continue your ministrations as best you can. I will pay more, of course."

"There's no question of that, Mr. Lamont," said Miss Emerson stiffly. "We will ensure her safety at no extra cost, but an increment cannot buy her happiness."

The drawing room did not seem cool now; Lamont was sweating in his morning coat. "I am grateful to you for sending for me, Miss Emerson. At this time, however, professional and domestic circumstances prevent me from taking Dorothy home."

"Is Scotland so inhospitable then?"

"At the present moment—yes," Lamont said. "Now, may I see my sister? I must leave London by the evening train. Regrettably, I'm involved in a complex inquiry and can't spare more time."

"More time," the matron said. "Ah, yes, of course."

"Miss Emerson . . ."

"This way, sir. I'll escort you immediately to your sister's room."

Lamont bit back further excuses and silently followed the woman across the hallway and up two flights of stairs to the shadowy corridors of the second-floor lodgment.

⁂

Dr. Mackay was adamant—Stalker could not sit in the sun. Alex had always loved the strong yellow sunlight of the summer season. Now he was the prisoner of four walls. Contamination threatened from the very source of life; he could do no more than stare longingly at the sunshine from the big lugged armchair by the stove. It said much for his workmates' loyalty that they too were willing to forgo the restorative sunlight on their wan faces to keep Alex company. There were four of them in the Stalkers' kitchen that magnificent afternoon.

"Aye," Alex said, "I'd like fine to see a bit of sky again."

"You're doing well to be in that chair, man," Callum told him.

"I know what you mean, though, Alex," said Colin Pritchard. "I never tire of the sky. God, but I resent climbin' into that cage on a fine night at the back shift."

"Huh!" said Callum. "I never like climbin' into the cage at any time."

"I've seen some bonnie sunsets over Blacklaw," mused Alex. "Aye, and some bonnie dawns as well." His wheezing was the only sound in the room. "It brings to mind the old yarn my father used to tell about how the stars were the lights from the lamps of all the colliers who had gone to heaven."

"Heaven?" said McNeillage. "I hope I'm not bound for Paradise and one of them harps. I'd feel a deal more comfortable with a shovel in my hand."

"What's the time, lads?" Alex asked suddenly.

"Near three o'clock."

Alex shifted restlessly. "When in God's name will they be done and bring through a verdict?"

"When they're good and ready," said McNeillage. "Not all the angels in heaven can hurry along a board of inquiry. It'll be tomorrow—or the next day."

"What I want to know," said Donald Pritchard, "is where Lamont's gone to. He was spotted leavin' yesterday on the early train."

"He'll have booked passage for America rather than pay us our dues," McNeillage said.

"Maybe he's petitioning in Glasgow, drawin' the traders and masters to his aid in case the decision goes against him."

"It'll make no difference," said Alex. "The boss won't be needed here until the shouting's all died down and the verdict's posted. Aye, we've achieved something in memory of those who died." Murmurs of agreement rose from his companions. "Since I've been lying here, I've come to realize what our fight's all about. We've moved an inch out of the hole. The next step, whatever it is, can only take us upward, nearer to the sunlight."

Donald Pritchard slapped his thigh. "By God, Alex, if they had you at their big-city rallies, they'd hear some real common sense."

"I've spoken my last in public," Alex said quietly.

"Get away with you," said Callum. "You'll be back on the drossbox by Christmas."

"It's dishonest to blind yourself to fact. And the fact is, I'm crippled. I've still got plans, though. They'll have to stand in my stead."

"Are you weary, Alex? Will we go now?"

"No, stay. I'm not tired, just. . . ."

Quickly Callum said, "Tell us your plans, then, Alex."

"Kate will go to the sortin' troughs, like Mirrin. Betsy will be leavin' school in a few weeks. She's pretty enough to find a job in Hamilton, in a shop maybe."

"And Drew will be on full wage in a year or two," said Colin Pritchard.

"Drew," said Alex, his hands clutching the chair's arm, his chin on his chest. "Aye, there's Drew."

"Never fear, we'll make a collier of the lad somehow," said Callum.

"That you will not," Alex Stalker declared.

"Then, what . . . ?"

"He's what I've struggled for," Alex growled. "He's the face I'll put toward the future. He'll do for us what we can't do for ourselves."

"What's that?" McNeillage asked.

"Fight the bosses." Alex lifted his head, the bitten flesh tight to the bone. "He'll learn to fight them where they stand, shoulder to shoulder with them, on equal footing in their bloody councils and secret chambers. He'll fight them in the courts of law."

"But . . . ?"

Alex grinned malevolently. "Drew's the one who'll do it."

"If he can," said McNeillage.

"Can?" said Alex. "You forget that Drew Stalker is my son. He may be the last, but I think that he'll prove the best of the bunch in the long run home."

❧

The view from the second-floor window was impeded by ugly iron bars and a mesh grid screwed into the beading. The room itself was large, comfortable, and clean. Dorothy was eight years Houston's senior. She too was tall, but where her brother was broad and hard-muscled she was gaunt. The bones of her wrists were like ivory; her hair, which only a year ago had been sloe-black, was streaked with gray now. She stood motionless by the window, squinting at him uncertainly. With an expression of loving tenderness, which nobody other than his sister had ever seen, Lamont hurried to her and took her in his arms.

"Dorothy, you look lovely."

"Oh, Houston!"

"What is it about you? I know, you're wearing a new gown."

"Am I?" She seemed bewildered by the compliment. "Am I, Houston?"

The thought that someday she might not even remember him chilled him. He drew her to the satinwood and brocade sofa, close to the tall hearth with its basket of crushed paper flowers. "I do like your hair in that style."

The flattery won her over; she patted the coils of hair with girlish vanity. "One of the ladies did it for me. Will you . . . will you stay with me today, since I look so nice?"

"For a little while."

"Today, all day?"

"Dorothy, I . . . yes, of course."

"Have tea with me. I'll ring the bell like Mama used to do, and a servant will bring us cake. She won't be as nice as Nursie was, but she ain't so bad." Lamont listened to her chatter. It pleased him that she seemed so bright. He had expected more deterioration.

It was difficult not to talk to her of his own concerns, to explain why, after an hour in her company, he would have to take his leave. What could Dorothy know of disasters and boards of inquiry? He questioned whether she even remembered Blacklaw at all now. This crisis could not have come at a more unfortunate time. He had so many problems at home. On Monday he had been interrogated on the clauses in his deposition to the board. It was not a court of law, of course, and did no more than make recommendations on its findings. Every master and every miner, however, would take those recommendations as the Gospel, more damning than any judge's verdict. Dorothy and Blacklaw had become divorced in his mind and must remain so. In a sense, he had been glad to escape the oppressive tensions of his mansion and his colliery. Donald Wyld knew where to find him, though there would be no release of the "verdict" before Thursday at the earliest. Frequently he wished that he could shuck off Blacklaw, Edith, and Strathmore, and escape with Dorothy to the peace of a small country cottage. He did not believe that his sister's madness was wholly without grace.

"Houston, I am a prisoner."

"No, Dorothy. Here you are free."

"Flowers are my only friends."

"What?"

"I'm being kept from visiting my friends. If I don't talk with them, they will pine and die."

"If you peep out of the window," said Lamont, "you'll see that the flowers are hale and hearty. In the autumn, as you know, they will sleep."

"I can't talk with them."

"Shall I ask Miss Emerson to bring some in a vase?"

"No, no. They are dying then, and I hear them whimpering. Only in the earth are they alive, Houston, as we are alive."

"Dorothy, don't excite yourself, please."

"Why will you not let me out?"

He caught her hands and held them to calm her. "Soon you will have a garden of your own. I promise."

"When?"

"Soon, Dorothy."

"A garden? The dust will smother it."

She had remembered the smoke from the chimneys and the dust from the pit that had rendered the soil so infertile in the house where they had been children, an angular house much closer to the workings than was Strathmore.

"There will be no dust in your garden. Tell me, Dorothy, what will you grow there?"

She frowned. "Little flowers, with sweet perfumes. Scents are the voices of flowers, you know."

He encouraged her and she soon lost herself in an endless rote of flower names culled from the expensive books he sent her from time to time. "Lily of the valley, violets, columbines, carnations, pansies, honeysuckle, irises, blue lupins, roses, marigolds, hyacinth . . ." On and on she went, listing flowers, shrubs, and trees, all in a jumble, yet with a poetic sense of the beauty of the names. Lamont listened, impatient yet loving.

For an hour he sat with her, prompting her happiness or soothing her anxieties, telling her lies, making false promises, letting her wander unchecked through the confused and colorful vistas that massed in her brain. He did not need to consult his watch—an inner urgency told him that he had no time left. Squeezing her hands, he eased himself to his feet, inching away from her slowly, carefully, sadly. His heart sank as she cut off her flow of words and accused him, "It's not a day yet."

"I'll come again, very soon."

"Make them let me out." She twisted away from him, cowering into the crook of the sofa. "You promised."

"Shall I send you another flower book?"

"You did not answer my letter," she said.

"But you haven't written to me lately, my love."

"I did. I did. I wrote when they. . . ." She leaped to her feet and clutched at his arms. "Houston, I dream things. I dream you've forgotten me, that I'm all alone."

He held her tightly. "Dorothy, do you remember Scotland?"

"With . . . with the dust."

"Think, think hard, not just of the dust."

"Hills."

"Yes, and you remember Mama and Papa, and Nursie and Mrs. Tindall."

"I *think* so." She beamed. "You mean *home*—where *you* live."

"Yes."

"I know the address I put on your letter."

"That's the place."

"Are there flowers?"

"Green lawns and trees and many flowers."

"Take me home, Houston. I'll look after your flowers."

"Yes, Dorothy, I'll take you home soon."

"Soon, soon, soon, soon. *Today*?"

"Watch for the flowers sleeping," he said. "When they waken again, I'll come and take you home."

"Tomorrow?"

"Yes, tomorrow."

On the strength of that lie she allowed him to leave. She was invariably calmed by her faith in his ability to right all wrongs and restore the color of her days of innocence and youth.

❧

The waiting chaise swayed as Lamont scrambled aboard. He had missed the local connection and offered the driver a sovereign to race the twenty miles to London to catch the overnight train for Edinburgh. Miss Emerson, however, delayed him, standing primly by the wheel.

"Well, Mr. Lamont?"

"Dorothy seems well enough," he said crisply. "Keep her here."

He tapped his cane on the rail. Miss Emerson stepped quickly back as the carriage rolled forward over the raked gravel. A minute later the chaise bowled through the gates. Lamont looked back at the brilliant flower beds, at the high wall with its gridded window behind which, so he imagined, he could just make out his sister's wraith-like shape. As the residence dropped out of sight, however, the coalmaster's world of dust, slag, disasters, and rebellion caught him up again, and nagging concern over the results of Hutchinson's inquiry. Dorothy, flowers, and broken promises were soon consumed by his urgent need to be home.

☙❧

The manager's office had it first, via a sealed envelope containing a résumé of the "Report of the Findings of the Inspector of Mines Committee on the Blacklaw Colliery Explosion." The news was too potent to be contained for long and soon spread like wildfire throughout the yards. Maggie Fox brought the news to Mirrin. "It's true," she said. "As true as I'm standin' here."

"They found *no* blame?"

"No, Mirrin. The inquiry cleared the master completely."

"But what did it *say*?"

"A quantity of foul air must've accumulated in a short time, after Mr. Wyld's mornin' inspection. Some collier with a naked light . . ."

"Whitewash," Mirrin hissed. "It's a whitewash."

"Mr. Lamont took all reasonable precautions," said Maggie. "Hey, Mirrin, what about compensation now?"

"We'll get nothing, not a brass farthing."

"Mirrin, what about . . . ?"

But Mirrin had swung away. She was dangerously composed, though her lips showed livid white against her flushed skin. She walked to the manager's office, strode up the steps to the door, and knocked imperiously.

A gaffer opened it cautiously.

"Is Mr. Wyld here?" Mirrin asked.

"He's not back from the inquiry rooms."

"Jock Baird?"

"Aye."

"Get him."

"Now look here, missy. . . ."

"Get him."

Jock Baird was gaffer of the night-shift crew. A widower and father of four rapscallion sons, he spent most of his free time drinking tea in the office. He was known to be a fair and forthright man; even her father respected him.

"What is it, Mirrin?"

"Mr. Baird, I want a look at the inquiry report."

"It'll be printed in full in the *Advertiser* tomorrow."

"Please, Mr. Baird, just one quick look."

"For why, lass?"

"So that I can tell my father it's a written fact."

Baird nodded and pushed open the door. "Come in."

The gaffer pointed to the document lying on the table, two long pages covered in neat script. "Read it," he said, "but be quick."

There were a dozen men in the room, all concerned with the running of the pit or its clerical administration. Clouds of tobacco smoke formed bilious auras around the oil lamps, light from the windows hardly penetrating the haze. The men watched Mirrin, some furtively, some angrily, but none tried to prevent her as she lifted the paper and scanned the itemized contents. Baird stood protectively by her side. Mirrin turned the page and read on until she reached the signature of Ian Hutchinson, Her Majesty's Inspector of Mines. Carefully she laid the paper on the table and smoothed it with her fingers, leaving an appropriate smear of coal dust across it.

"Thank you, Mr. Baird."

"So now you know it's true, lass."

"Aye, now we know."

Baird opened the door for her. She went down the steps and veered right, skirting the groups of miners already gathering at the pit head. She took the lane between the stores and strode on out of the gate into the main street. She did not understand her own calmness. All she knew was that she felt compelled to be home first with the news, the bearer of that information that in all likelihood would bring her father to his grave.

◈

The kitchen was shining, black planes of the stove sheened like velvet, brass edgings gleaming like gold. The straw mat and patchwork rug had been washed. Sink surround and tabletop were bone-white with scrubbing. The chair's red coverlet and the bed's alhambra spread fell into obedient folds. In the center of the bed, arms by his sides, Alex Stalker went quietly about the business of dying.

From her chair by the hearth, Kate stared blindly across the kitchen, a piece of knitting neglected in her lap. The house was quiet, not silent, though; her mother's purring snores came from the back room, the fire crackled intermittently, and her father's breathing was wheezily audible. Kate ached with weariness, her nerves numbed by the shocks of the evening. First Mirrin had brought the news, then Alex had raged and collapsed. Dr. Mackay had been blunt: "Heart's gone. Nothing to be done now." Few men could have stood up to the horrors of that spring and survived as long as her father. She could not grudge him a gentle passing.

That night they had gone through the rites of excessive cleaning with which Flora Stalker met every crisis, staving off by activity the realization that before the week was out she would have lost her husband as she had lost her sons. Flora slept now, with Mirrin, in the back-room double. Drew and Betsy were asleep in the cramped attic. Even her father slept, tranquil at last. Outside, the Blacklaw streets were deserted. Only the familiar *churr* of a steam wheel in the distance suggested that the pit too was breathing gently in the dark of the early morning.

A stirring, a halt in her father's even breathing brought Kate to his side.

His eyes opened.

"Hello, Daddy."

"Kate?"

"Aye."

"Is it morning?"

"Nearly."

"Is it fine outside?"

"Clear skies," she said. "Will I fetch Mam?"

"Are they ... all ... asleep?"

"Aye."

"Good," he murmured. "That's ... good."

"Do you feel better?"

Only his lips moved, and his eyes searched her face intently not for sympathy but for a signal of her loyalty. "Kate, promise me...."

"What?"

"Drew."

"What about Drew?" She put her ear close to his mouth. His voice was an effort of will, husky, coming from deep in his shrunken chest.

"Promise me," he said, "that you'll keep him at school."

"Aye."

"And see that he goes to university."

"But . . ."

"Kate, please."

"I promise, Father."

"University, to study . . . study law. A lawyer, that's to be Drew's trade . . . lawyer."

"Our Drew?"

"Listen, listen, lass, my mind's not . . . not rotted yet," he mumbled. "I see things so clear. Education, law, those must be the weapons. . . ."

"But it will cost so much money. . . ."

"Find it. Earn it."

"I will."

"Promise again."

"I . . . I promise."

She gave him her hand. His skin was hard and dry.

He said, "It'll not be . . . easy. But you'll do it, Kate. You'll see that it's . . . done."

"I've never broken my word to you as long as you . . . as long as you lived, Daddy. Not now, I won't now."

"Give's a kiss, chick."

She kissed him gently on the brow. He sighed and closed his eyes. For an hour Kate sat with him, then returned to the chair by the stove and watched the clock tick away the minutes of the night.

When at dawn she crossed again to the bed she found that her father had died in his sleep. Even though she had watched with vigilance and love, she could not say with certainty just when he had drawn his last breath. Now only one of the Stalker men remained.

Outside, in the pearl-gray daylight, the night-shift workers trudged wearily home.

❧

It was a pretty hat—the blocked crown gave it elegance, the wings of moiré ribbon at the sides added height and style. Flora Stalker's fingers caressed the pliant material. It was only the second hat she had ever owned; both had been bought by Alex.

The one she had worn on her honeymoon, cherry-red with a bead ornament, had been Alex's favorite; saucy, he called it, and assured her that its color matched her lips. Their honeymoon had lasted three days, three whole days away from Blacklaw. They had gone across to Portobello on the east coast; blue-green water, a salt breeze whipping it into snowy peaks. They had gone out in a rowing boat, and she had not known whether to cling to Alex or the cherry-red hat, and he had said that the hat was worth more in hard cash than he was. On their last evening by the sea he had dug a fan-shaped shell from the sand. This keepsake, rough and silvery as the sea itself, was still in her dresser drawer, a reminder over the years that there were more things in life than poverty and dirt, fear and anguish. Today, however, she had no need of the talisman. Every moment of those happy years was clear in her memory.

At the interment, though many emotions churned in her breast, she had not shed a tear. She could not begrudge Alex his peacefulness, his freedom from pain and struggle.

The clink of cups in the kitchen reminded her that her duties were not quite over. In a moment one of the girls would come to check that she was all right. Yes, she must go through now, sip a cup of tea from the china pot, which, like her hat, was reserved for special occasions. She hesitated, though, seriously giving thought to her new state of widowhood. Even now she had much to be thankful for. She was not all alone like some of the wives in Blacklaw; she still had the girls—and Drew.

Crossing to the bed, she unfolded a length of old lace curtaining, wrapped the black hat in it, and placed it on the high shelf of the wardrobe. It would not gather dust for long, would appear on her head at weddings, christenings, and perhaps at other funerals. But the cherry-cloth hat with the nice beaded ornament—no, it would stay wrapped on the high shelf forever. She would never wear it again.

❧

When the last of the kindly neighbors had gone and the dishes had been washed and put away, when Drew and Betsy had been hustled off to bed, the three Stalker women were left alone in the kitchen. Throughout the day the memory of her promise had troubled Kate. She had almost been tempted to lock the vow away in her heart and never mention it to a soul. But her conscience could not have endured that deceit. The promise had been made; she must find a way of keeping it, no matter the cost.

There was no urgency in revealing her father's last wish. Mirrin and her mother were both worn out tonight. Against that, however, Kate balanced the insidious power of routine—in a few weeks, without being aware of it, they would slip into new patterns of living and it was too easy for her to neglect her promise.

"Before we go to bed, there's a matter to discuss," she said.

Mirrin groaned. "Not tonight, Kate."

"It can't wait," Kate said. "It won't take long."

Mirrin sighed and flopped into a wooden chair, skirts

rucked up to bare her long, smooth legs to the heat of the dying fire. "It's a funny time for mysteries, Kate."

"Last night," Kate began, uncertainly, "last night, just before he died, Father and I had a talk."

Flora sat forward. "You didn't tell me."

"I'm telling you now," said Kate. "Daddy made me promise something, extracted a solemn promise from me. He . . . he made me swear that we'd keep Drew on at school."

"Aye, he was a great one for education," Mirrin said.

"But can we manage without Drew's wages for another whole year?" asked Flora anxiously.

"That's not all," Kate went on. "Father wants us to find the cash to put Drew through university."

"Our Drew?" Flora said. "Never!"

Mirrin's eyes narrowed. "And what did Daddy suggest he study?"

"Law."

"Hah!" Mirrin exclaimed. "Of course!"

Flora's jaw gaped. "Our Drew—a lawyer? Oh, no, Kate, no. That's not the thing for the likes of us."

Mirrin snorted. "Daddy would argue about that."

Her mother's reaction was as anticipated—it was Mirrin whom Kate watched most closely.

Mirrin said, "Did he advise you on how we were to find the money for this program?"

"Earn it, he said."

"Four women?" said Mirrin. "How can four women earn that kind of cash?"

"I think poor Alex was wanderin' in his mind at the last," said Flora tearfully.

"Not him." Mirrin sank back in the chair and cushioned her head on her wrists. "Old Alex was a fox to the end. He knew exactly what he was doing when he wheedled that promise out of you, Kate."

"How dare you speak ill of him, and him not cold," Flora cried.

"If he could hear me, he'd be flattered," said Mirrin. "He intended it to be this way, don't you see? He's right, as usual. That's what we *should* do—send Drew to a university."

"It's . . . it's unthinkable!" said Flora angrily. "Our Drew isn't cut out for that."

Mirrin sat forward and stabbed a finger at her mother. "Don't *ever* talk like that again, Mam, not in my hearing. What's wrong with you? You know perfectly well that Drew has the brains for it."

"No doubt he's clever enough. . . ."

"But he's not 'good' enough, is that it?"

"I didn't mean. . . ."

Mirrin darted a glance at Kate. "Drew has the intelligence. What he lacks is the opportunity. Can we give him that? Can four women find a way to give him that?"

"I promised Daddy we would try."

"Then we'll have to try," said Mirrin firmly.

"But what would it all cost?" asked Flora.

"There's a lot to it," said Mirrin. "We'll need to find out the proper courses of study, the fees, the price of suitable lodgings. Then there's books, clothes, matriculation dues . . . a whole host of things."

"The dominie would be able to advise us," Kate suggested.

"Then go and talk to the dominie," said Mirrin. "He'll tell you if Drew's got what it takes to make a lawyer, the qualifications he'll require for entry, and how long the degree course is liable to take."

"But a lawyer . . . in our family." Flora's protest was less adamant now.

"If it's to be managed at all, it will mean sacrifices from all of us," said Kate.

Mirrin shot to her feet.

"By God, though, wouldn't it be worth it in the long run? A collier's son in legal robes—that's what Father had in his mind's eye. It's bound to come one day. Change, radical change to our thinking, that's what we need. Why shouldn't our Drew be the one to do it?"

"Will the lad agree?" Flora said.

"Oh, he'll leap at the opportunity," said Mirrin. "I know him—he's fully aware of his abilities, and the last thing in the world he wants to do is go down a pit."

"I'll find some sort of work, maybe at the troughs," Kate said. "You'll have your wage, Mirrin, and Betsy can go up to Hamilton, or into service, if she can find a good position."

"I suppose my fingers still have some skill with a needle," Flora said dubiously, glancing at her hands. "I can find work at sewing."

"First add up what it will cost, Kate," Mirrin ordered. "If colliery wages aren't enough, then we'll find ways and means of earning more. Father left instructions plainly enough, and we're not going to ignore them. After all, we're Stalkers, and the Stalkers never go down without a fight."

"Is it agreed, then?" said Kate.

"Of course it's agreed," said Mirrin.

"Mother?"

"I'd like to think it possible, but. . . ."

"Don't be so afraid, Mam," Mirrin said. "We can do it."

"Lamont will want us out of this house, now that your father's gone," Flora said.

Mirrin brushed that item aside. "Daddy used to talk about putting a face toward the future. Now I know exactly what he meant by it."

"But Mother's right," Kate said. "What can we do about the house?"

Mirrin stared down the embers in the grate for a long moment, then glanced up, grinning.

"Just leave that to me," she said. "I'll deal direct with Houston Lamont."

CHAPTER VI

ABOVE Strathmore the sky was pale blue, like a bolt of the best silk. The morning was hot and still, the oaks like painted screens on each side of the drive. The mansion's broad steps were pipe-clayed, the door's brass fittings brightly polished. Flat, rectangular glass flanked the portico, matching the line of windows across the breadth of the house. Mirrin wiped her hands on a handkerchief, squared her shoulders, and rapped on the lion's-head knocker. The sound echoed away into the depths of the mansion with such solemnity that she did not dare knock again.

Annie opened the door. She was wrapped in a coarse canvas apron, and smuts of black lead on her cheeks told Mirrin which of the morning's chores had been interrupted.

"Good morning, Annie. Is Mr. Lamont at home?"

"Aye."

"I'd like to see him, please."

"Eh?"

"I want a word with Mr. Lamont."

"You can't just come here askin' for the master, Mirrin Stalker, 'specially at the *front* door."

"Just tell him a . . . a lady wants to see him."

"A lady! Huh!" The skivvy shuffled back into the hall and vanished around the newel post at the bottom of the staircase.

Mirrin could not resist peering into the sanctum. She was disappointed to discover that the mansion, though larger, was not much grander than the kirk manse. The linoleum was the color of cold pease brose, the paneled doors scratched. A huge carved hallstand crouched in a corner, above it the portrait of a bearded man as grim as one of the prophets in the Sunday School's book of Old Testament engravings.

Annie returned. "You're to step this way."

Mirrin was shown into a room to the left of the entrance. She had expected elegance—plush, velvet, walnut, deep Indian carpets—instead she found herself in a Spartan, uncarpeted office, with only a long yew-wood table and a dozen cripple-back chairs as furniture. Lamont was standing at the head of the table. His face seemed stronger, coarser than she remembered it from their two previous meetings.

"Why have you come to my house, Miss Stalker?"

At least he remembered her name; that was something.

"To discuss business, sir."

"I don't normally discuss business in my home."

"If I'd come to you in the manager's office, our business would have been known to half Blacklaw before nightfall."

"I've no time to spare, girl," said Lamont. "Get on with it."

"It's about the cottage."

"I thought as much. There are rules, you know. You can't expect me to grant favors."

"I'm not asking for favors. I'm willing to work for the entitlement," said Mirrin.

"The troughs aren't classed as a householder's post."

"Then *give* me a householder's post."

"How can I?"

"Because you're the boss, Mr. Lamont," said Mirrin.

"Just give me the chance and I'll draw a hutch or tip wagons—anything a man can do."

"What, I wonder, would the men have to say about that?"

"I don't care what they say."

"I see," said Lamont. "That's hardly good 'Socialist' philosophy, is it?"

Mirrin restrained herself, saying, "Find me something, Mr. Lamont, anything that'll let us hold onto the house."

"And set a precedent? Impossible."

"It's not much of a price to ask for three lives," Mirrin said.

Lamont's head jerked as if she had pricked him with a knife. He said, "I owe your family nothing, young woman. The official inquiry cleared me completely. You have no claim on me."

"Is this your way of paying us back for the trouble my father caused? You hated him, didn't you?"

"I respected his rights. He served me well. Of course I didn't 'hate' him."

"He hated you," Mirrin blurted out.

"Be that as it may," said Lamont. "Your father gave service for his pay, and that's all I ask. Besides, he was a *practical* idealist. One always knows where one stands with a man of principle."

"My sister will be working at the troughs soon," said Mirrin cautiously. "Do two women not equal one man?"

"No," Lamont said, hesitating. "But do you not have a brother, Miss Stalker?"

"Aye."

"And he, I imagine, will be signing on in a month or so, when school term ends? I'll let you hold the house until then, after which your brother can register as the householder."

"Drew—my brother—he's not for the pit."

"Why not?"

Mirrin regretted her rashness. It was too soon to air their plans for Drew, particularly to Lamont. "It was my father's wish that Drew be kept at school."

"Indeed!"

She waited for his criticism, his statement that education was a luxury that folk like the Stalkers could not afford. Lamont's silence confused her.

She said, "I . . . I won't keep you any longer."

"Wait."

He glanced down at the table and drew an uneven circle in the dust with his fingertip. His voice was oddly bemused, as if he were puzzled by his own decision.

"I'm not devoid of sentiment, Miss Stalker," he said. "I appreciate the confusion the tragedy has caused and the suffering it's brought to my people. As you say, two women in the Stalker family work in my employ. Provided your sister keeps her job at the troughs and you agree to work for me, then I'll grant you continued tenancy of the cottage."

"But I *do* work for you."

Mirrin was astonished at his capitulation. The realization that she had beaten the system caused her such overwhelming relief that laughter rose in her throat. "Aye, that's a bargain, sir. Two for the price of one."

"You will continue to work for me?"

"Aye, of course I will."

Lamont extracted a handkerchief from his cuff and dusted his hands with it. "Annie, the girl who let you in, is leaving our service in a week's time. Your first duty as housekeeper will be to engage her replacement."

The smile froze on Mirrin's face. "Housekeeper?"

"Housekeeper," said Lamont.

"Where?"

"Here, of course, in Strathmore."

"But I'm no domestic. I mean, I'm not trained."

"You'll learn," said Lamont. "You've worked in a hotel, therefore you know something of domestic procedures. When my wife returns from her visit to Edinburgh she'll organize proper instruction."

"But . . . but why employ me?"

"You underestimate yourself, Miss Stalker. You are very much your father's daughter—energetic, conscientious, and honest. In addition you know the people here and will be able to manage them much better than I can."

"So that's it. You want me to crack the whip just to make life easier for you?"

She could no longer tell whether he was serious or making fun of her. "That's not the only reason, Miss Stalker. As you've already pointed out, your father had certain militant ideas, which, I assume, he passed on to you. The safest place for a rebel is right under my nose."

"You're not suggesting that I spy for you?"

"I've more sense than to ask that," said Lamont. "Loyalty is one quality I respect, wherever it falls due."

Mirrin let out her breath. The terms had caught her completely off-guard. If it hadn't been for Kate's rash promise to their father, she would never have agreed to such a proposition. There would be tongues wagging in Blacklaw if she accepted; but gossip never buttered much bread with her. She was so strongly inclined to snatch at the chance that she hesitated. Impetuosity could be fatal in making this decision. Housekeeper to the Lamonts was an elevation in status beyond her wildest dreams. If, however, the coalmaster was engaging her to tell tales on her comrades, he would be sadly disappointed. She looked beyond him at the mass of scarlet-blooming shrubs above which clouds of bees hovered in the motionless heat. There were so *many* imponderables. Surely he must realize that, given the opportunity, she would fill his ears with the kind of things that no boss cares to hear and that she would never waver in loyalty to her own folk.

"Well?" Lamont said. "Do you accept the position?"

She dabbed her brow with her wrist. Perhaps it *would* be possible to let Alex Stalker rest quiet, for Lamont's militant and her hero to lie in the same grave forever.

"Our cottage would be safe? You'd promise that?" she said.

"For the duration of your employment."

"How long have I got to decide?"

"I'd like your answer now."

"I need a bit of time to think it over."

"Why?"

Mirrin shook her head, freeing her soft dark hair from under her collar. "To be frank, Mr. Lamont, I don't quite trust you."

Lamont nodded, apparently undisturbed by her honesty. "I'll give you a day, Stalker. I must have your decision by noon tomorrow."

"Very well, sir," Mirrin said.

∽

Houston Lamont watched the young woman make briskly down the driveway. The overcoat was trim on her full figure, and the cut of it suited her, though no woman in his social circle would have ventured out in this heat in a serge garment. It was kirk garb, a symbol of respect. He was wrong to criticize the mores of folk whose nature he did not really understand. Edith, his wife, regarded the colliers as landed gentry regarded game, adjuncts to income, valuable but individually dispensable. He too had been conditioned to view them collectively. His father had always maintained that the colliers' unity was both their strength and their weakness. That dictum took no account of the tides of circumstance or the individual traits of the men and women in the narrow houses. Stalker, for example, had had more wit than many a

Queen's Bench lord and more fire in his belly than a tap-room of traders and agents.

Mirrin Stalker passed out of sight under the massy oaks. Lamont closed the front door and made his way to his study at the rear of the house. The tall windows opened to an enclosure of rye grass that rippled in the wind. On the littered desk was a tray of decanters and a globe lamp. Lamont seated himself in the leather chair behind the desk, swiveled it on castors, and tugged the bellpull to summon Annie. The coffin-shaped grandfather clock ticked loudly. On its face were two tiny miners who on the stroke of the hour swung their tin pickaxes in jerky unison while a small barrow traveled on a wire around the crown of the dial. He had never liked the piece, but Edith found it "amusing." He wondered what his wife's reaction to the new housekeeper would be. He was weary of Edith's choice of servants—tired, shabby, ugly little mice who scuttled about the house in terror of him.

Good domestics were scarce in the county. Though he paid them as much as any Edinburgh merchant and fed them unstintingly, it seemed that he could not keep servants for any length of time. As if to personify his thoughts, Annie knocked, and on his instruction, entered. She stood disconsolately by the door, eyes glued to the carpet. It was very difficult to think of her as a child, though she was only thirteen years old. All girls in Blacklaw were not so puny as this, though dog-labor in the pits and the hardships of homemaking and childbearing tended to age them early.

"You're leaving us then, Annie?"

"Aye, sir. M'mother an' me are going to Ayr."

"Do you have relatives there?"

"M'uncle's a shoemender. He'll take us in 'til we can find work."

It was odd, Lamont thought, how that careless spark deep below the earth had blasted away the foundation of so many lives. Annie and her mother, who had lived in Blacklaw for many years, were now on the footpath to vagrancy, in search of a lost security that, God knows, had been frail enough in the first place. A collier's existence was damned precarious. His own life, when he considered it in context, was hardly more secure.

On impulse he opened the desk drawer, took out a cashbox, and unlocked it with a key from his fob. He removed a sovereign and held it out to the girl. Dumbly Annie contemplated the coin.

"Take it," Lamont said.

"What . . . what for, sir?"

"As a bonus for your good service."

"But . . . but . . ."

"Come, Annie. Take the coin and put it away safe. Hurry now, I'm waiting for my morning tea."

Annie stood staring at the large coin. Impatiently, Lamont tossed it across the room and watched the girl stoop and retrieve it from the carpet. She held it gingerly as though afraid that it might explode.

"Oh . . . sir!"

"Off with you, and fetch my tea."

"Oh, Mr. Lamont, sir."

"Be quick, girl, before I change my mind."

"Aye, sir."

Expressing her gratitude in a sudden flood of tears, Annie scuttled out of the study.

Lamont sat back and linked his fingers behind his head. The generous gesture did not make him feel smug or charitable. He could not understand why he had given the child a whole sovereign—a shilling would have been quite enough.

It did not occur to him until many months later that

Mirrin Stalker's influence had already begun to make itself felt in his house and in his heart.

❧

"As far as I can remember they've never had a house-keeper before," said Flora Stalker. "Plenty of servants over the years, but never a real housekeeper."

"Annie's leaving," said Mirrin. "Who'll still be there?"

"Nelly Burns in the kitchen and the McCormick cousins," Flora answered.

"Well, there's three good reasons for Lamont wanting a housekeeper," Mirrin said.

"Working for Lamont at the pit's one thing," Flora said sourly, "workin' for him in his house is quite another matter. I'm opposed to you goin' there, Mirrin."

"If I don't we'll be pitched out into the street," Mirrin answered. "Then what'll happen to all our plans for Drew?"

"But what'll folks say about Alex Stalker's daughter workin' in Lamont's house."

"They can clatter as they like," Mirrin retorted. "It's our security, not theirs that's at stake."

"I think you *want* to take this job," said Kate.

"It's the sane thing to do," Mirrin admitted.

"But why did he pick you?" said Kate.

"I think he wants me to keep him informed of what's brewin' in the village. I told him, though, he'd never make a spy out of me."

"No sayin' what Lamont'll make out of you before he's through," Flora said.

"Mother!" Kate exclaimed.

"Lamont's not that kind," said Mirrin. "He'd drown himself before he'd lose dignity over scruff like us."

"Huh!" said Flora Stalker.

Kate said, "What'll you do, Mirrin? Will you accept?"

"I haven't made up my mind."

"Well, whatever you decide," said Kate, "I'm sure you know what's best."

"Aye, the way a mouse knows what's best for the cat," grunted Flora Stalker.

"I'll sleep on it," Mirrin said, and went through to the back bedroom where Betsy was already snoring.

But the short hours of darkness did not provide an answer. When dawn came she was just as uncertain as she had been the night before, though the indecision did not lie close to her heart. Her nerves tingled, and all her instincts drove her toward the choice that logic would not quite accept. Her gaze strayed from the window to the swan-shaped stain on the ceiling, to the cupboard with its meager row of shabby skirts and scarves, to Kate's plain features drugged with sleep, to pretty, vain little Betsy's curls on the cot pillow. She had seen all this a thousand times before and would see it all again, no doubt —but never in quite the same light.

Suddenly she knew that she desperately wanted to take the post in Lamont's grand mansion. Even a temporary exposure to a mode of living so different from her own could not fail to affect her. With startling clarity she realized how much she hungered for change.

She swung herself soundlessly from the bed, gathered her best clothes from the hooks, and crept out of the bedroom. Hidden from the alcove bed in which her mother now slept, Mirrin dressed carefully; then quickly, silently, and with utter resolution, left the narrow cottage and set off uphill to begin her new life in Strathmore.

Part Two

CHAPTER VII

THE passage of years had left no dramatic marks on Dominie Guthrie. He had looked middle-aged since his graduation from Glasgow University thirty years before. His progress from infant master to head of Blacklaw School, through a swamp of local and national reforms, had only deepened the wrinkles around his eyes and made his hooked nose more patrician. He had also slipped back into boyish untidiness, and each succeeding generation found him a shade more disheveled. This casualness disguised a brain that became proportionally more astute, more acrimoniously disposed toward the strictures of officials who governed him from afar. His study smelled of damp paper and tobacco. His collection of charred clay pipes filled several earthenware dishes on shelves and ledges, receptacles that also acted as bookends, paperweights, holders for pins, chalk, sealing wax, pen nibs, and wriggly rubber bands. A stone jar, once thick with Reever's Best-Quality Orange Marmalade, bristled with a posy of pencils and pens, and three glass inkpots on a stained blotting pad cast a rainbow aura across the open attendance ledgers on the desk.

"Kate, is it not?"

"Yes, Mr. Guthrie."

"And what can I do for you, lass?"

A discreet nudge from Drew on the chair by her side

forced Kate to collect herself and embark on the subject that had brought her to the school.

"It was my father's wish, Dominie, that my brother should find a place at a university, to undertake the study of law."

She knew that she had spoken stiltedly, but the dominie, the doctor, and the minister were used to this strained form of address, which, in the case of more obsequious parishioners, reached heights of verbosity close to unintelligibility. Mr. Guthrie made no attempt to hurry Kate along.

"We hoped you'd give us your advice on the procedures for undertaking such a course," Kate said.

The dominie stroked his nose—which was perhaps why it had sharpened over the years—and considered his reply. Drew's rigidity was palpable, on the verge of causing him to tremble.

"Make Drew a lawyer," Mr. Guthrie said at length. "That's a tall order, Kate. I'll admit that your late father's ambition for his son is highly praiseworthy, but my advice is to put the notion clean out of your head."

"But why, sir?" Drew blurted out.

"It's too impractical. It can't be done."

"Why can't it be done?" the boy demanded.

"That's enough, Drew," Kate said.

The dominie fixed the boy genially. "You're disappointed?"

"Yes, Mr. Guthrie."

"You're a bright lad, Stalker. You shouldn't have associated yourself with this singular idea in the first place."

"What's to stop . . . ?"

Forbes Guthrie's eyes hardened, and Drew obediently fell silent.

"You're intelligent, and you have a capacity for work," the master said. "I could find you a clerk's job at Northrigg, a foot on the managerial ladder."

"I don't want to be a clerk. I want to be a lawyer."

"Drew, don't talk to Mr. Guthrie in. . . ."

"Let him have his say, Kate."

Drew pulled back his stooped shoulders until he seemed as tall as the dominie himself. He was pale as tallow and his eyes were wide, yet his voice remained as steady and grave as a kirk elder's. "I've studied hard, sir, not just because my Da made me. I saw the sense in it. I want more than I can find in Blacklaw, more opportunity."

"Many lads of your age prate on about 'opportunity.' "

"Aye, Dominie, but *I'm* willing to do something about it."

"What age are you, Drew?"

"I'll be sixteen in a month."

"You'd have less than a year to work for the examination—and it's a stiff one. You'd need special tutoring," the dominie said.

"Would you tutor me, sir?"

Kate once more attempted to curb her brother's tongue, but the dominie forestalled her interruption. To Kate it was like watching two strangers perform a legal ritual—cold, verbal, and astonishingly mature.

"What if I say no?" Mr. Guthrie asked.

"I'll make my own way to Edinburgh, find a job, earn enough to pay for a crammer, and save. Somehow, Mr. Guthrie, I *will* become a law student."

"You could apprentice yourself to a legal firm."

"As a clerk, I suppose? There's no real advancement from that position," Drew said.

"We do have some money saved, Mr. Guthrie," Kate put in.

"Do you have the faintest idea what this venture will cost," the dominie asked, "or how long it will take?"

"Five years," said Drew.

"And we'll meet the costs—somehow," Kate assured him.

The dominie pursed his lips and honed at his nose irritably. "All right, if that's how keen you are, I'll undertake to tutor you for the preparatory."

"The entrance examination?" said Drew.

"Aye, the entrance examination for Edinburgh University," said Mr. Guthrie, sarcastically adding, "Would you have it in writing, sealed by a notary?"

Drew sank back in relief, and Kate leaped to her feet in delight. "Oh, Mr. Guthrie, if you only knew what it means to us, and what it would have meant to my father," she cried.

"If the plan comes to grief, don't blame me," the master said. He got to his feet and clapped his hands as if to call a rowdy class to order. "Now, I wish to state the terms. Stalker, I'll give you a full course in Greek and Latin, from scratch. You'll also be expected to increase your proficiency in other major subjects. We'll work at times suitable to me, and you will make yourself available at these times, outside your advanced school curriculum. The fee for my services is two shillings per week, payable in advance, please."

"I'll pay you now, sir," said Kate.

"Ah, no!" said Mr. Guthrie, embarrassed by his own seeming greed. "Bring it along on Thursday evening, Drew."

"Thank you, sir," said Drew quietly.

"Aye, well, I hope you still have cause to thank me a year from now," the dominie said. "The truth is, I don't see how it can be done."

"Oh, it can be done, sir," Kate said. "That's one thing I learned from my father—anything's possible if you only have the will."

The dominie snorted dubiously and showed them to the door.

❧

Kate and Drew walked home. In her heart Kate knew that the dominie had been right in his assessment, yet she could not help the confidence that lightened her step and made her view the future with fresh hope. She had her job at the troughs. Her mother was in command of the house and taking in a bit of sewing. And with Mirrin earning too, it seemed that her father's impossible dream might after all be transformed into reality. The only real cloud on the horizon had to do with Mirrin's job as the Lamonts' housekeeper.

For the first few days Flora had treated Mirrin as some kind of pariah, a traitor. But that mood had diminished into truce, and the big woman was even showing natural signs of curiosity as to what went on in the coalmaster's mansion. Privately Kate was uneasy. Putting Mirrin in Lamont's province was like waving a taper near a pocket of gas. She prayed that the inevitable explosion would be long enough delayed to see Drew out of Blacklaw and settled to his studies in Edinburgh.

She glanced at her brother. Dressed in his Sunday suit, with a shiny, rounded collar, face scrubbed and hair slicked down with some of Betsy's precious toilet water, he seemed far too composed and mature ever to fail at anything he had set his mind on. She realized that she had never really regarded Drew as a child in need of care, comfort, and understanding.

"Are you happy, Drew?"

"Of course."

"Your daddy would be proud of you."

"It's too late for him. Besides, it doesn't matter. The past is just the past."

"It's the past that makes us what we are now," said Kate.

"I think I'd do better to bear in mind that it's the present that makes the future," said Drew. "Did you know that Guthrie tried to be a lawyer and failed?"

"Drew Stalker? How d'you know that?"

"Father told me."

"How did Daddy find out?"

Drew shrugged. "It's true, though. Guthrie's shelves are loaded with dusty old law books. One of them has an inscription on the flyleaf: 'To my beloved son Forbes, on the occasion of his acceptance into the Faculty of Law of the University of Glasgow, this year of 1836.' I saw it one day when he sent me for fresh chalk."

"You had no right to look, Drew."

Drew sighed at his sister's pettiness. "It's useful information. It's his reason for agreeing to help me. It's also the reason why he doesn't like me much."

"What a thing to say!"

"It's a fact," said Drew. "Guthrie doesn't like me because he knows *I* won't fail, with or without his help."

Kate had no heart to debate with the boy. His callousness drained her of her jubilation at Guthrie's offer. She could not really blame Drew for being what he was— whatever that might be. In her brother recklessness and kindliness had been beaten thin by the wheels of ambition. Her father was really responsible for this trait, and Alex was no longer alive to guide the boy. All that was left for Drew was the legacy of his father's single-mindedness. Even so, it shamed her that he should treat Mr. Guthrie with such thinly veiled contempt. The lessons would be beneficial in more ways than one. The dominie's ability to shape decent, honest young men was more proved than his skill at making a lawyer out of a collier's son.

However it turned out a year hence, Kate reckoned that the two shillings paid each week would be money well spent.

ভ~ৎ

Mirrin leaned against the kitchen dresser and fanned herself with a towel. She was stripped to bodice and petticoat, her bare feet discolored with dust that shifting the massive dresser had stirred up.

"Have we finished then?" asked Mattie hopefully.

"We've only just started," Mirrin replied.

Mattie groaned.

Mirrin mopped her neck, shoulders, and breast with the towel. "Is that not more convenient, Mrs. Burns? You'll be able to reach your crocks and pots more easily now."

Mrs. Burns sniffed and grudgingly admitted that moving the dresser had been a good idea. The cook was a stout woman in her midforties who had remained defiantly widowed since her young husband had been killed in the Crimea twenty years before.

"I'll say this, Mirrin Stalker," she remarked, "you're the only housekeeper I've ever known who'd roll up her sleeves and work."

Mirrin laughed. She had changed in the past weeks, happier in her new job than she had been since leaving school. The variety of work about the mansion left no time for boredom. Soon, however, there would come a point when the domestic reorganization was over and she would be faced with the harder task of acquiring poise and polish, qualities that a housekeeper could not do without. Edith Lamont would not put up with her as she was. The mistress was constantly criticizing her lack of deference to her superiors and her indiscretions of speech and manner.

According to Mrs. Burns the Lamonts' house, managed by a hodgepodge of customs borrowed from manuals and journals, was not quite up to scratch socially. In spite of its size the mansion contained only a dozen rooms. Mrs. Burns had a cozy basement flat to herself, and the McCormick cousins, the only other resident servants, shared an attic in the west wing above the tomb-like room that had once been the nursery. So far Mirrin did not stay on the premises, but tramped home each night between nine and ten. Soon, though, she would have to take up residence, be on call at the end of the bellwire twenty-four hours a day for six and a half days in the week.

Little Annie's position as upstairs maid had not been filled. Much to their chagrin the duties of attending the wants of master and mistress were divided between the cousins. All in all, Mirrin accepted Mrs. Burns's pronouncement that the Lamonts' house was "neither one thing nor much of t'other." Edith's struggle to pattern her home on models of Edinburgh society failed dismally because of her husband's indifference. Not that that was the only reason for the makeshift gentility of the place— a prevailing atmosphere of bitterness and near hatred tainted the house like a bad smell. Servants, no matter how ignorant or desperate for employment, could not endure that contagious morbidity for long. What the house needed, in Mirrin's opinion, was a bit of laughter about it, occupants for its shrouded guestrooms and children to chase over its polished floors and immaculate lawns.

"Mirrin, had you not better put something on?" It was typical of Hannah McCormick to feign offense, while peeping enviously down her bodice. If Hannah ever graduated to housekeeper, God help the poor scullions under her charge.

The McCormick girls were not from Blacklaw. They came from a hamlet thirty miles away. Mirrin had difficulty remembering which cousin was which. The shorter and younger fussed about her chores singing snatches of "Nearer My God to Thee" like a drowning mariner, while the taller, Hannah, was the real religious fanatic. To aid her memory Mirrin composed a silly jingle: "Hannah, tall, goes to church. Mattie, short, sings too much." If they ever really riled her, she might shock the pair by reciting it aloud.

"I'll dress in a moment," Mirrin said. "First, let's move the broom locker into that corner."

"Aaaaaaw," Mattie whined. "What for?"

"To put the small table in its place by the door, a rest for the breakfast tray while you open the door. Then Mrs. Lamont will have no call to complain about spillings on the tray cloth. Right, girls—backs into it."

With much grunting and groaning, the cupboard was duly pushed across the kitchen and aligned with the corner walls. The effort left the girls winded and surly. Only Mirrin had enough pride in the minor achievement to stand and admire the closet's new location.

"And why, Miss Stalker, are you parading yourself in my kitchen in that disgusting state of undress?"

The mistress of the house had entered the room silently. In contrast to Mirrin, Edith Lamont was enshrouded in the silks and velours of a fashionable day dress, the weight and mass of which seemed to project her through the doorway on waves of lavender. Her indignation was enhanced by the sinister rustlings of the dress itself.

"Because it's dirty work, madam." Mirrin never used the contraction, emphasizing the *d* to impart a certain drollery to the separate syllables of the word.

Mistress and maid had met by design on a half dozen occasions. Now they sized each other up mistrustfully, seeking the best means of attack. Without undue haste Mirrin buttoned on her blouse and skirt.

"My husband is seldom down here, you know." Mirrin ignored the innuendo. Edith Lamont went on, "May I remind you that this is not some miners' slum where lax habits are commonplace."

Aye, thought Mirrin, the knives are out at last. She smiled sweetly. "I'll endeavor to correct my friends in the village, madam, after they return from their fourteen hours of digging your coal out of the ground."

Edith frowned, feeling the barb. "By whose authority has the furniture been moved?"

"By my authority, madam. Mr. Lamont asked me to attend to the welfare of the staff."

"By causing upheaval?"

"Everything is neatly squared away," Mirrin explained. "And more conveniently located for the staff's use."

Mirrin surmised that Edith Lamont had heard rumors of her fiery temper and was trying to goad her into an outburst. Determined never to give this woman an excuse to dismiss her, Mirrin remained firm but polite as she demonstrated the advantages of the new arrangement.

"Now that you have squandered the whole morning in the effort," Edith Lamont said, "I suppose it had better stay as it is." Her gaze now fixed on Mirrin's dark, tangled hair. "In addition to remaining decently clad, however, you will wear a cap at all times while engaged on household duties, upstairs and down—a strong cotton cap with an elastic trim."

"Am I to appear before guests that way, too?"

"Of course."

"Hmmmmmmmm!" said Mirrin dubiously.

Stirring like a small ornamental conifer in a cold breeze, Edith rustled her skirts. "Do you object to my instruction?"

"I don't object. I'm just wondering what the guests will think."

The point was moot—the Lamonts entertained only rarely. Edith appeared to have forgotten this fact in her urge to unravel the source of Mirrin's enigmatic reluctance to wear a cotton cap.

"The . . . guests?" asked Edith.

"I wouldn't want them to think us 'countrified.' "

Edith was shocked. "What do you mean, 'countrified'?"

"According to Lady Peacock's *Manual of Domestic Duties, Decorum, and Accounts,* only housekeepers of farmers ever cover their hair—except in kirk."

"I don't believe you."

"It's there in black and white, madam. Mr. Lamont himself gave me the manual to study, to improve myself. Lady Peacock says the wearing of caps by housekeepers is vulgar and gauche."

The argument now was not about vanity or cloth caps but concerned Mirrin's precise status in the household.

Edith considered. Obviously Stalker had outsmarted her and she must compromise to save face. "You will wear a cap below stairs."

"Just below stairs?"

"Yes."

"Aye, madam. Thank you for correcting me."

A suppressed giggle came from the stillroom. Edith's mouth clamped into a wirelike line as Mirrin called, "Mattie, Hannah, less of that noise. Get on with washing the bottles as I told you to do." She dropped an incomplete curtsy to the mistress. "If you'll pardon me, madam, I must check that the water's warm enough."

Edith Lamont inclined her head graciously, though Mirrin knew that inwardly she was seething with indignation.

"By all means, Stalker."

Slapping down the skirts of the day dress, Edith backed out of the door and closed it behind her, not loudly. Mirrin remarked the restraint and marked it down for emulation.

On tiptoe she crept into the stillroom, and as she had suspected, found Hannah and Mattie hugging each other and stuffing hands into their mouths to hold back their glee. In spite of their dread of Edith Lamont they had at last found something to make them laugh. Mirrin could not seriously rebuke them for it.

From behind the door Mrs. Burns asked, "Does it really say that in the book, Mirrin?"

"Well," Mirrin replied, "if it doesn't, it should—don't you think?"

The cousins collapsed once more, and it was quite ten minutes before Mirrin could bring herself to chivvy them back to work.

❧

"Lady Peacock's *Manual of Domestic Duties?*"

Houston Lamont lowered his newspaper an inch. "What of it, my dear?"

"Did you present a copy to the Stalker girl?"

"I did, together with Beeton's *Household Management.*"

Edith sewed in silence.

Houston said, "Has she been discussing the volumes with you?"

"After a fashion."

"I'm glad that she shows such an interest in her work."

"To my mind, Houston, she is not suitable material for a housekeeper."

"She is young and inexperienced. In time she will acquire some of the airs and graces that you seem to consider necessary adjuncts to proficiency."

"I doubt it."

"You don't like the girl, Edith, do you?"

"She is impudent."

"Has she spoken ill to you?"

"Obliquely."

"Perhaps you are just a little oversensitive."

"Why do we need a housekeeper?" said Edith.

"To ease the burden on you, my dear."

"A steward or a butler would be more in keeping with our position."

"A manservant would have to be brought from Edinburgh," Lamont explained, "and would cost the earth. In a quarter the Stalker girl will be less uncouth. By Christmas she will be presiding like an expert. I didn't select her at random, you know."

"No," said Edith, pointedly, "I am sure you did not."

"She's nimblewitted and keen to learn."

"And pretty."

"She is certainly prettier than any other servant we have ever employed." Lamont lowered his newspaper and glanced at his wife. "Is that the crux of your complaint against her? If she were ugly, would you be less antagonistic?"

"Are you implying, Houston, that I'm envious of a collier's brat?"

"Not at all."

Edith laid down her sewing frame. "Houston, if I asked you to dismiss her, would you do so?"

"Not without good reason."

"She is . . . insubordinate."

"I'm afraid, Edith, that I would need proof."

"My word isn't good enough now?"

"I have a use for this girl."

"I thought as much!"

"Edith, guard your tongue."

Houston was rather enjoying his wife's display of envy. He had intended to explain his purpose and thus calm some of her petty fears—but now decided to let her think what she liked about his motives. Let her connive against the Stalker girl for a while. It would keep her from sharpening her tongue on him. He was in closer touch with life below stairs than Edith imagined and had learned from Mrs. Burns that Mirrin Stalker was, as he had supposed, industrious and scrupulously honest. She would never tinker with the provisions or "come to an arrangement" with local vendors, to pocket the spare profit herself.

"Have you found a suitable room for her yet?" he asked.

Edith's eyes widened. "To have her live in the house?"

"Housekeepers usually do, Edith."

"We have no room here."

"The garrets?"

"Damp and drafty," said Edith.

"But surely good enough for a mere servant?"

"Yes, I suppose so, if you're so set on accommodating her."

"We could put her in the nurse's room," Houston said.

"How can you suggest such a thing!"

"It's high time those rooms were put to use."

"How . . . how unfeeling you are."

"I wouldn't reoccupy the nursery itself, Edith. I understand your attitude on that point. But what harm can there be in reopening the side bedroom? It's decently removed from our quarters."

Edith tossed the sewing frame to the carpet and jumped to her feet. Houston had seldom seen her so roused.

"I'll not have it," she cried. "I will not have it."

"Gordon's been gone from us for a long time now," Houston said, mentioning his son's name for the first time in many months.

"How *dare* you bring my poor boy's name into this conversation? *How dare you, Houston?*"

"We will discuss the matter again when you are in a calmer state of mind," Houston said, reaching his hand to the bellpull. "Shall I ring?"

"For her?"

"For brandy."

His wife's complexion had the brittle tint of ivory, her eyes were feverish with fury. For once he did nothing to appease her. Why was it that he had no knot of pity for her in his stomach? He could look at her tantrums with utter detachment and aplomb, watching her fight to regain that expressionless state that was the seal of a lady of breeding.

As if reading from a handbook on etiquette Edith said

stiffly, "I have a slight indisposition. I will retire early if you have no objection."

"None at all."

Houston rose, crossed to the door, and opened it for her. She glided over and paused while he dutifully kissed her cheek.

"Good night."

"Good night, my dear," he said. "I trust you will have recovered by morning."

He watched her cross the hall and make her slow, sedate way up the staircase; then he closed the drawing-room door, returned to his armchair by the fire, and with a feeling of ease and comfort, rang the servants' bell. In less than a minute a knock sounded on the door.

Without lowering his paper, Lamont said, "Enter."

She wore a black serge overcoat and no hat. Her dark hair, freshly combed to judge by its sheen, hung in a soft bunch over her left shoulder.

"Is it nine o'clock, Mirrin?"

"A few minutes after, sir."

"Even so," he said mildly, "if you elect to answer the bell in person you must not appear in your overcoat. It takes only a moment to slip out of it. That is the proper thing to do."

"Sorry, sir. I was just on my way out."

"You may go home then, Mirrin, but please ask one of the maids to bring me the decanter."

"Brandy, sir?"

"Yes."

Mirrin held the door with her knee and gestured into the hall where Houston glimpsed both maids with trays in their hands. The taller stepped forward and transferred her tray into Mirrin's hands, and Mirrin, as she had been taught to do, carefully closed the door and carried the tray to him. She brought the wine table closer to his armchair, laid the tray upon it, and deftly unstoppered the cut-crystal decanter.

"A half measure, sir?"

"Thank you."

She poured, with great deliberation, an exact measure—according to Lady Peacock's manual, no doubt. On the tray were two glasses, a flagon of spring water, and a dish of sliced lemons. Mirrin stoppered the decanter, then offered Houston the glass.

"Put it where I may reach it, Mirrin."

"Yes, sir."

"You may go off home now."

"Thank you, sir."

Lamont watched her go, then, as she turned to close the door behind her, said, "Mirrin, what was on the second tray?"

"Whiskey, sir."

"What if I had asked for port?"

"That would have been your hard lu . . ." She caught herself in time. "That would have taken a little longer, sir."

"I see," Lamont said. "Good night, Mirrin."

"Good night, sir," Mirrin cheerily replied. "Sleep tight."

Behind his newspaper Houston Lamont smiled.

❧

A fortnight's summer weather broke at last. When the colliery hooter blared to signal the end of the day shift, heavy rain rattled mercilessly on the workshops' tin roofs. Kate knotted the scarf about her head, and sniffing and shivering miserably, contemplated the downpour from under the eaves. A persistent cold had drained her of energy. She was afraid that the infection might slip down into her lungs. She could not afford to be laid up, not with Drew's lessons to be paid for and a weekly sum to be salted away out of the family's collective earnings. It had been a distressing period for the Stalkers, Kate most of all. Blacklaw folk did not take kindly to the way in which the Stalkers were shaping up to the crisis, to the rumor that Drew was being educated for a university career, to the knowledge that Mirrin had sold out her ideals for a high-paid post in Strathmore.

Head bent against the driving rain, Kate ran out of the yards and onto the pavement. Blurred lamps showed already in the house windows. There was something so pathetic in the sight of such homely symbols that Kate shed tears as she hurried along. When she collided with the man the blow was almost hard enough to fling her to the ground. Only Rob's quick action prevented it. He caught her around the waist and cradled her for a moment against his black, crackling oilskins. Thus clad, the young man seemed larger than ever, like some coal giant just escaped from the shaft.

"God, Kate, are you practicin' for the Powderhall sprint?"

"I'm cold an' wet an' wantin' home."

Rob did not release her but peered more closely. She did not raise her head.

"You've been cryin'." He swiftly unbuttoned the big oilskin coat, spreading it wide. "Here, come inside. I'll walk you down the hill, fine an' dry."

It was easier to capitulate than to argue. Kate snuggled under the oilskin, arm about Rob's waist, leaning on him. Step for step they hurried down to the narrow house where he stooped and entered the closetlike hall, shaking the coat behind him as a crow shakes its wet wings.

"Mam's out," Kate said.

"The kettle's boiling, though," said Rob. "Look, lass, you skin out of those wet clothes, an' I'll brew us some tea."

"Scrounger," said Kate, cheered by his company.

In dry clothing, her chair drawn close to the fire that

Rob had coaxed into flame, she felt much better. Rob handed her a mug of hot sweet tea, which, as she gulped it down, cleared away the last of her depression.

"I'll say this for you, Rob, you make a braw cup of tea."

Rob seated himself in the armchair that had once belonged to Alex Stalker. He spread his knees and inclined forward uncertainly.

"Come on, Rob, what's on your mind?"

"Well . . ."

"Is it Mirrin?"

"Aye, it's Mirrin," Rob admitted. "I haven't clapped eyes on her for weeks. Is she sleepin' up at that damned house now?"

"No, she still sleeps here. But she works long hours."

"Old Alex would never have stood for that."

"Mirrin has more of my father in her than you realize," Kate said. "All she's doing is hurrying on the day m' father dreamed about."

"I don't set much store by dreams, Kate."

"Maybe that's why you're still. . . ."

"Still a collier?"

"I'm sorry, Rob. I shouldn't have said that."

"I've heard all about the dominie's lessons and what Alex intended for Drew's future. But it'll be bloody years before the lad's in a position to fend for himself," Rob blurted out. "And I don't want Mirrin workin' in that man's house."

"It's her choice."

"Look, Kate, it's no big secret. I don't want her in Lamont's house, 'cause I want her in mine—as my wife."

Kate rubbed her brow. She had been glad of his company when he was cheerful and hearty, but she had not the strength to cope with his bitterness.

"You've been into that with her, Rob?"

"Of course I have—a dozen times."

"And she gave you an answer?"

"Aye."

"Then there's nothing I can do."

"You could talk to her."

"It would only make matters worse," said Kate. "Mirrin's stubborn. She has a mind of her own."

Crestfallen, he stared at her for a moment. Suddenly she realized just what Mirrin meant to this frank, handsome young man. The independence that was so much part of Mirrin's personality was the very facet of her character with which Rob Ewing could never come to terms.

Rob slapped his thighs and got to his feet. He lifted his oilskins from the sink.

"Rob," said Kate. "Listen, I'll tell Mirrin you were asking for her. If you really want to see her, she's here most nights by half past nine. I'll have a word with her, though I can't promise it will do much good."

"Thanks, Kate," Rob said. He paused, looking down at her. "Maybe I'm not . . . well, forceful enough for your sister. Do you think that could be it?"

Kate shrugged. "I'm not clever enough to know what makes folks tick, Rob—least of all Mirrin."

"Aye," Rob said, nodding. "That girl's a law unto herself."

He smiled then and gave Kate a gentle buss on the cheek. "Look after yourself, lass," he said.

"You too, Rob."

And then he was gone.

For a half hour Kate sat by the fire, sipping tea, thinking vaguely of the years that had already slipped away behind her, and wondering what the future held for them all. It was not until Flora returned that Kate realized she had not sneezed since leaving the yard. At last her cold had broken and would be gone by the weekend. With luck she might survive to see the winter after all.

CHAPTER VIII

FOUR letters rested on the tray that Mirrin Stalker brought into the study and to Lamont's astonishment withheld from him. He glanced up at her angrily. Her defiant mood so matched his own, however, that he elected to avoid an encounter and slumped back in his chair.

"My letters, Stalker."

"Can I have the evening off, sir?"

"Ah!" said Lamont. "Have you asked Mrs. Lamont?"

"She says I can't."

"Then I cannot contradict her."

"I haven't had an evening off in the two months I've been here."

"Haven't you?" said Lamont. "Why do you wish the evening off? Is it important?"

"There's a wedding in the village."

"A relative?"

"Just a friend, sir, sort of. A girl who used to work near me at the troughs. I'd like to see the poor fish she managed to land."

"When do the celebrations begin?"

"At seven o'clock, sir."

"Did you explain your reason to Mrs. Lamont?"

"No, sir. She . . . Mrs. Lamont did not give me the opportunity."

Lamont considered the situation. Clearly the girl was entitled to an evening off. If it had not been for Edith there would have been no problem at all. Obviously, if he countermanded his wife's order, she would make his life a misery for a week or more. Ruefully, he realized that she would probably do that without an excuse.

"If Mrs. Lamont refused you an evening off, Mirrin, then that must be the way of it," he said. "On the other hand, you may leave early tonight—say, at a quarter after six, provided you organize the serving of dinner before you go."

Mirrin knew better than to grin. Instead, she lifted the letters from the tray and placed them neatly on the desk.

"May I inform the mistress t'that effect, sir?"

"No," said Lamont hastily. "I will do that—later."

"Very good, sir," said Mirrin. "Will that be all?"

Lamont nodded.

He hardly noticed her leaving. His attention had been caught by the scrawled address on the plain buff envelope before him. Deliberately, he left it until last. In the light of Dorothy's letter, the rest of the post was inconsequential. With a sad heart he cast his eye over the illegible scribble that was her notion of a long, informative, loving communication.

Far back, during her first months in Miss Emerson's care, her letters had been like this. It seemed that his sister was once more slipping down into madness. Was it somehow his fault?

Thrusting himself to his feet, he pushed back the chair and crumpled the letter in his fist. The study fire had not been lit that morning, and he crushed the paper ball into his pocket and started out of the study in search of some ready flame upon which to cast the letter and be free of the pain and guilt that it carried like a curse from poor Dorothy's prison in the south.

The dining room, though seldom used, was the servants' favorite room, and they maintained it diligently and lovingly. Perhaps they liked to work there because it was a sanctuary from Edith's domain of drawing room and parlor. Certainly it was the house's most formal chamber.

Heavy mahogany furniture glowed with lavender oil and beeswax. Mirrin's cherry-red smock was in warm contrast to the room's sober appointments. Light reflected from the dining table's surface, giving her face a luminous quality. He had not noticed before how clear her skin had become. She was humming contentedly to herself as she worked, smoothing soft little nuggets of perfumed wax into the pores of the wood and buffing them down with cloths.

The fire had been lit in the hearth but was not yet bright enough for his purpose. He pushed the letter deeper into his pocket.

Mirrin, startled, looked up at him.

"Go on with your work."

She applied herself more strenuously to the cloths.

"You like this room?"

"Yes, sir."

"Why?"

"It's got an air of history, I suppose, sir."

Lamont was surprised. "Very perceptive of you, Mirrin. In effect, this is the only room in the house that remains completely unaltered since my great-grandfather's day."

"How long ago was that, sir? A hundred years?"

"Much longer. He purchased Strathmore from the Earl of Northrigg, whose own grandfather had the misfortune to be a supporter of Bonnie Prince Charlie and was consequently dispossessed of the entitlement by the Crown."

"But it must have been restored to him?"

"Yes, by the generous Duke of Hamilton when the earl was in desperate straits. There are several histories in the library you may borrow if you wish."

"Thank you, Mr. Lamont. I'd like to learn more about the gentry."

"I take it you're well versed in proletarian history?"

"Aye, my father drummed enough of that into me."

"Then perhaps I should adjust the balance," Lamont said. "See here." Taking the girl's hand, he guided her fingertips to a long, shallow scar on the mahogany that a century of wax and elbow grease had not been able to heal. "Feel the indentation?"

"I've noticed it before and wondered about it."

"It's part of my history, the history of Strathmore," Lamont said. "Can you guess what made such an enduring mark?"

"Tell me, sir?"

"An ax."

Mirrin's eyes widened.

Good-humoredly, the coalmaster continued his story. "The ax was intended to cleave my great-grandfather from tip to tail, like a herring. Fortunately the young man's aim was wide of the target."

"What young man?"

"A suitor to my grandmother, the favored daughter."

"Why could he not just marry her?"

"The young man was not considered . . . stable enough to take into the family fold."

"You mean he was a collier?" said Mirrin in disgust.

"No, as it happens he was a tenant farmer. That occupation wasn't enough to condemn him in my great-grandfather's view. By all accounts Charles Houston was a shrewd judge of men. He was opposed to the match on more personal grounds."

"So the poor farmer tried to do your forebear to death?"

"Quite!" Lamont stood at the head of the table, playing the roles of both victim and attacker. He showed more animation than Mirrin had ever seen in him before, as if ancestral drama quickened his blood and expelled his own immediate problems.

"Can you imagine it, Mirrin? The table was set with glittering finery, a dozen guests, my grandmother in her silken evening gown, my great-grandfather presiding at the head of the board, here. Abruptly, the door burst open and the wild-eyed farmer lunged into the room, a hewer's ax upraised, madness twisting his handsome features. My great-grandfather hardly glanced around. He just swayed an inch and let the big blade hack past him, shattering crystal and fine plate and burying itself in the table."

"Go on. Go on."

Lamont's arm was stretched across the table, chest upon the edge. "Swiftly, without flinching, my great-grandfather snared the young man and pinned him down in the spilled wine and broken glass. With one hand he held him, waving away guests and servants."

"Until the constables arrived to cart the poor lad off to the clink, no doubt."

"The constables weren't summoned," Lamont said. "No, there was no more violence, and no retribution—at least not that evening. My great-grandfather had his own method of dealing with the situation. He knew how to turn the incident to his own advantage."

"What did he do?"

"My great-grandfather sent his steward to fetch a purse of ten golden guineas. He offered the purse to the young farmer on the condition that he leave the county at once and not show his face in Lanarkshire again."

"Of all the patronizing . . ."

"The farmer accepted at once, without hesitation. By midnight he had decamped, lock, stock, and barrel."

"I'd rather have gone to prison," said Mirrin.

"And so, I think, should I," said Lamont.

"Is this just a . . . a story, sir?"

"No, it's the truth."

In the moment that the couple faced each other, Lamont saw all the antagonism drain from the girl's face. In sudden confusion she gathered the polishing cloths.

"I . . . I must go, sir."

"But, Mirrin, I thought you would have shown some curiosity concerning my grandmother, the girl abandoned for ten golden guineas."

"I suppose she married somebody 'suitable' and had lots of bairns to please her father."

"Indeed, she did marry," said Lamont. "She married an elderly coalmaster from Fife, a gentleman with capital to invest in securing leases in Lanarkshire."

"So he got himself the guineas and the lady?"

"And the son he needed to clinch the contract," said Lamont. "Soon my grandmother presented her husband with a male heir—my father."

"Just as well for you, then, Mr. Lamont."

The coalmaster was too serious now to smile at her jest. "Four months after the birth, however, my grandmother came down into this very room one October midnight. She came silently, dressed in the gown she had worn on the eve of her jilting. She had acquired—from God knows what source—a vial of laudanum, which she carefully poured into a wineglass and drank—drank, every drop. The maids found her early next morning, sprawled across this table—stone dead, of course."

Mirrin's cheeks drained of color. For a moment she said nothing; then, unexpectedly, she laughed harshly. "Poor woman. I suppose they blamed the strain of child-bearing and salved their consciences that way."

"Even the consciences of coalmasters cannot be so easily salved," said Lamont. "On receiving the news my great-grandfather suffered a spasm of the heart. He died a week later."

"He deserved it."

"I daresay. But I cannot help wondering what I would have done if I'd been faced with his decision."

"It's maybe lucky, then, that you've no children to. . . ."

Mirrin gasped in horror at her indiscretion. She wished

that the floor would gape and swallow her up. The remark had been so tactless, so cruel. In confusion she murmured, "I . . . I must go, sir," and fled in shame to the safety of the kitchens.

Lamont felt no animosity toward Mirrin. Tactlessness and honesty had the same root. She had spoken her mind without regard for the barriers of rank that divided them. The fact that she was ashamed of hurting him spoke well for the girl and for their relationship.

He walked down the length of the table, brushing the surface with his palm. The history had amused Mirrin at first. Would she be as amused if he told her of his childhood, of Dorothy? He had spoken to nobody of Dorothy. Edith would not listen, brushing away his attempts to discuss his sister; her impatience was more cruel than the girl's frankness.

The sun had swung out from behind the oaks, pinpointing the rock garden's starflowers and the tiny leaves of the plant collection. He could almost see Dorothy upon the lawn, Dorothy as a young girl again, graceful, full of laughter and merriment, in the happy days before the ax had split her reason so many years ago.

Digging the crumpled letter from his pocket, he smoothed out its folds and once more scanned the childish scrawl. It meant nothing, mere ciphers of emotion pared away from logic and the grammar of restraint. The random words seemed to shout out for understanding—*loving sister*.

Loving!

Sister!

Carefully folding the sheet, he pressed it into his vest pocket. To burn the letter now would serve no purpose. His loneliness had made him vulnerable to the ghosts of yesteryear. Now that the past was unsealed he would be haunted by its sad, sweet memories throughout the day.

Alas, there were no vials of laudanum, no murderous

axes, and no occlusions of the heart to give his conscience ease.

∾

Behind the cottages of Blacklaw's main street a strip of waste ground forked around the kirkyard to form a lozenge of flat grassland and provide a setting for the village's outdoor gatherings. The lot was screened from the pit by blackthorns and whinns, though the sounds of industry were loud when the wind blew from the west.

Festivities were under way by the time the Stalkers arrived. The groom's pals had come straight from the shift, pausing only to wash off the worst of the dirt at the Lantern's pump. Maggie Fox's family, however, had trigged themselves up to honor the bride and to swank their superiority over the Williams tribe, who were Welsh by origin and lived in squalor in a clutch of raddled tin shacks in the shadow of the Clayburn coups.

Though times were hard, housewives had done their best with frugal provisions, and a feast of plain and filling fare was spread out on trestle tables crowned by two mammoth tea urns borrowed from the kirk hall. There were churns of milk too, gifted by one of Billy Williams's nine brothers who was herdsman at a local farm. Music came from fiddles and concertinas—jigs, reels, strathspeys, and sentimental songs popular in Scottish music halls. Couples were dancing on the bald earth patch in the center of the lot. The best time for hugging and kissing would be after dusk when the eagle-eyed old grannies hobbled off home. There were few colliers in evidence as yet; it was a known fact that weddings incurred a dreadful thirst in a man. Grooms of yesteryear shifted off furtively in twos and threes to sample the ale in the Lantern, leaving their wives gathered at the tea urns to speculate on how long it would be before Maggie Fox paraded a swollen belly around the streets.

The bonnie bride was soothing her nerves with measures of neat gin and wrestling impatiently with the yellowed veil, an heirloom, which hurt her head with its wire frame.

A mug of tea in one hand, a slice of dumpling in the other, Mirrin came up the line of well-wishers, regal as a queen. Holding her supper at arm's length, she pecked at Maggie's cheekbone.

"I didn't think you'd have the nerve t'show up," Maggie muttered.

"I wouldn't miss your big day for a barrowful of dross, Maggie," answered Mirrin sweetly. "Besides, I'd like to meet the lucky lad—*if* you know where he is."

Setting the gin measure on the table, Maggie cupped a hand to her mouth and bellowed, "*Billy.*"

It had been a long day for William Williams. When during the course of the afternoon his courage waned, there was always a Williams ready to administer a splash of the time-honored remedy for nuptial nerves. During the late afternoon Billy had napped in the rented shack, blown with the effort of toting Maggie's hamper up from her parents' house. He had wakened with a dry mouth, in a panic again, crying for his brothers to rescue him. But now it was evening, the shadows were long, the breeze cool, and Billy's emotions were under control, his senses suitably dulled.

"*Billy Williams, I want you.*"

Laughter exploded all around the lot.

Billy didn't mind. It was nice to be wanted. He eased out of the crowd and ran over to his brand-new wife.

Mirrin was prepared for a clown or a rough lout, not for the large, flat-featured youth who stood swaying and beaming, full of liquor and love. His tight blue suit and short-pegged trousers made him comic, yet the effect of his happy, moonstruck smile daunted Mirrin by its sincerity. She glanced curiously at Maggie's narrow, petulant face under the veil. Tonight there would be no miracles of bliss for them—Billy was too drunk and Maggie too abrasive. But in a week or a month, when the tin shack had been disguised as home and the couple had grown used to each other—what then? Perhaps there would be a sort of love between them in the lulls that hard living allowed, and even spiteful Maggie Fox would learn the true meaning of the marriage contract and have more tenderness than she deserved.

Mirrin put her hand on Billy's shoulder and kissed him. "Good luck to you, Billy Williams. You've a good wee wife there, you know."

Billy grinned and nodded.

Maggie waited for the insult, the sting in the tail, and when it did not come she was startled and embarrassed.

"Good luck to you too, Maggie," said Mirrin, and shifted past the couple, filling her mouth with tea and dumpling to allay her temporary envy of the girl she had always disliked.

For a while after that, Mirrin stood alone by the thorns, watching the festivities like a stranger. She realized now that Kate had not exaggerated the high feeling that ran against them in the village. It hardly mattered to her, and would matter less when, as must soon happen, she was resident in the mansion. But her sister and mother must feel the slights badly.

Betsy was dancing, too dainty for the hulking collier who swung her about in the crook of his arm. Betsy had started work last month in Dalzells' Emporium in Hamilton, a counterhand in the large, fashionable department store. Kate and Flora were helping at the tables, dishing out milk for the bairns. Most of the food would be gone before the menfolk trailed back from the pub. Drew was hovering on the fringes of a crowd of first-year pit apprentices who, in their moleskins and leather belts, were pretending to be men. They were his former classmates; yet he was so different from them that Mirrin could not blame them one bit for ignoring him as they did. Soon, she imagined, he would drift back to his attic and his books, alone as usual.

Gloaming darkened the whinns. A pitch torch flared, then another. The lads lighted small bonfires around the lot, and the tunes were carried now by the fiddlers. The tempo was lively. Young bucks, up from the pub, swelled the dancers. One wedding soon led to another, so the old wives said. Across the sward Maggie danced with her Billy, holding him tightly.

A touch on Mirrin's sleeve brought her around.

Loony Lachie Abercorn bowed low and produced a green glass bottle with a red rosebud nodding from a ribbon around the bottle's neck. Loony shook the gift vigorously, signing that it was for Mirrin.

"For me, Loony?" said Mirrin. "Who sent it?"

Loony grunted excitedly and pointed across to the edge of the ring of light. Rob Ewing was outlined against the bonfire's flame. Guiltily, Mirrin realized that she had not seen Rob since her father's death. Kate had spoken of him a night or two ago, but Mirrin had been too tired to listen properly.

Mirrin separated the rose from the bottle, which, so the label said, contained French wine. Did Rob suppose that she was so sophisticated now that only expensive presents would please her? Disentangling the ribbon, she wrapped it around the rose stem and gave it to Lachie. Lachie could not believe his luck. He performed a mute show of gratitude; then, on Rob's instruction, trotted off to exhibit his prize to anyone who would give him a little attention.

"How is it with you, Mirrin?" Rob asked.

"Fine, Rob, and with yourself?"

"Well enough. Would you be for dancing?"

"I'm not supple enough for that."

"Has housekeeping turned you into an old crone, then?"

"I can still put one foot in front of the other."

"Will you take a stroll with me, then, since it's such a soft night?"

"I warn you, Rob, you'll set all the tongues wagging."

"To hell with the gossips." He took her arm. "I'm right glad to see you again, Mirrin."

They skirted the kirkyard and crossed a corner of the goat pasture. The sounds of the fiddles dwindled as the couple approached the edge of the track that led over the hill to Northrigg. Grass and weeds had nibbled it to a dusty footpath. Leaves of rowan and birch contained the twilight and closed out completely the sawing music and the din of the colliery. Bats flittered across the nave, embodiments of dusk and quietness.

Rob put his arm about Mirrin's waist.

"Do you . . . object?" he asked.

"No, I rather like it."

She had given him the wine bottle, and he carried it in the pocket of his jacket. Saying nothing for a while, they walked along the track. Leaves held in the heat of the day and the perfume of wild flowers.

"Mirrin, you're bonnier every time I see you."

Mirrin was half afraid of her own emotions. "I don't believe that tale about absence making the heart grow fonder."

"I believe it," Rob said. "Every word of it."

"Rob, Rob," Mirrin murmured. "You'll only be hurt again."

"It would be better to be hurt than to have this . . . this nothingness," Rob said. "I want you every day in life, Mirrin."

She remembered Maggie Fox and Billy, and the loving in the young man's eyes, and how Maggie held her man tightly, so tightly.

She said, "You'd soon hate the sight of me."

"No, Mirrin, never that."

She paused, turning in against him. "Just what do you want, Rob?"

"Marriage."

"Wedding, bedding, and bairns?"

"Aye."

"And to get me out of Strathmore?"

"I asked you long before you went there."

"I know you did."

"Consent to marry me, Mirrin?"

"No, Rob."

"Christ!"

Once more he had forced her to refuse him outright. In so doing he had spoiled the romantic interlude, which, if he had been less proud, he might have used to bring him closer to his objective and its fulfillment.

Catching her roughly in his arms, he drew her from the path. "Listen, Mirrin, I've loved you for as long as I can remember. For a while I was content to see you there in your father's house—but not now. It's all I can do to struggle through the days without you."

"Please, Rob, don't."

"It isn't enough. Don't you see that, damn you?"

Mirrin was afraid. She could not deny the forces of her body. Perhaps—she thought later—Rob's violence was simply a response to her own passions, a kindling of impulsive longings so potent that they burned away his inhibitions and pride. His hand caught her hair and pinned her head. He crushed his mouth to her lips, kissing her savagely.

Fear vanished from her. Her eyes widened. His skin was pitted and scarred. She could smell the collier's odor of sweat and mineral harshness, feel the breadth of the big muscles across his back. Everything sane and rational was banished, thrust from her mind. He dragged her deeper into the shrubs, stumbling, and for a moment only, breaking contact.

"Wait, Rob, wait."

But he gripped her again and swung her around and pushed her down into the tall grasses. She too was caught by need, a need as great as his. Her fingers adroitly unhooked the buttons of blouse and bodice. She lifted herself enough to shed the garments—and free her breasts. Braced on her hands, she lolled back again, and Rob was upon her, his body black against the deep lavender afterglow that filled the sky overhead.

Moths glided from the broken stalks as Rob's weight thrust her into the grass. She saw only roots and fibers struggling from the earth, the intimate secrets of their tenaciousness and strength. Grass fronds tangled her hair. She thrashed in mute response as pleasure ranged in her loins like some wild creature loosed at last from bondage.

Rob's breathing was ragged. His fists kneaded her breasts. He arched his back. Fresh spasms of pleasure engulfed Mirrin. Pain too—pain and pleasure confused her. The only real fear in her was that Rob would revert to sanity and haul himself away, leaving her trapped in that cage of need, drowning in her own womanhood.

The urgency of Rob's hunger was direct, masculine, and selfish. Pain and pleasure separated in Mirrin with a suddenness that made her cry out and snare him with her arms.

It was quickly over.

He sank his weight upon her with a shuddering sigh, slid gently to one side and rolled into the grass. Half naked, and open, Mirrin waited while reason floated down into her brain again like a coin dropped through water.

"Did . . . did I hurt you?"

Mirrin did not angle her head. "Not enough to complain."

"Uh!"

Her arms were leaden as she reached for the straps of bodice and blouse, and clumsily now, rebuttoned them.

She propped herself up to untuck her bunched skirts—then she rested.

Rob was still hidden in the grasses. She could see only his crossed knees and one polished boot kicking the air gently. Was it shame, drowsiness, or indifference that kept him apart from her now? Now—when she would have welcomed an embrace and some loving words.

"So I was the first," he said.

"Aye. What did you expect, Rob?" she said. "Choirs of cherubim?"

"Wás it . . . was it all right?"

"How would I know?"

He sat up, hugging his knees, and stared across at her. "Don't worry."

"I'm not worried," Mirrin said.

"I mean, that's it," Rob said. "You'll have to marry me now."

"Are you proposing again?"

"I doubt," he said smugly, "if a proposal's actually needed any longer."

She could not believe that he was not making a joke of it. "Oh, Rob, a girl likes all the trimmings."

"Maybe you'll have more trimmings than you count on."

She peered into the gloom, searching for his face.

At length she said, "And just what the hell do you mean by that?"

"I mean, you might have a bairn."

"Is that why . . . ?"

"No, no," Rob said. "Now, Mirrin, if you'll just say what date suits you, I'll approach the minister, and. . . ."

She was on her knees now. "You're *serious*?"

"I've never been more serious." He spoke in a sepulchral tone. "Better if it's soon, to save folk counting on their fingers, you know."

"Rob . . . ?"

"I apologize for what happened," he said. "It's not the way I would have wanted it, really."

"Just enough to make me change my mind?"

He regarded her solemnly, head cocked. "It's the least I can do, Mirrin. Besides, it's not as if you can object. I always wanted to marry you."

"Make an . . . make an honest woman out of me, will you?" Mirrin leaped to her feet in fury. "You *bastard*! You smug, arrogant *hypocrite*! You mealymouthed, pious . . . God, I thought you were full of . . . of *love*. Love! There's nothing in you but *camphor*. You stink of it, *camphor and hypocrisy*."

"Careful what you say, Mirrin. I'm under no legal obligation. . . ."

Reaching, he gripped the hem of her skirt. She lashed out with her foot. His hand flew to his brow where the blow caught him.

"*You're* under no obligation?" Mirrin raged. "*What about me?* Am I supposed to crawl over hot coals and *beg* for you to marry me . . . just because I'm a woman, nothing but a bit of . . . of flesh for you to put it in every time the mood's on you?"

"Mirrin, don't talk like that."

"I'll talk how I please. And I'll marry who I please," she shouted. "No, don't come one inch closer or I'll let you have the other shoe, right in your smiling mouth."

"You might regret behaving this way, Mirrin."

"If I'm expecting, you mean? I don't care. But just to put your mind at ease, Rob Ewing, I'm no more expecting than you are."

"How can you be so sure?"

She spoke sibilantly, with a venom that cowed him. "Because I'm a woman and know about such things. If you must have the lurid details, it's because I'm due a bleeding tomorrow."

As he got to his feet she drew back from him, stumbling onto the path. He did not come after her. He stood stock-still, hands hanging limply by his sides. She thought, then, that he looked more stupid than any one of the Williams boys and less of a man even than Lachie Abercorn.

"I'll tell you this, Rob," she said. "I did what we did only because I wanted to, not because you forced me. No, I liked it for itself. It might have been better with another man—it might have been worse. But the fact of it doesn't grant you the right to be the *last* man ever to give me pleasure. Do you hear what I say—*pleasure.*"

"It's true what they say about you, Mirrin Stalker," Rob shouted.

"I don't want to hear." She clapped her hands to her ears. "I don't want to hear any more."

"You're a whore, Mirrin. Maybe sometime you'll be honest enough to be a real one and not just a fake."

"Tell them, then," she cried. "Tell all your randy pals what I was like. It'll be good for my business. You tell them, Rob Ewing, when you're propping up the bar in the Lantern, swilling bloody ale and thinking that you're the gods of the earth. Such a story will do your social standing no end of good. It'll make you *seem* like a man, *even if you're not.*"

She turned and fled from the glade, which, a half hour ago, had seemed so tranquil and romantic. Now it was trammeled by memories of rumors about the kind of girls who went there and what was done to them. She understood it all, every last syllable of it, and it made her afraid.

For fifty yards she kept to the path, then, thinking that he might attempt to follow her, she plunged into the thicket and ran heedlessly through the brambles and ferns and rank, clinging weeds.

❧

Betsy knocked on the attic door. It was hardly a proper door, more like a miller's trap set into the camber of the roof.

"Drew?"

"Come on up."

He opened the trap for her, and she scrambled up the short, steep ladder into her brother's sanctum. The tiny room was warmed by the lingering heat of day and by the strong beams of the candle-lamp. Improvised shelving supported the collection of books the dominie had given him. On the little table placed directly under the skylight notes were written in an open jotter. The young man's handwriting had become neater, more mature. It showed no sign of the irregular rhythm at which he worked—a blend of confident haste and pedantic uncertainty. Already, as the dominie intended, Drew was acquiring the habit of painstaking thoroughness, which would become the bedrock of a legal career.

Tonight he had exchanged his Sunday suit for the woolen robe his mother had knitted him. He seated himself on the edge of the iron cot in the corner.

"You're back early."

"It wasn't much of a dance," said Betsy.

"Where are the others?"

"Mam and Kate are helping with the washing up."

"God, I don't know why they bother to maintain the pretense," Drew said. "After all, it's fairly obvious that as far as this village is concerned the Stalkers are *persona ingrata*."

"Is that Latin?"

"Aye. It means nobody wants us here."

"The lads were quite nice to me," said Betsy. She shook her curls prettily. "Mirrin's missing, did you know?"

"Really?" Drew said laconically.

"She went off with Rob Ewing—down that path."

"What path?"

"Where . . . where the lovers go."

"Did she now?" said Drew. "Well, she's safe enough with Rob Ewing."

"I wouldn't be so sure."

"She's not interested in *him*."

"Depends what you mean," said Betsy. "Mirrin's no different from any other girl."

"No different from you, Betsy?"

"What *do* you mean, Drew?"

"Mirrin's worth more than a collier's bed."

"That's not a . . . a nice thing to say."

"But it's the truth," said Drew. "What's more, I think she knows it."

"You mean, she's after somebody more important?"

"Possibly," said Drew.

"Who?" said Betsy eagerly. "Who is it?"

Drew smiled enigmatically and sidestepped the question. "Tell me, sister, how do you like working in Dalzells' Emporium?"

"Fine."

"You must meet lots of attractive young men there."

" 'Course I do."

Drew leaned forward suddenly. "Then be careful."

"What?"

"Be careful how you handle them," he said. "I don't want you throwing yourself away on some nonentity, nor do I want to see you winding up in trouble."

"How dare you say that to me."

"I'm the man of the household now, Betsy. Somebody has to keep an eye on your welfare."

The girl's eyes narrowed. "I'll do what I like. Listen, it's all very well for you, Mr. Big Shirt. You'll be off to Edinburgh in ten months, out of this dump. But I'm stuck. I like Dalzells' well enough, but I don't intend to be a counterhand for the rest of my life."

"Meaning that you intend to marry yourself off to the first man who makes eyes at you and seems to have a shilling in his pocket."

"Really, Drew, I find this conversation most offensive."

He reached out and took her hand. It was hardly a gesture of fraternal affection, only a means of ensuring that she did not stalk off in high dudgeon before he had had his say.

"Edinburgh's the place for you too, Betsy," he said. "I meant it when I told you that I would send for you just as soon as I'm established. . . ."

"But that'll be years yet."

"Not so long as all that," Drew told her. "Besides, you're very young."

"An' you're exactly the same age, remember."

"Don't fall into the trap, Betsy," Drew said. "You're as pretty as any lady one's liable to meet in the city. I don't want you cheapened and coarsened by . . . by promiscuity. . . ."

"And what does that mean?"

Drew sighed. "Betsy, Betsy! It's for your own good. Don't do anything foolish. Don't throw yourself away."

Perhaps she would have argued with him further, not out of the conviction that he was wrong but simply to fish for more compliments. Betsy had long ago understood the value of her face and figure and had no intention of risking her job, her reputation, or her prospects by giving in to the blandishments of the ardent young counterhands who swarmed around her as though she were a pot of honey in a beehive. Even a few customers—husbands of wealthy ladies, usually—had made discreet approaches to her, all of which she had treated with innocent disdain. No, she would be patient, cautious, as Drew advised. Edinburgh, as her brother said, was the proper milieu for them both—better by far than Blacklaw or Hamilton, places rife with colliers and farmers and other vulgar traders.

The twins' conversation was cut short by the sound of the kitchen door opening below and Kate's voice saying, "Don't fret about Mirrin, Mother, she'll be perfectly all right."

"I can't help worryin' about her," Flora Stalker said. "She's always been so headstrong and wild."

"Aye, but she's got plenty of common sense," Kate said. "It's my guess she had a tiff with Rob Ewing and she's gone to spend the night with one of her friends."

"She has no friends, no real friends," Flora pointed out.

"Then she'll have gone back to the mansion. It's after midnight, Mam. She has an early rise. Like as not, she'll sleep with the maids and be ready for an early start."

"I wish I could be sure," Flora said.

Drew touched Betsy's arm. "You'd better go."

"Yes."

"Mind what I told you, Betsy. Be cautious."

Betsy nodded, opened the door, and lowered herself down the steps into the tiny hallway below.

Drew did not return to his studies immediately. He sat motionless on the cot listening to the desultory conversations of the womenfolk for a while, then drifted into plans and plots of his own devising. How could he use Betsy to his own advantage? He had qualms that his twin's acumen would not be as sharp as his own, and he felt that he might need her sometime in the future.

As for Mirrin, he spared her no real consideration. Long ago he had recognized in her a will to match his own and a bland indifference to him as a person and brother. No, dear Mirrin was quite able to look after herself. Provided she did nothing to endanger her job at Strathmore, Drew thought, Mirrin could do what the devil she liked.

❧

The brass lamps of the Regency pleasure carriage were silvered by the moon, which had risen over the stable roofs and now squared the cobbled yard with light. Grooms slept soundly in the musty dark of the gable attic. Tack hung from blocks along the lime-washed walls against which Lamont's rigs were ranked, conveyances splendidly polished and preserved like museum pieces, reminders of Great-grandfather Houston's passion for speed. Here were marshaled phaetons, early landaus, slender cabriolets, dogcarts, high gigs, and even a gilded Continental chaise in which the old man had raced about his holdings at the risk of a broken neck. Horses not pastured in the meadow behind the gardens were stalled in the ell wing. The sharp, aromatic odor of the stalls mingled with the smell of plush, leather, and axle oil in the long coach house, and the animals' drowsy champing gave Houston Lamont a sense of companionship that eased the weight of his depression.

Houston came here often after dusk, ostensibly to inspect the carriages or smooth the horses' coats with curry comb and dandy brush. More often he came only to find peace to brood, seated in shadow under a buggy hood or in one of the closed coaches. The place was full of happy memories of rainy afternoons and games of make-believe grandeur when he and Dorothy had been children. None of that magical quality remained in Lamont now, only nostalgic regret that it had gone. A more vivid memory was of the aching loneliness of his first college term, cut off from Blacklaw and his sister. Since then he had found warmth and affection scarce commodities in his life, even during his courtship and the early years of his marriage to Edith.

That night he was not using the coach house as a refuge from Edith. She was safe in Glasgow, visiting acquaintances. He had retreated, rather, from the strict feminine ambiance that had closed around the mansion like a fog as the years went on. In the stable yards he could be himself, free of the weight of responsibility that he, as a coalmaster, must don each morning as a knight might don war armor.

The night air was warm, the half-open doors admitting moonlight. An owl swooped low and silent over the cobbles, casting a brief shadow on the pale walls. Lamont reclined on the carriage bench, head resting on the inside of the hood, feet propped on the painted iron rail that, so his father had once informed him, was designed to prevent ladies and gentlemen "coming together" in the darkness. The carriage was long, broad, and shallow and smelled not of paint but of iron and horsehair. He had been sprawled on the bench for over an hour, moving only to light a cigar, then to stub out the butt on the wheel rim when he had smoked it down. Soon he must stir himself, he supposed, and go back indoors to bed. Laziness deterred him from making the effort. In fact he had just stretched his hand to the riding pillar to hoist himself up when a shadow blotted out the light from the doorway. Lamont opened his mouth to challenge the intruder, then, recognizing Mirrin Stalker, lowered himself down into the darkest corner of the coach.

The girl hesitated, then came uncertainly forward. Clearly the lass was not herself. Her skirts were wrinkled, her hair disheveled, and she walked haltingly along the line of the rigs, unaware of his presence. He was not yet inclined to reveal himself, curious as to what his housekeeper sought in the stables at this ungodly hour of the night.

At length Mirrin paused, leaned against the shafts of a phaeton, and covering her face with her hands, wept.

Lamont discreetly cleared his throat.

Mirrin whipped around.

"Who . . . who's there?"

"Lamont." He felt oddly guilty, as if he were the intruder.

"Ah!" Her exclamation was one of relief.

"Are you unwell, Mirrin?"

"No, Mr. Lamont."

"May I ask what brings you here at this late hour?"

She wiped her eyes with her cuff and swept the straggles of hair into a semblance of order. "I wondered if I might be permitted to sleep in the stables, sir? It's not that long until morning."

"Have you no bed at home?"

"Aye, sir, but . . ."

"I take it," Lamont said, "that the wedding festivities became somewhat rowdy?"

"They did that, sir."

"You're not hurt, Mirrin, are you?"

The question was logical, yet somehow indelicate.

"Just tired," Mirrin said.

"There's plenty of spare room in the house."

"No, sir," said Mirrin quickly. "I'd just as soon put my head down here for an hour or two."

"It's not long until winter, Mirrin," Lamont said. "You must stay in Strathmore then."

"I will, sir."

"I'll see to it that you have a room of your own."

"When, Mr. Lamont?"

"As soon as you wish."

"And the mistress?"

"She will . . . agree, I'm sure."

Lamont was no longer drowsy. He felt as though a bright lamp had been lit in his brain. He was tempted to comfort the girl, take her in his arms and soothe her. Then it occurred to him that she must think him odd to be immured in a coach in the middle of the night.

"I often come out here," he said curtly.

"Aye, Mr. Lamont."

"Why did you come?"

"I don't really know," said Mirrin. "It was the only place I could think of. I suppose it's like home to me now, in a way."

"Very well," said Lamont, "if you insist on spending the night in a carriage, try this one. It's the most comfortable of all."

Mirrin allowed him to help her into the carriage. Sighing, she sank back against the leather cushions under the protection of the hood.

"May I sit with you a little while, Mirrin," said Lamont, "or are you too weary?"

Had the servant a right to refuse her master? How often he had heard that debate trotted out by a lecherous coalmaster to excuse the seduction of a parlor maid. He did not approve, and when the talk turned bawdy, found an excuse to leave the company. He was called a prig behind his back, but the slanders did not upset him. To him, colliers had always been a class apart and his servants parcel of that class. Now, in relation to the Stalker girl, he began to understand how callous his previous attitude had been. Without waiting for her answer, he climbed up onto the bench. The painted rail's curlicues modestly separated them. He brought out his cigar case and fired up.

The hood framed her, but there was just sufficient moonlight to illuminate her eyes, the contour of her breast, and her hands folded in her lap. In her smudged clothing she was much like a gypsy—brazen and passive, bold and servile, a bewildering mixture. Or was that bewilderment in him a mirror of his own unrest?

"All these coaches and carriages belonged to my great-grandfather."

"The same great-grandfather, Mr. Lamont?" Mirrin asked. "The one who was nearly murdered by the ax?"

Lamont laughed. "He was not without his foibles, you see. Collecting wheeled vehicles was one of them. My sister and I . . ." He cut off abruptly. Mirrin had probably heard rumors about Dorothy. Sternly, he reminded himself that he did not wish to discuss that subject.

"Tell me about your sister, sir."

The question was ingenuous, not sly.

He paused, peering at the coal of his cigar.

Mirrin said, "I'm sorry, Mr. Lamont. It's not the sort of thing you'll want to talk about, perhaps."

"Dorothy, my sister—she lives in England." He blew out smoke. In spite of the railing he was close enough to Mirrin to touch.

The smoke made a pale cloud against the light from the doorway. Though she was seldom far from his thoughts, Dorothy's name had hardly crossed his lips in the past five or six years. The pressure of restraint had cracked him deep below his consciousness. He did not decide to unburden himself—rather, he was drawn into it by Mirrin's sympathy.

"What have you heard of my sister?" he asked.

"Only that she is ill and hasn't lived with you since . . . since your marriage."

"She was sent to a proper place to receive due treatment and care. For her own good."

Mirrin's silence was not disapproving.

Lamont felt like a swimmer about to plunge into a mysterious river, trusting himself to unknown currents, not now knowing where they might carry him or where he might eventually surface.

"Dorothy," he said, "is not of sound mind."

That frank statement triggered the destruction of the wall of silence he had built up over the years. A moment later he found himself blurting out many things about Dorothy's illness and his own sufferings and guilts.

The monologue was frequently incoherent. He spoke

of his childhood, of his separation from Blacklaw and Dorothy, of her gradual dissociation from reality, of her ever greater dependence on him. He spoke, though more guardedly, of his marriage, of the birth of his son, and of Gordon's untimely death. He spoke of many other deaths and exits, of Dorothy's exile, of her flowered prison in Kent, of the recent revival of symptoms of full-blown lunacy in her. For almost two hours he talked, unprompted and uninterrupted. It was close to morning before he finished.

Mirrin said nothing.

Had his droning confessions of failure and doubt proved so dull that she had fallen asleep? The cigar between his fingers had gone out. He groped for the matchbox and lit a stick and rolled the tobacco in the flame. His mouth was dry, yet he felt lucid, still, and calm, not at all embarrassed by the intimate nature of his revelations.

"Are you . . . awake, Mirrin?"

"Aye."

"I'm sorry. I've talked too much and far too long."

"If you love your sister," Mirrin said quizzically, "how can you stand to be apart from her?"

"I told you—Dorothy needs care and attention."

"And she needs love."

"May I remind you, Stalker. . . ."

He could not finish the reprimand. At this time and in this place they were not master and servant. If anyone had told him that he would confide in a collier's daughter, he would have accused him of making a joke in bad taste.

But this girl could speak of love without coyness, without confusing it with lust or duty—devils that plagued him and had brought him into moroseness and misery.

"Yes," he sighed. "It's true. She does need love."

"You should have her here, in Strathmore, with you."

"I can't."

"There's many folk in our village who could do with some care and attention," Mirrin said. "But they can't have it. Instead, they make do with love. It's not a substitute, Mr. Lamont. It's a mainstay. Are you afraid to admit that?"

Houston Lamont did not answer.

Mirrin went on, "What causes the harm? Is it money, or power, or pride? I know what my father would have said, sir, but my father was a simpler man than he was given credit for being. He had no truck with men who evade responsibility."

"Do you think I evade responsibility?"

Mirrin said, "I saw a girl married tonight. She's not much to look at and she has a tongue like a viper. But she's discovered that she has the capacity to love and to summon love in return. I think you're frightened of that, Mr. Lamont. Do you believe that it will weaken you in some way? Is that why you let love come last?"

"You can't imagine how much I loved my son."

"I loved my father and my brothers," said Mirrin. "I still love them and always will. But I don't blame myself for what happened to them."

"No, you blame me instead."

"I did at the time—but not now."

"What changed your mind?"

Mirrin hesitated, then shook her head. "That's immaterial. They're dead and buried. Your sister is alive. Look, if she was a collier's daughter, do you suppose she would be cast aside? No, Mr. Lamont. Maybe we couldn't give her 'care and attention' but at least we'd have the gumption to acknowledge her as one of us. That's the difference between your folk and my folk—we hold our failures dear and cherish them."

Lamont rose, making the coach sway.

Mirrin looked up at him steadily. "You're all your

sister has in the world. Why don't you bring her home?"

In the lattice of shadows the coalmaster's face seemed ravaged and tormented. "My . . . my wife. She just doesn't have the temperament to cope with. . . ."

"What's temperament got to do with it?" Mirrin said. "Speak plainly, sir. You mean the mistress won't have Miss Dorothy here because she's afraid of how people will talk? That's not temperament, that's the most selfish kind of fear."

"No, I can't agree. I can't. . . ."

"I've listened to you tonight, sir," said Mirrin evenly, "and heard more than the words. I heard the way you spoke them, and I think I understand. Are you not the master of Strathmore? Why can't you do what you *know* to be right?"

"Where are your free principles now, Mirrin? Don't they matter anymore?"

"Oh, they matter," Mirrin declared. "But not where love is concerned. That's first and above all. In that house there are no servants and masters—we're all as equal as we wish to be."

Houston leaned across the railing and placed his hand against her cheek. Perhaps he would have kissed her, shared sorrow and anger, kindled the fire that had been between them in the hours after midnight. Mirrin did not resist. But it was too soon, and chance prevented it.

The clatter of the hired chaise rose from the stable arch, and the driver's hoarse "*Hoooaaah*" came loud on the still morning air. The timing of the arrival could not have been more flagrantly coincidental.

"Edith," said Lamont. "She must have returned to Hamilton last evening and missed the local connection."

He got down from the carriage, then turned.

"You will stay, Mirrin," he asked. "Stay in Strathmore, I mean?"

"Yes."

Lamont smiled ruefully and shook his head at the irony of fate that, for better or worse, had snapped the temporary bond between them.

❦

Mirrin watched the coalmaster hurry through the side door. A lane would take him to the washing house, and a corridor would lead him directly upstairs. It was almost comical to see the master of the mansion behaving like a sneak thief. She sank back into the cushions, exhausted yet strangely relieved. Something momentous had happened, something much more important than the loss of her maidenhood. Rob's lovemaking and her flight through the woods seemed far into the past already. The self-pity and despair that she had nurtured before her return to the coach house had gone, and she spared hardly a thought for the squalid adventure in the wake of the wedding party. If anything, she felt more sorry for Rob than for herself.

She lay resting in the pleasure carriage until the first blackbird tuned his pipes in the trees behind the house and the lintel became visible against the lightening cobbles. She climbed stiffly from the coach and went into the yard, filled a bucket at the pump, and stripping to her petticoats, washed thoroughly in the fresh dawn air. All around her the birds were wakening and the high crests of the oaks were gilded by the sun. Behind her the tall walls of the mansion soared, giving her the security and protection she craved, so different from the community of pit-head troughs and the changing moods of the village.

Slipping on her dress, carrying her shoes and stockings, she returned the bucket to the nail on the stable wall and walked through the dewy grass toward the kitchens.

In a moment, before the cook and maids were up, she would return to the kitchen and take out the prim black dress that marked her as a housekeeper, and put it on.

She might even hide her hair under the daft cotton cap this morning just to keep the mistress happy, if such a thing were possible.

She tried to envisage the woman who figured so large in Lamont's life, to picture his sister as a child in this green playground, safe from the world's hardships. But the image would not congeal. It wavered into the face of Houston Lamont as he now was—stern, brooding, and yet as solid as the blocks on which Strathmore was built. It was almost as if *he* had made love to her that night, not Rob Ewing. The transference did not disturb her. She allowed its comforting warmth to spread within her heart.

CHAPTER IX

EDITH Lamont was a seasoned traveler. She approached each journey, long or short, with an autocratic attitude to porters, firemen, engine drivers, and refused to be rushed by such commonplace things as timetables. As that summer progressed toward autumn her excursion rate increased. Traveling alone, without even a maidservant, Edith spent many nights away from Strathmore.

Farewells, fond or otherwise, had been made between husband and wife in the latter's bedroom at an ungodly hour of the morning. Houston seemed uncommonly anxious to be about his business at the colliery and had breakfasted without any formality at all. He had quit the house on the stroke of eight. As he tapped his topper onto his head and ran down the steps to the waiting chaise, Mirrin heard him sigh audibly. She did not imagine that the sigh indicated regret that Edith would shortly be off on a trip to Edinburgh and that he would be left as a "taffeta widower" for five or six days.

Silk had come increasingly into the panorama of high fashion, and Edith, scorning tweeds, was dressed like a lady of fashion as she emerged ready for her journey. Her flounced bustle was neatly draped at her rear, and her dress shimmered pale blue in the sunlight. The hall clock indicated that she had two hours on hand to drive the miles to Hamilton where she would catch the one o'clock connection for Edinburgh. Being, as always, relieved of the stresses of unpunctuality, Edith put in the time by having a last malicious skirmish with her house-keeper.

Since breakfast Mirrin had had to endure the mistress's carping. Only the thought that she would be free of the harangues for at least a week enabled her to rein her temper and remain polite, obedient, and apparently attentive to Edith Lamont's instructions. Pencil and tab-let in her gloved hand, Edith noted all marks of slovenli-ness, and at the front door, handed the list to Mirrin at the end of the tour. There was something horribly incrimi-nating in Edith's insistence on detailed inventories, and Mirrin could not help but remark that Mr. Lamont would still be on the premises to keep an eye on things.

Edith glanced up sharply from her stationery.

"And what do you mean by that remark?"

"He'll be able to keep check," said Mirrin.

"Do you imagine that my husband has nothing better to do with his time than police the domestics?"

"I didn't mean that, madam," said Mirrin. "I meant only that he will be able to keep stock of expenditure."

"That is the housekeeper's task."

"Aye, madam," Mirrin sighed.

"Do the chores bore you, Stalker?"

"Not at all, madam."

Edith pushed the paper at her, and Mirrin accepted it.

"You, Stalker, are responsible."

"Yes, madam."

Outside, the carriage horses snickered and stamped impatiently, and Sandy Willocks, the driver, ordered them to be still.

Edith moved out into the sunlight and billowed down the shallow steps to the driveway. Archie, the young groom, had already opened the carriage door and stood at attention by it. His footman's pose was at odds with his tousled shock of hair, patched jacket, and baggy breeks. Mirrin had recently realized just how far down the social scale Edith Lamont really stood, how much of a mockery reality made of her aping of the gentry. By Blacklaw standards Edith was a fine, wealthy lady. Among real blue-bloods, however, she would immediately be recognized and graded, like inferior coal, as a middle-class trader's wife. This grain of understanding comforted Mirrin and strengthened her resolve never to give the little tyrant the satisfaction of putting her in a temper.

Not one to admit defeat, Edith had saved her cannon for a last, unexpected salvo.

She stepped into the open carriage and signaled to Archie to lock the door. The boy did so, then vaulted boisterously into the seat beside Sandy, demonstrating a lack of decorum that, at another time, would have drawn a stern rebuke from his mistress. But Edith had another matter in mind.

The gloved hand lifted, and a crooked finger beckoned.

Mirrin stepped close to the bright black flank of the carriage, looking up at the woman.

"I do not wish to leave in a spirit of ill-feeling," said Edith. "Do you wish me to explain *why* I have documented the contents of the house?"

Caught by the verbal snare, Mirrin said nothing.

Edith smiled. "It is a protection against dishonesty."

"I hope, madam, that you don't think the staff untrustworthy?"

"Oh, no," said Edith. "I'm sure my domestics are all quite honest."

"Yes, madam."

"It's the honesty of their friends that is in doubt."

"Friends?"

"Come now, Stalker," said Edith, with an icy little laugh. "I *know* what servants get up to when left unsupervised."

Mirrin, puzzled, frowned.

"When Mr. Lamont is out at business, and you have the house to yourselves," Edith explained, "it would not be unnatural for you to 'entertain,' shall we say, your admirers."

"Listen, Mrs. Lamont. . . ."

With an airy wave of her hand, Edith brushed the protest aside. "It happens in the very best establishments. Why, after last summer's European tour, Lady Catherwood returned to find that her parlor maid had been *obliged* to marry in her absence, and that all the evidence indicated that the . . . ah, the deed had been done under Lady Catherwood's roof."

"I'll watch over the servants' behavior very carefully," promised Mirrin.

"And who will watch over you?"

"You need not worry on that score, madam."

"I cannot believe that such a handsome girl as you has no admirers."

"That's as may be," said Mirrin thinly. "But they'll not enter this house, by invitation or otherwise."

Again Edith blessed her housekeeper with an ingratiating smile. "I'm sure you are sincere, Stalker. But the temptation will be very strong, will it not? Indeed, you could hardly be blamed for seizing the chance of. . . ."

"There will be nobody here but the staff while you're gone, madam, nobody to tap the liquor or filch the cheese, or carry away the silverware—nor do anything else, either."

"Good." Edith looked at the tip of Sandy's whip and almost snapped her fingers to tell the driver to wheel away. She paused, however, and gave Mirrin one last moment of attention. "You do *have* 'admirers,' do you not?"

"Not in the way you mean, madam."

"I've heard of a young collier—Ewing, would it be?"

"A friend of my father's . . ."

"And of yours, too, I think."

Edith's tone exuded sympathy, a conspiratorial bond in such *affaires du coeur*. She might even have been instructing Mirrin to encourage her admirer to use the mansion as a place of debauch.

"Yes, a friend of mine too," admitted Mirrin.

"If he is a young, sturdy fellow, perhaps he will not be able to keep away from you."

"I think he will," said Mirrin. "In fact, madam, I doubt if you could drag him through those gates with a steam engine, whether you're here or not."

"Does he not care for you?"

"Aye," said Mirrin. "But he's been well schooled in respect. He knows his place—just like the rest of us, madam."

Edith snapped her fingers. Sandy flicked the whip. The carriage wheels grumbled over the gravel.

Mirrin could not hold back.

Running a few steps, she caught up with the carriage before it gathered speed. Hand on the door, Mirrin lifted herself so that her words would not be lost, even though Edith sat rigidly facing front, eyes fixed.

"Mrs. Lamont," Mirrin called. "If it comforts you, I'll give you my word that no man will bed down in this house in your absence—no man, except Mr. Lamont."

Edith's upper lip lifted like that of a vixen. She tapped Sandy on the collar with the crook of her parasol.

"Drive. Drive, I say."

Mirrin dropped back and watched the handsome carriage gather speed and roll through the gates at the foot of the driveway. She partly regretted the impulse that had urged her to have the last word, a last word that implied a power she did not possess. Yet she felt triumphant, full of glee that she had defended herself so adequately and had, in the final swipe, given better than she had got.

Turning, she strode back to the house, entered by the front door, and locked it behind her.

Rob Ewing, indeed! From which source had that rumor reached Edith's ears? It was absurd, anyhow. Rob Ewing did not dare show his face in the Stalker house, let alone accost her here in Strathmore.

Mirrin's parting shot had had more than a crumb of truth to it. This was Houston Lamont's house, not Edith's. No other man had a right to sleep here without the master's invitation. Startled by the thought, Mirrin gave herself a little shake of warning, then, checking her watch against the hall clock, took herself down to the kitchen to join Mrs. Burns in a much-needed cup of tea.

∽

Dominie Guthrie lit his pipe, a long-stemmed clay with a chipped and blackened bowl. The tarry tobacco burned with a smell like singed rope. Drew had grown accustomed to the reek, to ink, chalk, and the oily effluvia of the lamp, which was lit early these nights now that summer was dimming. The schoolmaster relaxed with his pupil. Heels on desk, book in his lap, head wreathed in pungent smoke, he expounded at random on subjects far removed from the academic curriculum. The dominie was a downy bird, as much concerned with the development of Drew's thinking capacity as with his memory. Drew, in turn, no longer held the teacher in awe but listened with fierce concentration even when the old man appeared to be engaged in mere casual reminiscence.

On the desktop, laid on a pad of blotting paper, was an object like a small, shriveled gray cauliflower, which the dominie had identified as a human brain. To his credit, Drew did not shrink from the medical trophy, which, said the dominie, had been in his possession for so long now that it had probably come from the cranium of a caveman. He had used the object to strike up discussion, tapping the preserved, plasterlike husk with his pipe stem to illustrate the areas where the most illusive mechanisms were supposed to reside.

"A miraculous container," he said, "storing a vast quantity of material of unknown worth."

"Is not the memory of limited capacity, then?" Drew asked.

"Medical science believes that there's no limit to the faculty," said Mr. Guthrie. "The problem is in knowing how to tap it."

"It's not what's stored there, but how to get it out?"

"Right as rain, Drew."

Puffing on his clay, the dominie waited patiently for the lad's next observation. When it came, it caught him unaware.

"My father," Drew said.

The pipe stem hovered an inch from the master's lips.

"My father was ruined by memory," Drew said. "He could never be quit of the past. It sort of choked him."

"What do you mean, Drew?"

"Remembering the struggles and hardships of his youth."

"But they were real hardships. Your father, like most men in this part of the world, had a hard life."

"But was it right of him, Dominie, to miss out the middle?"

"I don't take your meaning, Drew."

"He lived in dreams of the past and the future. But in between—it seems to me that there was just a hollow space, nothing."

"The present, you mean?"

"Up when the hooter called, an' out to work."

"Much as you do—only he went to the seams and you go to your desk."

"Aye, but at least it's my own future I'm slavin' for," said Drew.

The dominie set the pipe in a saucer, took his feet from the desk, and leaned his elbows on it instead. He had no comment to make on Drew's remarks. A multitude of implications crowded behind the statement. How could he explain the intricate system of ethics on which past, present, and future, work, accomplishment, and reward were founded?

"What's more," Drew went on, "I can hardly remember *him*. Maybe that's how it happens—you put old memories down under new ones and bury them."

"Undoubtedly."

"But I *should* be able to remember my own father," Drew insisted. "I can hardly remember one word he said to me in all those years."

The dominie cleared his throat. "Strange as it may seem, Drew, you'll remember him much more clearly as you grow older, recollections will restore themselves. When you are my age, you'll recall your father with more clarity than you ever believed possible. I've no means of proving it—just take my word for it."

"I don't *miss* him, Dominie. Is it wrong of me not to miss him?"

"You have your mother and sisters, of course."

"They're . . . all right," Drew said, "but . . . but I just don't seem able to care much for them either. It's funny, when I think about my father, I realize that if he were still alive I wouldn't be here at all."

"That's an illogical assumption, Drew."

"No, it's the truth, Mr. Guthrie. He'd never have managed it. Oh, I might have got as far as classes in Hamilton, and a job as a clerk, but that would've been my limit.

Da would have kept on dreaming of something better, something different for me, but he would never have been able to make it come true."

"You're being unduly hard on your father, Drew, and on yourself."

"My sisters are doing this for me only because they promised *him.* That was the best thing he could manage —to extract a daft promise with his dying breath."

"I'm . . . I'm sorry, Drew."

"Sorry for what, Mr. Guthrie?"

"That I can't help you understand."

"It's not important," said Drew abruptly.

"No?"

"It's over and done with. Nobody can change that."

With sudden brusqueness the dominie swept the papers on his desk into a cardboard folder and thrust it across the top at Drew. "Additional exercises. Same time on Thursday?"

Drew rose, strapping his books together. "Yes, Mr. Guthrie." He crossed to the door.

"Drew?"

"Aye, Dominie?"

"The first conjugation in all Latin primers is *amare*, the present indicative active of the verb 'to love.' Have you ever wondered why that is so?"

"Because it's the simplest grammatical example."

"Perhaps there's another reason," Mr. Guthrie suggested. "If you think of it, Drew, please let me know."

"I will," Drew promised, but as the dominie suspected, the young man never did.

❧

Edith Lamont opened her eyes, saw that it was broad daylight, turned her back to the window, and burrowed deeper into the pillow. She stretched an arm across the vacant area of the double bed, not seeking her husband so much as the comforting assurance that she was alone. Her sojourn in Edinburgh was a fortnight into the past, but the gay life of the capital had seemed full and rich and had left her discontented. By contrast Blacklaw was a sump of boorishness in which it was impossible to find a single soul not tarred by vulgarity. The Cunninghams, with whom she had stayed, thought as little of Houston's manners as she did, and regarded his obsession with coal as rude and unhealthy. Their sympathy, though courteously veiled, flattered Edith and strengthened her spite against her husband.

On her return to Strathmore she had interrogated Mrs. Burns as to anything untoward that might have occurred while she had been away. But servants were loyal to their own kind, and the cook would admit to nothing. Edith's suspicious nature was not appeased. Patiently she had waited and watched for some sign that Houston and the Stalker girl had evolved a relationship other than that of servant and master. She almost hoped that it might come to pass, thus giving her a perfectly acceptable excuse to separate herself from him completely and live out the role of a wronged wife in the city, generously financed by the allotment she would extract from Houston's guilt.

The door opened.

She heard a footfall on the carpet, a heavy tread, and pretended to be asleep.

"Edith?"

Pinching the sheets to her breast, she raised herself a little.

"I've brought your morning tea," Houston said.

"Have we no servants in this house?"

Houston placed the tray on the bedside table. "I want a private word with you, Edith."

She rubbed her eyes. Her husband was dressed for the city, in his smart frock coat and narrow-check trousers. He decanted tea from the silver pot into a bone-china cup, added milk and sugar, and even stirred it for her. His air of determination disturbed Edith and dispersed the remnants of sleep.

"My robe, if you please."

Obediently, he brought the quilted silk robe from the chair and waited, teacup in hand, while she sat up in bed and put the garment on. Settling sheets and blankets about her, she sat upright like an invalid. He gave her the cup.

"Thank you."

She sipped the liquid, then eyed him narrowly, suspiciously. "Well?"

Houston said, "I've written to Miss Emerson today, to inform her that I will call for Dorothy in one month's time and bring my sister home."

Edith's head suddenly seemed too heavy for her slender neck and dropped back with a tiny thud against the padded board. Tea spilled from the cup into the saucer, and a few drops stained the linen sheet.

"Houston," she gasped. "Do I understand you correctly?"

"I intend to bring Dorothy home."

"You'll only unsettle her."

"No, she'll be happier here."

"Are you mad?"

"My mind's made up, Edith."

"*Your* mind is. . . . What about me, Houston? Am I not to be consulted at all?"

"I already know your opinion, my dear."

Edith threw the cup and saucer onto the tray, swept back the sheets, and pranced out of bed. "My opinion is that your sister isn't fit to be . . . to be. . . ."

"Dorothy needs my care, and my love."

"Who put this ridiculous notion into your head?"

"It's been in my mind since my last visit to Kent," Houston said. "Dorothy is virtually a prisoner there.

At least she will be able to walk in the gardens here."

"I *forbid* you to do it, Houston."

"It's already done," Houston said. "Dorothy must come home."

"And what of me?" Edith said. "Is this my home no longer?"

"I don't expect you to attend her."

"I suppose *you* will do that?" Edith sneered. "Manage a colliery *and* look after a lunatic?"

"The servants . . ."

"Ah!" she exclaimed. "It's that Stalker girl, isn't it? She put you up to this, to defy me?"

"I assure you that Mirrin Stalker knows nothing of my decision," Houston said.

"Where will we put her, your sister?"

"In the nursery wing."

"No, Houston! No!"

"Mirrin will take up full duties as housekeeper. Her room will be close to Dorothy's. You will not have your sleep troubled nor your life disrupted in any way—of that I assure you, Edith."

"Have you told the Stalker girl of your plans for her?"

"Not yet."

"Perhaps she will not agree to serve both as housekeeper and night nurse."

"In which case I will employ another person to care for Dorothy's needs."

"It appears that you have worked everything out very carefully in my absence, and that you leave me no choice."

"None."

Edith realized that threats, tears, and temper would serve no purpose now. In all the years of their marriage Houston had seldom defied her. She had come to regard his pliancy as weakness; suddenly she had an inkling of the true quality of his capitulation.

"Very well, Houston, if that's your decision, I'll not stand in your way."

He bowed formally but gave no other sign of gratitude.

"I'll be in Glasgow today, Edith. Is there anything you require?"

She shook her head.

Houston hesitated, then quietly left the bedroom.

Edith's control lapsed at once. She staggered to the bed and leaned across it like a woman startled by the pangs of childbirth—yet she suffered no real pain. After a minute or so, she gave up the fruitless posturing. The battle had to be fought cleverly if she hoped to regain that which she had lost—her position of authority and her husband's devotion.

The identity of the enemy was no mystery.

The Stalker bitch was her opponent.

She would begin at once. She would summon the carriage and be driven to Hamilton where, in Dalzells' Emporium, she would purchase the kind of dresses that would restore her softness and the winsomeness of her youth.

Pushing herself from the bed, Edith Lamont rang the bell and waited, with furious impatience, for one of the servants to answer her call.

CHAPTER X

IN September, only six months after the tragedy that had reached into every home in Blacklaw, Mirrin left the narrow house at the main street's end. She had imagined that she might grieve at the moment of departure but to her surprise found that her feeling was one of relief. Perhaps it was the sight of her brother Drew that stifled sorrow at leaving home. The way in which the young man lolled, silent and arrogant, in the doorway almost made her wish that her severance with this place might be permanent and total. Mam and Kate, of course, were carrying on as if she were starting a trek to Timbuktu and not just moving a mile up the hill. She would be home once or twice a week to visit. Family fetters, as she had discovered before, were not so easily broken. Her loyalty now was only to her mother and to Kate. The twins were beyond redemption—Betsy an empty-headed little snob, and Drew a hopeless case of galloping ambition. She took her seat in the dogcart in which Archie had stowed her luggage and rode out of the colliers' row toward the bronze-leaved oaks without a single pang of conscience.

September, in her book, had always been a hopeful month, and she loved the mellow season. Besides, every passing week took her farther from the horror of the spring, ripening her from the brash, upstart girl she had been then. At times she wondered how much of a part Houston Lamont had played in helping her to mature. It was less what he had done for her in practical terms than his effect on her as a man that puzzled her. The old enmity toward him as a coalmaster had all but gone. She felt a strange, abiding loyalty to him and enough confidence in him to assume that within a day or so she would be thoroughly settled in his household.

Among the first of her chores would be the preparation of the nursery wing, that part of the mansion that had been deserted since Lamont's son's death. It gave Mirrin a peculiar satisfaction to march through the tomb-like chambers with brooms, mops, and dusting feathers, letting in light and air. Her own room was in this wing too, larger than she had anticipated and very comfortably furnished with pieces that Lamont had unearthed from attics and cellars.

Mirrin could not be sure how much she had influenced the coalmaster's decision to bring his sister home from Kent. Their conversation in the coach house had been so intimate that she could not quite reject the possibility that she had helped edge him toward the purpose that had eventually caused him to defy his wife. It was common knowledge in the servants' quarters that there had been a confrontation between Houston and Edith Lamont. Mirrin's most stern warnings could not quell the gossip that chattered about among the maids, the cook, and the gardeners, all of whom were agog with the news that Mr. Lamont would shortly be installing his daft sister in the house.

Houston had given Mirrin the news personally. Since that moonlit night in early August, the master had often found opportunities to talk with her, even to confide in her, and she felt his attitude toward her was now as confused as her own toward him.

Edith Lamont's spiteful outbursts had apparently been calmed by the impending arrival of the sister. Her wardrobe was stocked with colorful new gowns, and, so Betsy had told Mirrin, her account with Dalzells' had come to over fifty pounds, more than a collier could earn in a year. Outwardly, Edith's manner might have softened a little, and she no longer scolded the servants and Mirrin, treating them with a cold formality. Beneath the surface, however, Edith's mistrust had turned to hatred, a fact of which Mirrin was instinctively aware. She did not relax her guard for a moment.

During the week when the master was in Kent, the atmosphere in Strathmore became electric with anticipation. Removing herself still farther from domestic concerns, Edith spent most of each day in her bedroom, fussing and primping with her new clothes and accessories. Charitably, Mirrin told the maids that Mrs. Lamont intended to look her best for Miss Dorothy's homecoming; in her heart, though, she recognized the spirit of competition.

Lamont brought Dorothy home by easy stages, cosseting her in grand hotels in London, Newcastle, and Edinburgh. Her baggage arrived by railway carrier an hour in advance of the branch-line train from Hamilton. Sandy and Archie had the big coach in the station yard by noon and had honored the occasion by tricking themselves out in new shirts, hacking jackets, and gleaming black boots. The queen herself could not have arrived to a grander welcome.

But Miss Dorothy was exhausted by her long journey and unsettled by the dimly remembered sights of Hamilton and the glowering Lanarkshire landscape. The assembled staff caught only a brief glimpse of the master's sister as she was whisked from the coach and up the steps into the mansion.

Edith, who had sense enough to feign compassion at this sentimental moment, undertook to attend her sister-in-law personally, and for the rest of the afternoon the servants' curiosity remained unappeased.

❧

Mrs. Burns sprinkled parsley into the potato pot and tested the temperature of the basic sauce. She wore a starched apron and a cap of spotless white linen; linen cuffs banded the sleeves of her dress. To judge from the aroma that wafted from the great stewpan she had excelled herself in the selection and dressing of the pair of fowls and had coaxed them to a state of tenderness before which the most invalid appetite must surely quicken. Hannah was set to stir the sauce while the cook, with a frightened glance at the clock, fiddled with the valves of the ventilated oven within which a rich lemon pudding was just about to erupt deliciously over its puff-pastry rim.

"If I'd known they were goin' to be late," the cook wailed, "I'd have settled them with cutlets and a cold chocolate mold. It'll all be ruined if they don't come down soon."

"Poor daft lady doesn't know about such things as dinner," said Hannah.

"Eight o'clock I was told," said Mrs. Burns, whose sympathy at that moment was all with her fowls and lemon pudding, "and eight it should be."

Mirrin entered the kitchen, straight-backed and unflustered, her black dress making her seem much older than nineteen.

"They are coming down directly, Mrs. Burns," she said. "I take it the food is prepared?"

" 'Course it is," Mrs. Burns beamed. "Is the sister with them?"

"Yes, it seems that Miss Dorothy—as we will call her —has recovered enough to join the master and mistress for dinner. Trays, please, Hannah. Then fill the soup tureens, both of them, and don't forget to fix the lids on tightly to keep them hot."

Much activity followed, and at one minute past the hour of eight, when Edith and Houston descended the stairs with Dorothy between them, they were greeted by Mirrin's sonorous announcement, "Dinner is served."

"Thank you, Mirrin. We will take it at once," said Lamont.

Mirrin was hardly prepared for the gentleness of the woman who took her seat on her brother's left at the long dinner table. Wisely, the full length of the board was not utilized, and only half was covered with the embroidered cloth, so that the three members of the Lamont family sat within touching distance of each other. As Mirrin conducted the serving of the dinner, she studied the new arrival closely. Dorothy's likeness to her brother was marked, but in her the man's brooding silences were replaced by a naive and slightly apprehensive vacancy of expression. There was little conversation, though Lamont occasionally clasped Dorothy's hand as if to reassure her that there was nothing to fear in this house. Edith was reserved, her smile fixed.

At the meal's end, Mattie cleared away the pudding plates and conveyed the master's congratulations down to Mrs. Burns. Mirrin laid out the fruit bowls and nut dishes and poured the wine, which Lamont himself had uncorked and decanted earlier in the evening. As she did this, Mirrin became aware that Dorothy Lamont was staring at her.

"Dorothy, my dear," said Lamont, affably, "this is Mirrin Stalker who looks after the house. It was she, I believe, who arranged the spray of flowers in your room. I told her how fond of flowers you are."

Mirrin was unprepared for the radiant smile that lit Dorothy's face, causing the years to drop away and be replaced by an almost childlike prettiness.

"I . . . I . . . I do like flowers, Mirrin."

"That's nice, Miss Dorothy. In summer the gardens are

full of them. We still have quite a display as you'll see tomorrow."

"I like your hair."

Mirrin was abashed by the woman's frankness.

Edith's fingers tightened on her wineglass.

Tapping her hand on top of her head, Dorothy said, "My hair is too soft. I do try to arrange it, but . . . it's too soft. I wish. . . ." The wish too was too soft and could not be formulated into a proper expression.

"My young sister has soft hair," said Mirrin gently. "But she cheats a bit and uses curling irons to make it stay in shape."

"I do not think," said Edith, "that hair is a suitable subject for dinner-table conversation. You may take away the fruit, Mirrin, and attend to the kitchen."

It was as though a cloud crossed Dorothy's face. She responded not so much to the words as to Edith's sharp tone, seeming to cringe into herself. It was all Mirrin could do to stop herself taking the poor woman in her arms to comfort her. Houston, however, swept the conversation on in defiance of his wife's objection.

"If curling irons are the answer, Dorothy," he said breezily, "then why should you not purchase a pair?"

The cloud whisked away, and his sister smiled in delight. She would have badgered Mirrin with many more questions had not Houston prudently signaled to the housekeeper to gather the fruit and take it from the dining room.

Outside, in the hall, Mirrin paused. Anger and compassion flickered in her—anger at Edith's tactlessness, compassion for the poor wandered creature who was so vulnerable that the slightest wrong word could hurt her like the claw of a gin trap. In Dorothy Lamont there was an infinite capacity for happiness. But, thought Mirrin grimly, damned little of it would ever come to the surface if Edith had her way.

There and then, Mirrin promised herself that she would do all in her power to ensure that things went well for the master's sister.

⬥

The autumn of the year seemed to make amends for the trials imposed by the spring. The sun shone warmly late into the year, and the leaves changed color gradually as if reluctant to give way to winter. As late as mid-October there were still roses upon the shrubs, haws and rowan berries glowing red along the hedges, and huge, sturdy margarets to be found in the garden's sheltered spots. Mild weather and a bountiful harvest gave the colliers a chance to recover their health and gird themselves for the cold months ahead.

Behind Strathmore's walls the Indian summer benefited Dorothy Lamont. She settled rapidly into her new surroundings, undisturbed by shadows of the past or by tensions that her presence intensified in the household. Archie, who also had a simple outlook on life, was her favorite. Proudly he showed her around the stables and held the horses while she stroked their velvety muzzles. Mrs. Burns produced elaborate puddings, as ornate as Parisian *chapeaux*, and received the reward of all conscientious cooks —words of praise from the family, including Miss Dorothy.

Houston imposed no restrictions on his sister, set up no lines of demarcation. She mingled with the servants and joined freely in their chatter, helped the gardeners, fed the dogs, cats, and hens in the little farmlike cottage where the greensman lived. In a remarkably short space of time, gloom seemed to lift from Strathmore and the lilt of forgotten merriment return to it. If only Edith Lamont could have put aside her pride and petty jealousy, that golden autumn might have endured unimpaired forever.

To Mirrin, Miss Dorothy's unaffected joys were so childlike that her awkwardness and instability were almost forgotten. But Dorothy was not a child. As a woman of close to middle age, Edith could not help but view her as a competitor for the love that she, mistress of the house, demanded as her exclusive entitlement. Only Mirrin and Houston, sensing Edith's growing hatred, were aware that Dorothy had brought more than happiness to Strathmore.

Edith, however, was instinctively intelligent and recognized the true cause of her relegation in status. She chose to feign a sweetness, which, by reason of its patent insincerity, alienated Lamont still further. Gorgeous dresses adorned her stocky body. Creams, lotions, expensive perfumes, and rouges appeared on her dressing table and were duly applied to her features. The effect was too vulgar to appeal to her husband, and coupled with her gushing exhibitions of affection, quite sickened the coalmaster.

In spite of his wife's reaction Houston was close to finding happiness. In his sister's company he discovered the unstinted warmth that had so long been missing from his life. It was this effect on Houston that pleased Mirrin most of all and tugged her inexorably closer to that day when their confused feelings would crystallize.

If only matters had been as good in the narrow house. Mirrin's concerns at Strathmore were tainted by anxiety over her mother's health and Kate's problems. The villagers' sniping had not dwindled much, and Flora, who had always enjoyed the community's respect, took it much to heart. She treated Mirrin coldly now, as though she blamed her for the loss of face. Mirrin was powerless to improve the situation. She had committed herself to furnishing money to put Drew through the university. She could not be expected to do more. But it seemed more was required of her.

Kate accurately put her finger on the prime source of

worry one Sunday afternoon when she and Mirrin stole a half hour together in the weedy garden behind the colliers' row.

"Everything's hanging on Drew passing this examination," Kate said.

"He'll pass," Mirrin told her.

"Aye, or kill himself with overwork."

"He's not sick, is he?"

"No, but he's drawing so much out of himself, I'm frightened by it."

"Have you had a word with Mr. Guthrie?" asked Mirrin.

"It's not Drew's studies that worry the dominie, it's Drew himself."

Mirrin needed no explanation. "How Drew's turned out is none of our doing, Kate."

"Maybe not, but what'll become of him if he fails?"

"Listen, Kate, our Drew's too cunning to make a wrong move. He won't fail."

Kate nodded bleakly. "So, what'll I do if he passes?"

"So that's it? You're worried about money?"

"What if he wins an entrance to the university and then we find we can't afford it? Oh, we're saving all we can, but it might not be enough. I'm frightened that *we* may fail *him*."

"We can do no more than we're doing now."

"No, I know. It's not your fault, Mirrin."

"No more is it yours, Kate."

"I wish I could be sure."

"Well, we've six months to worry about it," said Mirrin. "How much is Betsy contributing?"

"Not as much as I'd hoped. She buys ribbons and scent and things. I can't blame her. It must be very tempting for her, working in a place like Dalzells'."

"I *could* ask for a small increase in my wages," Mirrin reluctantly suggested.

"I wasn't dropping hints, love."

"I know," said Mirrin. "But it's possible Mr. Lamont might give me a shilling more, since I'm helping to look after his sister."

"Every penny would help."

"Aye," said Mirrin. "I just wish it was for your benefit, Kate."

"Oh, Drew's not so bad. Wait until he's a rich and famous advocate, he'll see us right for our old age then."

"Not him. He'll pretend we don't exist."

"No, Mirrin!" Kate was a little shocked. "Drew's loyal, if he's nothing else."

"We'll see. The truth of it is, Kate, I'd willingly pay him just to stay out of my life from now on."

"He's our *brother*, Mirrin."

"More's the pity."

∝

The India rubber ball and frayed old racquet had been dug from a garden shed. The game did not suffer from the equipment's imperfections. Unobserved, Mirrin stood by a tree at the edge of the lawn and smiled at the sight of the coalmaster puffing after the ball. He picked it up, hid it in his large hand, then turned to Dorothy, twenty yards across the grass, and raised both arms.

"It's gone," he declared. "You must have hit it straight out of the county. Shall I send a carriage to look for it?"

"It's . . . it's in your hand, Houston."

"Never."

He advanced foxily across the lawn. But his sister had already learned the rudimentary deceptions that made the game so much fun and did not release the racquet handle or expose the painted flower tub that stood in lieu of a wicket.

"It's in your hand, Houston," she cried gleefully. "In your hand."

Houston lumbered a few paces, swung his arm in a huge circle, and delivered the ball in a floating arc toward the tub. Dorothy flailed at it, missed, then, as the ball trickled along the ground, stopped it with the sole of her shoe, took aim, and clouted it across the shoulder of the lawn into a distant flower bed. Lamont gave every sign of being flabbergasted; not annoyed, however—any irritation had a distressing effect on his sister. Ruefully, noisily, he applauded the drive. "A fine effort, Miss Lamont."

"Is it lost, Houston?"

"I daresay we can find it."

"Be careful not to hurt the flowers."

"I'll be most careful," Houston promised as he crossed the lawn.

Mirrin emerged from behind the oak. Cheered by the sight of the play, she had sloughed off the cares that her visit home had incurred. Dorothy's gaunt figure was filling out, and she had lost many of her nervous habits. As for Houston Lamont, he appeared not to have a care in the world, as if a lifetime of sunny Sunday afternoons stretched into the future. Edith disapproved of games on the Sabbath, even though the family had attended morning service in the village kirk and would go again to the evangelical meeting that evening. Mirrin did not attend church and stayed behind with Dorothy who, it was felt, might be disturbed by the minister's references to death, hell, brimstone, and damnation, the nexus of all Scottish sermons.

Lamont did not notice Mirrin. He continued toward the flower beds, then, veering suddenly, caught Dorothy around the waist, hoisted her from the ground, and swung her in a wide circle.

"Houston, don't dare. Houston, put me down."

On the final turn, the coalmaster caught sight of his housekeeper, and slightly discomfited, set Dorothy lightly to the ground again.

"See," he said, directing Dorothy's attention, "here's Mirrin come to see who is making all the noise."

"Are you enjoying yourself, Miss Dorothy?"

"Yes, Mirrin. We are . . . we are playing a *game*." She displayed the racquet. "I hit the ball with this."

"Yes, I saw you. A grand hit it was, too."

"Dorothy," said Lamont, "see if you can find the ball."

Mirrin and Houston watched the woman cross the grass, step gingerly into the flower bed, and begin to poke about among the leaves. Her attention was soon diverted by a pair of mauve butterflies, then by the discovery of a cluster of tight yellow rosebuds, which promised late blooms. As she explored the minutiae of the garden she chattered away contentedly to herself.

"What a difference these past weeks have made to your sister, Mr. Lamont. You must be pleased with her progress."

"I am, indeed. However, I can't help wishing. . . ."

Houston did not finish the sentence. Mirrin nodded in sympathy. She was an expert in wishing. Her kind survived on it. It was strange, though, to hear a coalmaster admit to such a weakness.

"Miss Dorothy will be needing some winter dresses soon," Mirrin said.

"A splendid idea, Mirrin."

"I hear from my sister that Dalzells' has just taken delivery of a stock of the latest fashions."

"We'll all bundle into the carriage one afternoon next week and go there."

"Perhaps Mrs. Lamont would prefer to supervise?"

It was a delicate decision. Edith would have a dilemma on her hands. She would hardly like to be excluded from a shopping trip. On the other hand, she would not wish to be seen in Hamilton in charge of a weak-minded person. Dorothy's behavior in response to new situations was not predictable.

"I'll . . . ah, speak with my wife," Lamont said.

Mirrin cleared her throat. "I'm sorry to have to ask it, Mr. Lamont, but. . . ."

"What is it, Mirrin? Are you unhappy here?"

"No, sir, it's certainly not that. I was wondering if . . . if you could see your way to paying me a little extra each week. I think I'm worth it now, sir."

"Mirrin," Houston said seriously, "if I had told you the truth some three months ago, you would have thought it an excuse. Perhaps now you will understand. Times are bad, for masters as well as men. If it ever leaked out that I pay my housekeeper more than I pay my foremen then every hothead in Blacklaw would be howling for my blood."

"It would only be a shilling, sir."

"You don't need it, do you?"

"No, sir, I don't need it."

"But your brother does?"

"Aye."

"I'll consider it, Mirrin," he said. "You do well here, Mirrin. But you're not really the stuff that ideal servants are made of."

She felt a prickle of resentment; was he patronizing her? He had a right to patronize her, of course. She had elected to become a servant and must accept the sharp divisions that occupation incurred.

"What stuff am I made of, then?" she asked.

"You don't truly believe that you serve my family, Mirrin. You believe that you help us."

"Is there a difference?"

"A vast difference."

"The difference between the slave and the hireling?"

"Yes," said Houston Lamont. "But we may differ on which is which, Mirrin."

"I'm sorry I asked, sir."

"Don't be quite so willful, Mirrin. I haven't given my answer yet."

"Aye, sir, I think you have."

The discussion was interrupted by Miss Dorothy, who, having found the ball, tripped up from the flower bed now with racquet and ball hidden behind her back.

"I . . . I can't discover it," she said, trying to stifle her grin. "Lost, Houston. You look."

Houston frowned at Mirrin, head on one side; then he gave all his attention to his sister, falling back into the pattern of play.

Mirrin had almost forgotten her request for an increase of a shilling. It astonished her when, the following Saturday noon, the twist of brown paper that contained her wages was heavier by a florin.

She said nothing, of course, to anyone, and gave all the money to Kate.

༄

The coalmaster's warning was the first intimation to reach Mirrin's ears that the market was unstable. If she had been at home the rumor might have reached her sooner. As it was, the steady and alarming fall in the price of coal continued throughout November and brought despondency to collier and management alike. Meetings kept Houston Lamont engaged until all hours of the night. Day after day he was obliged to tighten his grip on his workers and fight bitterly with their militant leaders. For all his telling, however, he could not make them understand, or accept, that they were all at the mercy of a national deflationary spiral. In trade with ironmasters, shipping magnates, and mill owners, he struggled to grab the best prices for his material, and for the sake of contracts, which would enable him to keep full employment, shaved his personal profits to a minimum. Throughout the first drab month of winter he saw little of his family. Up in the cold hours before dawn, back late at night, like most men of Blacklaw, he cared only for a warm fire, hot food, and sleep.

No matter how late the hour, however, he found Mirrin Stalker still in the kitchen. Long after the cook and maids had retired, Mirrin would be sure to have the drawing-room fire blazing and a meal bubbling on the kitchen stoves. Soon Lamont came to prefer the companionable warmth of the kitchen to the empty upper rooms and took his supper informally with his back to the stove and his boots drying on the rack. Mirrin treated him as she would have treated any collier home from a double shift at the pit, with a blend of jocular bullying and a practical demonstration of sympathy.

By the month's end, the nightly suppers had become a habit. The couple were relaxed with each other, and Lamont unloaded the burdens and cares that the day had brought.

"I can't seem to hammer it into their thick heads that the slump is not my fault," Houston said.

"But it is your fault, Mr. Lamont."

"I thought you'd changed your mind about coalmasters."

"I'm still the same girl at heart," said Mirrin. "The difference is that I now understand both sides of the case."

"I don't *want* to cause them misery, you know."

"What'll happen if the price slump continues?"

"I'll be forced to reduce the labor force."

"That'll mean loss of wages, homes, and dreadful hardships."

"I can't go on sustaining losses out of my own pocket."

"But you can't expect a collier to consider your problems when they seem so much smaller than his own."

"Not smaller," said Houston. "Larger and more complex."

"Be that as it may, the collier sees you tearing past in a coach pulled by horses that are better fed than his bairns and. . . ."

"Mirrin, even if I sold my stables and carriages *and* Strathmore," interrupted Lamont, "and plowed the proceeds into supporting an idle pit, the added capital would only stretch to a few extra weeks' wages."

"I know that, Mr. Lamont. But the collier only relates himself to you. You're more than an employer. You own the village, provide the bread and the milk and the bit of meat. When you cease to provide, then you are condemned as a selfish exploiter."

"Is that how you see me?"

"Of course not."

"What else do they say about me?"

"I hope you're not asking me to spy?"

"I'm just trying to understand the root of the colliers' mistrust."

"My brother calls it the natural result of a feudal legacy."

"Yes, I've heard that explanation before," Houston said. "But I can't change matters overnight. Somebody must always hold the reins of power."

"Miners aren't ignorant, Mr. Lamont. Most of them can read and keep abreast of affairs in the newspapers. They know fine that coal prices are low and that pits are closing everywhere in Scotland. They just pray that it won't happen here, continue to hope for the miracle that will bring back prosperity."

"Then why are they afraid of me?"

"They are afraid that you'll cut the work force prematurely just to save your grand mansion."

"I've always tried to do what's best for the villagers."

"How can you expect a miner, born and bred in hunger and disease, in disaster and insecurity, to believe that

you're really on his side? The pit can never be the enemy.
You and your kind must stand in place of the devil.
You'll never change that, Mr. Lamont."

"Yet I must try? Is that what you mean, Mirrin?"

The girl did not answer.

She turned to the cooking range and scooped a ragout
from the pot, added potatoes, peas, and small yellow
turnips to the plate, and put the plate before the master.
He began to eat.

Diplomatically, Mirrin changed the subject.

She said, "Miss Dorothy bought some new gowns
today."

"I'd quite forgotten," said Lamont. "How did she fare
in Hamilton?"

"She was as good as gold, and quite charmed the
drawers. . . . I mean, she was a great favorite with the
assistants in Dalzells'. I doubt if they've ever had a customer more appreciative of their wares."

"What color of gown did she choose?"

"I won't spoil the surprise by telling you," said Mirrin.
"She'll have the day dress on tomorrow, if you happen
to be home. But the evening gown will be hidden away
until the Christmas festivities."

"Was my wife with you in Hamilton?"

Mirrin shook her head. "Mrs. Lamont did not feel . . .
up to it. Archie drove the gig and helped with the parcels.
At the emporium a doorman with a big umbrella stood
out and covered us as we entered, and snapped his fingers
like a pistol crack to summon a manager to attend to us."

"I take it you both enjoyed yourselves?"

"Aye, we did that."

"And what did you buy, Mirrin?"

"Nothing. I had enough fun helping Miss Dorothy,"
Mirrin said. "She needed out, Mr. Lamont. After being
shut away for so long, she needed to mix with people."

"She can't be allowed out alone."

Mirrin hesitated. "No, she can't."

"Perhaps," said Lamont wistfully, "someday."

He mopped gravy from his plate with a pinch of bread, popped the bread into his mouth, and sat back, sighing contentedly. Mirrin put the mug of tea before him. He could not quite stifle a yawn, and as if to account for it, the cook's clock whirred and struck eleven. Lamont lit a cigar and blew smoke toward the lamp.

"It's very late, Mirrin."

"Aye, you must be tired."

"I am. But I was thinking of you."

"One thing you learn as a collier's daughter, and that's how to survive on a short night's sleep."

"You may go to bed now, Mirrin."

"Not just yet, Mr. Lamont. I've the stove to stoke and the crocks to wash."

"Then I'll finish my cigar and leave you to it. I may be late again tomorrow, Mirrin. I'm attending a traders' meeting in Glasgow."

"I'll save supper then."

"Mirrin, why do you do this?"

"Do what, Mr. Lamont?"

"Wait up for me. It isn't strictly part of your duty, you know."

"Maybe not as a housekeeper," Mirrin answered. "But if I was the woman in any man's home, I'd do the same for him."

"Yes, I expect you would."

A moment later Houston got to his feet, stretched, and said, "Has Mrs. Lamont been long in her room?"

"Since nine o'clock, sir."

"Good," Houston said. "She'll be fast asleep by now."

❧

Hastily, Edith Lamont laid the wax candle on the table, closed the door with her finger against the lock to silence

the click, and hurried back to the double bed. She paused
long enough to adjust the shoulder of her nightgown and
expose a portion of her breast, then slid into the bed and
drew the quilt over her face. In spite of the woolen socks
she wore, her feet were icy. She curled into a fetal position and tried to suppress the shivering her vigil by the
open bedroom door had brought on. She had reaped no
reward from the watch, heard nothing from the kitchen
except the clack of pots and pans. An hour had elapsed
between the arrival of Houston's coach and the time he
finally elected to come upstairs. What had really happened in the hour, Edith could only surmise.

For a month now Houston had been eating his supper
below stairs like some common jobber. The evidence of
her ears and eyes was enough to convince Edith that her
husband was under the thrall of the vulgar girl who had
usurped her authority. She did not now have enough
confidence in herself to confront Houston with a direct
accusation. Instead she had devised trials for him, set
traps with a cunning no man could foresee. But the
gowns and jewels and perfumes had gone unremarked; he
had even failed to complain about the size of the bills
from Dalzells'. When she asked for money he gave it to
her without a word; his generosity was sufficient to confirm her belief in his guilt.

Feigning sleep, she lay with eyes closed and breast
bared in a halo of heady perfume. Since childhood she
had been instilled with the notion that a wife was her
husband's helpmate and must not be bold in her demands
—as if any decent woman would. A good wife, however,
must acquiesce when her husband wished to exercise his
conjugal prerogative, be as modest and decorous as possible considering the ugly position Nature required for the
satisfaction of man's ruttish instincts. But after much
observation Edith had reached the conclusion that men

were sheep easily led astray by forward women, and that they found such lascivious flirting irresistible. Fire, she reckoned, was the weapon best used against fire.

The creak of the corridor boards told her that he was walking softly in order not to wake her. He opened the bedroom door. The sounds were familiar. She did not need to open her eyes.

The edge of the mattress sagged. She could feel his scrutiny and did not move. The candle was snuffed out. The weight of his body in the bed; the whispering of the sheet as he made it tight about him; the bed was broad and he lay away from her, on his back, hands clenched on his chest.

In the darkness Edith gently stirred, manufacturing tiny noises to indicate that she was not quite awake. Houston did not move. She rolled on her side and brushed against him. Politely he inched away. She shifted again, depending on the dip of the feather mattress to draw her into the hollow and bring her breasts against him.

Houston's breathing was rhythmic.

Edith was rigid with tension. Every communication between her body and that of her husband caused her to flinch. Though her need of him was wholly physical, she would not surrender to it or even acknowledge it as such. She put it down as part of the trial, the testing. Vaporized by the growing warmth of her body, the perfume on her bosom released a fragrance that added to her own desires—yet had no effect at all on the man by her side.

"Houston," she murmured.

His ribs moved. She felt the twitch of his elbow, which indicated that he had slackened his grip on the waking world.

"Houston, my dearest."

Just as she plunged to the side to plaster herself explicitly against him, he wallowed and turned from her, adopting the position that prepared him for sleep, and to Edith's mind, effectively rebuffed her advances.

Her arms trailed over him.

He started.

"Houston, hold me."

"Hm?" he growled drowsily. "Yes. Good night, Edith."

Pulling a corner of the sheet about his ears, he sank instantly into sleep. Within a minute he was snoring in a manner that Edith could only regard as self-satisfied and boorish.

Drawing herself away, she turned and bit her knuckles to hold back tears, vowing that she would make him suffer for his indifference. It did not occur to her that her softening had come too late, far too late.

I'll make them all suffer, she told herself—Houston, Dorothy, and most of all, that pretty Stalker bitch.

CHAPTER XI

SNOW fell four days before Christmas. It sifted down through the birch boughs and the arms of the oaks, stippled the briars and bramble coverts, and slid sleekly from the waterproof leaves of the holly bush around whose base the women ranged. Flakes adhered to Dorothy's sheepskin overcoat and to the fibers of Mirrin's shawl. Gradually the falling snow obliterated the crenellated edge of the pit heads and the smoke of the colliers' rows. It moved relentlessly over the brown River Shennan, across the breadth of the valley, and soon absorbed the woods, marooning the holly-pickers on an evergreen knoll. Mirrin wished now that they had brought Archie on the expedition. The billowing snow caused an early dusk, and the wintry afternoon seemed strange and hostile.

Dorothy sensed it too. She whimpered a little as Mirrin packed away the shears, and glancing around, chose the path above the river as the shortest route back to the estate.

The ground was spongy with leaf mold and slippery. Mirrin held Dorothy tightly, guiding her awkward steps along the high banking. Below them the river was as still as gelatin. Dorothy ceased whimpering and clung bravely to Mirrin's arm. The melancholy afternoon had blotted out her happy anticipation of Christmas, however, and she did not respond to Mirrin's strained cheerfulness and talk of carols and candles and gifts.

They reached the division of the track. One fork dipped toward the bridge north of the village, the other threaded through a coppice to the back gate of Strathmore.

Suddenly Dorothy stopped.

"This way, Miss Dorothy."

The woman's face was warped by horror.

Fear gripped Mirrin too. "What is it? What's wrong?"

Nasal whining sounds and a mechanical shaking of her head were all the answers that Dorothy Lamont could give. Setting down the holly basket, Mirrin clasped the woman in her arms. On this occasion Dorothy could not be consoled. She pushed Mirrin violently from her and broke into a run, the wicker basket, still clenched in her elbow, bouncing against her hip.

"Miss Dorothy, wait, wait."

Running, Mirrin followed the woman along the upper pathway. Where the first straggling oak tree stalked down from the estate, Dorothy Lamont halted. Pitching herself against the gnarled trunk, she buried her face in her hands. As abruptly as the fit had begun, it passed away.

The River Shennan lay below the slope, screened by drifting snow.

Mirrin leaned against the woman and gently inquired as to what had so frightened her. Dorothy's features were relaxed, and her terrible glassy stare had melted into tears. She stammered unintelligibly but could not formulate the source of her terror.

Stroking and patting her cheek affectionately, Mirrin said, "Never mind, we'll soon be safe home by the fire."

And they soon were.

A fire burned brightly in the grate of Dorothy's room. It cast sunny reflections over the tea things that Mattie had set out on a card table, with a stand of honey scones and cherry cakes and bread and butter.

By nightfall the whole incident seemed to have been

forgotten, to be buried in Dorothy Lamont's memory forever, and she smiled and laughed again and talked of Christmas.

Even so, Mirrin stayed with her and devised amusements to keep her entertained until a half hour before dinner when Hannah relieved her for the rest of the evening.

⤐⟿

Incongruously dressed in a floral tea gown, Edith Lamont stood before the fire in a pose that reminded Houston of the stance of a former governess, a witch of a woman who had terrorized Dorothy and had almost driven him to suicide. Edith's fury was palpable long before she opened her lips.

Turning his back, Houston strode to the breakfast table, drew out a chair, and sat down.

Still Edith did not speak.

Outside the snow had thawed slightly, and fretted the edges of the lawns prettily. It was colder than ever, though, the sky laden with more snow. Even while he was sucked into his wife's mood Houston prayed that the fall would not be deep enough to bury the surface trucks, though Donald Wyld had told him that one nightlong blizzard would give him the best excuse in the world for closing the colliery. He could then shut down production, salving his conscience—three days before Christmas—by calling off the month's rent tithes. So occupied with calculations did he become that he had almost forgotten his wife.

"Did you spare me one thought last night?"

He glanced up at her; then, to indicate that he had no time to waste on petty squabbling, speared beef onto his plate and forked it neatly into fragments.

Edith's fists were like hooks on the ruck of her dress.

Houston ate quickly.

"One single thought for me," Edith yapped.

"When one is in Glasgow," said Houston patiently, "one only spares a thought for getting out again."

"Do not be glib with me, pray."

"Ah, you're full of seasonal good cheer this morning, Edith. It's a pleasure to breakfast with you." Nonchalance spiced his sarcasm.

"I warned you, Houston."

"Edith, for God's sake, what's wrong now?"

"That . . . that . . . harlot . . ."

"Oh, not again!"

"It seems you cannot have enough of her."

"What foolishness are you handing me now?"

"Do you deny that you spend a part of each night with her?"

"Of course I deny it."

"I have heard you—*together.*"

"You've heard nothing of the kind, Edith."

"In the kitchen."

"Ah, so that's it, is it?" he said. "My dear, I *eat supper* in the kitchen. It's warmer than the drawing room or study or that damned tomb of a dining room. I have been much occupied with. . . ."

"Yes. Yes, you admit it."

"Occupied with business," said Houston precisely. "It's unfair to expect the staff to wait late on me."

"Only that Stalker creature."

"Would you have me dine on cold ham and rice pudding every evening of the week?"

"I would have you dine with *me.*"

"I . . ."

"*And sleep with me.*"

"Edith, do I understand correctly? Are you accusing me of having carnal relations with our housekeeper?"

"Dare you deny it to my face?"

"Aye, I *dare* deny it. I deny it most emphatically."

"Hypocrite!"

"Edith, I think you must be ailing. . . ."

"Ailing of grief that my husband should conduct himself like a rake under my roof."

Houston rattled down his knife and fork; then, changing his mind, lifted them again and speared a third slice of beef, which he ate with apparent relish.

Edith trotted across the carpet and clamped her fingers on the chair back.

Houston no longer tried to make sense of the avalanche of accusations. She had openly accused him of lusting after Mirrin Stalker, even of conducting an affair with the girl. Everything that his wife now said was only embellishment on the original demented theme.

Finishing his meal, he paused to casually light a cigar, then rose, wished his ranting wife a pleasant good morning, and without another word, left the room.

It was not until he had entered his carriage and Sandy Willocks had cantered the horses onto the gravel drive that the import of Edith's slanders really struck him. The morning air was keen, smelled of impending snow, and a stiff breeze chastised the oaks. Looking at the scene, Houston realized that he felt no anger. Indeed, he was full of unaccountable vigor, tempered by a peculiar sense of having sinned himself free of guilt.

Leaning from the window, he looked back at the house.

Mirrin was by the pump in the kitchen yard. He had only a fleeting glimpse of her, just enough to sweep off his hat and wave, and to receive a wave from the girl in return.

Laughing, he sank back against the leather and stuck the stump of his cigar in his mouth at a raffish angle. He could not fathom why he suddenly found Edith's behavior so ridiculously comic. It was as though a window had opened in his heart. Perhaps it was the pace of the coach, or the weather, or Christmas. Perhaps it had to do with

Mirrin Stalker. Damnation! He might as well admit to himself that it *did* have to do with Mirrin. Edith could rage from now until doomsday, but he would not forgo the pleasure of his late-night suppers in Mirrin's company. And if it came to more? Only Mirrin had any say on that score.

The coach lurched drunkenly and skidded a little.

Houston's heart lurched too, not with fear but excitement.

Craning from the window, he saw sprays of snow flung up from the verge and the coal-black eagerness of the stallions as their polished hooves gouged up mud from the mushy snow pelt.

"Sandy?"

"Aye, sir."

"They're lusty animals. Let them take it as they will."

"It's verra slippery this mornin', sir."

"To hell with that," Houston shouted. "Go on, man, give the stallions their heads."

"Aye, sir," Sandy answered, and switching his whip across their cruppers, spurred them into the main street like a Roman charioteer.

∽

The most deceitful of lovers could not have contrived the circumstances that, that same night, gave Houston Lamont and Mirrin Stalker the freedom of Strathmore. In a sense it was Edith's own doing. She was the principal conspirator in creating a climate of love in which she could have no share.

At eleven that morning she appeared in the hall in all her finery and announced that she would be lunching in Glasgow prior to calling on her friends in fashionable Radnor Terrace. Archie jogged the buggy to Blacklaw station and saw his mistress safely off on the Glasgow train. Before he had returned as far as the kirkyard gate, however, the blizzard had swung down with the shift of the wind to the north.

By four o'clock that afternoon the whole central plain of Scotland was drowned under a thick blanket of snow.

Managers and gangers, acting on Lamont's orders, dispatched bellmen into the streets to rouse the night-shift men to the shovels. Winter emergency procedures for securing the colliery against the weight of snow and the floods of a sudden thaw were put immediately into action. All afternoon every collier and clerk worked like a slave in the driving snow. By the time twilight had inked out the landscape the bulk of the safety work had been completed.

At home in Strathmore, Mirrin was engaged in stocking up for a snowy blockade, which might be of long duration. Marshaling the services of grooms and gardeners, she had the log shed filled, extra provisions fetched from the village, and generally set up such frantic industry around the mansion that a stranger might have supposed that a barbarian horde was sweeping across the country. Instead, it was only the old enemy, winter, which put the fear of death in all hearts.

Though there was a fine blazing fire in her room, Miss Dorothy too experienced the urgency and awe that smote the household. Perhaps some echoes of childhood chimed in her, like the notes of a music box. Sad-eyed but calm, the woman stood motionless by the window, watching the flakes swirl across the garden. Whatever she remembered of cold Christmases gone by, she kept to herself.

Since the disturbing outburst by the river, Mirrin had kept a close eye on Dorothy Lamont. She did not leave her long alone that busy afternoon, and at five o'clock, when the December dark was down, had her brought to the kitchen where a special tea was arranged for her beside the stove. In spite of Mirrin's efforts there was no warmth to be found upstairs in the mansion. It was as though the snow had brought ghosts with it to drag their icy robes throughout the empty rooms.

In the kitchen it was quite different. Fat loaves and black-crusted sultana buns were pulled smoking from the ovens. Sponge tiers were carefully beaten and put in to rise. Dorothy was allotted the task of counting the minutes on the clock to ensure success to Mrs. Burns's efforts. When all the groceries were shelved, when the last of the logs had been stacked away, when the horses had been fed and stalled, and the sponges rescued from the oven just in the nick of time, then estate workers and servants convened in the kitchen. There they revived their circulations with hot chocolate and rum biscuits and amazed themselves with tales and speculations on the general subject of snow.

At length Mirrin packed them off about their duties and organized dinner for the mistress, though doubting that the solitary place in the dining room would be occupied that night.

"Na', Mirrin," Archie agreed. "She'll not be back this night. I haven't heard the peep o' a train since three o'clock. The line's blocked, and the road's blocked, so unless she flutters home like a hoodie crow, we'll not see the missus this side o' tomorrow's morn."

"Will the master get home from the pit, Sandy?" Mirrin asked anxiously.

"Och, aye, but not by carriage, I fear."

"Then take the lantern down the hill a bit and greet him with a light."

"When, Mirrin?"

"About eight o'clock should do. And wrap up well, Sandy, I don't want you frozen to the path like a plaster saint."

Eight came and went, and outside all was still and silent, the night filled with the snow's milky quietness.

From the mouth of the kitchen yard Mirrin could make out Sandy's lantern through the trees.

At nine Dorothy could no longer stay awake. Mirrin accompanied her upstairs and saw her into the warm bed. She sat with the woman for a little while, but sleep came quickly to Dorothy and Mirrin was soon able to return to the kitchen. Hannah and Mattie were next to retire, and Mrs. Burns, who had not left the kitchen all day, complained that the cold had quite worn her out and soon retired to her basement room, leaving Mirrin alone.

It was ten thirty before Houston stumped into the kitchen. He had borrowed Donald Wyld's spare boots and a ragged tweed cape. Even so, he was soaked through by his tramp from the colliery. Before he dried off and sat down to supper, however, he decanted a gill of whiskey from the cellar keg and gave the little bottle to Sandy, whose vigilance and patience were thus amply rewarded.

While Houston changed his clothes, Mirrin ladled out his supper. Wrapped in a woolen robe, the master sat at table and ate without a word. When he had appeased his appetite he tilted his chair, and exactly like any collier, set his heels on the edge of the range. Only when he had lit his cigar and poured himself a glass of brandy did he inquire after his wife.

"Mrs. Lamont went into Glasgow, on the noon train."

"She'll be stranded, no doubt." Houston shrugged. "She has plenty of friends in the city who will see to her lodging for the night."

"I hope this snow doesn't last long," said Mirrin. "Have you closed the pits yet?"

"Not yet. Provided we can keep stuff moving on the surface, we'll struggle through. It's the thaw that will bring the real danger."

Houston stretched. Beneath the robe his chest was matted with dark hair. Cord breeches shaped themselves to his muscular thighs, and his feet were snug in soft leather slippers. "Did my wife speak with you this morning, Mirrin?"

"No, only with Hannah."

Houston nodded and said lightly, "Edith believes that we are having an affair."

The girl turned slowly from the stove and stared at him.

"An affair?"

"Yes, a carnal relationship."

"Do you want me to leave, Mr. Lamont?"

"God, no!"

"But . . . ?"

"We've done nothing dishonest, Mirrin," Houston said. "Even so, perhaps my wife is more perceptive than either of us realizes."

"In what way?"

"I believe myself to be in love with you, Mirrin."

The girl said nothing. Steadily, she poured boiling water from the kettle into the teapot.

Houston said, "Now you may leave if you wish, Mirrin. I'll honor my bond on the cottage for your family, and if you wish, I'll find you alternative employment."

"But why?" Mirrin blurted out. "I don't *want* to leave Strathmore. And *she* has no right to accuse you. . . ."

"Mirrin, Mirrin, don't you understand? I'm in *love* with you. It's not impossible, but it is difficult. You're an honest girl, and this isn't an honest situation."

"It's up to me to decide what's honest."

Shrugging apologetically, Houston said, "The strange fact is that I don't feel guilty."

"Why should you?" Mirrin demanded. "I've taken nothing that belonged to your wife, nothing."

"But what you have given me. . . . I'm sorry."

"Stop saying you're sorry."

He looked up at her, then glanced away.

The girl set down the teapot and headed past him toward the door.

"Mirrin, don't go."

"I can hear Miss Dorothy."

Houston sighed. "You must have ears like a cat."

She paused, stepped back from the door, and reaching down, gave him her hand. He clasped it, kissed it, then released her.

For some minutes after Mirrin had gone, Houston stared into the embers in the grate. He experienced no lack of certainty and no remorse. In bringing his doubt to the surface he had begun the process of cure. Whatever Edith might say, whatever Mirrin might elect to do now, at least he had declared himself honestly.

At length he rose and went quietly upstairs to his sister's room.

Dorothy lay on her side, lips parted, a narrow frown cleaving her brow. Mirrin held her hand, crooning a Highland lullaby to her, low and soft as the winds of the western seas.

"She had a dream about the river and the snow," Mirrin whispered. "I don't know why it should distress her. It's so like her favorite song, the song of the river flowing into the sea and the snows melting on the hill. But it's over now. She's asleep again."

"I'll sit with her, Mirrin."

Mirrin carefully disengaged her hand and shifted back from the bed, allowing Houston to take her place.

The fire was low in the hearth, and though the drapes were fastened across the glass, the room was full of the formlessness of the falling snow. The upstairs rooms were no longer chill. It was as though the kitchen's warmth had at last spread throughout the house.

For a half hour Houston sat with his sister. He did not touch her but waited until the frown smoothed from her brow and her parted lips closed and she slept peacefully.

Rising, he changed the night candle and checked the fire guard. He felt contented; strangely so, for he was moved by memories of the many nights when he had returned home late and looked in on his son in the nursery. He remembered it now without rancor, without anguish, and smiling faintly, left the bedroom.

At the corridor's end, a tall, diamond-paned window cast a slot of light across the doors of darkened rooms, rooms sealed off with their cargoes of dusty toys and infant's clothing. Many children in the village would be glad of these toys and clothes, he supposed. But he could not be so cruel as to deprive Edith of whatever consolation the little relics gave her. Turning his back on the nursery, he walked down the corridor toward the dark well of the main staircase.

The glow flooded out ahead of him.

He hesitated, glancing at the open door of Mirrin's room. Even then, he did not suppose that she had left it open by accident.

"Mirrin?"

There was no reply.

The door was wide open, not ajar. Three branches of the candlestick each held a new tallow. The wicks bloomed with pure yellow flame, shedding light across the bed. The colors were like the rich oils of a new painting, thick, bright, and substantial, and the composition, framed by the posts, reminded him of an intimate portrait.

Mirrin was seated on the bed, the spotless white sheet drawn up to her waist. Within the scant cotton shift her breasts were free and heavy. Her hair draped her shoulders. She looked straight at him.

"Mirrin?"

She smiled, not in calculation, not lewdly.

She smiled warmly, and gave a slight apologetic shrug as if to ask forgiveness for the theatricality of her invitation.

Houston felt again as he had done that morning, full of strength and assurance.

"May I come in, Mirrin?"

"Please do," Mirrin said.

The master entered the bedroom and with rueful formality closed the door on the outside world.

Part Three

CHAPTER XII

THE old pine table was now highly polished, back-breaking chairs were repaired and trimmed, respectable enough to grace a kirk vestry. The warped floorboards had been covered with carpet, the chimney swept, the grate black-leaded, and a fire lit in the iron hearth. It was to the boardroom that Houston and Donald Wyld retired after lunch on a raw afternoon a couple of days before the close of 1875. The purpose in adjourning to the boardroom in preference to Lamont's study was that it contained a table large enough to support all the great ledgers, files, and printed data that the men required to plan their strategies for the difficult days ahead.

Long bills of figures were spread side by side with docketed reports of union conferences, and the two men moved around the table like billiards players selecting shots. Houston's concern for maintenance of the status quo was based on pride. He fought for his pits, not for his men—yet the two were so inextricably linked that he could not contemplate them as separate entities. Owner and manager were well aware that whatever their personal inclinations they could not hope to stand aloof from national crises. Throughout the afternoon they mulled over facts and figures, and about the time the lamps were lit, reached the sorry conclusion that they were limited to two courses of action, and that their decision posed a difficult moral dilemma.

Houston flung himself onto the nearest chair and leaned his elbows on the annual tally sheets. "How will the colliers react, Donald?"

"Violently, I fear."

"Do they not see how well treated they are here?"

"They're blinkered horses, Mr. Lamont. They see only Blacklaw and the backs of their own larder shelves."

"I wouldn't dare admit it outside, Donald, but the tonnage lost last March might have been a blessing in disguise," Houston said. "It puts us decently behind in the slow-horse race."

"Too much coal, too few markets."

"Precisely."

"Aye, sir, but how can you tell a collier that there is too *much* coal when all his life he has been ordered to dig up more and more of the damnable stuff?"

Glumly, Houston surveyed the mass of charge sheets that littered the table.

"What shall I do for the best?" he mused. "If I were a collier, what would I prefer to settle for?"

At that moment a discreet knock on the door disturbed them. So long had the pair been shut off from society that they were startled to realize that the usual household routines had gone on outside during the course of their discussion.

"Come."

Mirrin entered. "I thought you and Mr. Wyld might care for some refreshment, sir."

Houston blinked. For four hours he had not spared a thought for Mirrin Stalker, yet in the preceding week she had hardly been out of his consciousness for a moment. She was neat, demure, ladylike in her dark garments. He felt inordinately proud of her, as if he had somehow rescued and redeemed her as a model for all colliers' daughters. Foolish! he told himself. Foolish, and patronizing!

"Tea, I think, Mirrin," he said. "Donald, would you prefer something stronger?"

"No, thank you. We've much to do, and thinking needs a clear head."

Houston looked at Mirrin, trying not to let his feelings show in his expression. "A large pot of tea, Mirrin."

The girl bowed and went out. Houston glanced curiously at the manager. Donald seemed unaware of a deepened relationship between his boss and the girl. Houston was strangely disappointed by the realization that their lovemaking must at all costs remain a close-guarded secret and could never be openly acknowledged. Beneath the housekeeper's formal garb was the body of a lithe and sensual young woman—and he had possessed it. She had given herself willingly to him. Now he wanted to boast of his love for her.

During the four or five minutes it took Mirrin to return, he skirted the subject with outrageous daring. "Do you recognize my housekeeper, Donald?"

"Alex Stalker's lass, is it not?"

"She suits the role, don't you think?"

"Aye, sir. I wonder what her father would say if he could see her now?"

"He would howl in dismay, I fancy," Houston said.

"Oh, Stalker was not one to stand in the way of progress. He might have been a militant but he learned sense the hard way and grew wiser as he grew older."

"I wish we had someone of his caliber now," Houston said. "I think he might have supported me."

"Stalker would not have supported *you*, Mr. Lamont, though he might have understood the necessity of your decisions and have interceded with the men."

"I wonder what Mirrin would advise."

"Mirrin?" said Wyld, caught off guard. "But she's a woman and has no sway with the colliers."

"Let's ask her advice. We're not obliged to take it."

"She may tell you only what you want to hear, sir."

"Why do you say that, Donald? Do you imagine that I've broken her spirit in some way? Oddly, I put great trust in that girl's integrity."

Wyld shrugged, dubious. "Well, it can do no harm, I suppose."

A minute later Mirrin nudged into the room with a trolley laden with a tea serving. The men said nothing as she poured. Wyld was seated at the top end of the table. Houston stood now by the hearth. He suspected that Mirrin might be aware of the element of tension in the air. But even when she handed cups to the men she did not meet their eyes.

"Shall I leave the trolley, sir?"

"Yes, thank you, Mirrin."

She turned toward the door.

"Mirrin? Perhaps you can assist us," Houston said.

"In what way?"

Houston glanced cautiously at Wyld.

The manager said, "Tell me, Miss Stalker, if your father was alive, how would he react to a proposal to cut the basic wage?"

Mirrin's eyes widened. "He'd be leapin' mad," she said. "How much of a cut?"

"Probably a shilling and sixpence per darg," said Houston.

"Is this to keep your profits intact, sir?" asked Mirrin.

"No, Mirrin, merely to preserve the pit in full employment."

"The alternative," said Donald Wyld, "is to pay off."

"Aye," said Mirrin. "I knew the situation was serious."

Wyld said, "It's one or the other, Miss Stalker. How do you think the villagers will feel about it?"

"Why don't you ask them, Mr. Wyld?"

"I've already consulted with the management. They leave the decision to Mr. Lamont," Wyld said.

The radical fire was in Mirrin's eyes once more. Her head was tilted back, and for a moment Houston thought that she intended to bawl them both out like a taproom militant. "Nobody ever *asks* the colliers anything. They always get *told*."

Houston was a little surprised. Was this the same warm and loving girl whose bed he had shared a week ago? Then he felt proud of her, even of her temper. A hundred women of Mirrin's caliber could rule the bumbling world of borough politics, a thousand could take over the governing of the whole country. He had been wrong to imagine that he had softened her. She was still a rock, quarried out of the granite of the Scottish working class.

"It was unfair to involve you," he said placatingly.

"I won't apologize for my answer, Mr. Lamont—even though it's little use to you."

"Why do you say that, Mirrin?"

"You asked it casually, and there's nothing casual about putting families out in the street," Mirrin answered.

"It's not just Blacklaw's problem, nor is it a trick of the bosses," Wyld explained. "Something must be done."

"Then I'd say keep full employment at a reduced wage," Mirrin told him. "It's what my father would have advised. Give a man a home and a place to work and he's still your man, no matter how hungry he may be. But throw him into the gutter and you've rejected him and all he stands for—and that's the crime."

"Ah!" said Lamont.

"And if you reject one man, you may soon find it expedient to reject others in less stringent circumstances. Thus you sacrifice all sense of unity and loyalty."

"I certainly see the logic in that," Wyld admitted.

"Aye, but you're a manager, not an owner," Mirrin rapped out.

"Do you mean, Mirrin," said Houston, "that a collier may still feel secure even if he's living in poverty?"

"Aye, if he has a job and the hope of improvement," said Mirrin. "The biggest fear of all, as I've said, is rejection."

"I won't reject them," Houston promised.

"Until it suits you," Mirrin blurted out.

"Mirrin, am I in the habit of rejecting . . . ?" Houston bit off the end of the sentence.

"I'd hardly know that, sir. I haven't had time to find out."

Silence gathered in the room. Mirrin blushed, not in shame or embarrassment, but with the frustration of imagining herself patronized.

"With your permission, Mr. Lamont," she said, "I'll get back to my duties."

Houston nodded.

When Mirrin had left the room he said, "What do you think, Donald?"

"She has a point."

"Which particular point?"

"About the innate fear of being flung out."

"So?"

"I think we can now plan our procedure," Wyld said. "Though I believe we should wait awhile before we put it into action."

"Why?"

"In February the rate of sickness is usually at its highest."

"Good God! Not even Mirrin thought of that," Houston said.

"Perhaps she's too honest," Wyld said. "I will say this for her, though, she's still as spirited as ever. Frankly, sir, I don't know how you put up with her."

"No," said Houston, lighting a cigar. "I'm not quite sure myself."

☙

February's frosts brought more hardship to Blacklaw folk than the snows of Christmastime. The year of 1876 had been ushered in by rain, and customary celebrations dampened, both by the weather and the memory of the black tragedy of the year that was gone.

Throughout January coal prices continued to fall. At various meetings Donald Wyld explained the coalmaster's proposals but the maneuver, instead of boosting Houston Lamont's image, made the colliers suspicious. If *they* were being consulted on policy, the situation must be grave indeed. Houston himself attended the meeting that gave him his answer, a stormy gathering in the kirk hall. He answered their questions as best he could but refused to make the final choice himself. He left the men for half an hour and when he returned was informed that the miners' ballot agreed to accept a cut rate of pay. Lamont greeted the news with a curt nod. Somehow his manner suggested that he had, by duplicity, committed them to doing just what he wanted, while foisting the decision onto them.

As it happened, the Arctic weather of February did slice the labor force by a third, and fit miners and their womenfolk, haunted by the phantom of unemployment, worked twice as hard for their money.

Even Mirrin Stalker, on whose advice Houston had given free choice to his men, could not determine whether the master had foreseen this pass or not. Though she shared his love, there were some confidences that he still kept secret even from her.

❧

Frost gripped the land and stretched it taut, split it and healed it superficially with ice. Blacklaw kirkyard was truly a place of the dead. Nothing moved under the leaden sky, and the trees were as rigid as the headstones.

Wrapped in a shawl, Kate Stalker stood by the grave

that held the remains of her father and brothers. It had
been several months since last she had come here to weep
for the menfolk. Grief had not lasted, and she had been
freed from guilt by the memory of one of her father's
favorite adages: "A man's never dead until he's forgotten."
That platitude comforted Kate, who knew that Alex,
James, and Douglas would not be forgotten in her lifetime.

That February afternoon she wept less for those below
ground than for those upon it. Times had never been so
bad, nor money so scarce. The Stalkers were better off
than many families. Indeed, without the burden of the
promise they would have survived comfortably enough.
But the promise hung over them all like a sword. There
was no escaping it. Not that she wanted to escape. Drew
deserved his chance. In spite of his superciliousness he had
worked harder than any of them. In a week's time, however, the young man would make the journey to Edinburgh. They could not afford to send someone with him.
As it was, the fare, cost of meals, and a night's lodging
would deplete their savings considerably. Bowed over the
grave, Kate tried to smother that part of her that prayed
that her brother would *not* pass, would not win admit-
tance to the Faculty of Law in the coming May term.
Failure might sap some of Drew's confidence in himself,
but at least it would leave the family intact. If he did pass,
and she knew in her heart that he would, then she would
be confronted with a breach of faith so serious that she
would never be able to hold up her head in Blacklaw
again.

The truth was that she did not have the capital to see
the project through. Their savings had proved woefully
inadequate. Without the money he just could not accept
a university place. By rights she should tell him now. But
she could not deprive him of a glimpse of his goal. She

clenched her fists in frustration and drew the shawl tightly about her head.

"Careful, lass, you'll tear it."

Callum Ewing was hunched in a threadbare jacket, his thin, sharp face tucked down to keep the icy wind from his chest.

"Come on now, Kate. It's not like you to be weepin'."

Before she could stop herself she had clutched at the man, her father's old and trusted friend, and clung to him while sobs racked her body. "I wish. . . . Oh, God, I wish. . . ."

Callum comforted her. "There now, lass. Tell old Callum what ails you so sore."

"It's Drew. We haven't the money. An' I promised Father."

"Forget that promise."

"I can't."

"Drew's an educated lad now. He'll have no trouble finding a place on the management ladder."

"Callum, you don't understand."

"I understand pride when I see it."

Kate pulled away. "Is it only Stalker pride, then?"

"Listen, what will it cost, this thing about Drew?"

"The dominie estimated twenty pounds."

"Twenty pounds! By God, Kate, you've set yourself a high target. How much is short?"

Kate would have confided in no other person in Blacklaw. But she trusted Callum. "We've only eight pounds saved, and it'll take a pound out of that to send him to the examination."

Callum shook his head. "If it had only been a pound or two, Kate . . . but twenty. I can't help, lass. It's too much."

Kate wept again. "Oh, Callum, I'd never have taken your money. But I'm grateful for your offer. No, I'll just have to tell Drew, sooner or later."

"Best make it later," Callum said. "You never know what might turn up."

"For the likes of us, what *could* turn up?"

Callum could find no answer to the girl's question. He put his arm about her waist and escorted her from the kirkyard.

"Perhaps it's a judgment on us for tryin' to raise ourselves above our station," Kate said.

"Rubbish! Believe that and you'll believe anything," Callum admonished her.

Kate squared her shoulders. "Well, at least it'll give the folks around here a good snigger."

"You're knucklin' under, Kate. Your father would never have done that. He'd have fought to the last gasp."

Kate nodded. Her lips pursed and tightened, and Callum was pleased to note, some of her former determination showed, even though tears continued to roll down her cheeks.

"Aye," she said. "I'll wait—and hope."

❧

The dominie slapped shut the book of Latin adjuncts. Drew sighed and leaned closer to the fire in the parlor hearth. The boy, thought Guthrie, looked as gaunt as a gargoyle; eyes red-rimmed, hair lank, hands trembling like a fever victim. The fever that burned in him, however, could only be cured by engagement with the inquisitors in the halls of academe. Whatever the long, hard period of study had done to Drew's mind, undoubtedly it had matured him physically. It might even be said that it had robbed him of his boyhood. If the examiners had been inclined to pick the most promising legal face, Drew would have been their natural choice. Already he bore a distinct resemblance to one famous hanging judge. The dominie kept such fancies to himself.

"Whatever you do, you must be bold—bold but calm,"

he said. "Read the questions carefully, choose to answer
those most favorable to your knowledge."

"I will," said Drew.

"Don't hurry. Impatience is the rock on which many a
student has foundered. Don't be intimidated by the pom-
pousness of your fellow students. Are you going alone?"

"Yes, Mr. Guthrie. I prefer it that way."

"I see."

The dominie lifted the lid of a tobacco jar that stood
in the litter on his desk, brought a silver piece from it,
and tossed the coin to his pupil.

"What's this?" Drew asked, startled.

"I doubt if you'll be quizzed on coin of the realm,"
said Guthrie, "but in common parlance that's a half
crown."

"But . . . ?"

"It's a lucky token. Buy good meat with it. If I rightly
recall, there's a cozy little tavern in Queen's Wynd. When
it's all over, Drew, go there and purchase a decent dinner
and a tipple of wine."

"Wine?" said Drew. "Are you tryin' to corrupt me,
Dominie?"

The dominie laughed. "Aye, lad, we all need a bit of
depravity in our lives from time to time. Make the most
of it."

Drew rose and buttoned his ragged jacket and tucked
in his scarf. He put the half crown carefully into his
pocket. "Thanks, Dominie—and not just for the price of
the tipple."

He held out his hand jerkily. The schoolmaster shook
it and clapped him on the back. "I wish you luck, Drew,
and beg you to remember that it's not over yet. You've a
long road ahead of you."

"Yes," Drew said, "but at least I've reached the beginning."

When the young student had left the parlor the old

dominie lit himself a pipe and wandered to the window. Outside, the playing yard was deserted. Sugared with frost, the children's slides showed like black fissures across an ice floe. Drew came out of the side door, hands in pockets, shoulders stooped. He walked at his usual introverted gait across the yard, then, suddenly, stopped.

The dominie watched curiously.

Drew glanced around furtively, then broke back and cantered toward the doors. He started his approach far out of sight and had worked up considerable speed before he reached the ice slide. He had not forgotten the technique. In perfect balance he skated down toward the gates, upright and arms akimbo, then dropped into a crouch and clutched his knees with his fingers.

The innocent joy in the boy's action made the old schoolmaster's heart leap; then Drew Stalker, student of law, whizzed out of the playground and vanished from sight.

❧

Houston closed the door and bolted it. There was no sound at all in the deserted corridor. Dorothy was sleeping peacefully, the servants were snug in cellar and attic, and Edith was "staying over" with friends in Port Glasgow. It did not occur to Houston to question his wife's motives in spending so much time in other folks' guestrooms, nor did he suspect her of having an affair. By now she had left him so far behind that he had no way of checking on her, even if he had been inclined to do so. But there were no lovers for Edith. She craved only the collective attention of society, its reassurance that, even without her husband's patronage, she remained a member in good standing of the influential class.

A single act of infidelity with Mirrin might have been put aside as a rash impulse. But his lovemaking needed no justification. It stood as a pact of love. The physical side of it, though gentle, had been highly satisfying to both of them. Now, uninvited, he had come to her room again. As soon as he turned from the door he saw that she had anticipated him. She had placed two new candles by the sides of the bed and turned down the coverlet. He was not angered by her preparations or the fact that she had anticipated him. Her eager acceptance eased his conscience and brought a surge of vigor to his loins.

Mirrin was clad in a cotton shift, shoulders, arms, and part of her breast quite bare. He tried to think of an appropriate endearment, but words had lost all their value. Obeying his instinct, he touched her instead. The movement was demanding but not insistent. Breath caught in her throat. She pushed herself against him, her breast against his chest.

"How are you?" he asked.

Mirrin smiled at the awkward formality.

"I'm fine."

"Are you cold?"

"No."

"May I . . . stay?"

"Yes."

"Mirrin, listen, it's. . . ."

She put her hand to his lips. "Hush," she told him. "There's nobody here but us now, Houston. Nobody to hear, see, or think anything about it. Just us. Let that be enough for you."

"It's more than enough."

He kissed her.

Sliding out of his arms, Mirrin stripped off her shift, rolled across the bed, and spread herself on the coverlet. Her hair spilled on the pillow. Any trace of false modesty would have made the pose seem sacrificial. In years she might be little more than a girl, but her breasts were high and heavy, waist curved into swelling hips, and belly with that plumpness that made it both tempting and beautiful.

She reminded Lamont of a Viking princess, full of courage and passion and pride, yet infinitely more womanly than the staid marionettes whom contemporary society classed as doyennes of femininity.

Mirrin lifted her arms to him. Tearing at the buttons of his shirt, he threw the garment aside, leaned to kiss her breasts and bury his face in her hair. Her flesh was soft and yielding. He was harried by his own need to press selfishly into her. But this, he sensed, was the stamp of the smoking-room boor who thought of nothing but his own quick pleasure. He caressed her body, flattering it with his touch. She moaned a little. Her lids fluttered closed, opened. She smiled as he stroked her breasts and for the moment neglected his own ardor. Her pleasure gave him pleasure. The heightening of her passion increased his own. There was no conflict, no selfishness here. He had never dared make love to Edith in this manner. In all his life he had never before attained such a pitch of sensual harmony with a woman.

Only when Mirrin cried out and raised herself against him did he wrap his body tightly against her. He did not need to seek her out. Her responsiveness obliterated all clumsiness. In an instant he was swallowed up in her completely. Rocking, he cradled her in his arms, hearing her rapid, throaty cries. He drove deeply into her again and again until a tide of passion gave him release and left him spent and gasping.

When it was over he inclined his head and found that she was studying him. Her eyes were soft, without mockery. He curled a strand of her hair around his finger. "I should have brought some wine."

"Next time," Mirrin said.

"I never dreamed we would be here like this again," Houston said. "In spite of what happened, despite your not having been out of my thoughts since the day you entered this house."

She wriggled closer and took him in her arms again. "I see. You planned it all. I am undone."

For a split second he thought she was serious and felt dismay well up in him. Then he saw that she was grinning.

"Don't be so sober about it, Houston."

"I don't understand you."

"It's because we're so different."

"I do not feel that now," he said.

"I'm not in the mood for a political argument."

"Not since we've found such an admirable means of settling our disputes?" Houston asked.

"I don't understand myself, to tell the truth," Mirrin said. "A year ago this would have seemed indecent and impossible."

"Change is the prerogative of us all."

"How daft you make that sound."

"Do you regret . . . ?"

"How could I regret it?" she said.

"Then that's all there is to say."

"But I don't feel guilty."

"Should you, Mirrin?"

"Everybody would tell me I should suffer agonies of bad conscience."

"Perhaps it's because I love you," Houston said.

"The magic potion."

"What?"

"That's what the village girls call love—the magic potion," Mirrin explained. "They say a lad can get anything he wants from a girl if only he uses a few drops of the magic potion—if he just tells her he loves her."

"I'm not lying, Mirrin."

"I know. Anyhow, I think the girls have it all wrong. If you ask me, the love must be in them."

"Is it in you now, Mirrin?"

"It is."

"Then say it."

"It's still difficult to say a thing like that to a coal-master."

Houston laughed and shook his head.

"Surely, Mirrin, you don't still think of me as a coal-master?"

"It's the result of long schooling."

"That's ridiculous!"

"I suppose it is," Mirrin said. "But we're in danger of becoming two people, two times two—four in all."

"Is that not true of all lovers?"

"Perhaps."

"Can't you say it?"

"I . . . I love you."

"There!"

"It doesn't help me being what I am."

"And what is that?" he said. "It's what you are that I love."

"A willing girl, or a collier's daughter?"

"Is that what you're afraid of, Mirrin, that I've some-how taken advantage of you?"

"It's difficult for me, Houston—not to give up my body, but to give up my principles," she said. "That's what I meant about there being two of you, and two of me."

"I am Houston Lamont, coalmaster, and I love Mirrin Stalker, a miner's daughter and my housekeeper. I'm not afraid of plain facts, or plain words, Mirrin. Are you?"

"I'm afraid I am, Houston. I've lived too long with slogans and rallying cries. I can't be so easy rid of them."

"This is hardly a romantic conversation."

"This can hardly be a romantic relationship."

"Why not?" Houston asked.

"Because of what we are. You can see that, can't you?"

Houston did not answer for a moment, then said, "Yes, I can see that."

"And on those terms?" she asked.

"We must take what we can—and expect no more."

"Yes," Mirrin said. "Now put out the candles."

Reaching, she snuffed out the candle on the left. After a pause, Houston thumbed out the flame of the candle on the right of the bed. Darkness enclosed them like a quilt. Mirrin hugged him.

"Now," she murmured. "Now, like this, Houston, we can be two other people."

"Yes."

"Lovers," Mirrin said. "Lovers, and no more."

◆◇◆

Drew stepped down from the carriage onto the platform at Hamilton railroad station and walked toward the ticket gate. His swagger, Mirrin thought, was something to behold. He looked neither right nor left, the faint, fixed smile on his face making him appear even more self-assured than usual. Mirrin, like Kate, was at odds with herself over Drew. She almost wished that he would take a fall, smash the shell of his arrogance. Yet Mam and Kate depended on him now. He was their sole source of pride. Many women were doomed to live vicariously through the achievements of their menfolk, not even obliged to love the puppets whom they manipulated from birth to grave, just to accept them as instruments of fulfillment. Now that James and Douglas were dead, all they had left was Drew. God knew that was little enough, Mirrin told herself as she watched her brother, still oblivious to her presence, leg it up the platform.

He would have gone on past her had she not caught him by the arm. For an instant there was a quirky flash of alarm in his eyes as she swung him toward her.

"Mirrin?"

"Who did you expect, the lord provost?"

"I thought you'd be at work."

"I'm in town for groceries."

"I see."

"Well?"

"Well what?"

"How did you get on in Edinburgh?"

"All right."

"Were the examinations difficult?"

"Not particularly."

"Go on."

"What?"

"Tell me about them."

"Not much to tell."

She waited for him to volunteer news. It had never crossed her mind that he would fail, of course. Recently Houston had informed her that any bright, intelligent lad could be sure of being taken into the college fold. Somehow that impartial opinion diminished Drew's ability in her eyes.

"I'm driving the dogcart," she said. "It's over by the cattle pens. I'll drop you off at the house."

As they walked across the station forecourt toward the cattle enclosures that backed onto the grain warehouses, Mirrin said, "You intended to walk home?"

Drew said, "No sense in wasting money."

"You mean you spent it all?"

"I didn't have much to begin with."

"Enough for tobacco, though," said Mirrin.

"Tobacco?"

"You reek like the dominie's study."

"All right," Drew said, "so I bought myself a cheroot. It cost a penny. Besides, the dominie gave me something for myself."

"I suppose you had a drink too?"

"Yes, a tipple of wine."

If it had not been Drew, Mirrin would have laughed at his boyish indulgences. But the fact that Drew had blown five or six pence on luxuries galled her. Every one of those pennies had been earned by the self-sacrifice of her sister and mother. Drew had squandered the price of a good family supper on booze and smokes.

"I wouldn't go developing any addictions if I were you," she said testily. "If you do go up to Edinburgh, you'll need every farthing just for food."

"If?"

"If you pass."

"Oh, I can't possibly fail," said Drew. "The dominie had me prepared for something really difficult—and it wasn't. In fact it was incredibly easy. In the oral examination in particular I felt very much at ease. Frankly, I really did rather well all around."

Mirrin was sorry now that she had gone out of her way to borrow the dogcart and arrange her shopping expedition so that she could meet him. If Kate had not been so keen for a member of the family to greet the young hero, she would not have made the effort.

She said, "That cart. Get in."

The small, elderly mare was obedient to Mirrin's inexpert handling of the reins and started off on the wide circle that would steer it out of the yard and into the upper end of the high street. Mirrin let the leathers ride lightly across her palms as Archie had told her to do.

Drew displayed no interest in his sister's skill, did not even appear to notice the busy traffic in the streets, as though the scene were so utterly familiar that it bored him. For March the air was very still. The smoke from the chimneys on Hamilton's outskirts rose unwaveringly into the sky.

For twenty minutes the couple rode in silence as the town dropped behind them. Mirrin navigated onto the back road where the trees were winter-bare against the bland cloudscape.

Suddenly Drew asked, "Did you tell Lamont you were collecting me?"

"Don't be so daft," said Mirrin. "He's far too busy to ask what his servants do with their time."

"But it's his cart."

"Drew, what's the point of this?"

"Mere curiosity."

"If you must know, I asked him if I could borrow the dogcart."

"And you mentioned me?"

"No."

"Oh!"

Mirrin squinted suspiciously at her brother.

"In Edinburgh," Drew said, "there were a surprising number of boys of my station in life, all of them striving for a university place."

"That doesn't really surprise me."

"Quite a number have patrons."

"Patrons?" said Mirrin.

"Sponsors, local gentlemen."

"Like Houston Lamont?" said Mirrin.

"Precisely."

"But you already have 'sponsors.' "

"Oh, you mean Kate and Mother," said Drew airily.

"It doesn't matter where the money comes from, does it?"

"Basically, no," answered Drew. "On the other hand, a proper patron would be more generous. . . ."

"I thought you just wanted to get to Edinburgh, anyhow."

"Of course," said Drew. "But when I get there I don't want to fall short of the accepted standards."

"You mean you want a full belly, cheroots, and wine."

"You're angry."

"God Almighty, Drew!"

"Ideas above my station?"

"Yes."

"Lamont isn't. . . ."

"Lamont isn't *what*?" said Mirrin.

"After all, he's helped us a lot since Father died."

"Drew, please shut up."

"Frankly," Drew persisted, "I wouldn't be averse to putting a straight proposal to him myself."

"You?" Mirrin cried. "You, you swelled-headed brat?"

"For twenty or thirty pounds per annum . . ."

"Shut *up*, I tell you."

Mirrin flicked the reins, urging the mare to a sluggish trot. She wanted this journey over before her rage belched forth in a torrent of abuse.

She had always felt guilty at disliking Drew so much. There was no reason for it. He had not been her father's favorite. The only close relationship he had within the family was with Betsy. Somehow, though he never appeared to make demands, Drew always wound up with the lion's share. He despised them all, had been born despising them, yet he had no scruples about using them to shake free of Blacklaw. He admitted no sense of duty nor affection. Now she saw him threatening Houston and her happiness. The warmth she had enjoyed in the past months might be stolen from her not by Edith Lamont but by her own brother's ambition. He would trample ruthlessly on anyone who would help him get what he wanted. His aims were shifting and expanding ceaselessly, that was the hell of it. He was insatiable.

She vented her spleen on the poor mare, which, having raised herself to a trot, once more subsided into a shambling walk, toiling uphill.

Northrigg was in sight to the west, and the dense smoke of Blacklaw showed not far distant.

Drew said, "I didn't mean to offend you. I want nothing from you, you know."

"But you'll take all you can get, won't you?"

"If you mean the money. . . ."

"What else can *we* give *you*?"

"I thought the money side of it was arranged?"

"Aye, so what more . . . ?"

"You like Lamont now, don't you?"

".I respect him."

"What, I wonder, would Father have said about that?"

"Father's well out of it," said Mirrin.

"Yes, it's idle talk under the circumstances," Drew said. "Still, it's all worked out very well, hasn't it? Kate's got work, and you're settled in the mansion. Come what might, that's not going to change. I mean, you respect him so much that he's bound to be aware of it. He won't toss *you* out into the gutter."

"All that," said Mirrin evenly, "is true."

"So, how much will the market bear?"

"*What?*"

"Lamont must have friends, influential friends. It would be beneficial to have contacts like that in Edinburgh. Letters of introduction."

"You're looking far ahead."

"Five years," Drew said, "won't be long in passing. Besides, I think it'd be best to establish contacts now."

"Keep away from Strathmore, Drew. I'm warning you."

"Very well, Mirrin. I just thought I'd mention it. I mean, if you . . . ah, *respect* Lamont enough in the interim. . . ."

She plucked the whip from its pod and slashed at her brother with it. The short, supple thong caught him across the brow and laid traces across the backs of his hands as he protected his face. For a moment Mirrin continued to slash at him; then, as abruptly as she had begun the attack, subsided. She tossed the whip into the well of the cart and tweaked the loose rein to bring the mare to a halt.

"What the devil's got into you, Mirrin?"

"Get out."

"Here?"

"Out."

"I thought. . . ."

"Out, I tell you."

Drew raised his brows and hopped over the side of the cart. Without so much as a glance at him, Mirrin slapped the reins. The dogcart trundled down into the broad valley of the Shennan, into the sprawling wasteland of the collieries.

Mirrin did not look back until the first of the truckers' sheds lofted above the track, then she swung around at the hill. Drew was walking briskly, swaggering down the stoop of the road. She had not made that much ground on him.

Trotting, she coaxed the mare into the avenue that would lead behind the shale coups and avoid the troughs and the village, bringing her to Strathmore by the quiet back route.

It was not Drew's gall nor his ruthlessness that maddened her. It was his ignorance of all human feelings. Whatever transpired in her life or in his, she would do not one whit more for him than her duty to the family demanded.

Duty without love, she knew now, could lead only to heartbreak.

CHAPTER XIII

SPRING came early to Blacklaw. A spell of wan sunshine melted away the frost and finally encouraged winter-weary wives to throw open their doors and drag down the rag stuffing that had lined their windows. Neighbor greeted neighbor and exchanged grumbles about ill-health and shortage of cash. Gutters were cleaned of winter trash, and the family footwear was "tacked up" to last the summer. With no wasted effort, and little reason to suppose that the coming season would show much improvement in their lot, the folk of Blacklaw greeted the spring.

Activity was hectic in Strathmore. Spring-cleaning began on the fifteenth day of March. Booming winds then provided good drying for the silks, velours, and linens that were stripped from their hangings and washed in the laundry coppers. Dust fled from brooms. Mops splashed suds into corners and chased out the spiders.

Dorothy greatly enjoyed the domestic upheaval. In spite of Edith's protestations Houston did not attempt to rescue his sister from the vulgar company. Servants, Mirrin in particular, gave the woman warmth and affection. He did not even object when Mirrin presented Dorothy with a large, frilly apron and cap to wear during dusting. This development so outraged Edith's sense of propriety that she surrendered her last hold on the management and withdrew from all contact with her staff.

Edith had changed much since Christmas. She spent many days away from home and most of the rest of her time in her room, primping and preening. It seemed almost as if her husband's love affair was being abetted by the mistress of the house, and Mirrin suspected that Edith was working on some plot to be rid of her.

Mirrin was unashamedly in love with Houston. She had given him her heart as well as her body, and there was no apologetic formality in their lovemaking now. A dozen times they had lain together, always in Mirrin's room, when Edith was safe away from home and the rest of the servants asleep. Houston was not injudicious in his attitude to the affair. He was too much in love with Mirrin to risk losing her by acting like a fool. In the long run he supposed that the relationship would terminate. He had heard of widowers and bachelors who had lived out love-marriages with servants and died in their eighties still clasping the beloved's hand—but there was no wife on the scene in those cases. It seemed inevitable that sooner or later Edith would ferret out the truth and find her colorful accusations had substance after all. In the interim he determined to enjoy the pleasures of that time in all forms and protect the relationship for as long as possible.

Everyone that Houston Lamont really cared about was happy under his roof. It was not as the ministers said—there was no evil in adultery; the real evil was in the denial of love. He had not known love in any form since Gordon's death, could remember precious little of it even before that period. Mirrin and Dorothy were the stars by which he charted his course through the reefs of Victorian morality.

The bright, blustery weather of that early spring robbed him of caution, however, and made him vulnerable, not, as it happened, to Edith's petty vengeance, but to the tragedy of the unforeseen.

❧

The goodfolk of Blacklaw decided that Loony Lachie was one thing and Miss Dorothy Lamont quite another. It did not take long for them to load upon the woman all her brother's sins. She didn't have the cheek, of course, to show her ugly face in the village. But she and the Stalker girl had been seen in Hamilton, spending the big profits that Lamont claimed he wasn't making. No, it wasn't right for the likes of her to be free to wander the streets like a normal person.

Whispering campaigns were something that Mirrin understood. She made sure that Miss Dorothy stayed safely within the walls of the mansion. In any case the weather was too bleak to tempt her out. It was well into the spring before the woman showed any inclination to spread her wings.

"I want to go out, Mirrin."

"We'll think about it tomorrow, Miss Dorothy."

"Today."

"I'm too busy today. Look, come and help Mattie polish the study table. You can wind the Brighouse clock if you like."

"I want to go out."

"I'll tell you what, Miss Dorothy. Go on over to the stables and Archie'll let you feed the horses."

"I've fed the horses this morning."

"No, that was yesterday."

"I . . . want . . . to . . . go . . . out."

"No, Miss Dorothy," said Mirrin firmly. "Not just now."

"Later?"

"Tomorrow."

"Later."

Mirrin sighed.

"Wait in the garden, then," she said. "I'll finish the

study cleaning and take you up to see the cats in the gardener's cottage."

Dorothy's head was held back, her eyelids lowered. She looked thoroughly autocratic just then; but her demand did not materialize.

She said, "Yes."

"Wait in the garden. I'll be with you as soon as I can."

Swishing the feather duster, Mirrin turned from the door at the side of the house. Miss Dorothy was hovering about by the empty flower bed. Mirrin went into the mansion to supervise the annual renovation of the master's sanctuary.

It was an hour before she completed her tasks and returned to the kitchen door in search of Dorothy.

By that time it was too late.

✦

All through the woods beyond the wall the leaf mat was shot through with crocuses and a second flowering of virginal snowdrops. The flowers coaxed Dorothy on. She nodded to the blooms, bowing and dropping words of praise for their pretty new dresses like some regal lady passing among courtiers. She soon shed the niggling guilt that her escape through the broken section of the wall had incurred and soon forgot that she had acted in defiance of Mirrin. The host of spring blossoms diverted her attention, and their pretty patterns lured her away from the grounds and into forgetfulness.

After a while her pleasure was marred neither by willfulness nor doubt, and she was emboldened by the sun into greater independence.

On the western slopes of the valley trees were struggling to bud and grass was showing green. Fern fronds spread golden skeletons across the rabbit paths where the contour dipped through banks of early daffodils down to the flooded river.

The Shennan rose in the Lowther hills. The snow melt had begun there three days previously, with the seep of water loudening and the level of the streams rising. The lesser streams had come cheerfully to flood, but the Shennan took on that dour uncoiling power that said that it fed the industrial Clyde. It flowed like a strong brown muscle across the Blacklaw line, surging between muddy cliffs and coal-black outcrops, giving out no obvious sounds save subtle gurglings and suckings as it sieved through drowned roots and branches.

Dorothy did not, this day, flee from the river. Her newfound courage and debt to the flowers kept her on the path by the water's edge. Only after ten minutes or so did the nightmare revive and the river begin to seem a gluttonous entity.

She stopped, swung around, and stared back uphill at the trees.

Ferns had covered her tracks. The daffodils' trumpets all pointed hither and thither. She chose a higher path, ran a step or two, then halted again.

During the winter, under Mirrin's guidance, Dorothy had begun to learn to confront the irrational impulses within her brain. She bit her lip and wrenched at her dress—but she did not flee in panic. Some force, some transient sanity held her above the long, rolling currents. Courage had narrow limits, however, and she would soon have balked and fled. But an unexpected distraction offered itself and lifted her mind from the threatening Shennan.

The child came over the brow of the hill.

The child was six or seven years old, dressed in a cotton smock, protected from the chilly wind only by a patched jacket trailing the ground. Her laced boots, several sizes too large, flopped comically as she skipped through the grasses. She had a pert, pretty little face, and her eyes were eager for adventure.

Her name was Jinny Sinclair.
In each hand she carried a posy of flowers.

⤨∽ఴ

Hastily, Mirrin untied her apron and hung it on the peg
behind the laundry-room door. It was not so warm as it
appeared outside, and she shivered a little as she walked
along the shadowed avenue and around the gable to the
front of the mansion.

"Miss Dorothy?"

Bland and deserted, the lawns leaned away to the oaks.
Mirrin called out again.

There was no answer except a very faint hollow echo
from the corner where the walls met.

She scanned the trees for a dart of color, which would
show up Miss Dorothy's day dress.

The sun was brittle and dazzling. Mirrin screened her
eyes and pivoted, staring back down the wedge of the
shrubbery to the drying greens behind the kitchens.

"*Dorothy?*"

Already walking, she called out again.

Passing into sunlight along the front of the mansion, she
increased her pace. The beech hedge rustled. She peered
hopefully toward the rose garden—but the breeze dwindled and left the leaves stiff and motionless.

Mirrin circled the mansion once, then headed up to the
gardener's cottage, searching the stables and carriage
house on the way. She did not call out Dorothy's name
now but moved silently. She did not enlist Archie's help,
though the boy was there in the stable yard, soaping tack.
By the time she reached the vegetable gardens she was
nagged by panic. The sensible thing to do was round up
the staff and organize a search for the missing woman.
Instinct prohibited it, some intuitive sense within her.
Perhaps she did not want to risk ridicule and the accusation of being careless with her charge.

No, it went deeper than that, was less personal.

At the cottage Mirrin searched diligently, silently, with a coolness she did not feel. Certain that Dorothy was not in that part of the estate, she returned to the house. Without a word to the maids she hunted through all the rooms from cellars to attics—and found no trace at all of the master's sister.

By that time Dorothy Lamont had been at large for close to two hours.

∞

"Pretty flowers."

"I picked them."

"You didn't hurt them, did you?"

"Flowers canny be hurted."

"They can if you don't pick them nicely."

"What's your name, lady?"

"Dorothy."

"My name's Jinny. I've got five big brothers."

"I have a brother too."

"I've had a cough."

"Are you better now?"

"Aye."

"Where do you live?"

"Blacklaw."

The bunch was made up of daffodils and crocuses, clutched so tightly that velvet petals were already shedding. In her left hand Jinny grasped a spray of pussy willow, the silken gray buds fat on the twigs.

Jinny Sinclair was like a patchwork doll with a fine china face. Dorothy stared at the doll's face, then at the pussy willow. The buds were the shade of a gown she had worn once, long, long ago.

She reached out to touch them.

Jinny cut off her chatter, snatched the bouquet of twigs and leaves away, pouting possessively. "They're mine."

"Where did you pick them, little girl?"

"Back yonder."

"Show me."

"I should be at school t'day, but I've had a cough. Mam put me out in the backyard. I cam' over the brig all b'myself."

Far across the valley a train hooted. Dorothy and the child both glanced up at the puffs of smoke that showed above the slate roofs, all that was visible of the village.

"Will we pick more?" suggested Dorothy.

"Aye, some for you, lady."

"Yes," said Dorothy eagerly. "Where's the tree?"

"Back there. Come on then."

The white willow tree clung to the river bank. A season ago it had been on high ground. But subsidence of the clay had brought it down, and now the Shennan, jealous of its new buds, chaffed and tore at it and would soon have it all.

Behind the willow, alders and bushy whinns were thick. Woman and child pushed through them and emerged on the narrow sward dominated by the willow roots on an outcrop above the river. Dorothy stared up at the whippy branches speckled with silver buds. The doll-faced village child was not in awe of the location. Tossing aside her spray and posy, she hitched her skirts, leaped catlike onto the trunk, and swarmed nimbly up into the fork.

The willow creaked and swayed.

Fear bolted through Dorothy Lamont; not a rational fear that a normal adult would have experienced at the girl's foolhardiness, but an accumulation of many terrors, some real and some imagined. At its core lay memories of the nightmare that had troubled her intermittently all winter long. Images merged, dream and actuality becoming one, as if she had at last caught up with herself. She uttered a warning cry.

Jinny Sinclair snapped off twigs and dropped them

down on Dorothy, who took the branches full in the face, slapping at them as if at snakes. The child giggled and broke off more twigs and showered them down. She was seated, cross-legged like an imp, in the fork of the bole and main branch, perched over the river.

Tears streamed down Dorothy's cheeks. She thought of Mirrin and tried to behave as Mirrin would have wanted. Still weeping, though in some sort of control now, she clenched her fists and commanded, "Come down at once."

Scornfully, Jinny tossed another handful of twigs onto the lady's head. She was safe enough up the tree. She seldom did what anybody told her and was not awed by this woman who cried for no reason.

"Come down, I say, come down this minute," Dorothy shouted, emulating Mirrin as best she could.

Grinning, Jinny kicked her heels. Her skirts were lumped about her thighs, her thin legs bare. Stepping closer to the cliff edge, Dorothy circled an arm about the willow trunk, and stretching, snared the child's ankle. Jinny wriggled and kicked. The grip was tight enough to hurt.

"Let me go."

"Then will you come down?"

"Naw."

The struggle was over in an instant, a frail tussle, with neither the child nor the woman finding much leverage. The child's petulant complaints, however, conjured the man from out of the woods.

Bounding forth from the whinns like a dwarf, he grunted and wheezed with laughter. Young, broad-backed, big-thighed; his head was huge and misshapen, and his slack lips dribbled saliva. Even as he came to rest on the sward his hand planted brass teeth into his mouth and his voice changed to a breathy, metallic wail. Blast upon blast chanting at Dorothy, he hopped forward, cheeks blown, arms swinging.

Dorothy released her hold on the tree and on the child's ankle. She tottered, sank, and toppled over the cliff.

The river's roar enveloped her, full of gobbling greed, like some massive animal. Sticky clay adhered to Dorothy's dress. Involuntarily, her fists closed on the tussocks of the verge and her muscles contracted, holding her body plastered against the cliff face. One shoe, hanging from her toe, was stripped off by the water and gulped down. She could still see the beast above her on the bank, though he paid her not the least attention.

The happenings linked into a continuous action. Even as Dorothy fell, Lauchlan Abercorn advanced to the bank, and Jinny, scrambling higher, lost her hold, crashed through the boughs and down toward the swift, horse-brown current.

Woman and child were only a few feet from each other. Jinny dangled from the lowest branch, snagged by her patched jacket. Her trailing knees scored up streamers of foam and released from the Shennan's depths a hideous hissing sound. Lachie's round head jutted over the cliff. He pushed the mouth organ forward in his teeth, arched his brows, and nodded.

Soft, wet clay cushioned Dorothy.

Lachie's face vanished.

Dorothy inched herself up the banking, digging with her knees. Beside her, the child pendulumed, screaming, slipping lower and lower until the river flickered at her heels.

The branch that Lachie found was three or four feet long. He poked it out over the river and wagged it. The chant of the mouth organ was his speech. The noise became more insistent as he projected the branch close to the child, and waved and beat, impatiently. But Jinny Sinclair was too terrified to understand. She did nothing to save herself. Suddenly, furious at his failure to communicate, Lachie thrashed wildly, flailing water and willows, inadvertently striking the girl, her arms, legs, head, as if to jar sense into her. The branch broke. Blood flowed from Jinny's skull. Still Lachie hacked and smote, prancing up and down, his boots shuddering on the clay.

The willow tree released its burden.

The smooth, flexible twigs bent. The bundle slid, neat and contained and limp. Brown water flopped open to welcome the child and closed over her hair. Nothing was left but an elongated dimple that swirled softly away downstream into the main channel.

Eyes closed, Dorothy waited, no great weight of terror in her now, nor much awareness of her own danger. The man with the metal mouth was no longer in sight.

At length she raised her head and opened her eyes, propped elbows over the edge, and with a weary effort, hauled herself up onto the solid ground. There was no sign of the creature, no sign of the little girl, nothing to remind her of what had occurred.

Bunches of flowers and pussy willow lay on the grass. She stooped and lifted them, wondering who could have been so careless as to cast them aside. Holding the spray and the posy close to her breast, she staggered on upstream, whimpering a little, then talking to the flowers for company.

❦

Angus Sinclair had been drinking in the Lantern since it opened. His mates were all on hand, so that, within an hour of being summoned by his eldest son, search parties had been marshaled and had swarmed out across the countryside to seek the missing child by the light of pitch torches. Rita, Sinclair's wife, and a posse of neighbors had combed the backs of the rows and all the nooks this side of the pit fence where Jinny might have hidden. It was full dark before Constable Neave arrived from Northrigg to conduct the investigation. Though full of sympathy, Neave was not, at this stage, unduly worried by the child's disappearance. One squint at the half-drunken father suggested that the wee mite was probably hiding out from fear of punishment for some minor mischief.

The change of shifts at the colliery made the job more troublesome and confused, but Forbes Guthrie had come up from the schoolhouse by then with some of the younger teachers. Armed with storm lanterns and an iron hailing funnel, they explored the scrubland along the old railway tracks. Waylaid on their way home from the shift, Rob Ewing and the Pritchard brothers were pressed into service, and Callum led an eager contingent of schoolboys on a hunt around the colliery sheds.

Some men took Jinny's disappearance seriously, others ruefully expected her to turn up at any moment and have her ear clipped for the bother she'd caused. After all, they reasoned, she had only been missing since noon. At last Neave and Sinclair and the four Sinclair brothers were left, with a sheaf of pitch brands, in the yard of the Lantern.

Angus Sinclair sunk the jug of ale that the landlord had brought him to calm his nerves, then resolutely shouldered his torch.

"What's left?" the constable asked.

"The river," said Sinclair lugubriously.

Five minutes later the little party set off for the bridge and the crumbling banks of the Shennan.

❧

Houston tossed his hat onto the nearest chair and closed the study door behind him. He had just returned from the colliery but had read in Mirrin's face the fact that some domestic crisis had occurred and selfishly assumed that Edith was at the back of it.

"For God's sake, Mirrin, what's wrong?"

"It's Miss Dorothy."

"Ill?"

"I'm not sure."

"Have you summoned the doctor?"

"Not yet."

"Why the devil not?"

"She went out on her own this afternoon." Mirrin's color was like chalk, and her fingers twisted the key chain at her waist as though it were a rosary. "It was my fault. I left her in the garden. . . ."

Houston poured himself a glass of whiskey and drank it in a swallow. At the back of his mind was the memory of the group of colliers he had seen from the coach window, six or seven of them tramping purposefully toward the river.

"Has Dorothy returned?"

"Aye, a couple of hours ago."

It was after seven o'clock now. He said, "What did she tell you?"

"Nothing. She was covered with mud, but she wasn't distressed. That's what I can't understand. She wasn't weeping, she just wouldn't say anything about where she'd been. I put her to bed. Hannah's with her."

"I must see her."

"Houston, I'm afraid."

"But she's all right. I mean, she's home now."

"I don't know why," said Mirrin, "but I'm scared to death."

"It wasn't your fault that she got out." He would have taken the girl in his arms but caution prevented it. "Don't blame yourself, Mirrin. We've never really made a prisoner of Dorothy, and the estate is no fortress."

Mirrin said, "I searched for over an hour. I found her in the far woods, wandering up from the river. She was hardly even aware of me at first. She had two bunches of flowers in her hands."

"No doubt she'd been picking them. You know how. . . ."

Mirrin clutched the man's sleeve. "Houston, those flowers had been *torn* from the ground. Dorothy would never do that. No, Dorothy didn't pick those blooms."

"God, do you suppose that some man . . . ?"

"No, she has no marks on her. I tried to question her, but she wouldn't say a word," Mirrin said. "I brought her in through the hall and took her to her room by the back stairs."

"Secretly, you mean?"

"Yes—but I don't know why. Even when I was looking for her I didn't tell anyone that she was missing."

"Mirrin, you *know* Dorothy isn't violent." He swallowed another glass of whiskey. "There appears to be no sense to any of this. I'll talk to her."

Mirrin nodded.

"Where's Edith?" Houston asked.

"In her room, I think."

"Does she know about Dorothy?"

"No."

"Very well, let's go upstairs. I'll see if I can wring some sense from my sister."

Dorothy Lamont was propped up in bed. Though her lids were heavy she was awake and had eaten a boiled egg and toast. The room, as always, seemed snug and secure.

Hannah rose as her employer entered.

"Has she spoken?"

"No, sir," Hannah answered. "Not a word."

"You may leave us now, Hannah," Mirrin said.

Hannah went out soundlessly, taking the tea tray with her.

Hands folded, Dorothy Lamont seemed to be entranced by the quilt pattern. She showed no nervous signs at all, was so passive that even her brother's appearance did not rouse her from her dreamy contemplation.

"Dorothy?" He seated himself on the chair by the side of the bed, lifted her hand. It was as limp as an empty glove. "How have you been today, my dear?"

Experimentally, he passed his hand before her eyes and found them blind with stupor.

"She's in a state of shock," he said. "Send for Mackay at once."

"Talk to her first," Mirrin suggested.

"Dorothy, how are you?"

The woman's passivity was sinister. Her hands lay like fallen leaves.

Houston swallowed. "Where did you go this afternoon, Dorothy? Won't you tell me?"

She did not answer.

"Did you gather flowers?"

She did not answer.

"Where did you pick such pretty flowers?"

Her eyes remained empty.

"Dorothy," he said more loudly, "what happened at the river? You went to the river. What happened there?"

For a long minute there was no response, then her lips moved, gnawing on the word: "*Riv . . . river.*"

The transformation was shocking. One moment she was wrapped in a trance, the next she was upright, rigid, clawing at the air in terror. Great bellowing screams issued from her gaping mouth until Houston, frightened beyond endurance, clapped his hand across her lips and pressed her back into the pillows.

In his mind was the vivid memory of the marching men, men marching toward the bridge that crossed the Shennan at its deepest point.

"Mirrin," he rasped, "send Sandy to the village immediately. I must know what happened there."

Mirrin ran to the bedroom door and flung it open.

The hat was a pigeon's wing set astride a velvet brim with a cut of ostrich feather to give it height. The winter dress was quilted silk with an apron front of shimmering russet. About the hem, though, was a band of damp mud, and Edith's polished shoes had clay on them. Her furled umbrella was raised to bar Mirrin's exit.

Edith Lamont surveyed the scene coldly. She did not seem surprised to see her husband struggling with his sister, and ignoring Mirrin, addressed herself to him in clear, calm tones.

"I have been to the summit of the hill, Houston," she announced. "There are men by the bridge, men with lighted torches. I believe they are searching for the body of a child."

"*Christ in heaven!*"

"Perhaps your sister Dorothy can shed light on the little mite's last resting place." Edith smiled icily. "Do you think that may be so, my dear?"

❧

A plaintive tune guided them through the darkness. Loony Lachie was seated on the middle spar of the wooden span, thighs clutching the post, legs and feet dangling over the black, sibilant river. Angus Sinclair would have attacked him on the spot if Neave had not forestalled him.

"That's Abercorn, isn't it?"

"Aye, the murderin' . . ."

"Who knows him best?"

The group had halted ten yards from Loony, who continued to make discordant music and contemplate the river. Darts of blood-colored flame reflected on the water from the torches. Sinclair thrust forward, bulling into Neave.

"Stay here," the constable said. "I'll do the talking."

Moving slowly forward, the young constable came close to Lachie, who, though fully aware of the uniform now, refused to acknowledge the intruder.

"Hullow, Lachie," Neave casually remarked. "Bit cold tonight, don't y'think?"

Four chords answered him.

Neave squatted on the boards. The light was behind him. Abercorn's eyes were as round as glass stoppers, and spit glistened on the board of the instrument.

"I'm lookin' for a wee lass," said Neave. "Can you help me, I wonder?"

The music ceased. Lachie bumped his brow against the post as if to shake the information to the surface.

"She's just a wee lass. I hear you know all the folk in Blacklaw. I'm from Northrigg m'self. Here, Lachie, d'you like my uniform?"

Loony squinted shyly and grinned.

"How would you," said Neave, "like a button for yourself?"

Lachie nodded. He admired the brass baubles on the man's long jacket with honest greed. Neave cupped his hand to his midriff and yanked off one button, twisting it until the thread broke. He held it out so that the daftie could see the design on the convex surface.

"D'you like it, Lachie?"

"Ah!"

"Now, I'll give you the button if you tell me whether you've seen the wee lass or not. Her name's Jinny. Her daddy's Angus Sinclair. Maybe you know him?"

His stumpy fingers made a beak as Lachie reached for the button.

Neave closed his hand on it.

"Where is she, Lachie, tell me?"

Loony made a low barking sound and spat the mouth organ into his palm. He wiped the metal on his sleeve and put the instrument carefully into his breast pocket. Sinclair was shouting. Only the common sense of his sons restrained him. Torches spluttered and cast the animate shadows of the searchers along the bridge.

"Where, Lachie?" Neave gently insisted.

"Dey—dey—dey."

Lachie struggled, extricated his legs, and excited, leaped to his feet. He hammered Neave on the chest and pointed down over the handrail into the water below.

"Dey—dey—dey—dey—dey . . ."

"In the water?"

"Dey—dey—dey . . ."

"Who put her there? Did she fall?"

"Dey—dey—dey . . ."

"How did she get into the water, Lachie?"

"Lay—dey," said Loony. Then, with chance clarity: "*Lady.*"

Neave leaned over the rail.

The patched jacket bulged with trapped air. The skirt had ridden up on the backwash from the prow of debris mounded against the timber piles below.

"Lights. Bring lights."

It was no bundle of rags, alas. He saw filigree strands of hair, and the little legs, pale and thin as sticklebacks, trailing in the hurrying water, all pulled out by the race.

"Oh, God!" he murmured to himself, then set about the sorrowful business of retrieving for examination the corpse of poor little Jinny Sinclair.

CHAPTER XIV

MIRRIN stood in the tiny scullery doorway, staring out into the darkness. Houston was still upstairs doing all he could to calm Dorothy and reason with Edith. In the kitchen she could hear the McCormicks' muted voices. She could not blame the girls for being curious; she had told them only that Miss Dorothy had taken a "turn" and was having fever dreams. Though there was no connection between the missing child and Dorothy Lamont as yet, the fact remained that the woman *had* been alone on the river bank at approximately the same time as the little girl had vanished. The coincidence could not be ignored. Edith had not been slow to underscore it.

Suddenly the scullery door burst open and Hannah, eyes wild with fright, beckoned Mirrin into the kitchen. Mattie was standing on tiptoe by the front basement window, peeping out.

"Men," Mattie declared. "A whole great mob of them."

"Where?"

"Storming up the drive."

"Will I fetch the master?" said Hannah.

"Not yet," Mirrin answered. "Mrs. Burns, be good enough to bolt all the doors."

"What does it mean, Mirrin?" the cook asked.

"A child was drowned. Some of the villagers seem to think Miss Dorothy's to blame," Mirrin said.

"But Miss Dorothy wouldn't harm a fly," said Mattie.

"The villagers don't know that," said Mirrin. "Where are they now?"

"Coming to the front door."

"Right. I'll find out just what's on their minds," Mirrin said.

"But it's Mr. Lamont's. . . ." Hannah began.

Curtly the cook told her to shut her mouth. Mirrin barred the laundry-room door, then ran upstairs to the hall. She paused to listen to the murmur of voices outside. She had heard enough crowds in her time to read its mood—uncertain, but on short fuse. She smoothed her skirts, flung open the heavy front door, stepped onto the broad step, and drew the door closed behind her.

It was hardly a mob at all, only a couple of adults and three half-grown lads. One of the men was Neave, the constable from Northrigg. His tunic was smeared with mud. The other man was Angus Sinclair, a shiftless collier with a reputation for being a troublemaker.

"What brings you here at this time of night?" Mirrin demanded. "The coalmaster doesn't like being disturbed at home."

"Where the hell's that bloody madwoman who done for my wee Jinny?" Sinclair yelled.

Mirrin placed her hands on her hips. "There's no madwoman here," she said, then addressed Neave: "Kindly explain, Constable."

"Our business is with Lamont," Sinclair shouted. "We've no truck wit' the likes of you."

"It's a serious matter, ma'am," said Neave. "A child was drowned this afternoon. We've reason to believe Mr. Lamont's sister was in the vicinity at the time."

"When was the accident?" asked Mirrin, heart pounding.

"Between three and five this afternoon," Neave said.

"Then Miss Dorothy couldn't possibly have been there."

"She was seen by the river," Neave said, eyeing Mirrin curiously.

"Impossible!"

"Don't listen to that bitch, Neave," Sinclair shouted. "She's Lamont's woman, everybody knows that."

Mirrin bit her lip, then said, "I appreciate that you must make a thorough investigation, Constable. . . ."

"Tell'r, Neave. Tell the bitch."

"The child, Jinny Sinclair, was found under the Shennan bridge," Neave said.

"What makes you think Miss Lamont was involved?"

"I . . . ah, I'm not one of your storybook detectives, ma'am, but I made a thorough search of the banks and found signs of a struggle—a stick with blood and hair on it. A brief examination of the body showed injuries which suggest that the wee lass was . . . well, struck repeatedly —in other words, murdered."

"And you seriously suspect Miss Lamont?" asked Mirrin.

"I suspect nobody just yet. But a witness says Miss Lamont was at the scene."

"And who is this witness?" asked Mirrin.

Neave hesitated, then said, "Lauchlan Abercorn."

"Lachie!" Mirrin exclaimed. "Don't tell me you give credence to an idiot?"

"One idiot to catch another," bawled Sinclair.

"That's enough, man," Neave warned, and Sinclair's sons quieted their father down as best they could. To Mirrin the constable said, "Abercorn wasn't able to tell me much, but he was quite emphatic that the lady from this house had been on the spot at the time. Now, can we question her, please?"

"I'll fetch Mr. Lamont, and you may talk with him, Constable. But this I will tell you, Lachie's wrong," Mirrin said. "Miss Lamont was unwell, and I personally put her to bed at half-past one o'clock. I will vouch for it that she did not leave her room all afternoon."

"Don't listen t'that one." Angus Sinclair scanned his sons' faces for support but met only embarrassment. He caught at Neave's collar. "I tell you, she's Lamont's whore."

Mirrin winced.

A hand closed on her arm.

Houston's face was pale and set, eyes narrow.

"I heard the gist of it," he said. "I understand your bitterness and grief, Sinclair, but I cannot permit you to invade my home and throw such vicious accusations at my family."

"Nobody's made any accusations yet, sir," said Neave apologetically.

"Who are you?"

"Constable Neave, sir."

"Are you responsible for leading these men to my house?"

"I . . . ah, accompanied them, sir, to ascertain that there would be no trouble. Officially, I'm making preliminary inquiries into the circumstances surrounding the death of Janet Sinclair."

"And why does that inquiry bring you here?"

"Your sister . . ."

"I told you once, Constable Neave," Mirrin interrupted, "Miss Lamont was not out of my sight all afternoon."

The Sinclair sons looked hurt and bewildered, anxious to take their sorrow home with them, to leave the coalmaster in peace.

Houston raised his hand. "I'll see to it that the matter is fully examined. None of you will be penalized. . . ."

"It's not for you to investigate, Mr. Lamont," Neave said. "It's a matter for the law."

Angus Sinclair collapsed sobbing against his eldest son's shoulder.

Houston said, "Take him out of here, Constable. I'll answer any questions you may have at my office in the morning. Sinclair, stay at home for a couple of days. Your wife will need your comfort. I'll instruct the clerk to pay your wage."

"Da," said one of the boys. "Come on away now, Da."

Sobbing, Sinclair was led off down the driveway.

The pitch brands were all extinguished now bar one that glimmered fitfully at the head of the column as the Sinclairs moved through the oaks toward the gates.

Constable Neave lingered on the gravel.

"Would there be anybody else, sir, who could corroborate this young woman's assertion that Miss Lamont was at home all afternoon?"

Houston did not hesitate. "My wife, of course."

"Aye," Neave said. "And may I have a word with her?"

"Not at the moment, Constable. She's nursing my sister, who is unwell."

"Thank you, sir," said Neave dryly. "And you too, ma'am."

Turning, he tramped off down the drive.

Mirrin and Houston watched until the uniform was out of sight, then moved back into the mansion.

No sounds came from the upper floor, and the hallway was deserted. Houston slipped his arm about Mirrin's waist and hugged her for a moment.

She stood meekly, quietly, tears in her eyes.

"I'm proud and grateful, Mirrin."

"Miss Dorothy did not harm that child," Mirrin said. "If I hadn't been sure of that one fact, I wouldn't. . . ."

"I know," Houston said. "I know."

"You'd better go to her now," said Mirrin, gently pushing him away.

❧

It was late now, and dark. Mice scraped at the wainscots in the nursery wing, and in hall and study the tall clocks ticked away the small hours of morning. In Dorothy Lamont's room the night candle guttered at flaws in the tallow, and Houston, lying back in an armchair, snored slightly. Dorothy slept too, very still under the weight of the bedclothes.

Farther along the corridor, the door of Mirrin's room creaked faintly as it opened.

The girl lay across the bed. She was still dressed in her black outfit, her hair spilling across the pillow. A candle in a water-glass holder had almost burned out, and the wick lay floating on a little lake of clear wax.

The door closed, and the lock clacked.

Edith Lamont wore a flowered robe, quilted collar high about her face. She had removed her nightcap and arranged her hair, had carefully rouged her cheeks and applied powder to her throat. She tucked her thin fingers into the robe's sleeves like a Chinese mandarin and said, "I wish to talk with you, Stalker."

Mirrin groaned and turned on her back. The motion was unwittingly sensual and submissive. She opened her eyes, then sat bolt upright.

Edith said, "You make an excellent liar, miss. Perhaps my husband was more shrewd than I imagined in bringing a collier's slut to Strathmore. It takes kind to deal with kind, I see."

"What do you want with me?"

"I heard every word of your 'performance,'" Edith said. "I took the liberty of listening at the upstairs window. They believed you, it seems."

"Why shouldn't they believe me? You know as well as I do that Miss Dorothy did not assault that child."

"How can any of us be sure just what that demented

woman may or may not have done?" said Edith. "However, I doubt that the matter will be allowed to rest there."

"There might be an inquiry," Mirrin conceded.

"Oh, there *will* be an inquiry," Edith assured her. "Are you, Stalker, prepared to follow one perjury with another? The young constable will certainly wish to take written statements from members of this household."

"The servants will back up what I say."

"Oh, yes, the *servants* will."

"Meaning that you won't?"

"I must tell the truth," said Edith silkily. "I must tell the constable, and the fiscal magistrate, and the high court if need be, only what I know to be fact."

"And what's that?"

"I'll inform them that there's a conspiracy among members of my domestic staff, that my poor feebleminded sister-in-law was *not* at home during the course of the afternoon, that she was, in fact, out upon the river bank and did not return home until five o'clock."

Edith floated to a small stool and seated herself upon it, replacing her hands in her sleeves.

"Our accounts," she said, "will be directly contradictory, of course. But I doubt that the authorities will accept the word of a mere housekeeper against that of a coalmaster's wife."

"Houston will never. . . ."

"Houston? If you mean *Mr.* Lamont, I assure you that he will have little alternative. After all, Stalker, do you suppose that I would display a motive—other than that of Christian conscience—to the law? What could I hope to gain by lying? I'll embroider my account with tears—but I will tell the whole truth. Do you see?"

"I see fine," said Mirrin. "But I don't see what you will gain from it."

"I'll *regain* my husband." Edith let the words hang in

the air for a moment, then continued. "The choice is yours, Stalker. You may protect your own position and watch the process by which precious Miss Dorothy is taken to a place of incarceration, is tried, is found guilty of a hideous crime, is convicted by law and duly removed to a criminal madhouse—or hanged."

"And the alternative?"

"Leave my house at once."

"I doubt that you would do that to Miss Dorothy."

"Would I not? I've waited months for an opportunity to correct the wrongs that have been done me. Houston may have one of you, you *or* his sister—but he cannot have both."

"What if I tell him . . . ?"

"Make *him* choose, you mean? But you're too respectful, too honest to do that, Stalker. Tell me, are you so damnably respectful when you're in bed together? Do you call him *Sir* when he fondles your body? Do you . . . ?"

"*Stop it!*"

"It's not within my power to stop it," said Edith blandly. "*You* must do that."

She rose from the stool, her skirts knocking it over.

Both women paused, listening, but the house remained silent.

"How long do I have to decide?" asked Mirrin.

"I imagine that the constable will return here tomorrow to complete the report. He will ask me to corroborate your story."

"Tomorrow," said Mirrin. "What will Constable Neave think when he discovers I've gone?"

"I'll explain that you've gone home on family business. He'll accept that from me."

"But what'll folks think?"

"Does that disturb you? It's not what they *think* that will do harm, only what they can *prove*."

"But . . . ?"

"Do not quibble," Edith snapped. "Decide what is best for my husband. My terms are clear. One or the other— Dorothy or you. Not both."

❧

For an hour after Edith Lamont had left, Mirrin sat on the bed, hands clasped and head bowed. The candle spluttered out but she made no move to replace it. Darkness consoled her and turned her thoughts in upon themselves, forced her to examine the quality of her love for Houston and her position in Strathmore.

At length she groped her way from the bed, found a fresh wax and lit it. By its light she stripped off the tailored black dress and unpatched petticoats. She folded the garments and laid them neatly across the bed. She coiled the key chain, threaded it through the ring, and placed the bunch on the pillow. Dressed once more in her ragged gray skirt and shabby jacket, she packed her few personal belongings into a bundle and carried them downstairs. She did not hesitate on the landing to look back into the nursery wing but hurried on across the hall, carrying the candle holder and the bundle.

The clock's tin miners jerked just as she entered and hewed out four units of time, carrying them away in the tin barrow forever. Decanters glowed in the candlelight, though the fire had died and the chillness that accompanied the spring dawn had already invaded the room.

Mirrin set her bundle by the door, went directly to Houston's desk, and rummaged on it until she unearthed a plain sheet of paper and an unused envelope. Leaning, she cleared space upon the desktop and picked a pen from the row of inkpots.

Clearly, there was no choice. Edith meant every word of her threat. In the end Edith Lamont had been more cruel than any of them could have predicted. She would not relinquish her chance advantage. If Dorothy were subjected to the humiliations of a public trial and committed to spend the rest of her life in a public madhouse, how much love could remain between herself and Houston? Houston might even blame her for persuading him to bring Dorothy home in the first place. No, he would not be so irrational as that; even so, he would be hurt, scored with wounds that would never heal.

In the many diverse ways in which a man and a woman could prove their love for each other, few were equal and none was fair. There was no method of testing in advance which of them nurtured the seeds of pain.

It must appear to be her decision, her decision alone.

In protecting Dorothy, ironically she must also protect Edith.

When she began to write she was disappointed to discover that few words were needed to mark the end to such an important phase of her life.

> *I am going away. I told the lie for Miss Dorothy's sake. I will stand by it if there is a trial or an inquiry. But I am not proud of what I have become since I first came to this house. Do not try to see me, please. I want no more to do with Strathmore.*
> *Mirrin Stalker.*

She folded the paper, slipped it into the envelope, and pasted down the flap firmly. She addressed it in large letters to Houston Lamont and printed the word *private* above his name.

She propped the letter against the inkpots, then lifted her bundle and went out of the mansion by the kitchen door.

❧

Flora Stalker wakened in the alcove bed. She could hear faint shouts in the street and for an instant was filled with the fancy that tragedy had once again struck Blacklaw. But she had no more sons to lose to the pit, and that selfish thought calmed her. She lay awake, wheezing slightly, and listened instead to the familiar bump of the water bucket as Kate carried in the day's supply from the pump.

"Kate?"

"No, Mam, it's me."

"Mirrin?"

Flora drew back the cotton curtain in surprise.

The fire was built in the stove, porridge put to boil. Even as she watched, Mirrin ladled water into the big kettle. Her sleeves were rolled up, and she was as busy and bustling as if she had never been away from this early round of chores.

"What's wrong, girl? What are you doin' here?"

"Nothing's wrong. I've left, that's all."

"Left?"

"I've quit Strathmore."

"Thrown out?"

"No," Mirrin snapped. "I left of my own accord."

"But why, Mirrin, why?"

"Because I wanted to."

"Can you not tell me the truth, Mirrin?"

"That is the truth."

Mirrin put the kettle on the hob and laid the caddy close to it. She turned and looked through the half-light at her mother's perplexity. "That's all the truth there is, Mother. Now don't ever ask me again."

"But . . . but, Mirrin, what'll you do now?"

"Work at the only job that seems to fit me."

"The troughs, you mean?"

"Aye, what else!"

CHAPTER XV

QUIETLY and without fuss, Jinny Sinclair was put to rest in a corner of the kirkyard early on a Thursday afternoon. The colliery was under full employment that week, and not many men were able to be present, nor did Constable Neave attend the funeral. He was occupied in drafting a report to the fiscal authority of the county, a task that took up more of his time than the actual investigation. If he had applied himself, he *might* have proved a case to answer; but he was no blood-monkey and consequently tempered his account of the "accident" with evasions and distortions of the possible truth. Neave reckoned that murder had not been done, that the lass had received her injuries accidentally, not through foul intent. He reckoned also that the Stalker girl had lied about Miss Lamont and later learned that for some unfathomable reason she had been dismissed service at Strathmore. By that time the report had been placed with the fiscal, and it was too late to reopen the case. Neave regretted the need to account for chance. The circumstances were unusual, but he wanted no complaint from Sinclair to blot his own record. So the constable did what he thought was best— and let it go at that.

Certainly, Constable Neave could not be blamed for what happened later.

There were more things than the death of a child to occupy the minds of the Blacklaw miners. It was clear that

Lamont had tricked them in some subtle way. The committee who returned from a delegate conference of colliers in Falkirk understood the duplicity. They also understood that Blacklaw was better off than most other villages in Scotland. Lamont had told them that the price of coal was low. In fact it had never been higher. The sorry state was that greed, not depression, accounted for the falling off in demand. The damned masters had pressed their pits into overproduction. Strikes now suited them. Strikes cooled the market. Any district representative who used the threat of strike action was playing right into the bosses' hands.

In Blacklaw there were enough honest men with enough common sense between them to foresee a period of lockouts and violent clashes, and they wanted to hold Blacklaw back from this chaos. Callum Ewing was one such man, backed by the Pritchards, and halfheartedly, by Rob.

Since Alex Stalker's death, however, militant politics had lost its savor for Rob. He could not decide whether he was pleased or sorry to learn of Mirrin's return to the narrow house. There were certain aspects of her return that intrigued him and gave him hope that within a season or two she would mellow enough to allow an approach. If only the daft business with her brother would settle itself too, then it would not take long for the Stalkers to become accepted again in humble Blacklaw and for Mirrin, allowing for her past, to be considered decent enough to marry a Ewing.

❧

The communication came in a thick cream envelope with an embossed seal on the back. Only Drew was unimpressed by the missive's outward trappings. The letter's contents, however, sent him into raptures of self-congratulation.

Since his return from Edinburgh he had thought less of

his professional ambitions than of the city itself. Though most of his two days there had been spent in the university's baronial halls, he had seen enough of the streets to convince him that Edinburgh was the hub of the civilized world and Blacklaw just a speck of fly dirt by comparison. As the days dragged past, however, he had lost confidence and whiled away hours dreaming of Edinburgh as a pilgrim might dream of the Celestial City, without much hope of ever reaching it.

One morning in April the letter arrived. Kate and Betsy were off at work but Mam and Mirrin were in the kitchen when he slit the envelope and extracted the paper, scanned its contents, clenched his fists to his ears, and shouted, "I *did* it! Damn me, *I did it*!"

In the family only Betsy was as elated as she should have been, and Drew shrewdly tempered his enthusiasm and poured out his plans in secret to his twin.

The dominie too was delighted at his pupil's success and throughout the rest of that month continued to meet him regularly, at no cost, to discuss erudite philosophies of law. It did not occur to Forbes Guthrie to ask Drew whether his family could afford to send him east. And it did not occur to Drew that his sisters would not keep their part of the bargain.

It was not for her brother's sake that Mirrin strove so hard to find work. It was not because of Drew that her failure to do so drove her into despondency. Everywhere she went in Lanarkshire the same notice greeted her: NO HANDS REQUIRED. She supposed that she could have persuaded Donald Wyld to give her a job at the Blacklaw troughs. But that kind of nepotism was not for her; besides, her name was bad enough in the village without making it worse by finding work when other women could not.

Mirrin's return home was a nine days' wonder. The malicious gossip did not escape Flora's ears. Shamed and

angry, she lost no opportunity of berating Mirrin—
though Mirrin could not decide whether her mother was
annoyed at her for taking the housekeeper's post or for
giving it up.

Nobody was brave enough to interrogate Mirrin. She
was more proud and quick-tongued than ever, her temper
on short fuse. Maggie Fox Williams got a flea in her ear
for suggesting that if Mirrin happened to be in the first
stages of motherhood—as Maggie was—a stray Williams
might be willing to make her an honest woman for a wee
cash consideration.

Lifting the basket of laundry, Mirrin carried it out to
the wash house at the back of the row. The fire in the
little grate under the stone boiler was almost out, but the
water in the caldron was hot. She began to feed clothes
into it, thinking of other things, anxious for herself and
for Kate. Poor Kate was so whittled down by worry
about Drew's future that Mirrin feared for her sister's
health.

She pushed the laundry carelessly into the suds. It
lumped and knotted. She had no right to feel sorry for
herself. What had she ever done to be proud of? The
boiler stick jabbed at the tangled clothing. No, she had no
scope for pride in anything that had happened to her in
Strathmore. She could not think of Houston now without
a shadow of guilt and growing animosity. The ingrained
habit of blaming the coalmaster was reasserting itself—
unfairly. Houston had not taken advantage of her—on
the contrary. It might have been to her credit that she
had saved Dorothy Lamont from a criminal madhouse,
but she had done so at the cost of honesty.

The rumor was strong in the village that Lachie Abercorn would soon be sacrificed to the legal machine and
taken off to an asylum for his part—whatever it was—in
the mystery of the child's drowning. She thought of the
simpletons of this world as its free spirits, of Lachie as the

essence of Blacklaw's liberty—a daft analogy, of course. He fed in the bakehouse or the back of the store, slept in the railway sheds or somebody's wash house, talked to the stray dogs and cats, and played his discordant music to his heart's content. He was free all right. In his grinning silences she recognized now a mute contempt for the whole slave system. And she, Mirrin Stalker, had perhaps put an end to that too. Everything she touched seemed to turn rotten.

Pounding the suds into agitated froth, she sent up clouds of steam to fill the low outhouse like a fog. She did not notice Kate's arrival, and lifting the stick, speared madly at the clothes in the caldron.

"Does that help?" Kate asked.

"Aye, it helps."

"Maybe I could have a shot," Kate said.

"What's wrong with you?"

"I've decided to tell Drew."

"When?"

"Soon, perhaps tonight."

"He'll go mad."

"I know," said Kate grimly.

"How bad is the financial position?"

"Very bad. He just can't go to Edinburgh. Besides, we could be turned out of this house now, now that you're not. . . ."

"Don't blame me," Mirrin snapped.

"No, no, love. I didn't mean it that way."

"I'm sorry," Mirrin said. "I'm all on edge. If only I could get some decent work."

"God knows there's enough of it in the world," said Kate. "It's payment that's so scarce."

Mirrin leaned against the boiler. Sweat glistened on her face and arms, and her blouse clung to her breasts.

"If Houston dares to put us out, I'll . . . I'll kill him."

"I don't think you mean that," said Kate.

"Don't I?"

"What happened?" asked Kate.

"Nothing," said Mirrin defensively.

"Was it him, or was it her?"

"Her, if you must know."

"Why? Did she resent you?"

"She hated me. She's a born hatemonger, Kate. And I was so happy there. I suppose that sounds odd coming from me, a Stalker, a collier's lass—but I *was* happy in Strathmore."

"With him?"

Listlessly, Mirrin stirred the sinking froth with the flat stick. "Especially with him."

Kate said nothing.

"You must never tell anybody, Kate," Mirrin said quietly, "but I love Houston Lamont. I loved him in every sense of that word. Mother suspects and thinks the worst of me, but it wasn't like that at all. Believe me, Kate, I don't regret it, not one single moment of it. All I regret is the fact that it's over. None of the rest of it was deceitful—only the way it ended."

Suddenly Kate's arms were about her, and the sisters were weeping. Their weaknesses and needs were safely enshrouded in steam. Nobody saw them or heard them. Nobody in all Blacklaw could possibly guess that the Stalkers' secrets caused them so much suffering.

"Perhaps you'll go back one day," Kate said.

"No, it's past now," Mirrin sobbed. "It's all over, Kate."

But once more she was wrong.

❧

Kate did not tell Drew the disastrous news that night. Mirrin would have done so herself but she did not want to usurp her elder sister's authority. Flora Stalker too was kept in the dark about the true state of affairs, and for another five days the situation remained unchanged.

Mirrin roved farther and farther afield in her search for work, and the talk about putting a face toward the future seemed as grimly ironic as Free Miners' gala days and the tattered bunting of the unions' parade flags. As if to rub in that fact, Mirrin was coincidentally involved with what seemed to her to be the last tangential act of bad faith to stem from her spell in Strathmore.

She had returned home after a hard morning's tramp around the Hamilton warehouses, none of which was employing new hands. Boots off, feet on the hob, she was resting and sipping tea when Flora Stalker barged into the kitchen from the street, loudly declaring, "It's a proper disgrace."

"What is it now?" said Mirrin.

"See for yourself."

Upset, Flora pushed on into the back bedroom and closed the door. Mirrin wondered what could possibly have stirred her mother to such indignation, and still in her stocking feet, went out curiously onto the pavement.

It was a cool, dull, hazy morning. Near where the street narrowed at the mouth of the kirkyard lane a group of women were jeering the antics of two men in biscuit-brown uniforms.

Still intrigued, Mirrin wandered uphill. The broken pavement pricked her feet, but she hardly noticed the discomfort, for her eye had been drawn to a horse van at the lane's end. A tight brown tarpaulin, bearing no name, was battened across its spars, and the horse, a docile, aged beast, waited patiently between the shafts. The uniformed men were patient too, flanking the kirk lane for all the world like whippet racers waiting for their dog to spring from its trap. It was no dog, however, that they had penned there.

Lachie had been cornered twice already. For more than an hour the chase had gone on, by fits and starts, shifting from the colliery coups, through the wasteland shacks, into the backyards of the village. Lachie's escape routes had less sense to them than those of a hunted animal. His dens, earths, and secret dreys were no longer safe for him.

The village women were ambivalent. Most of them did not trust Loony Lachie and yet resented the authority of the brown uniforms. Since word about the daftie's involvement in the little girl's drowning had got about, though, Lachie had been rejected by most of his former friends, so the wives chose to jeer at the uniforms but not to impede them in their civic duty. Reports were shouted as to Lachie's position, advice on methods of capture freely donated.

Mirrin gave a spluttering little cry. Loony was seated astride the kirk wall, the mouth organ in his hand. Grinning, he conducted some inaudible chorus with huge sweeps of his arms.

"Bring your ropes, then."

"Have y'not got batons?"

"Aye, we've got batons," retorted one uniform, "but we're not keen to use them."

"Scared you'll break them?"

"You would, too, on his thick head."

"What d'you think, Rab?" said one uniform to another.

"Hell, aye. I've had enough chasin' about."

"Righto! I'll fetch the gear."

The man strode purposefully to the van and a minute later reappeared with two long, polished batons and a net of hempen rope.

Loony stopped conducting, crooned softly into his mouth organ, and regarded the officials with interest.

One man shook out the net, spread it in the dirt, folded it again carefully, and draped it like a cloak over his arm. He stuck a baton into his belt and approached Lachie directly. His partner crept down the street and slunk through the kirkyard gate.

In a trice, Lachie was off, leaping from the wall and galloping around the corner across the backs of the rows.

"Bloody hell!"

Spectators found new vantage points. The uniforms united again at the lane's end, and Mirrin heard one say to the other, "Nothing for it, Rab, we'll have to net him and put him out." Their patience and efficiency horrified Mirrin. Even if it took them all day, she had no doubt that Lachie, broken and bleeding, would inevitably become their prisoner.

She walked forward. "If I bring him to you peacefully, will you promise not to hurt him?"

The parish officials looked at her. "Friend of yours?"

"You might say that."

"Can you get him for us, lass?"

"I think so."

"Righto!"

Mirrin went down the lane to the area of the backs. There was no visible sign of Lachie, but a woman leaning from a cottage window shouted and directed her to his hiding place. The young man had taken refuge behind a broken cart under thorn bushes. Mirrin stopped twenty yards short of the den.

"Lachie? Mr. Abercorn," she called, "will you give me a dance?"

He whistled, casual and unconcerned.

"It's me, Lachie, it's Mirrin Stalker."

Lachie's head popped up over the edge of the cart, like a puppet in a box.

"I see you, Lachie," Mirrin said.

The head vanished.

Talking quietly and persuasively, the girl went forward.

The tune started up, lively and discordant. A moment later, Lachie crawled from his retreat, leaped to his feet, and performed a clumsy, high-kicking dance. Not smiling,

Mirrin applauded in time to the rhythm, watching the bushes tremble.

"That's it, Lachie," she called. "That's the way."

The thorns parted. A uniform appeared. Off to her right was a second brown-clad figure. Stealthily they flanked Lachie.

"Dance, Lachie," Mirrin shouted. "Go on, dance."

The cavorting boots, tied around with string, flopped and flapped crazily in the dirt. He bit into the instrument, sucking and blowing. He raised his arms, pirouetted, once around, then again—then stopped.

The uniforms sprinted the last few yards. The net billowed, hovered in the air, and swamped the little broad-shouldered man. He fell to his knees, tearing at the mesh, entangling himself. Bunched up, he rolled on the ground.

Mirrin screamed as the official batons cracked ruthlessly on Lachie's skull. The women in the lane stopped cheering. Four times the men hit the daftie, and rendered him still. They did not so much as glance at Mirrin as they wrapped the net tightly around the unconscious body, strained and lifted and lugged their heavy burden down the kirkyard lane and heaved it into the back of the van.

The mouth organ lay in the dirt where it had fallen.

Mirrin lifted it. The women had all slunk away to their houses. There was nothing now to amuse them. Mirrin, running, came out of the lane into the main street. The nag swung its head and stared along its blinkers at her. Lachie was inside the hooded van, unwrapped, groggy. One uniform stowed away the net, his companion already on the driver's bench. Neither looked at Mirrin.

She loitered aimlessly on the pavement, clutching the mouth organ. She could see Lachie stirring within the van. Blood flowed from a split on his brow. He did not seem aware of the wound, though it bled over his thighs onto the planking. The official clanged the cage door, padlocked it, stepped around to the side of the conveyance, nodded curtly to Mirrin, said, "Much obliged," then went on around to his seat at the front.

Reins snapped. The driver's guttural command coaxed the horse into motion. Iron wheels rumbled on the cobbles. Within, Loony swayed, bemused and numb, against the shrouds.

"Lachie," Mirrin shouted. "Here, Lachie."

Sprinting, she grabbed at the bars, hauled herself up, and thrust the mouth organ through the grid. It landed on the floor, and the young man did not seem aware of it. His big, ugly head had a majestic dignity as he pillowed it on the tarpaulin, vacantly studied the girl, then closed his eyes and allowed two globular tears to trickle down his cheeks.

The horse trotted. The van gathered speed.

Mirrin dropped, fell sprawling into the gutter. She crouched there on all fours staring into the receding cavern behind the bars. Forty yards uphill, the van ground into the corner by the colliery fence. Mirrin got to her feet.

She turned to run home. The sound stopped her in her tracks. It filtered from the cart, faint, wistful, and sad. The van trundled out of sight onto the Lanark road. The plaint of the mouth organ lingered a little, dwindled, and was gone.

That was the last of Lachie's tunes ever heard in Blacklaw. He was never seen again at large and free in his old stamping grounds and innocuous haunts.

❧

Flora Stalker found her daughter crouched on the floor with her face buried in the cushion of her father's armchair. A sore weeping reached down deep into her and racked her terribly. Flora lifted the girl's tear-streaked face. She did not know how to comfort her. With sudden insight she realized that she had never had the proper words to give to Mirrin. Mirrin was so much like her father. A wave of tenderness engulfed Flora. She cradled the girl's head and crooned gently to her until the sobbing diminished and with a final rending sigh Mirrin was motionless.

"What is it, love?" said Flora. "Was it what they did to the daftie?"

"It was how they trapped him, laughed at him, beat him, and . . . and took him away from the places where he was happiest."

"It's like that for many of us," said Flora. "We think we're safe and secure, but all the time we're being swept away."

"Do you miss my father very much, Mam?"

"Aye."

"But . . . but what does that kind of hurt feel like?"

"I wish I could tell you, lass. There's no word for it. It's just . . . an emptiness, that's all."

"Does it not heal?"

"It changes," said Flora. "I suppose that's the healing."

Mirrin stared into her mother's face, the face of an old woman. What was left for her now, twenty-five or thirty years of emptiness? What memories could she have accrued to help her through the nights—a seashell, a cherry-cloth hat? Not much for a lifetime of labor and suffering. Suddenly Mirrin understood Drew's greedy ambition.

There were hills beyond the Lothians, rivers that did not flow into the Clyde, villages and towns where men did not have black dust in their pores. There were cities where women could still be young at forty, lively at fifty. There were far harbors where happiness was constant and not just a lull between tears. Honesty and industry might be extolled as the greatest of virtues, but what did it all mean if honesty and virtue were simply pared out of the needs and continual sacrifices of life itself?

"Mirrin, don't look at me like that."

"What?"

"As if you . . . despised me."

"I don't, Mother. No, I don't despise you."

Mirrin could not explain that she pitied her. Pity was worse than scorn.

She hugged the big woman, and comforted, got to her feet.

"Whatever happens, you'll be all right, Mam."

Flora nodded. She had heard that heartiness before. Mirrin had made up her mind about something, and no power on earth would stop her.

Nothing Flora Stalker, Kate, or Betsy might say would change Mirrin's mind and alter her decision to leave Blacklaw for good and all.

❧

That same night, only minutes after the shift hooter sounded, Jock Baird, a foreman, brought Mirrin a letter from the management.

"Eviction notice, I suppose," Mirrin said.

"May be," said Jock. "What'll you all do then?"

"Camp out," said Mirrin.

"Well, good luck to you anyway, lass."

"Thanks, Jock."

Her mother was out delivering completed needlework in Hamilton, and Drew had gone to the school to talk with the dominie. Kate and Betsy had not yet returned from work.

Mirrin turned the letter over in her hand. It was addressed to her. Somehow she did not feel dismay. The firm, upright hand told her that it was Lamont's writing. She slit the flap with her thumbnail, took out the sheet of colliery notepaper, and read its message.

Houston wanted to see her.

It was his first attempt to make contact with her in the weeks since she had walked out of his study in Strathmore. The note brought a picture of Houston to mind, unbearably vivid. She crumpled up the sheet and envelope and burned them in the grate, then went into the back bedroom and closed the door. She studied her face by candlelight in the fragment of mirror. She looked so tired. Her hair was untidy and her eyes lusterless.

For a minute she was tempted to reject him; then, with memory strong in her, pulled herself together and took her clean blouse and skirt from the wardrobe.

An hour later, in the gloaming, she set out to keep the appointment.

❧

Houston had chosen a coppice on the high ground north of the village as a suitably private rendezvous. There was a fine view from the hill. The Shennan was hidden, and the coppice was bounded by open farmland that joined the pastures behind the Strathmore estate. The day's cloud had lifted, and the sun was setting in golden glory, while Mirrin wended her way up the path.

A breeze rode over the shoulder of the hill, carrying no taint of damp and dust but only the scents of the new spring growths. Below her the girl could trace the patterns of the little gray dwellings arranged in the shadows of the coal heaps, sheds, and wheels. She could even pick out the narrow house, last in the row, the house in which she had been born. How many years it seemed since she had been a child romping tomboyishly in the fields behind Poulter's burn and on the ground where the railway now

spun its iron web. She did not dare count the years—
there did not seem to be enough of them to debit with so
many deaths and so much suffering.

She climbed; her strong young body made light of the
steepness. She felt comfortable in her everyday clothes, the
leather belt buckled around her waist and her sleeves
rolled up. Dressed like a collier's daughter, she was better
prepared to meet Houston Lamont than she would have
been in finery.

Though she was early, Houston had already reached
the rendezvous. The coach was hidden among the trees
by the track, and he waited by the only conifer in the coppice, brushy green branches reaching high above the
beeches. In the golden light, Mirrin saw that his features
were harder, leaner than before, and that his smile
of welcome did not now soften the lines of anxiety at his
mouth.

"I wasn't sure you would come."

"Don't I always do what you ask?" said Mirrin.

"Not always."

"I felt I owed it to you."

"Why?"

"Because of my letter," she said.

From his jacket pocket, Houston withdrew her letter.
He unfolded it. "Tell me, Mirrin, what manner of fool do
you take me for? Did you really think I'd believe *this*?"

"It's the truth."

"No, Mirrin. I want the truth, from your own lips."

"If that's all you got me here for, then it wasn't worth
the climb."

"Don't torment me, Mirrin. I know why you wrote this
letter and why you left so suddenly."

"Then . . . then, there's no more to say."

"Darling." The endearment no longer came easily. "Mirrin, do you think you can deceive me? I love you too
deeply not to understand."

Mirrin felt herself trembling. She did not want his arms about her, did not need them, was afraid to allow him to draw too close.

"It wasn't difficult to guess your reasons," he said. "I *know* what happened."

"Do you?"

"Concerning Edith."

"Houston, please leave me as I am."

"Is that what you really want?"

"It's as it must be."

"Dorothy asks for you."

"How is she?"

"Ill and depressed," Houston said. "She's slipped back. Perhaps I was at fault for encouraging her love. It can be a terrible prop, taking too much weight—love, I mean."

"Yes," said Mirrin, "but until it breaks. . . ."

"Until it breaks we must stand under it and trust it with all our hearts," said Houston.

"Is your wife happy now?"

"Edith will never be happy. I'm not sure she would have found . . . something, if our son had lived."

"At least she has you."

"Yes, I am there, in her house—one of her prisoners, like Dorothy. Like you too, I suppose. We talked of this once, do you remember?"

"I remember."

"Nobody is free," Houston declared with a vehemence that suggested that he had been forced to the admission. "There's nothing any of us can do to break down the walls."

"Not together, Houston, only apart."

Houston, with sudden brusqueness, took two long envelopes from his inner pocket and held them out to her.

"In one," he said, "you will find the title deeds to your cottage. Your family may stay in it as long as they wish.

Nobody will be able to break the legality of the deed exchange, I assure you. Only in the event of there being no Stalker left in Blacklaw will the property revert to me or to my kin."

"No," Mirrin exclaimed. "No, no!"

"In the other envelope," he went on quickly, "is a letter of introduction to a lawyer on George Street in Edinburgh. He will administer a grant of twenty pounds per annum to be drawn on your brother's name. In addition he will, if your brother passes his bar exams, article him as an advocate at the end of his university terms."

"No, Houston, no."

"My lawyer friend will also find suitable lodgings for your brother."

"I can't accept."

"Because you're too proud?"

"I don't want your charity, Houston."

"I wish to do this for your brother—for you."

"How did you calculate it, coalmaster—so much for sharing your bed, so much for perjury, so much for . . . ?"

She swung her hand to strike him. He caught her wrist and drew her against him.

"If I gave you Strathmore, its grounds, my horses, my colliery, and all the land you can see from this hill, Mirrin, it would still be short of the price of a bribe. What I give you is nothing, *nothing*. Don't you love me enough to see that much, at least?"

Part of his strength was hers too now, and she did not weep. She touched his face with her hand, gently impressing it upon her fingertips as if she were blind and had no other way of memorizing it.

"I'll love you as long as I live, Mirrin."

"Yes," she said. "Yes."

He kissed her once, then turned and strode away from her through the trees.

She heard the horse snort, the sound of the coach wheels, and the brushing of the leaves against the jet-black stuff of the hood.

Stooping, she lifted the envelopes from the grass where she had dropped them. Hope was so easy to record—the stroke of a pen on paper, the shape of a signature. Like a miracle, the answer to her family's problems was held in two little paper envelopes hardly weighing a goldsmith's gram. But to *her* problem there was no easy solution. Houston had no means of signing a deed to seal up love in perpetuity, all neat and lawyer's legal.

How could she ever learn to live with the accident of love, the error of giving her heart to a man who should have remained her implacable enemy for all time? At least in death there was an end to change, a kind of permanence. She could love her brothers and her father as they had been, untainted by the future. But what had happened between Houston and her had been both too simple and too complex to erase. The mark of it would rest on her heart forever.

Abruptly, she was running, stumbling and sliding downhill toward the village, toward the streets of the place in which she had been born and many, many months ago, had, for a brief, exultant moment, been young.

⌗

Kate could hardly have chosen a less opportune time to inform Drew that his plans would be scotched by lack of money and that his enrollment in Edinburgh University must be canceled. The young man had returned from the dominie's parlor in an unusually good mood. He had eaten his meal without hiding behind a newspaper and had even regaled Betsy with scraps of information on the bounties of the capital city. Even Flora appeared entranced by Drew's suave enthusiasm and listened attentively for once.

It was too much for Kate.

Suddenly she blurted out, "You're not going to Edinburgh."

"Of course I am."

"You're not."

"You can't stop me. I've been accepted."

"We've no money to pay the fees."

"Money?"

"Aye, money. You see, Drew, we don't have enough."

Pushing away his plate, Drew smiled uncertainly. "I must say, Kate, this joke's in rather poor taste."

"It isn't a joke. We can't afford it."

"Now, Drew, now," said Betsy. "She doesn't mean it."

"*Damn it, I do mean it,*" Kate shouted, clanging down the kettle.

"I gave you so much," Betsy cried. "What have you done with it all?"

"It's in the bedroom cupboard, every last brass farthing," said Kate. "If you don't believe me, Drew, go and look. You'll find the weekly accounts in the same jar."

Drew glanced from Betsy to his mother as if expecting them to contradict Kate.

"Best . . . best do as she says," Flora told him.

Drew rose and walked stiffly into his sisters' bedroom, leaving the door open. He flung open the cupboard and peered inside.

"Under the floorboards," Kate told him.

Crouching, the young man yanked up the loose plank, dug out the big stone flour jar, and carried it back into the kitchen. Knocking off the lid, he spilled its contents onto the table. Fishing inside the jar, he found the tally sheets, which Kate had kept assiduously week by week since the previous March. He flicked over the pages, then checked the total against the coins spread on the tabletop. "Is that *all*? Is that *everything*?"

"Yes, Drew, I'm afraid it is."

"*You cheats!*" shrieked Betsy.

Drew put down the jar, eyes filmed by disbelief.

"Why didn't you tell us you were short?" Betsy stormed.

She stood squarely before Kate, screaming at her. It was as though she spoke not only for her twin but even in his voice.

For a moment Drew did nothing. Kate pushed Betsy, sending the girl sprawling into a corner. She reached out and grabbed Drew by the hair and shook him violently. "Say something! Say anything!"

"I worked this . . . this house out of me," he began, oddly calm. "I worked to get out of here. Do you think I did it because of a promise? What about *your* promise, Kate? Why did you fail?"

"God knows, Drew, I tried," said Kate, releasing him.

Flora heaved herself to her feet, stretched out her hand to her son. "There's my wedding ring, Drew. We can sell it. It won't fetch much, but. . . ."

He slapped her hand away. "It's worth nothing. Look at it—worn thin. It was probably bought from some cheap tinker's stall in the first place."

Flora seemed stunned. Even Betsy ceased wailing. But Drew was in full flood now, and before Kate could stop him he had stretched his clawlike hand across the table. "I want what's mine. Where is it?"

"It's . . . not . . . anywhere," Kate stammered.

"Damn you," he said, seething. "You're just another thickheaded colliery bitch. If *he'd* been alive, he'd have made *sure* you kept your promise. Yes, I know. You loved *them*—Da, James, and Dougie. You'd do anything for *them*. All *they* had to do was snap their fingers, and you all jumped. But what about *me*? Is it because I'm not smeared with coal dirt and stink of sweat, is *that* why you hate me?"

Kate could not bring herself to silence him. Much of what he said might be true. His terrible accusations reflected so much on her that to stop him now would be an act of selfish pride. She sank back in a wooden chair, head hanging, and in that position of servility received all his slanders on herself.

For ten solid minutes Drew berated them. He cursed his father and brothers, his mother and sisters. He cursed his own misfortune at being the last-begotten son, and only a twin at that. He used words that none of them had ever heard before, some erudite, some foreign, some filthy, all plaited into a rope of obscene abuse with which he flayed the women remorselessly.

At length he stopped, turned, and walked out.

None of the weeping women stirred.

The sound of their son and brother was still loud in the narrow house. He stamped up the ladder to the attic. They heard him sweep books from the shelves, batter the bed, smash the candle-lamp, hammer the stout chair against the roof. The ferocity of his anger shook the house to its foundations. Even so, they could hardly grudge Drew this scouring out of the prison his ambition had built over the past year. It was as if they had released a demon of destruction, a manifestation of all the anguish and fury they had suppressed in themselves.

Finally the noises trailed into uncanny silence.

At exactly this moment Mirrin entered the kitchen door.

At a glance she took in everything that had happened since she had left an hour ago. The envelopes in her hand might atone for despair and redress the balance of their future. But Houston's gifts had come too late—the damage to the Stalkers was irreparable.

"Where is he?" Mirrin demanded.

"Up . . . up . . . upstairs," Betsy sobbed.

Mirrin threw Kate a withering glance, then hoisted herself up the ladder.

In the wreckage of the tiny attic, Drew was seated in a corner, on the floor, his back to the walls, knees drawn up. He stared at her, his eyes smoldering. "You," he said quietly. "You could have done it for me, Mirrin. You could have got Lamont, if you'd cared for me enough."

A year ago, less, she would have matched his rage with her own. But not now. Houston had taught her so much more than love.

Almost insolently she tossed one envelope at Drew.

He looked down at it; then, curiously, at his sister.

"Everything you want," Mirrin told him quietly. "It's all there—money, security, introductions to influential people in Edinburgh."

"But . . ."

"I didn't do it for you, though," Mirrin said. "Never, ever think that, Drew. And whatever Houston Lamont did, he did for me."

Drew scrambled to his feet. It was dark in the room, and the sister and brother were like specters of themselves, bleached of color by the gelid light from the skyglass in the slanted ceiling. He tapped the envelope against his mouth, very calm now, wary, speculative.

"How much?" he asked.

"Twenty pounds a year."

Drew sighed. The sound spoke of his satisfaction, a temporary feeding of his greed.

"Mirrin, how can I thank you?"

"You can leave this house," Mirrin said. "And stay away from it."

"Yes," Drew said. "Quite. Yes."

"You can stay away from me, from now on."

"You never did like me, did you?"

"No."

He shrugged; he would have traded them all for Lamont's letter.

Someday, Mirrin knew, Drew would claw his way to the top of his chosen profession. Someday in the not-so-distant future he would lord it over the weaker members of the jungle of legal gentlemen and would be feared and envied. The folk of Blacklaw, who had spurned him, would take pride in the fact that he had once been a collier's lad and one of them. But whatever Drew did, whatever he became in the years ahead, *she* would never be proud of him, nor forgive him for being born without the capacity to love.

She studied him now, seeing him with merciless clarity. His pale face seemed jaundiced in the light, his eyes cunning like those of a leopard freed from its cage.

"Look," he said.

He was not looking at her now, but past her, his gaze lifted to the open skylight. She glanced behind her and saw that the source of that strange yellowish light was in the sky.

"What is it?" she asked.

Drew righted the wooden chair, leaped up on it, and lifting the window to its limit, craned his head and shoulders out into the night air.

"*Good God!*"

Mirrin tugged at his elbow. "What is it? Is it the pit?"

"God, no!" he said. "It's a fire, a blaze."

"Where? Whose house?"

He looked down at her, his eyes round with astonishment.

"It's Lamont's house," he said. "Strathmore's burning like a beacon."

CHAPTER XVI

FOUR kegs of coal oil, filched from the cellar in the stable yard, were sufficient to do the deed. Even if he had survived, it is doubtful that Angus Sinclair would have been able to explain the confused motives that spurred him to take revenge on Lamont's property. Ale was at the back of it, of course, as ale was at the back of every piece of cruel stupidity that Sinclair had chalked on the slate of his life.

Later it was surmised that he had been driven mad by grief for his daughter Jinny. But that was as remote from the truth as the stars are from the earth. What first moved Sinclair was not sorrow but guilt. In his cups that evening, he had been haunted by the hellish specter of his own inadequacy. How deep his guilt went down, no man, not even Sinclair himself, could say for sure; yet it was there, like a taproot, worming through countless layers of ignorance and egotism into his very soul.

Dismissed from the colliery for flagrant drunkenness, he drank alone in the Lantern, shunned like a pariah dog. Five days on the trot he had tottered to the shed at the head of the shaft where his crew of winding-gear operators took the lives of their comrades in their hands. Four shifts Sinclair had been sent home with a flea in his ear by the general foreman and latterly by Donald Wyld. One more breach, he was told, and he could look for work elsewhere, or join the dregs of casual labor, without skill or privileges, hacking out dross with a shovel when his head was clear enough and his pockets empty.

And one more spree there had been, that very afternoon.

Now the tithed house must go; the family would be in the gutter; his sons would shun him like a leper lest they too became contaminated by his unstable reputation. Visions of a future without status foamed in Sinclair's mind as he drank away the last of his severance pay in the unhallowed halls of the Lantern bar. The publican did not deny a customer the right to go to perdition in a wash of beer, provided he paid his score by the round until the packet was empty.

No credit, no home, no status.

Behind him was a wife who keened for a dead child, a wee elfin face that had never clearly imprinted itself on her father's memory except as a drowned thing hauled from the river. Even then he had felt no genuine loss, only rage that death had dared unsettle his family life and rob him of the limelight he demanded as his right as a breadwinner.

Now, in the dreary mourning days, he considered himself rejected, a wronged man.

And like most colliers, he blamed the boss; not circumstances, but Lamont; not God, but the master of Strathmore.

The practical aspects of the crime no sober judge would ever have understood—the ease with which Sinclair obtained access to the mansion, the leisurely manner in which he hauled oil kegs from stable to study, all undetected by members of the household. Nobody could fathom this piece of pure luck, so, as the months passed and the horror of the event paled, Sinclair was credited with being an evil genius driven mad by capitalist injustice.

The plain truth was that he had come to Strathmore with the fuddled notion of begging Lamont for another chance. He had stumbled around the grounds for half an hour before broaching the house itself.

It was the sight of the coalmaster's wife through the uncurtained windows of the dining room that rankled in Sinclair, soured him, and in an instant brought his hatred to sharp focus. It was the way she sat, all heaped with finery, stiff-backed and plump, pale and proper, all alone at the long table, all alone before a sumptuous array of foods, a dozen candles burning, and two poor servants dancing attendance on her every whim. It was that tableau that razed his humility, and in the wreckage of his sanity, left only the overwhelming urge to destroy such complacency forever.

With the motive, such as it was, came a modicum of slyness and a boldness that no designing criminal would have dared apply. He had loitered in the gloaming for a half hour until the woman left the room and the candles were snuffed out. He had gone then directly to the front door, twisted the handle, found it open, and entered the hall. Without nervousness or undue stealth he had crossed the hall and entered a room that contained a desk littered with papers, a clock, and several armchairs. This room, conveniently, lay to the side of the house and faced out across a sheltered lawn and the stable yards.

The room was deserted, though a small fire burned in the grate and a lamp was lit. Decanters were ranked on a table by the desk. Sinclair unstoppered one and flung back the contents in one long swallow without recognizing the taste of the best French brandy. The spirits did not bemuse him; in fact they seemed to sober him a shade, to sheath his purpose in steel and give clarity to his every action.

Greedily, he unstoppered the other decanters, found port and sherry wine too sweet and cloying for his palate, and poured the contents over the rug like a libation to the gods. He rummaged on the desk. Cigars from a box among the papers; a match from a holder; the taste of tobacco, too strong, making him cough; the brown stub ground out angrily into the papers; a cloverleaf of red, spreading, wisping blue smoke.

Sinclair blinked.

Fire and purpose merged.

Lifting the lamp, he unscrewed the sandglass wick holder and splashed oil upon the desk. The saturated papers burned without vigor. Sinclair cast around for faster fuel.

Coal. He tried a bucketful of dross upon the pyre but it only stifled what flame there was. Searching for kindling, he opened the window, stepped out, and crossed to the sheds. So far was he sunk in his own purpose that he did not even bother to check the windows, and approached the grooms' attic without a shred of caution. By chance he found the fuel cellar at once, and carried the four stout little kegs of domestic oil, one by one, across the grass and dumped them through the window into the study.

Later Mrs. Burns declared that she had heard sounds about the hour of nine o'clock, and at the same time, Hannah McCormick claimed to have remarked to her cousin Matilda that Mrs. Lamont was in the study. Miss Dorothy, they knew, could not be abroad—she was locked in her bedroom on the first-floor wing.

Sinclair reentered the study and closed the window. He unbunged the first keg with a paperknife, and using the desk as an altar, dribbled oil all over it. For some reason it refused to ignite. The next two kegs were decanted with more deliberation across rugs and chairs and into the case of the Brighouse clock, whose tin miners particularly offended the sacked collier.

Slithering, Sinclair laved the whole room with oil. None of it seemed willing to burn. It hissed and steamed, and in the general area of the desk, changed into subtle gases.

The grate was bathed with oil from the last uncorked keg until the hearth was awash and stinking. Even the grate, however, would not jet out the one bright flame that Sinclair required to cauterize his anguish and give him release. He splashed on more and more of the viscous fluid, dabbling in it, slick with it, clothing smeared, hands, breeks, scarf, and hair all plastered.

God knows which tiny coal finally sparked the ultimate chemistry.

It happened in the space it takes to draw breath.

A sheet of lambent white flame spread through the air, enveloping hearth and mantel shelf, reverberating from the brass fender. The keg in the collier's fists was instantly encased, and instantly exploded, drenching him in scalding fire.

Swift as a lightning bolt, the room was shot through by living flame. The desk, a roaring plug, blotted out the window; the clock was devoured from the guts up.

Blinded, Sinclair saw none of it.

Burning like a torch, bucking and plunging in agony, his blundering shoulders finally found the door and carried destruction out into the hall, scattering it into the empty drawing room, into the parlor, seeding flame all through the ground-floor rooms, until with a last barbaric cry he pitched down and died by the stairwell wall.

❦

Edith Lamont stood nude before the full-length mirror in her boudoir. The faint sweet smell of smoke hardly impinged upon her consciousness, nor did she pay any attention to the noises below stairs. Since the Stalker girl's departure she had supposedly assumed a housekeeper's main responsibilities. So lax and self-absorbed had she become, though, that she let the mansion run itself and even neglected to attend to its security before retiring. For her, security was not a matter of bolts and locks but an inward quality, a sensation reflected back at her from her surroundings, like a mirror image.

She found no fault with the plump, sagging figure. The very gesture of standing unclothed in frank admiration of her own body gave her an unfailing thrill of wickedness. She had been disciplined to regard her body as something intrinsically evil; only in the past few months had she dared take pleasure in it for its own sake. She amused herself now with chiffon robes, silky underthings, ribbons, garters, and perfumes, adorning it for her own satisfaction like a voluptuary. She fancied herself a courtesan before whom men would grovel in worship; the game had become its own pleasing reality.

Even at this late stage in her dying marriage she might have jettisoned her prissy air and affected manners if only she had felt that she could win Houston back. But her husband had escaped her. The man who stalked into the dining room occasionally was a stranger, surly and withdrawn, indifferent to her very presence.

Edith now appreciated that the Stalker girl had only been part of the threat against her rule. It sickened her to see how Houston still lavished his affection on the gaunt, ugly creature who was imprisoned in the nursery wing. All the jealous venom she had expended on the collier's brat was now directed at her sister-in-law. But she would bide her time. The chance to be rid of Dorothy would come. Then, and only then, would Houston be driven back to her. And when she had him snared and safe once more, she would make him suffer for his indifference and transgressions against her.

After a time the stench of smoke became too strong to ignore. Indeed, behind her reflection a faint mist filled the bedroom, and a sound like the sloughing of a west wind rose from beneath her feet. A spasm of superstitious awe caused her to cover her body with a robe, lash it tightly around her in case the slithering caress of the material give away her naughty secrets and her sinfulness.

The bedroom door was locked, of course. Nobody would dare intrude. Even so she was motionless, breathless, listening.

Shouting below stairs. The sloughing sound was pierced by cracklings like burning leaves. Through a gap in the curtains she saw a carpet of color staining the lawn by the nexus of the east wing. With quickening pulses, she flung open the window and leaned out.

Flames licked the study window, massive flames, raw, red and hungry. Even as she watched, the casements splintered and spewed outward and flames scorched the ivy-clad wall.

Edith's shock was brought under control at once. Outside, she could count all three of her domestics—the McCormick girls and Mrs. Burns—and haring across the yard with clog buckets in their hands were the groom and the stable lad.

The gardener's dogs were barking and their clamor added depth to the pagan roar of the fire. Strangely, she experienced no sense of urgency or personal danger. The blaze appeared to be in Houston's study and would probably be confined to that area. As if to confirm her belief Archie tossed a bucket of water into the burning window bay and she saw the hot glow visibly diminish.

Nobody seemed to be in the least concerned for *her* safety.

And Dorothy?

Soon, no doubt, it would occur to the servants that Miss Dorothy, their precious Miss Dorothy, was still imprisoned on the floor above, and that realization would lead to all sorts of false heroics.

As swiftly as the original explosion, the concept of a solution to her own problem struck Edith.

She did not even pause to salt her jewels into a pillowcase, but plucking the key ring from her dressing table, unlocked her door and hurried left along the corridor.

As she crossed the head of the stairs, she glanced into the burning hallway, not with terror but rather with relief that the most obvious route into the house had already been cut off. The flames looked thin, like imitations, as they scuttered up the paneling and nibbled at the boards. A chair that she had never much admired was burning merrily. Smoke spiraled and crawled along the ceiling cornices. At that moment she could have walked down the staircase, picked her way through small puddles of fire, and made her escape sedately by the front door.

But Dorothy was still upstairs.

Edith was too vain to believe herself in real danger. Incredibly, she did not foresee that the blaze might take hold of the whole of her house. As she hurried into the gloomy regions of the nursery wing, her immediate plan was already lightened by speculations as to how she would have the mansion remodeled.

Dorothy was seated on the side of the bed.

There was much smoke in the room, little impish gouts of soot floating freely in the heated atmosphere. Oddly, Dorothy showed no signs of panic or distress. What seam of reason had been opened by recognition of danger remained a mystery. She sat quite still upon the bed, fully dressed, with a reticule of personal treasures packed by her side.

When Edith unlocked the door Dorothy got to her feet. She was disappointed, almost irritated by the fact that it was Edith and not Houston who had come to her aid. She asked for no explanation, though, and did not need to be coaxed into cooperation. Edith nodded and beckoned. Dorothy lifted the reticule and followed her sister-in-law out of the bedroom and into the recesses of the nursery wing.

It was darker there, single lamps cupped in honey-yellow auras where the smoke's seepage was most dense. The noise of the fire seemed remote, like the surge of the sea on a distant beach. Edith had no way of knowing that, by vents and ducts, the fire had spilled from the drawing room into linen closets and from there had taken hold of the dry old timbers of the shuttered wing. Below her, at that moment, flames were eating into the pillars and joists, sucking themselves along the lathes behind the plaster toward the kitchen stairs.

Stooping carefully, Edith unlocked the nursery door. She pushed it open and ushered Dorothy into the room. A weird ethereal radiance bathed the chamber's dusty furnishings, silhouetting the larger toys and hampers of clothing. It no longer smelled disused, but was impregnated by a quick, acrid scent like incense. The shouting from outside was momentarily loud, then faded. A handbell clanged wildly in a far corner of the estate.

Dorothy went meekly into the forbidden room. Her expression was controlled, showing only bewilderment, not fear or mistrust.

For an instant, looking at that face, Edith was touched by a physical pain so sharp that it caused her to halt and clutch at her heart. The shapes in the room—the high curve of the rocking horse, the rubber ball, the wooden railway train, the easel, the day cot still with its vermilion counterpane turned down—did not hurt her with memories of her son; rather it was the total capitulation of a woman who could not tell friend from enemy, whose mind refused to separate love from treachery, and who, by that gray trail, had escaped the hungers of the world.

If she had gone through with it at once, Edith Lamont would have succeeded in her plan; but a stirring in the heart, some dim resurgence of pity, caused her to hesitate, and the hesitation brought her defeat. That pause, that genuine moment of doubt in Edith, broke Dorothy's numb acceptance. Even as Edith stepped back toward the door, Dorothy caught her.

"Don't leave me here."

The woman's hand was lean, strong; the fingers bit into Edith's shoulder. Tension made Edith shout aloud as she found herself drawn hard against the body of the tall, faded, bony woman who was the source of all her innermost terrors. She stabbed and ripped at Dorothy with the key ring, but the assault made no impression and the woman refused to release her. Grappling and hugging, breast to breast, they edged like uncertain dancers back into the nursery.

The smoke was much denser now, coagulating along the cracks in the wainscot. Edith could taste it in her throat. It seemed, in those fantastic seconds, that she had tasted that burning, dusty flavor all her life, that it was the lode of all her repressions and frustrations. Crushed against Dorothy, she could not struggle. The keyring, dropped, was lost. Rasping, she fought for breath enough to scream, until her throat ached and her lungs felt as though they would collapse.

The rocking horse swayed violently. The ball bounced into the gloom. Dorothy's heel caught on a wicker hamper and she stumbled a little, giving Edith her one chance to break free.

She ran now, the silken robe clutched in her fist.

Everything had changed.

The corridor was a tunnel of reeking brown smoke. The servants' stairs were buried in it. From that impenetrable pit the massive, smothering tide of smoke took its motion. It resisted Edith and drowned her in its fumes. She whirled around and headed back for the main staircase.

As she passed the nursery door Dorothy loomed out, hands stretched and groping. She caught Edith by the

shoulder of the robe. Tearing herself free, Edith plunged
on through the stifling fog, Dorothy, wailing at last, trailing on her heels. Ahead the smoke was lighter.

But the light was fire, a fretwork barrier of fire.

It curled up from the eaves of the first-floor landing,
entwining the posts of the balustrade like the tendrils of a
scarlet vine. It flowed and flowered, and mounting higher,
merged with the flamehead from the stairwell itself. The
sheets were multihued, shot with spurts of ebony and
stinking brown, riddled with cavities and crannies where
the oak had collapsed inward and the paneling had
buckled out.

When she came to a halt, the rolling wave of smoke
engulfed Edith. Disintegrating, it streamed rapidly into
the heart of the holocaust, back into the ocean of fire
that had given it birth.

Edith's senses recoiled.

Arms locked about her waist, Dorothy caught her from
behind and hugged her tightly once more.

Dragging her sister-in-law's weight, Edith hobbled to the
brink of the fire pit that was all that remained of the hall.
Its skeletal structure showed—a door, an alcove, a window. The charred bones of furniture stood out dark and
fragile against the vivid veils of color. The staircase was a
waterfall of fire.

A blast of heat overwhelmed her—heat more suffocat-
ing than smoke.

Drawing Dorothy down with her, Edith fell.

Scalding heat was replaced by whipscores of intimate
agony. She no longer had the strength to struggle or cry
out. Her brain was closing like the petals of a shriveled
flower. She wallowed onto her stomach. Through stream-
ing eyes, she glimpsed Dorothy's body, crouched, patient
and waiting, upon the crumbling edge of the landing.

"Houston," Edith shrieked, "Houston."

There below, through leaves of flame, she saw her husband burst into the inferno.

❧

Mirrin was among the first of the crowd to reach the gates of Strathmore. Behind her, clattering past the schoolhouse, came the colliery fire cart drawn by a team of four strong horses. A dozen miners clung to the rails, swaying as it canted on nearside wheels. Water tubs tilted in their racks. Furled hoses shuddered and buckets and ladders chattered as the vehicle leaped over the rutted junction and slewed onto the gravel of the drive. Mirrin could hear the hoarse sawing of the horses and the deafening clang of the bell, Rob Ewing, poised on the buckboard, yelling, *"Fire! Make a way! Fire!"* as the cart thundered past.

Strathmore was blazing, filling the night sky with hellish light. Tall brick chimneyheads spouted sparks like miniature volcanoes. The east wing was already so eroded that parts of it were avalanching outward, spilling hot slates and timbers across the lawn. In the flower beds the stalks of last summer's flowers smoldered like rows of Roman candles. The main door, above its shallow steps, was wide open, blackened by smoke; behind it was a cavern of orange flames so bright that it hurt her eyes to look into it.

One thought pounded at her mind.

Houston!

The carriage was there, by the gable, the terrified stallion rearing in the shafts as Archie and Sandy fought to control the beast and lead it out of the fire cart's path. From the stables came a bedlam of animal sounds; the grooms had not yet released the other hacks. Chains of bucket carriers had been organized to pass along cogs from the yard pump, but the silver splashes of water made no more impression on the fire than darts of flint. The sloughing, roaring, and sliding rushes of the fiery mass were terrifying, and even the most adventurous of the village children stood well back in the protection of the oaks.

Soaked coalsacks gave the rescuers some small defense against the intense heat as they labored to unroll the canvas hoses and connect them to the pump. The Pritchards and Hendersons manned the swan-necked handles, slaving at their task but achieving only a laggard column of water from the racked tubs for their efforts. The water cascaded across the steps, hissing, transformed at once to steam.

Now that she had reached the scene Mirrin was at a loss. She wanted Houston, wanted to see with her own eyes that he was safe—and yet, even in the center of such drama, she was mindful of her role. Wandering along the skirts of the lawn, past sweating firemen and volunteer helpers, she found Hannah McCormick kneeling in prayer, hands clasped and eyes turned to the glowing sky.

Mirrin caught the girl by the shoulder and pulled her to her feet. "Hannah, where's Mr. Lamont?"

Hannah's mouth gaped.

"Dead. They're all dead and gone," she droned.

"*What?*" Mirrin shook the girl roughly. "Hannah. The truth. Where are they—the master and mistress?"

"Inside."

"*Oh, God!*"

Mirrin swung away.

Mrs. Burns, arms around the sobbing Mattie, was ten yards away. Mattie still wore her neat black dress and apron, and the cook's flat linen hat was hung comically on one ear.

"Where is he?" Mirrin cried.

Within the west wing of the house, tongues of fire broached some new source of energy and boomed and bellowed thunderously, shooting fresh showers of sparks and flames high into the air.

The onlookers cowered. Rob Ewing flinched and dove full-length upon the gravel as a cascade of tiles poured from the roof. He was on his feet in a moment, wrapping the sackcloth around his head once more. The men were backing the fire cart, horses prancing madly, hoses ineffectually spewing water onto the gravel now.

Mirrin placed herself squarely in front of the cook.

"Tell me what you saw," she demanded.

"Miss . . . Miss Dorothy and the mistress are inside," said Mrs. Burns. Fat tears rolled down her cheeks. She continued to hug Mattie and pat the girl comfortingly. "I'm certain they didn't get out."

"Tell me about Houston," Mirrin pleaded.

"He . . . he went in."

"When?"

"Three or four minutes since." The cook shook her head at such squandered courage. "I . . . I think Miss Dorothy and Mrs. Lamont were in the hall . . . somewhere there. He . . . he went straight in, through the front door."

"And didn't he come out again?"

Mrs. Burns shook her head once more.

Dazed, Mirrin shuffled a few paces past the cook and stared at the raging facade. If Houston had dared enter there, then there could be no hope. No hope.

Swaddled in a large tarpaulin, Rob Ewing was crawling under the protection of the steps, inching his way on his belly. She could see no purpose in the maneuver. It seemed like futile bravado, and she experienced anger at the young collier's heroic gesture—before she understood its meaning.

Knurls of incandescent wood sprinkled the tarpaulin, which crouched up now, and like a gray-green crab, scuttled up the steps to the rim of the fiery cave. It settled, flattening again, then, with jerky sluggishness, began to retreat. As it came, the Pritchards bathed it with a stream of water from the tubs, clouding it in steam. Ten yards, fifteen yards, the tarpaulin progressed across the gravel, painfully, slowly.

She looked up.

The outer wall bulged, cracked, and splintered a buckshot of bricks far out at the front. It held, though, held vertical just long enough for Rob to shake loose from his tarpaulin carapace and drag the man's body clear. Then the wall fell, a solid slab, backed by a magma of fire. The onlookers, a vast crowd of them now, yelled and fled back, far back into the trees. The fire cart's horses took fright and dragged away, hauling the brakes, making forty or fifty feet before the colliers halted them.

Through the hale of debris Mirrin walked, moving into the gale of searing heat until she reached Rob. He was on his knees, bleeding from the head and dazed. Under him was Houston Lamont.

Between them the collier and the collier's daughter lugged the unconscious coalmaster another ten yards, then managers and firemen and Dr. Mackay took over and the girl only glimpsed Houston's face, blackened and gnarled, before she was pulled aside.

They took him away on a stretcher in the back of the coach, Donald Wyld and Mackay in close attendance. She did not know, until Rob told her, that Houston was still alive. Even then, she could not be sure that she would ever see him again this side of heaven.

By dawn, when the rains came, there was nothing left of the mansion of Strathmore, nothing but a jagged, smoke-wreathed area of burned brick and charred timbers, which hid the Lamonts' final secrets well.

CHAPTER XVII

THE destruction of Strathmore was more than a nine-days' wonder. Houston Lamont's life, or at least his future, was at stake. Even if he did not succumb to his injuries, the fact that a collier had been involved in the tragedy put the fate of the pit in the balance. A new owner, some very distant relative, perhaps, might be a harder taskmaster than Lamont had been. Opinion was divided. Some still saw Lamont as a villain who had reaped a harsh but just reward. The majority, though, prayed that things might soon be restored to an even keel, with the boss back at the helm. Gossip and information mingled inextricably. Wild speculations were rife in the village throughout that spring and summer.

Donald Wyld took on the running of the colliery, attending to all the affairs that the coalmaster had previously kept to himself. A lawyer traveled from Hamilton to take charge of the process of law involved in the inquiry and the preparation of an accurate fiscal's report on the accident. This lawyer also arranged the interment of Dorothy's and Edith Lamont's remains in the family plot in Hamilton's most prestigious cemetery. Houston, in a private nursing home near Glasgow, was too ill to attend the funeral. All these matters were reported, with restraint, in the Hamilton *Advertiser*, which eventually gave out the news that Mr. Houston Lamont was not now critically ill and had been removed from the danger list.

STRATHMORE

For the time being, Mirrin had to be content with such public sources of information.

The administrative lawyer paid off Strathmore's staff. Mrs. Burns went into service in fashionable Edinburgh. The McCormick cousins returned to their home village. The gardener and grooms were found jobs on the Duke of Hamilton's policies. May passed into June, and June into July, and still Lamont did not return to Blacklaw unless, as a few sworn enemies suggested, it was by cover of night.

Two pieces of private news did reach Mirrin, however. Four weeks after the tragedy a letter arrived from an Edinburgh lawyer, dryly confirming that Andrew Stalker would be the recipient of twenty pounds per annum, thus indicating that Houston was well enough to fulfill his promise to the boy. With that letter came the draft deed for the Stalkers' house, a detailed document as valuable, to Kate and Flora, as a chest of sovereigns. Much to Mirrin's sorrow there was no personal enclosure from Houston himself.

Donald Wyld, however, sent word via Kate that a vacancy was due at the troughs and that the job would be hers if she cared to apply. Mirrin returned to work on a Monday in mid-May. As she left the colliery that same evening a note was handed to her by the gateman. In Donald Wyld's writing, it cryptically stated, "Mr. Lamont is now out of the hospital and has gone abroad to recuperate."

Mirrin was tempted to approach Wyld for more news, but somehow she did not trust the manager.

Weeks passed. Work continued. Minor crises of trade came and went. The national market revived a little. Poverty was never so grim in summer as in winter. Besides, the Blacklaw colliers had adjusted to lower wages by tightening their belts.

Still, Mirrin was troubled. She did not know how seriously Houston had been injured. More important, she could not judge how deeply Dorothy's death had scarred him. Even Edith, now that she had gone, might weigh on Houston's conscience. Had he "gone abroad" to recover his health or just to lay an excuse for quitting Blacklaw for good and all? It would not be the first time that a coalmaster had sold out his rights and standing properties and settled his capital into another form of business.

Would he ever return to Blacklaw? Would she ever see him again?

Uncertainty went against the grain of her character. She detested the troughs and could not bear the malicious chatter of her companions. By August, Mirrin had reached a stage in which she felt her very sanity threatened by indecision.

After all she was no longer a child. Her twentieth birthday was not so far off. Flora was nudging her to marry and settle down. Rob Ewing had called several times at the house, ostensibly to visit Kate. Things were slipping back into the old familiar patterns. Her months at Strathmore were beginning to seem like a dream. Only her love for Houston remained unchanged.

That night on the hill, only a few hours before the tragedy, she had reconciled herself to putting love behind her. All her life, it seemed, she had really denied love, had let it come last. By that rebuttal she had won security for her mother and Kate, had put her brother on the path to becoming a gentleman. But those achievements, however worthy, had drained her, and she went through the days now in a waking trance, feeling little.

A week before the annual August fair, however, she found that she had drifted into a decision. She would stick to her intention, would leave Blacklaw and strike out on her own again.

Once her mind was made up, strength, determination, and some of her former spirit returned. On the day after the fair she would leave for England. On that day too Drew would set off for Edinburgh, to introduce himself to the lawyer who would become his mentor and to enroll in Edinburgh University. She chose that date because Drew's departure seemed to mark an end to duty.

And as for love? That, she told herself, was an illusion, an impossible goal, as tantalizing and elusive as a desert mirage. What future could there be for a collier's daughter? The coalmaster could never be free. He was bound to the code, bound to his class, just as she was part of Blacklaw and always would be, wherever she went in the world. Deep into this spoiled earth her roots went down; they must feed and sustain her as her father would have wished. She might leave, but she would never forget.

If Houston did return, did love her, did still want her, they would still be trapped. He could not fly in the face of *his* upbringing, could not risk making more of her than a clandestine lover.

No, there was no hope after all. She would leave her home place after the August fair, put all the sufferings behind her—and Houston Lamont with them.

‿⟋⟍

The name of Fair Mile field was older than the hamlet of Blacklaw. It was mentioned in historical annals going back six centuries. The field was a stretch of flattened grassland on the moor, which roofed the subterranean vaults of rich black coal, two miles from Blacklaw and three from Northrigg. For as long as records had been kept, an August fair had been held there, a tradition that gave the colliers a sense of continuity with the golden age of the past. The year of the Blacklaw disaster was the first in living memory in which the August Saturday had not seen a trek of packmen, tinkers, and miners out to Fair Mile. That year the moor had been too tainted by soot thrown out by the March explosion. But the season of grief was over, and the weather had cleansed the land.

From the crack of dawn the men of two communities met on the field to shore up booths, mark out tracks for races, tug-of-war tournaments, and tossing the prop. In the lee of a line of small trees, boards were laid for dancing. Paper lanterns and bunting were strung around and benches put out for the fiddlers and bandsmen who would provide the music.

Though impoverished, the colliers struggled to put aside their uncertainty and depression and enter jovially into the spirit of the carnival. Farmers' daughters came down out of the hills with cheese and junkets to sell. The tinker kind assembled to make a week of it, hawking all the beats from Hamilton to Blantyre. There were pipers too, Highlanders, who would squeeze out a rant for a copper or two, and a fellow from Ayr, dressed like Rabbie Burns, who would recite the bard's works most stirringly for a capful of small change.

Within the Stalkers' house there was little excitement, however. The following morning Drew would embark on his journey to Edinburgh—his valise stood packed and ready by his bed. Mirrin too was leaving by the Sunday coach. Surprisingly, neither Mam nor Kate had put up much argument when she announced her intention. They would never fully understand what sacrifices Mirrin had made. Besides, they had all been confused and strained by Drew's torrent of abuse. The family was split, and nothing could really mend it. That brave promise, made fifteen months ago, had taken too much from them all.

Flora Stalker went off before noon, carrying her contribution to the children's picnic. In the latter part of the day, Drew and Betsy set off together for the dancing. They were hardly children now, but smart young adults, set apart from their former schoolmates.

Arms linked, the Stalker twins walked sedately up the

length of the main street and through the kirkyard lane, neither one sparing so much as a glance for the corner where their father and brothers were buried. They were too engrossed in discussing the future to be conscious of the past that had shaped it for them.

"Perhaps," said Drew, "I was a trifle harsh on them."

"Most of what you said was perfectly justified," said Betsy loyally.

"If only Mirrin hadn't been so tardy in wheedling my grant from Lamont."

"How do you suppose she did it?"

"Can't you guess, Betsy?"

"Ah, but guessin' isn't knowing, is it?"

"The evidence is plain enough."

"You sound like a lawyer already."

"I shall be soon."

"You won't forget your promise?"

"What promise?" said Drew. "Oh, my promise to send for you? No, I shan't forget. In the meantime don't do anything foolish."

"Like what?"

"Marrying some clerk."

"I won't, don't worry about that," said Betsy. "I've come to the conclusion that the Stalker girls aren't the marrying kind."

"Oh, I imagine Mirrin will marry one day soon," said Drew.

"You mean, because Lamont's . . . free now?"

"Never!" said Drew. "You can't expect a coalmaster to marry a . . . a. . . ." He shrugged. "No, she'll wind up with Rob Ewing."

"Good thing too," said Betsy. "Our Mirrin's not cut out for better than that—in my opinion."

"And you are?"

"Of course I am."

Drew paused and inspected her critically. She had

grown even prettier, more dainty and more poised. There were plenty of pretty girls in Edinburgh, but few as attractive as his sister. With decent clothes and careful grooming she might prove quite an asset in furthering his career.

"Indeed, Edinburgh's the perfect place for you, Betsy, as it is for me." He secured her arm again and led her on toward the crowds and the bunting.

"Promise, Drew," she insisted.

"Yes," he said casually, "I promise."

Dusk spread intricate shadows over the framework of stalls and tables and the debris of the afternoon's festivities. In the fading light the bunting no longer seemed shabby but took on the texture of silk, rippling in the little wind that had sprung up from the west and brought with it the threat of rain.

Prizes had been given out, blankets, cooking pots, and food donated by local gentry. Games and races had been the highlight of the day's events. Poverty, however, showed in the baking and knitting competitions, which had hardly been worth judging. But that was history now, of no concern to the couples who drifted through the gloaming to join in the dance. Children and old folk had gone home, though the older boys and girls still dodged about the empty stalls, taunting the tinkers. Barrels of beer, carted up from the Lantern, were the focal point for miners who had just come off shift. In the short lull before the evening's program began, there was laughter, noise, and true to the colliers' tradition, voluble arguments on every possible subject.

Mirrin watched from the edge of the boards by the tinkers' booths. She noticed Drew dancing with Betsy, leaving a trail of whispered comment in their wake. Kate was dancing with Colin Pritchard. Young miners had no interest in such an "old" woman! Kate's only hope of marriage now was to one of the senior bachelors, the kind who sought a housekeeper rather than a bedmate. Such a marriage contract might not be so bad after all, Mirrin thought; that quiet sort of love might even survive the gray rains of Blacklaw.

Night came down. Lanterns now seemed to shed their light over a painted frieze of all the days of her life, good and bad.

She noticed Maggie Williams trying to drag Billy away from the beer table; saw Donald Wyld in heated argument with Callum; Davy Henderson, upper lip sprouting a wispy mustache, dancing with Edna Brown and thumping McLaren on the back every time they passed each other on the floor. Dominie Guthrie and Dr. Mackay were examining the medicinal benefits of whiskey sipped neat from a leather flask. But the faces missing from the throng meant more to Mirrin than memories—James, Dougie, and her father; Loony Lachie too. She would have liked to see the folk from Strathmore incorporated into the swirl of the dance—Mrs. Burns and Mattie and Hannah and Archie. Dorothy would have enjoyed the color and the music and the strange warmth that the colliers generated in this annual get-together.

"Mirrin?"

She came abruptly out of her reverie.

Rob stood before her, healthy, handsome, and as solid as ever. Involuntarily she slid her shoulder around the booth, drawing herself away from the crowd.

"Is it true you're leavin', Mirrin?"

"First thing in the morning."

"Hamilton again?"

"Not this time, Rob. Much farther afield."

"Surely not for good?"

"That depends."

"On whether you find work?"

"On whether the world's a more hospitable place outside Blacklaw," Mirrin answered.

"You don't really want to go, do you?"

"Yes."

"But you don't have to, Mirrin. You can do everything you want here, in Blacklaw. It's where you rightly belong."

"How do you know what I want, Rob, or where I belong? I no longer know that myself."

"Once, Mirrin, long ago, I asked you to marry me," the young collier said. "It was wrong of me to ask you then. I . . . I think I know now what you meant when you refused me."

"I'm not for you, Rob."

"Because of what I did?"

Mirrin shook her head. "It's not that. I was never for you, Rob."

"I still love you, Mirrin."

"That will pass. You'll marry some other lass and forget all about me."

"I doubt it," Rob said. "I'm scared of what will happen to you, Mirrin. Stay here, with me. Be my . . . my wife?"

"No, Rob. I can't stay. There's more to it than you know."

"Lamont?"

"Go on, Rob." Mirrin gave him a gentle shove with the palm of her hand. "Good-byes are not for the likes of us."

He studied her critically. She saw surprise in his eyes, surprise at discovering that his feeling for her had waned —not all of it, but enough. He could, she realized, manage without her, and could even endure the memories.

"Go on," she murmured.

Rob nodded and swung away.

While they were talking the music had ceased.

Rain drifted heavily across the deserted boards. The

colliers and their womenfolk sought shelter under the big black tarpaulin that protected the tables. They were still hopeful that the cloud would pass and reveal the stars once more.

Mirrin knotted her scarf and slipped down the aisle between the stalls. A wrinkled crone peered up at her from under the turtle basket, held out her hand. "Fortune, missy? Good fortunes told."

"Not me, old one," Mirrin said. She paused, fished a halfpence from her pocket, and dropped it into the tinker's lap. "I think I prefer to keep my future to myself."

A silver piece landed on the damp grass. The crone was looking past Mirrin, her wise eyes bright and knowing. A familiar voice said, "Take it, old woman, and do as the lady says. Leave her future to me."

Mirrin did not dare turn. The tinker woman chuckled and slid back out of sight. Mirrin's heart leaped as she felt the man's touch on her shoulder.

"Mirrin, look at me."

Houston's face was scarred, a medallion of puckered flesh clasped on his cheek drawing down the eyelid. She gasped and lovingly reached up to touch the place.

"Will it heal?"

He shook his head. "Does that matter now, Mirrin? I'm well again."

"Houston," she murmured, almost disbelievingly, "why have you come here?"

"I heard from Donald Wyld that you were leaving Blacklaw."

"Yes, tomorrow."

"I want you here."

"It's not . . . no, Houston, it's not for us. I can't be deceitful."

"In a year," he said, "about the time that the sale of Strathmore is settled and my house in Hamilton built. . . ."

"You're selling Strathmore?" Mirrin interrupted.

"Yes. How can I live there now?"

"And the colliery?"

He smiled. The brooding, taciturn look had gone from his face, and the scar, strangely, gave wry humor to his expression.

"I intended to sell," he admitted. "I went to London with that purpose in mind, to find a wealthy buyer. But I could not bring myself to do it. And then, in Brittany, where I went to recover, I could think of nothing but returning. Blacklaw is in my blood, is part of me, Mirrin."

"I'm glad," Mirrin said.

He did not touch her now.

"And you are part of me too," he said gently.

"But there's no future for us, Houston."

"I say that there is, if you allow me just a little time, my love, just a little more time."

"And then, I suppose, you will take me on as your 'housekeeper'?"

"As my wife."

"How can you . . . ?"

"I'm the coalmaster," he said sternly. "The coalmaster can do as he wishes."

"Can he?" Mirrin said. "Then will you dance with me?"

"What?"

"Dance with me, here, now, tonight?"

"Mirrin, we will be . . . seen."

"If you love me," she said, "you will want to be seen with me."

Confused, he shook his head. "I . . . I can't."

"Are you afraid, Houston? Is that it?" She took his hand. "You don't have to be afraid."

"Later, Mirrin, but . . ."

"Tonight."

Light from the ring of lanterns cast a pale wedge upon

his face. She could see the stamp of the past on him, the haughtiness and pride, and the sorrow too; then it was gone, wiped clear. He lifted his head and clasped her hand tightly, and with a firmness that almost lifted her from her feet, drew her away from the shadow of the booths and out into the dancing arena.

Laughter and chatter stilled at once. A long, gasping sigh of astonishment rose from the colliers' throng. Houston did not pause now, did not hang back. He drew the girl behind him, overriding her sudden reluctance, drew her on into the very center of the boards.

"Miss Stalker," he said loudly, "will you dance with me?"

"Yes," Mirrin murmured, then, taking strength from him, cried out, "yes, I'll dance with you, Mr. Lamont."

The crowd was aghast, muttering, but Mirrin paid them not the slightest heed. Houston stood before her, his arm out, smiling down at her as if they were alone in all the field.

She linked her arm with his.

He snapped his fingers. "Fiddler, strike up a reel."

The music began, tentatively, then increased its tempo, fierce and fast and assured.

Houston caught Mirrin in his arms and danced with her, drawing her to him and releasing her in perfect rhythm to the music. They had eyes for no one as they danced alone on the shining floor.

But after a time the colliers and their women clapped their hands and some came down to join the couple under the paper lanterns in the softly falling rain.

"Mirrin," Houston said breathlessly, "will you give me my year? Will you wait for me?"

"Aye, sir," she said. "Forever."

Far across the moor the rain cloud passed, drifting away to the east over the colliery fence, the railway sheds, the kirkyard lying silent under the shadow of the winding wheels. Beyond Blacklaw's rows and dun-colored hills the world lay waiting.

But Mirrin no longer cared.

BESTSELLERS
FROM DELL

fiction

- [ ] THE NINTH MAN by John Lee $1.95 (6425-12)
- [ ] THE CHOIRBOYS by Joseph Wambaugh $2.25 (1188-10)
- [ ] MARATHON MAN by William Goldman..... $1.95 (5502-02)
- [ ] NIGHTWORK by Irwin Shaw $1.95 (6460-00)
- [ ] THE DOGS by Robert Calder $1.95 (2102-29)
- [ ] WHERE ARE THE CHILDREN? by Mary H. Clark $1.95 (9593-04)
- [ ] PASSION'S PROMISE by Danielle Steel $1.95 (2926-07)
- [ ] THE GANG by Herbert Kastle ....:. $1.95 (2786-06)
- [ ] WHEN THE LION FEEDS by Wilbur Smith ... $1.95 (9497-01)
- [ ] SHADOW OF THE CONDOR by James Grady $1.95. (7771-02)

non-fiction

- [ ] BRING ON THE EMPTY HORSES
      by David Niven $1.95 (0824-04)
- [ ] MIRACLES OF THE GODS
      by Erich von Däniken $1.95 (5594-19)
- [ ] MY LIFE by Golda Meir $1.95 (5656-14)
- [ ] RENDEZVOUS WITH DESTINY
      by Elliot Roosevelt and James Brough $1.95 (7420-15)
- [ ] BELLEVUE by Don Gold $1.95 (0473-16)
- [ ] DR. SIEGAL'S NATURAL FIBER PERMANENT
      WEIGHT-LOSS DIET
      by Sanford Siegal, D.O., M.D. $1.75 (7790-25)
- [ ] A WORLD OF MOVIES by Richard Lawton ... $7.95 (9690-06)
- [ ] CUISINART™ FOOD PROCESSOR COOKING
      by Carmel Berman Reingold $4.95 (1604-16)

Buy them at your bookstore or use this handy coupon for ordering:

She was born to dazzle the world,
he was born to change it—
together they shared . . .

PASSION'S PROMISE

by Danielle Steel

As one of the world's richest women, Kezia St. Martin was the pampered darling of the international Jet Set. But Kezia had a secret life, and secret longings to have all her lavish world provided—and more.

Then she met Lucas Johns, bold, dynamic, an ex-convict, now a crusader. He was a hero to many, a threat to even more. To Kezia he became the only thing that mattered, and the brief time they shared together was passion's sweetest hour—the golden hour that glows just before dark.

A DELL BOOK $1.95 (2926-07)

The jaws of horror were closing on her again-- and this time there was no escape!

Where Are The Children?

by Mary H. Clark

Nancy Harmon had fled the evil of her first marriage, the macabre deaths of her two little children, the hideous charges that had been made against her. She changed her name, dyed her hair, moved from California to New England. Now married again, she had two lovely new children and a happiness-filled life . . . until the morning when she looked for her children and found only one tattered red mitten and knew that the nightmare was beginning again.

"Absolutely riveting horror!" —*Publishers Weekly*

"An extravagantly plotted page-turner. It will make you hold your breath!" —*Kirkus Reviews*

A DELL BOOK $1.95
(9593-04)